A Fine Line of Distinction

In Search of Roots

Ron Wooten-Green

RESOURCE *Publications* · Eugene, Oregon

Resource Publications
A division of Wipf and Stock Publishers
199 W 8th Ave, Suite 3
Eugene, OR 97401

A Fine Line of Distinction
In Search of Roots
By Wooten-Green, Ron
Copyright © 2006 by Wooten-Green, Ron All rights reserved.
Softcover ISBN-13: 978-1-6667-0343-6
Hardcover ISBN-13: 978-1-6667-0344-3
eBook ISBN-13: 978-1-6667-0345-0
Publication date 2/22/2021
Previously published by Publish America, 2006

This edition is a scanned facsimile of the original edition published in 2006.

Dedication

This book is dedicated to the brave men and women, Union and Confederate, who stood and fought, those who in conscience could not serve, and those who courageously decided enough is enough.

This book is also dedicated to those brave men and women, Gay and Straight, who have stood and fought the good fight of proudly being who they truly are without prejudice towards those who are different from themselves.

Table of Contents

Foreword

As you, the reader, will note in the epilogue this novel would not have even been an idea, if it were not for the Hambidge Center for the Creative Arts in Rabun Gap, Georgia. In 2003 the Hambidge Center provided me with the opportunity to spend one whole month with no worldly distractions to focus on the writing of this book's original manuscript. To the extent that *A Fine Line of Distinction: In Search of Roots* is worthy of publication, a great debt of gratitude is owed to the Mary Hambidge Foundation in Atlanta and the gracious staff at the Rabun Gap center.

To say thank you, or to say that I am grateful, just seems to devalue the incredible support rendered by the staff at the Museum of the Confederacy in Richmond, Virginia. When I emailed my request for certain categories of information, as well as the hope that Linda and I could have two days at the Museum's library, I had absolutely no idea what I would find upon arriving. A large conference table with piles and piles of books and file folders awaited us. The Museum of the Confederacy is one of the richest historical resources in this country.

Much gratitude is also owed to the National Park Service staff at the Antietam and Kennesaw Battlefields. They never tire of answering questions, providing directions, and making resources available to their inquisitive visitors. My sincerest thanks also go the staff at the Calhoun

County Courthouse in Morgan, the staff at the Calhoun County Library in Edison, and the staff at the Sandersville Genealogical Research Center, as well as the staff at the Washington County Courthouse in Sandersville—all in the State of Georgia.

To Dan Bishop, Peter Anderson, Bob Morse, and John and Sandra Kelly who read a more recent draft of the manuscript, all I can say is "I owe you one!" To my wife Linda, who has read many versions of what you the reader have in your hands now, what can I say? More than any other person, this book "lives" because of you. Finally, if it were not for what one of the characters in this story, William Drayton Sheppard, did in the Fall of 1862 there would have been no such book written, and there would have been no Linda Wooten in my life.

Ron Wooten-Green
Las Vegas, New Mexico
June 2006

John Sheppard & Phanelty
(Patrick, Augusta, Charles)

John Sheppard & Ava Brittan
(Sarah, Charles, John, Hudson)

William Drayton Sheppard ←———————————→ Martha S. Sheppard

Augustus Eugene Sheppard ←———— → Sadie Ann Manry

John Price ←———→ Annie Belle Sheppard   Bessie Sheppard ←————→ Will Wooten   9 other children

---

eter Bird   Anna (?) Wooten Barnes ←— — — —→ Hooten-Tooten Wooten   Simon Burney Wooten ←———┐   →Elizabeth Roach

enry Bird & Nancy   Henry Manry & Jane   James R. Wooten   David L. Wooten ←———→ Elizabeth Colley   Sally

Bessie Sheppard ←——————→ Will Wooten

nnie Bird ←———→ William Manry ←———→ Martha Ann
                                    Keel Culbreth

———— (James Henry Manry , Benjamin F. Manry, John Bird Manry)

Irvin Bird Manry ("B. Papa") ←———→ Ann Collier

Theo   Sadie Ann Manry ←————————→ Augustus Eugene Sheppard (Gene)

John Price ←———→ Annie Belle Sheppard Bessie Sheppard ←——————→ Will Wooten   9 other children

Jonathan Barnes

James Barnes

Harvey Barnes & Ruth Bowen

Horace Barnes ←----------→ Caroline Thompson ←----------→ Johnny G. Barnes   William   Mariette   H

----------- (Leonard & Horace, Jr.)

Dave's Great ←----------→ *Anna (?) Wooten* ←----- ┬ -----→ *Hooten-Tooten Wooten*
Grandfather Barnes

Dave's Grandmother Barnes (?) ←

Annie Barnes Benson ← ┬ - - - -→ *Frank Benson*

Dave Benson ←- - - - - -→ *Gary Lee*

Italicized names = *fictional characters*
Broken lines (--------) = fictional relationships

Chapter 1:
Voices from Beyond

No one dies alone…
Those who have loved us,
(and those who loved those who have loved us),
will be there to greet us when we die.
[Elizabeth Kubler-Ross, "On Life After Death," in *On Death and Dying*,
Quality Paperback Book Club, 1992]

September 12, 2000

Anna is dying, and her son's life will never be the same. "David! David! David!" she calls insistently from the bedroom.

Dave hears the plea from above the roar of his electric shaver, turns the switch, and steps into the bedroom. "What do you want, Mom?"

Looking startled as she turns toward her son, this skeletal version of a once robust and large framed woman grips the rails to her hospital bed and positions herself to face her questioner.

"What do you mean? I don't want anything, except to get better; but we both know that won't happen, don't we?"

Dave feels a lump forming in his throat. It always happens this way: the stabbing sensation in the chest, followed by the obstruction in the throat. It always happens when his mother's bluntness about her imminent death unmercifully smashes Dave's avoidance like a rock through a window. She has always been this way, blunt and to the point sometimes bordering on rudeness and insensitivity.

A "stubborn, pig-headed German," Dave's father often said. Well, no one was ever absolutely certain she was of German descent, but the Wooten in her family tree was assumed to be of German origin; and that had proven good enough for Frank. Simple answers to complex questions were always good enough for Dave's dad.

Leaning against the doorsill and rubbing his chin in puzzlement, Dave responds, "No. You're right; damn it; but I still believe in miracles, Mom. I have to."

Suddenly, Dave is seized as if by a giant with a vise-like grip around his chest, squeezing out his breath—and, the tears. *Damn the tears. I can't let myself do this. I have to stay strong; she has enough to worry about, she doesn't have to worry about me.*

Wiping the tears by brushing his face with his upper arm, and hoping she doesn't notice, Dave uncontrollably stutters: "I h...h...h...ate it, Mom."

"Come're Dave. Put this damned bedrail down and sit awhile with me."

As Dave sits on the spot his 72-year-old mother smoothes out for him, she takes him in her arms. *This is really stupid. She's the one who is dying. She's consoling me; but I need this.*

Somehow the gripping tightness enveloping his chest is gone. Shifting slightly to look directly at this mother who is being a mother to the end, Dave asks: "But why did you call me a few moments ago?"

"Huh?"

"Mom, you called my name. I don't know much, perhaps, but I did learn from you fairly early on to recognize my own name. You said, *David.* So, here I am."

Anna stares at Dave with a look that is so very familiar to him. It is the same puzzled expression that always says, without voicing it as such, "are you nuts?"

"I did not call you, David," she protests with an emphasis on "David" that reverberates in her son's ears as if it were a clap of thunder. "Think about it, *Dave.* How often have I called you *David* in your 52 years? Once? Maybe twice?"

"More than that actually, Mom. When you would be angry with me as a kid, I heard 'David!' a few times. But Mom, I heard you clearly. You called out my name three times, 'David! David! David!' just like that."

Silence. Anna, who prefers to be called Annie by her friends, is looking toward him, but not at him. Her stare seems to be taking her to a different world; and Dave wonders if she even heard what he said. Lately, it has been like that. "Increasingly Mom is with me and then she is gone to some other place," he wrote in his journal just last night.

Dave moves from the edge of the bed saying, "I know what I heard, Mom. I know your voice when I hear it; and you and I are the only people here." As he says this, Dave notices a changed expression in her face. It is the same incomprehension he recalls seeing that day in 1980 when his father announced that they were going to have to give up the farm. Dave, ever since then, has tried to blot out that scene: a woman, who always had a firm grasp of reality, one who always had a word to say, struck speechless.

"What is it Mom? What's going on?" Dave asks as it occurs to him that Anna was, on that very day in 1980, the same age as he is today.

He remembers noticing for the first time, the evening of the family farm's death notice, how his mother's hair had somehow, without prior warning, turned gray around the temples; and the wrinkles around her eyes, never before seen (or at least noticed) took up permanent residence. It was only moments ago, 20 years later, that Dave observed a man graying around his temples and wrinkles around his eyes. The general outline of the face was familiar; only the details were new. The new, of course, was the old Dave getting older, and making his presence felt through the telltale mirror. Despite his persistent fair complexion, the earrings in both ears, his physical fitness maintaining the prized slight build, and his efforts to keep up with the latest clothing styles, Dave's moment of truth at the mirror stunned him to near-speechlessness. In his mind he is still peering into the mirror of his own mortality.

"I don't know, Dave," she replies curtly. "Ah, Dave. Hello, are you there? Earth Mom calling Dave," Anna adds as she realizes Dave is somewhere else mentally. She will never know how this son of hers has just experienced a moment of truth.

"Believe me, Dave, I was not calling you. I was not calling for you; and right now I am too damned tired to think about it. Now you just go off and do what you have to do, and leave me alone. I may be old. I may be sick. I may be weak. I do know I am dying. But as your mother, I retain some rights unto myself. Now be off and if I need you I'll call you as I've always called you, *Dave*. So, wherever you were just now you may return. Just don't space me out when I beam you up, calling from Planet Earth."

Soon thereafter Cathy, the hospice nurse, arrives and Dave takes off to go to the library for a few hours. Between the nurse's visit, then Callie, the home health aide coming to give Anna a bath, followed by Dave's special friend Sharon, he knows his mother will be well cared for.

However, as he backs the car out of the driveway, Dave slowly comes to the realization that people are standing on either side of his car waiting patiently for him to get out of their way. Grinning with the sheepishness of a child caught where he ought not to be, Dave motions for his stymied neighbors to pass by. Looking at his watch he realizes he has sat here for at least five minutes waiting for the cars to go by.

But there are no cars. There hardly ever are any cars on this street anyway. All this while he has been hearing the echo of his mother's call: "David! David! David!" All this while he has been trying to figure it all out.

If she is not calling me, or for me, then who? What is going on? Why does she deny it? I do know what I heard. What is this? Life sucks. Not only is my Mom dying, but also I am getting old.

Around noontime, Dave returns home—a regular routine now days. As a freelance writer he has a need to do groundwork research for a writing project. On the other hand, as an only child, he has a need to be home for lunch, and all the meals. He knows that others could do it. Sharon would be perfectly capable of feeding her, but... *No, she eats better for me. Yeah, right! Who the hell am I kidding? She isn't eating anything for anyone under any circumstances anymore. Mom is dying for God's sake.* As this thought winds its way through his consciousness, Dave grips the handle to the front door as if his hand is frozen to it.

"'Mom is dying for God's sake?' How in the hell can she be dying of cancer for *God's* sake? What does God get out of this? I need her. I need Mom as much as I need Gary. But she is dying; and it really sucks."

"What sucks?"

Dave is shaken by the sound of another human voice in this his own private world—a world of late composed mainly of pain and puzzlement, agony and anxiety. Following the sound of the voice, Dave sees Sharon through the screen door standing in the archway separating the living room from the dining room.

"Oh, nothing much, just the world. I was just talking to myself."

"Well," Sharon laughs, "I hope you don't mind my listening in. I think it sucks that a person as young as Annie is already facing death. I mean I used to think that 72 was old, but your mother's mind is just as sharp, I imagine, as it ever was. If she did not have cancer, she would be very healthy. That probably sounds stupid. What I'm trying to say is, Annie could have had 20–30 more years of an extremely productive life. It does suck. I mean it really sucks."

"How is she Sharon?" Dave asks choking back the lump in his throat.

"Well, okay, but she has been calling out for you a lot."

"What do you mean?"

"Well, she simply calls out 'David, David, David,' over and over again. I have told her that you were at work and that you would be back later. But you know, Dave, it is as if I am not here; and, when I told her you would be here shortly," Sharon pauses scratching her head, "it's as if your coming had nothing to do with her calling out your name. I just don't know how to describe it. She did sleep some and now she is awake and sitting up waiting for you."

Sharon pauses waiting for Dave to respond, but he does not. That is certainly not unusual. *Sometimes talking to Dave is like talking to the wall. Well, his mother is dying. That is part of it now, but it has always been like this. Why do I bother?* "Dave, I'm no nurse, but I don't think Annie has much longer to go."

Dave's only response is to put his head down as he moves toward Sharon, or so she thought. Dave moves toward her only because she stands between him and the hallway to his mother. Sharon reaches out to embrace him. He brushes by her as if she were a drape in the doorway.

Sharon seems to shrink as she watches Dave shuffle his way to his mother's room. She turns now to pick up a photo she has seen many times on the bookshelf near the hallway. It is an old photo of a very young woman about her own age. It is Annie. For the first time, however, Sharon notices, really notices, the remarkable resemblance between herself and Dave's mother. *God, is that what I am? Dave's insurance policy against the loss of his mother?* Sharon is crying as she walks out the door.

Dave has a picture in his head; he knows what to expect: It is Anna in bed with her favorite bright yellow bathrobe, jade green turban covering her nearly hairless head, sitting up with the help of the adjustable bed and three pillows supporting her back. He is delighted to know he will find her so. Yesterday she was non-responsive. In fact, he was not even sure she was breathing: *She's gone,* he thought as he sucked in his breath; and then he saw the covers move. Relief chased anxiety from the room.

As Dave walks down the hallway toward their bedroom, he hears a one-sided conversation going on: "Well, who are you? What do you want?" She is sitting up, just as he imagined. However, she is gazing to the side of her bed opposite the doorway, nodding her head and looking back and forth, occasionally emitting a grunt of apparent acknowledgment, "Hmm, huh hah."

Dave clears his throat and steps into the room, "What's happening Mom?"

"Oh, Dave these people have come to visit," she says with the excitement he recalls hearing in her voice when she announced that the rhododendron thought to be dead had experienced a resurrection. *That was ten years ago. How I wish we could return, recapture her vibrancy and pump it back into her body. What do I do now? Do I try to keep her grounded in reality, or do I just go with the flow? This is weird, but I need to find out who she thinks has been (is?) here.*

"Who are they, Mom? Tell me about them. It must be good; you seem excited."

"Well, you are going to find this really strange, because it is really strange. First of all I don't have a clue who these people are around here. I don't even know if they are male or female. But I do know this: I will get to know them and they have promised to take me there."

What the hell! This is a bit much. "They have promised to take you 'there'? Where is there?"

"The Plantation, Dave, they said it is such a beautiful spot."

"The Plantation? What Plantation?"

"I don't know what it is or where," Anna laughs. They haven't told me, yet; but they will, I'm sure."

This is really interesting. "Have you ever been on a Plantation?"

"Dave," she laughs, "I have never been to even one Southern State."

"Didn't I hear that your Grandma's ancestors came from the South somewhere?"

"Yeah, I guess so. But right now I'm kind of tired again. You know it gets so very frustrating to be so tired all the time. I guess those people kind of wore me out; but they are good people, Dave, even if I don't really know who they are."

Dave gives his mother a kiss on the forehead and strides toward the bathroom when she says, "Those people know David."

"They know? Okay what do they know?"

"No, what I mean is they know David. They know the David you have said I was calling out for. In fact, he is with them."

September 13, 2000

It is 3 A.M., and Dave is gradually realizing that his mother is talking. He turns his head from the pillow on what used to be her bed and opens his eyes to observe her sitting up and carrying on an animated conversation with people whom he cannot see. He says nothing, just chuckles quietly to himself as he recalls a comment his deceased father often made: "I didn't recognize my own wife that day when she had her mouth shut." *Come to think of it, I never heard Dad repeat that good-humored remark, ever, after the loss of the farm.* Dave watches and listens with the attentiveness of a child being introduced to chocolate candy.

Shifting his position slightly and silently not wanting to interrupt the "conversation" in progress, Dave leans on one elbow with a good view of his mother's left profile. She is smiling nodding her head in agreement with what is being "said," and obviously enjoying herself. Suddenly, she turns toward Dave:

"Oh, Dave, you are awake. He said you should find out."

"Find out what, Mom?" A shiver goes up and then down the full length of his spine. *This is spooky. I am not alone in this room with Mom. We are not alone.* "So, I guess we are not alone in this room."

Anna smiles her mischievous broad and knowing grin, and begins to sing, "Sometimes people leave you, halfway through the wood."

Then, with the well-practiced routine between mother and son, Anna extends her arm toward Dave who picks up the cue and sings the closing line from one of their favorite songs in Steven Sondheim's musical, *Into the Woods*, "No one is alone."

"Well, Dave, that was David. He says you are a good man and a smart man. He says you can find Ben and Johnnie. He said something about a fox and a gap in something. You would like him Dave. David likes you."

"But who is David, Mom?"

"I don't really know, but he says I look just like her."

"Like who?"

"I don't know. He didn't say."

"Mom, was there anyone else here?" Dave asks with an aire of resignation.

"Dave, it amazes me that you cannot see them." With a flourishing sweep of her right arm, she explains, "they are right here, but only David has introduced himself." With that comment and her sweeping non-verbal depiction of the number of her visitors, Anna's whole body visibly sags.

Dave jumps out of bed, or tries to. Instead, he becomes hopelessly entangled in the sheet. "Damn, I never did learn how to make a bed properly, even in Boy Scout Camps or Air Force Basic Training—always getting demerits for my damned bed."

Anna laughs her distinctive wild and boisterous laugh, the laugh that was so characteristic of this woman, a laugh that required so very little to activate.

"There goes Annie again," was the very common response of those anywhere around her at such moments. In fact, as Dave recalls, his father said it was her laugh that first attracted him to her in 1944 as a sixteen-year-old. *Maybe, if he could have kept her laughing, things would have been different for both of them—and for me.*

Dave wonders whatever could have happened to the laughter. Whenever laughter visited the family home, it made a prompt exit as soon as Frank walked in. Until those fateful moments when it seemed that a Swat Team of One would arrive to kill the joy, Anna's laughter brought with it a state of peace and well being, security, and that precious sense of being loved. Then, it would all end. The door would open. The very sound of Frank's heavy footsteps coming up the gravel walk brought a foreboding that would rush in where promise had hastily escaped. Disapproval and anger would then overthrow a regime of tolerance and love.

Still laughing at him, Anna notes "You look like the Ku Kluckers, David, talked about."

"Really? What did he say about that?" Dave inquires hesitantly.

"Oh, not much. I'm very tired Dave. Get yourself untangled and get over here to help me, Oh Grand Mucky Muck."

After getting her situated in bed, lowering it and making her comfortable, Dave returns to his bed. *How long will this go on? I haven't had a good night's sleep in so long. I can't remember what it was like to sleep through the night. God! It seems like every morning around this time she has got something going on. I am so tired, so damned tired, so tired, so...*

"Dave... Dave! Do you hear me?"

I don't believe this: "What now Mom?"

"I'm sorry Dave. I'm a real bother aren't I? A real pain in the neck. I know that and I'm so sorry. But there is one other thing you need to know. David said you need to find Ben and Johnny B."

"Yes, I know. You told me that, but who, for pity's sake, are Ben and Johnny B?"

"I don't know Dave; I just don't know. But David said they are to be found either with a fox or near a fox. I don't recall which. But...well... one other thing, Dave: David sounds worried and sad. Maybe a fox is attacking or stalking Ben and Johnny B, whoever and wherever they are. Don't ask me. I've told you all I know."

"And perhaps more than you know, right?"

No response, she is sound asleep. Dave pulls the blankets up over his head

18

and drifts off to sleep thinking and rethinking: *Ben & Johnny B. are with a fox in a gap. Chased by a fox? This is really helpful. This is strange. Why me?*

September 14, 2000

Dave once again comes home for lunch with the intent to stay home for the rest of the day. When he had left for the library he noticed a major change in his mother. She barely responded to him, except for refusing anything to eat and taking only a sip of water. It was their neighbor Ginny's turn to stay with Anna this morning and Dave told Ginny he had reported a change to the hospice nurse. The nurse would be coming by about mid-morning.

As Dave enters the house, Ginny greets him with a broad smile saying, "You said Annie was different today, Dave. Well, she sure is. Ever since you left she has been 'high as a kite.' She has been talking almost constantly, but..." Suddenly Ginny turns real serious, shoulders stooped low with her hands stuffed deep into her slacks pockets, looking at the floor rather than at Dave.

I don't think I want to hear this. Ginny is going to tell me she thinks Mom has gone over the edge, that the cancer has gone to her brain.

"Dave, she is seeing people around her that I cannot see. She isn't just seeing them she is carrying on conversations with them. She mentioned names, names of people she obviously is seeing in her bedroom: Sadie, Annie, David, Ben and Johnny, WD, Horace & Johnny G. One other name I heard but I am not sure if it is a person or a place."

"What name is that, Ginny?"

"Marsh. Do you know who she is talking about or to?"

"No, I sure don't, Ginny. I sure don't. I had a Tech Sergeant by the name of Marsh when I was in the Air Force, but Mom never met him. I will try talking to her about all of this." *But this is really getting interesting—each day more and more so. Marsh, I haven't thought of him for years. He was like a father to me—probably because he had a son like me. Marsh knew. He just kept his mouth shut. That was before the "don't ask, don't tell" policy. Guess Marsh didn't need to ask.*

However, as Dave walks into the bedroom, Anna is in a deep sleep. *Well, so much for that discussion. Think I'll just get a bite to eat and read the paper. When she wakes up, I'll see if she will eat something.*

The kitchen is in disarray. In a hurry to get to his work at the library, Dave had left the dishes in the sink. Now, he stands at the sink, the water running over the plates as he passes them mindlessly through the stream of hot water. There is something about the water as it pours out of the faucet. Dave stands and stares. A searing burn sensation begins as a small ping-pong ball-sized feeling in the middle of his chest. It grows larger and larger moving upward into his throat. His right hand grips the side of the counter. Leaning forward, his left hand grips the faucet; and Dave weeps.

It is his memory of the many times, as a kid, when he would see his mother standing at the kitchen sink gazing out the window. She would be holding on to the edge of the sink, looking off into the unknown distance. While playing ball out in the yard with his friends, Dave recalls often looking up to see his mom at the window. His friends were known to comment, "Hey, your Mom likes to watch us play, doesn't she?" Dave's stock reply was, "Yeah." But he knew better.

He recalls one very special incident when he was about seven years old, playing silently in the living room with the pretty blonde-haired doll left by his cousin, Sandy. Slowly, it occurred to him that his mother was talking out in the kitchen. Curious to know whom she was talking to, since he had not heard anyone come in, nor had he heard the phone ring; Dave tiptoed out to the doorway. There he saw his Mom at the sink saying, "Then why did you name me Anna, Mama?"

A mother's intuitive sense apparently kicked-in at that point. She knew she was not alone. When she turned away from the sink, Dave saw the tears. "I was just talking to my Mama. You'll do the same someday, Dave."

September 15, 2000

The mid afternoon sun is gently glancing off the large picture window creating on the east wall a shadowed silhouette of a Mission-style rocking chair along with its current occupant. The newspaper on his lap looks more like a skirt as it is projected onto the wall. Dave is asleep.

Anna's voice gradually breaks through his exhausted consciousness. His body remains inert as he listens with a mild, almost detached, interest. *There she goes again. Wonder who she is talking to now?*

"It is so beautiful, David. It is breathtaking. It is just like all the pictures I have seen."

Dave puts the newspaper down and starts to get up from the chair. *No, think I'll wait a bit. See what else happens.*

"But why should he? Dave doesn't know where to go and I... but what can

20

Dave do? I don't understand. Oh, yes, I will tell him. He will do it. I know he will."

Dave leaps out of his chair with the rocker left in motion at full speed. *Okay, what the hell is going on?* As he approaches the bedroom door, Dave witnesses his withering mom sitting upright, nodding her head and glancing around the room as if she were following the movement of people.

"Mom? Mom?" She does not appear to hear her son; nor does she seem to see him. "Mom, who were you just talking with?"

She jumps as if she had touched a frayed and live electrical cord. "Good God, Dave, where did you come from?"

"I live here you know; or at least now I do."

"I'm sorry, so sorry to have interrupted your life, Dave. But, I want you to know this old lady so appreciates what you have done and are doing for her." Looking Dave squarely in the eye she takes his hand and with seriousness that he has not seen since she informed him of her cancer diagnosis: "Dave, when this is over, you must promise me you will do one last thing for this Old Pain in the Butt. Please?"

"Do what, Mom? You know I will do anything for you. But what do you mean 'when this is over'?" *Shit! That was stupid. I know what she means, but maybe I don't.*

"What I mean, Dave, is that after I die, I want you to do what David is asking. Make note of it all and go. Please? It is really important. I mean I don't care what you do with your life after I am gone. You and Gary can move to Saudi Arabia, whatever. But I do care about this."

"Okay, but you really have to help me, because I don't have a clue what's going on here. You said I should 'make note of it all.' Well, that's one helluva good idea. Let me get my journal. Do you feel like talking about all of the folks you have seen and all that you have heard from them?"

"Yes, Dave, I'm feeling pretty good right now. Let's do it, but one other request."

"What's that, Mom?"

"Would you play that CD of 'La Boheme' one last time, right now?"

With Puccini now playing, Dave enters his studio to snatch up his journal, but as he does so he is thrown back to another moment in a time gone by.

* * *

September 15, 1985

Dave and Gary, Anna and her friend Claire were seated at the Village Inn having an opera post-mortem, along with coffee and pie. The discussion had about run its course, when his mother piped-in with a comment that took him back to the kitchen sink when he was seven: "You know, I can really relate to Mimi," Anna said to no one in particular.

Claire responded with a twinkle in her eye, "Oh, yeah. You mean that time when you lived with that young artist in the bohemian section of Kansas City?"

Gary, at that moment, snorts into his coffee, nearly losing his grip on the cup, and with tears of laughter running down his face, blurts out: "Hey man, you two and my Mama are about the same age. So, whenever you were living in Bohemia, KC, my Mammy was a living in Ghetto, KC. Fact is, she's still there."

There are those times in our lives when we find ourselves laughing at that which is not funny—laughing at the bizarre, the macabre. There are also those moments when we laugh only because someone else is laughing, when we do not even know why the other is seized by the happy malady. This is one of those times.

Anyone observing this foursome enraptured in hilarity would easily think those lives were worry-free. No one would suspect that the heavier set woman with the multicolored scarf wrapped elegantly around her neck, the one who seems most seized by fits of laughter is seized as well by a fit of wonder and doubt.

"Lee, you are so funny; but it is not funny."

"Mother! For God's sake! Gary! His name is Gary. Gary Lee. Not Lee Gary! When are you ever going to get it right? Another 30 years?" Dave's face turns a telltale red. His voice is sharp.

Gary reaches over to take both Dave's hand and Anna's, "Hey man, it's okay. It's okay. I've been called worse things believe me, like Boy, Fag, Nigger, Ass Hole, and even Opera Lover."

Dave smiles. Anna bursts out into her patented rollicking laughter. "You know, of course," she says, "that my former friend here made that up. Claire, sometimes I have a hard time remembering why I like you. I mean, there have been many a moment when I too wondered why I was called Anna, as Mimi wondered why people called her Mimi."

"Well," Claire chimes in; "people call you Anna or Annie because that's your name. Seems pretty simple to me."

"I suppose it would to someone as simple as you, Dear Claire, " Anna retorts in good-humored sarcasm, "but the fact is my mother, Anna, often wondered the same thing. She had no idea why her parents named her that; yet, she turned right around and perpetuated the practice. There always seemed to be more to it than an idle naming. And I think that is what Mimi is getting at. There was an unsolved mystery in her past."

✳ ✳ ✳

Dave steps toward the door of the study when he stops dead in his tracks. *That was almost* exactly *15 years ago. That was the day I got my first article accepted in a real magazine. I will remember the date always: SEPTEMBER 15, 1985. It was also the same night that Gary and I vowed our commitment to each other.*

Returning to the bedroom with his trusty journal, Dave pulls the chair closer to the bedside, elevates his legs to a comfortable position on the bed, opens the book with pen in hand and begins:

"Okay, Mom, let's start at the beginning. You have talked about David, Ben, Sadie, Annie, WD, Horace, Johnny G, and Johnny B. Who are they?"

"I'm not sure, but I know they are family. That, I know for sure."

Dave's glance at his mother convinces him beyond doubt that her visions are indeed rooted in her family. "And they are all dead, aren't they Mom?"

"Yes. They are all dead, Dave. But I will be going with them soon. They are waiting for me. They are all very good people. They are around here to help me when it is time to go. But you can find them." Now with her familiar pleading tone, she adds, "You need to help them, Dave, but I'm not sure what it is all about either."

Help them. How can I help the dead? "So, they are family but do you know how or what their relationship is to you, to us?"

"No, but they have come a long way."

"A long way?"

"But I don't know how far. I do know though that they need healing."

"Mom if they are dead... Well, I just don't understand how the dead can be healed."

"Dave, it's just that a lot happened and they need to get things right. If you will just go to Lookout Point, perhaps they will be forgiven."

Anna has rendered this last statement with a chilling certainty that Dave recognizes from times past. It is the same level of certainty when she informed him that:

• his father was dying.

• she was going to find a job after Frank had died.

• he had no need to hide his sexual orientation from her and that she loved him for who he is.

• she knew the chemo was not working.

• she was not going to make it.

"So, they all 'need to get things right.' What does that really mean, Mom?"

"I don't really know that either, Dave, but they are not the only ones you know. Ben and Johnny B. are really lost and it has something to do with some fox. David was in 71 fights and lost the last one. Sadie Anne lost it all. So did WD and Horace. David says Johnny G. was really good to him."

"Whoa. Slow down. Have you talked to Sadie, WD, Ben and Johnny B, Horace and Johnny G as well?"

"Well, sort of. Some of it I just know. But yes I have seen them."

"Can you describe them?"

"No, I really can't. But they are all wonderful people. I just wish you could see them, meet them. It just blows my mind that you do not see them, Dave. It doesn't seem like I should even have to tell you all this."

"Well, I'll say one thing Mother Dear; you sure as hell aren't hurting for company these days. And they all need to get things right?"

"Yes, Dave," she responds and taking Dave's hand in hers, adds: "So do you, and you know, Dave, I'm totally amazed at how you, Horace and Johnny G look so much alike."

"Really? What do you mean by that? What do you mean that I need to get things right?"

"I really don't know, but you will know. You will know Dave. I am getting real tired. I need to lie down."

"One other thing," Dave adds as he lowers the bed, "I overheard you talk about something being so beautiful."

"The Plantation."

"The Plantation? You saw it?"

"Oh, I more than saw it," she laughs weakly. "I was there. It amazes me that you do not see it yourself, Dave." Turning her head slightly upward, she adds, "It's right over there. I can see it so clearly."

"Okay, but where is it on the map?"

"Not...far from...Knockaway...Knockaway...Knock..." Anna is asleep. *Rats! I forgot to ask her about "Lookout Point." Just as well I suppose. That's probably near "Knockaway" too. I think I know how to track this sucker down, but it has to wait.*

September 16, 2000

"Calhoun? Okay, I'll tell him. Yes, and Morgan, too?"

Calhoun & Morgan. Calhoun & Morgan. Calhoun & Morgan. Calhoun and...? Dave lifts his head from the pillow, wipes the crustiness from his eyes, and glances toward his mother's bed. She is sitting up nodding her head again as if she is engaged in a conversation with someone.

Oh, my, what now? Calhoun & Morgan; or, by the gods do we finally have a first and last name for someone? Is it Calhoun Morgan? Morgan Calhoun?
"Good morning, Mom, what's up?"

"Well, you should be I guess."

"Huh?"

"It is eight o'clock, Dave. You are usually up and out of here by this time."

"Damn! I've got to get going. The nurse will be here any minute. Damn!"

"Dave, don't hurry. Just relax. Take it easy. You'll be okay. But before you come home, will you stop by and pick up my tickets?"

"Tickets? What tickets?"

"Oh, you know, my tickets for the train."

"Train? What train?"

Annie looks at her son with a puzzled look, as if he had totally missed the point—a "how-can-you-be-so-stupid" kind of expression, furrowed brow, penetrating eyes running deep into his heart. "Geez, Dave, sometimes I wonder about you. The Albany to Albany train." Anna is nearly shouting. "But, I may not be here when you come back."

"Okay, the tickets, the train. You bet. By the way, what's the deal with Calhoun and Morgan, or is it Calhoun Morgan?"

"Oh, I don't really know, but David said to tell you that's where it is."

"That's where what is?"

"Dave, I'm telling you I don't know. Now will you get going and get my tickets?"

"Okay, sure," a very confused son says to his most confusing mother.

"You don't believe me do you, Dave?"

"No, Mom, I believe you. I just don't understand what's happening here. I feel about as confused as I did in about fourth grade when math and I were on two separate planets and Miss Tooley's best efforts only confused me even more. I simply had no idea what to do or how to begin."

"Oh, I know Dave. This old woman is confused herself. I'm not really sure what is going on either, but I know it is good. I think we're getting there. Just don't give up on your old mom. Huh, Dave?"

Dave is now in his mother's arms, sobbing out the wordlessness of love.

Moments later Dave is dressed and putting his coat on when the doorbell rings. It is Cathy, the hospice nurse. He walks her down to the bedroom. "Look who's here Mom. Your favorite nurse of all time."

"Hi Cathy. Dave is going to get my tickets for the train today. It's time to do that you know."

"Well, when it's time to get the tickets, it's time to get the tickets. It's like a friend of mine said just the other night, 'When it's time to boogey, it's time to boogey woogey,'" laughs Cathy. Dave joins this comely good-humored nurse who never dresses in whites by snorting out, "that's a good line, Cathy. Think I'll borrow that if you don't mind?" Neither of them seems to notice that Anna is not laughing.

Leaning over to kiss his mother goodbye, Dave says, "I love you, Mom. See ya later."

"Later. I love you too, Dave. Just don't forget the tickets. I can't believe how tired I feel. I have never felt this way before. I feel so cold."

As Dave walks out of the room, he glances back to have a good look at Cathy. She is always dressed so attractively. Today, it is a long tightly fitted almost silky multicolored dress with slit skirt. Cathy looks as if she was poured into the dress; or is it that the dress was shrink-wrapped over her? *Some guy who is into that sort of thing is going to get a real prize in her.*

Tickets. Train. Calhoun. Morgan. Train Tickets. Calhoun, Morgan. Morgan, Calhoun... "Oh damn!" Dave realizes he is still parked in the mouth of the driveway; and there they are—*the same folks as before, cut off at the pass, waiting for me to get the hell out of their way! This is really embarrassing! I've got to get a grip.*

Dave has a twenty-minute drive to the library, much of it through the rolling Ponca Hills. This is a time he has grown to treasure—a time to get his breath, a time to reflect on life, a time to reflect on death: his mother's death.

While the sun was shining so brilliantly on the landscape when he began this daily trek eastward, it suddenly disappears under a commanding black cloud. Everything changes. The day, which appeared to be so bright and promising, feels dark and foreboding. A chill runs down his back. He feels a quickness to his pulse, a rush of blood to his head, a tightening in his chest: "I may not be here when you come back."

Slamming on his brakes, Dave blurts out, "Dear God. Mom is dying. I mean really dying. She was trying to tell me she is dying and that she won't be there when I return!"

Fortunately for Dave no cars are behind him. None except for the patrol car two blocks back. The police officer observes the brake lights, and notices the car moving off to the side of the street. Pulling along side the suspicious vehicle, the officer sees a middle-aged man in a business suit, cell phone in his hand, weeping like a baby.

"Annie died," Cathy said, "not long after you left. She just sighed a great sigh and died just like that. It was as if she consciously sucked in her last big breath, let it out and decided to never take another one. I tried to call your cell phone, but it just rang and rang."

"I knew it, Cathy. All of a sudden, I knew. I could feel it. That's why I called. You couldn't get me, because I had forgotten to turn my phone on."

"Dave, there are two other things. Just before she took her last breath she said: 'Tell Dave I will see him on Hartford;' and, I should have seen it coming Dave, when she talked about getting tickets for the train. People who are dying often talk about planes, trains and automobiles as their means of getting to heaven. I think your mother's train arrived ahead of schedule, that's all."

"Are you okay, Sir?" the policeman asks.

"Yes, Officer, just great," Dave says with mixed anger and sarcasm as he heaves his phone out of the window. "My mother just died, and I wasn't there."

Chapter 2:
Mapping the Journey

We,
local and ephemeral as we are,
Are not for one moment contented in the world of time
Nor confined within it;
We keep on crossing over and over
To our predecessors,
To our descent,
and to those who apparently come after us.
(Rilke, quoted by Anne Morrow Lindbergh in *The Flower and the Nettle*)

September 23, 2000
    David
    The Plantation
    Ben & Johnny B
    (Need to Find Them)
    A Fox & a Gap
    Sadie Ann
    Marsh
    Need to help them
    Need to be healed
    Lookout Point
    David: 71 fights & lost I (the last one)
    WD
    Johnny G was good to David
    THEY need to get things right & so do I
    Knockaway/Nockaway

Calhoun
Morgan
Calhoun Morgan
Morgan Calhoun
Hartford
Annie
Horace & Johnny G

"There," Dave exclaims as he slams his pen onto the table. "I think that does it. Everything Mom ever mentioned that didn't make sense during her final weeks of life. But what does it all mean? Damn, I wish she could have told me. I wish she could tell me now. Dear God, if only she could tell me now. I wish I could see her one more time."

Okay, now I need to be methodical. I'm going to make sense out of this. She said it was really important. It was somehow important to her that I pursue this puzzle.

"Well, Mom, I'm going to give it my best shot.

"So, what do I really know? Well, the answers would appear to lie somewhere in the South, because that's where plantations are; or at least were. But that's all I know. Of course there is one other thing: all of those people she mentioned are dead. If any of them were really plantation folk, the chances are they would have lived somewhere around the Civil War period, give or take 50 years maybe. That would mean 1810–1910. No problem. This should be a piece of cake. Just track down every David who ever lived in any of the Southern states over that 100-year period; then move on to the others; and swish—the job is done, and I can get on with my life. Mom, you have cursed me."

As far as Dave can see, the burning question is whether there were any Davids, Johnny Bs, Horaces and Johnny Gs, WDs, Sadies, or Annies in the family tree? Is there a family tree? The problem is there is simply no one to turn to. His father was never interested in tracing a family history. In fact Frank had said many times, "I'm not interested in any family tree. I'm sure we would find more than a few hanging from it. Maybe even a queer or two."

Always, never was there any exception, Dave knew, as one knows thunder follows lightning, that the line, *I'm sure we would find more than a few hanging from a tree*, would be followed immediately with *maybe even a queer or two*. The difference between his father's two comments and lightning accompanying thunder is that Frank's lightning always struck and its victim was always Dave. *Maybe even a queer or two* invariably was accompanied by Frank's heart-piercing, soul-penetrating, and unmistakable disdainful stare at his son.

Dave's Grandmother seemed to know only one thing about her family and that was that her mother had briefly been married to a man from the South. His name was Wooten. The suspicion always existed in the family lore that while Great Grandpa Barnes raised the child as his own, "everyone knew" she had been sired by a "foot-loose Hooten-Tooten Wooten."

Very little is known concerning the Barnes lineage. All that Dave knows for sure is that a distant relative was killed in the Civil War and another had fought in the Revolution. Therefore, as he often heard it said, "when you have a daughter, she will qualify for membership in the Daughters of the American Revolution." Dave would just grunt and think to himself, *No way, No way. I will never have a daughter, unless and in the very unlikelihood that Gary and & I would adopt one.*

But is that why, or part of why he continues his relationship with Sharon? *It would be foolhardy to adopt a child with Gary at our age. But Sharon is much younger. She* could *have a child. I mean* we *could have a child. No. This is stupid.*

The more Dave ponders the idea of pursuing the family tree, the more it feels as if he is entering a forest blindfolded and being expected to identify each of the unseen trees by name—Latin names at that! He sits with the list of "clues", staring at the paper, looking but not seeing, when suddenly it hits him: "Yes! Calhoun and Morgan! Back to the Atlas. Calhoun & Morgan may be cities, towns, villages, or counties. At least it is a place to begin."

Dave is in his element now. He spreads the Atlas out before him on the coffee table that Gary designed and painted years ago, a bright multi-colored and glossy representation of their favorite pastime, music. The book of maps, pens, and notepapers are obliterating the cleft notes, piano keys, and music scores imprinted on the table's surface. The flames from the fireplace feed the ambiance of the moment, enflaming the very thought of chasing down the many leads Dave is determined to pursue.

For Dave having a research project to do is like being an alcoholic, an addiction that takes over his life. While an alcoholic may dream of the next drink, Dave's night-dreams and daydreams take him to the next step, the next lead, and the next possibility. Sleep is not feasible until the lead is checked out. And then? Well, there is no end to it. There is always another lead. This project, he realizes, literally may have no end to it at all.

Opening the Atlas to its index, Dave proceeds in his methodical way by beginning with Alabama and immediately hits the target: Alabama has both a Calhoun County and a Morgan County. *This could be it, but there was something about the way Mom said it. I think one of them is a county and the other is a town. If so, Alabama is not it. But who the hell knows?* "I bet you do Mom, but you aren't saying are you?"

Dave moves on to Florida and finds Calhoun County. Making note of it, his search takes him to Georgia where he finds something similar to Alabama: Calhoun and Morgan counties. Then the lights flash, the bells ring—a researcher's dream, the Golden Nugget, the Pearl of Great Price, the Mother Lode, the Treasure at the Bottom of the Sea, the Holy Grail: Calhoun city. *Gadzukes! This is probably it: Morgan County and Calhoun city. I just feel it in me bones. But not to panic, stay with the program.*

Stay with the program he does: Louisiana—Morgan City; Mississippi—Calhoun County, Calhoun City, Morgantown; North Carolina—Morgantown and Morganton; South Carolina—Calhoun County and Calhoun Falls.

Tossing his pen on the table, Dave sits back into the sofa feeling inside like a Panther stalking its prey, circling closer and closer ready to strike. There is a certain exhilaration for any researcher, whether historian, scientist, or genealogist, when one knows without really knowing that pay dirt is one click away, or on the next page. It is like being a child on Christmas morn, seeing the long anticipated package under the tree, knowing without really knowing for sure what is inside, so eager to rip the wrappings off, but savoring the anticipation.

Dave slowly, deliberately, picks up the Atlas; fans the pages open to the Georgia index. Calhoun County at M-4 is not even close to Morgan County at F-7, but Morgan County might work with Calhoun city at C-3, but no—they are too far apart to be related as David imagines his mother's meaning. His hopes about dashed, Dave finds Calhoun County in South Georgia. It is a small county to the west of Albany and to his total surprise finds Morgan, the county seat of Calhoun County (population 5013). *Damn—this has to be it. Calhoun is obviously a small county and Morgan must be really small—not even listed in the index. So what? Where do I go from here? The Internet, that's where.*

It is late, nearly midnight. Dave is feeling the exhaustion of a man who has been weighted down by the intensity of caring for his dying mother, the stress of experiencing all of the stages of grieving and loss at least a dozen times over, and seeing her lowered into her grave. Added to it all now is his compelling urge to solve the problem bequeathed to him as an apparent part of the estate. He takes the Atlas and his notes to bed with him. Pulling the map of Georgia onto his lap, he stares at the rectangular form he has outlined with a highlighter: CALHOUN COUNTY. His gaze soon becomes a trance in hot pursuit of the body's need for the sustenance of sleep.

September 24, 2000

For the first time in months Dave sleeps not only through the night, but also without moving; and well beyond any Saturday morning sleep-in, ever. Indeed, he may have gone even longer allowing his body to restore itself from the ravages of sleep deprivation, had it not been for one of the most startling experiences of his life. His mother so fully alive: vibrant and vivacious, laughing, so fully herself. She is sitting in her recliner reading a book. Putting the book down to her lap, she speaks to Dave: "Dave, you did it. David is waiting for you. Go. I'll see you on Hartford."

But now to Dave's utter sadness or terror, if not terror, then certainly the kind of panic Dave has rarely experienced, he realizes that she is leaving. She is walking away. Dave screams, "Mom, wait, wait! Wait for me." She keeps walking, turns her head slightly to look at Dave, smiles, and resumes her journey. "Mom, no don't g…"

Dave picks himself up off the floor. Stunned and bewildered, his heart beating so fast he feels flushed, he wipes the sleep from his eyes only to feel the wetness of his tears. The dream was so real. Dave simply remains on the floor trying to understand what has just happened, beyond the fact that he has fallen out of bed. *Hell, I didn't just fall out of bed; I must have jumped.*

"My God, that was so real. She was so real. What was that all about? I don't know, but I do know that I need to journal that one."

All the while that Dave is showering, shaving, making the bed, fixing coffee and brunch his entire mind and soul are wrapped up in the dream. It was a dream that somehow seems to have been more than a dream, an event.

Dave takes his coffee and his journal to the screened–in porch. It is a beautiful autumn day. The maple leaves are carpeting the ground. The hot sun is baking the leaves. A pungent aroma fills the air and the lungs of those who breathe it. It is the kind of day that intoxicates those who enter its sacred passages, especially those who walk blindly but willingly, and innocently into a sanctuary such as this.

There was a time when St. Bernard's Catholic Church was Dave's sanctuary. St. Bernard's was home to Dave. St. Bernard's was where he went to elementary school. St. Bernard's was where he and his friends would go to shoot baskets on the playground or in the gym. St. Bernard's was where he and Anna worshiped on Sundays and two or three times during the week. St. Bernard's was where Dave served as an altar boy. St. Bernard's was where Dave would go when he was troubled.

Dave recalls, as he sips his coffee now, how he would as a twelve-year-old walk the half-mile down the road from the farm to town—a town literally built around the Catholic Church. In those troubled times known as pre-adolescence and the ever-worse adolescence that soon followed, just the sight of the huge church so solidly grounded to the earth gave this tormented youth the reassurance that all would be well.

Walking up the front walk, seeing the cross guarding the roof and beckoning Dave toward the ornate but welcoming doors, sometimes in itself was enough to wipe away the doubts and fears—enough, even, to soak up the tears. The red-tiled roof warmed Dave's heart as well as the interior of the church.

Father O'Connor was always there when Dave needed him. Never too busy to talk. Never too preoccupied to listen. Really listen. But all of that is over now. Father O'Connor is dead; and to Dave so is the Church, or at least a Dead End with signs that say "No Vacancy"—"No Admittance"—"Stay Out". For Dave, the sanctuary of his youth is now a gated community and "his kind" is kept at bay.

Today, however, he should have seen it coming. A few years before he had purposefully "walked" straight into a similar moment—a turning point moment. It was a similar kind of day, but Dave had walked to Memorial Park, an expansive green space in what Omahans nostalgically continue to refer to as "mid-city" when in fact at least two-thirds of the city lies to the west of the park. Bringing his journal with him, he walked toward the Rose Garden intending to grab a bench and journal amidst the beauty of the multicolor display, and breathe in the intoxicating aroma of hundreds of roses. Alas, a wedding was going on. Dave felt the pang of disappointment, but knew exactly where he would go now.

It was one of his favorite spots in the park. It had always seemed to him that this particular maple tree had demanded this panoramic view as its own entitlement, its reward for some unknown civic deed like the Soldier Monument some 50 yards behind and at the very crest of the hill. Unknown deed? Well, the "Soldier" had fought for freedom; the tree had fought off encroachment. "It is a wonder," Dave thought to himself, "that this park even exists." This tree and the dozens of other trees seemed to Dave to act as a regiment defending the park from urban housing invasion. More to the point, this tree and the park itself were defending the past from the future—a sanctuary for the present moment.

Sitting at the base of the tree and leaning his back against its trunk, Dave began to write. He had come to this park intending to journal with his deceased dad. It had been a contentious relationship—at times bitter and unbridgeable. But Dave had decided he would try to sort out some of those issues by way of his journal.

The pen began moving; he was speaking with his dad as if his father was present right there under that tree; as if his father was sitting on the other side of the tree. They were really communicating for the first time. Yes, for the first time in Dave's life he felt like he understood his dad. For the first time he felt like his dad understood him—maybe even accepted him. Maybe.

However he didn't see it coming then. He doesn't see it now.

Propping his legs up on a black wicker ottoman Dave takes in the multidimensional view always fascinating, even mesmerizing to him—a view through the front yard and down the street, trees and houses framing multiple scenes of color and form. "Life is so simple from here," Dave says to the rabbit nibbling away at the grass only about 5 feet from where he is sitting. "So simple, but I fear my life is going to get really complicated. How would you like to trade spots, my little furry friend?"

The rabbit, apparently uninterested in the tendered proposition hops off. Dave grins, "I don't blame you fella. You know a good thing when you got it." With that Dave opens his journal and begins to write:

Mom, what happened? You just walked away from me. I pleaded with you to stay. I know you can't stay. Not really. I know you are gone. I know this is my grief, my pain over losing you. But what, pray tell, was that all about?

Dave, I just wanted you to know that you did it—that you have it figured out. I didn't know when I was with you that David will be waiting for you in Morgan, Calhoun County, but I do now. I will see you on Hartford, Dave. You are on the right track. Don't stop. Trust me, Dave. I love you.

Mom, I love you too, but what is this all about?

You will find out, Dave. It is not just for me, or even for David. It is something you need to do for you. You will see.

As Dave places the pen down with the journal still open and held against his raised knee, he notices with amusement a flock of five wrens drinking and bathing, playing and frolicking in the birdbath. "Wish I had it as easy as you guys," Dave says to the birds. At the sound of his voice, the wrens are instantly in the air with a flutter.

"Wish I could take off like that; just go, don't even think about where to, just go to it wherever *it* may be—go there wherever *there* may be. In fact, I wish I could be as free as a bird to go there even if there is no there there."

Looking around, Dave cannot help noticing three squirrels sitting up with their front paws poised in an inverted prayerful posture. "Look, you guys talk to yourself too. I've heard ya—chortling to yourself when none of your buddies are around. Well, if you can talk to yourself, so can I."

On Hartford. On *Hartford.* *Not* in, *nor even* at, *but* on. So what in the hell does that mean? Maybe I need to get the Atlas out again. But no, somehow I don't think she means a town or city or village or county. I just don't know.

✳ ✳ ✳

That evening Dave is seated in front of his computer monitor typing Calhoun County, Georgia onto the search box. Moments later a list of possibilities appears on the screen. Tapping Calhoun County Dave suddenly has a photo of the Calhoun County Courthouse at 111 School Street, Morgan, Georgia, staring him in the face. While it is a pretty photo, one that reminds him of his mother's high school in Mexico, New York, the web page does not offer much promise. It has not been revised since 1997. But the photo!

The photo somehow provides a sense of reality to the journey that Dave knows in the depth of his soul he is about to embark upon. Now he knows where he is going and he has a clear picture in his head of what the destination will look like. He can hardly wait to drive into the town of Morgan and have a clear vision of that Federal style courthouse. Who knows, perhaps there is some clue to be found in the mix between the Courthouse in Morgan and the former private academy turned public high school in his mother's hometown. *The "Albany to Albany Train" Albany, Georgia to Albany, New York?*

Returning to the original resource list, Dave taps onto Calhoun County Government. This one seems more promising. Under "maps" he taps "M" and then "Morgan", but the result is a nearly blank page. No new information. Scrolling back, he decides to tap on one of the other three major towns in Calhoun. He finds "Edison"—taps the mouse, and is dumbfounded by what he sees on the screen. Here is a map of Edison, Georgia, nearly as sketchy and blank as Morgan is, but with one startling difference: the one and only street identified by name is *Hartford Street*.

"My God. This is totally unreal. Mom, you said you would see me 'on Hartford'. Hartford, here I come."

As Dave is showering, the excitement builds—feeling on the inside as tingly as he would feel on the outside if it were a cold shower pummeling his body. Turning the handle to the off-position, and reaching for the towel on the hook near the shower curtain, Dave's arm remains poised in mid-air: *Shit, what am I thinking? I can't just go. I'm not like those birds. I have to complete that article. But wait, yes I can. I can write that from anywhere. You do have a laptop, Dummy. In any event, there is sure to be a library in Morgan. It is the county seat after all. Maybe, I'm more like those birdies than I thought. Besides, Gary will look after the place.*

"What I do need though is to do whatever research I can accomplish from here on Mom's family tree. *I can try the Internet's* Ancestry.com *and see what I can find.*

Predictably, Dave takes his prized seat at the computer and goes to the genealogy website. His search for information on Anna Barnes goes nowhere. "This is really helpful," Dave says as he slams a partially open door to his computer desk shut. "I know that trying to locate information on women in genealogical records is not well rewarded, but Mom's family didn't just drop out of nowhere. I mean, I never heard that they landed here as passengers in a UFO! Although, with one too many beers, Grandpa was a little strange."

Just for kicks, I'm going to try David Wooten; *see what that may catch.* The catch for David Wooten with a birth date of 1920 +/- 20 years yields only four "Gene Pool" records none of which seem promising, but there are 88 individual records for a variety of David Wootens. As Dave scrolls through the listings, most with little to no information attached, his eye falls on three listings for *David L. Wooten, born October 4, 1839, date of death March 31, 1909, Morgan, Calhoun County, Georgia.* Dave concludes there is an almost certain chance that David L. Wooten is the man he is after. David L. Wooten will, as his mother said, be waiting for him in Calhoun County—maybe on Hartford Street, in Edison, Georgia.

Dave pulls out the Atlas again and, together with the maps acquired from the Internet, realizes that the most efficient route to Calhoun County from Omaha will take him directly to Edison—and Hartford Street. Picking up the receiver, Dave waits for his editor to come to the phone. After a short wait

Dave says, "Bill, I need to take some time off. Another project has come up and I need to get onto it right now. I'm heading South. I'll be in touch."

The next call is to Gary's hotel in Santa Fe. Dave explains to him how he has run onto some leads to what his mother was talking about prior to her death. "Gary, I'm going to be gone, perhaps, several weeks. I just want you to know that not being able to be with you, to see you, to hold and to be held by you…well, damn it, I would not be doing this unless I could not not do it."

"I know, Guy. Look I understand without really understanding. The thing is, if you tell me you have to do this, then damn it you have to do it. I cannot and do not want to hold you back. Besides, if your mom is behind all this, the last thing I want to do is get in her way. That's like standing in the middle of a railroad track with a runaway train coming down on ya. I'm stupid a lot of the time, but I'm not that stupid."

"Gary, you are a true friend."

"Yeah, well, I hope I'm something more than just a friend."

"Gary, you know you are everything to me. Look, I've got to pack up and get some sleep; but I will keep in touch with you, constantly. Thanks again for being there for me."

"Hey, Dude, no problem. Besides, this trip I'm on is turning out to be a longer venture than I had planned. Maybe we will both be returning to Omaha at the same time. But, have you called Sharon?"

"Not yet. Why?"

"Well, she is our friend, right?"

"Yes."

"Actually, she is more your friend than mine. More your friend than ours. Do you think she knows?"

"Of course she knows. I mean, what do you mean by 'do you think she knows?' She just likes to be with us."

"No, Dave. Sharon likes to be with you and you have to face into that, Ol' Buddy. If we, well you more than we, are not careful Sharon is going to get hurt."

"What the hell are you talking about, Gary? Sharon is just a friend."

"Uh huh. I've heard you say that about me when we are out in straight company. The fact is Sharon is much more than 'just a friend' to you and you know it."

"Gary, you have me really puzzled now. What the ever-loving hell are you getting at?"

"Dave, for Buddha's sake, she looks like your mother, she talks like your mother, and she cooks like your mother. She is an incarnation of your mother.

You and your mother have always been so very close. With Sharon it will never end, and I'm not sure I can compete with that. Frankly, I won't even try; at least for very long. I love you, but I feel the time has come to say what I just said. I know I have hurt you, Dave. I'm sorry, but I won't take it back."

Dave has gone from standing by the phone to sitting on the edge of an over stuffed chair to sitting on the floor, from smiling to looking glum, from feeling eager to jump into an imagined pool to fearful of even putting his toe into the water. "Gary, I don't know what to say."

"You don't have to say a damned thing, Guy. Just think it over, but while you're thinking also remember that I love you. "

At about 9 the next morning, just before locking up, Dave places a call to Sharon at home. He knows she is at work. He could call her there, but decides not to bother her. "She's probably at a staff meeting. She wouldn't have time to talk anyway, even if she is at her desk," he reasons aloud.

The fact is Dave does not want to talk to Sharon—and, he knows it. He listens to her voice on the answering machine, hangs up, and dials her work phone. The receptionist answers only to hear a click. "Wrong number, I guess," she says to Sharon who is standing at her elbow.

He redials Sharon's home phone and says, "Sharon, this is Dave. Just want you to know that I will be out of town for a few weeks. I'll be in touch. Going South to do some research. Take care."

He imagines Sharon coming home later around 5:30, punching the messages button and listening to his message. He cannot picture her dress. All he can "see" is her walking away at the very sound of his voice. Dave hangs up and walks out the door feeling a weight in the middle of his chest, as if his center of gravity has suddenly dropped into his heart.

* * *

A young woman returns home from work. She is wearing a blue dress that sets off her glowing blonde hair like the sun rising above a body of aqua blue water. She appears to be in her mid 30s with the poise of a woman who knows the meaning of life. A smile comes upon her face at the sound of his recorded voice. The smile fades as she yanks off her dangling bracelet and flings it across the room. "Why? Why do I bother?" she cries as she collapses into a recliner nearby.

Her Yorker, Sammy, leaps into her lap and snuggles into her neck. Sammy whimpers echoing the sighs and muffled cries of his owner. As the sun goes down, increasingly darkening the unlit room, Sammy continues licking the salty tears of his wounded mistress.

Chapter 3:
The Struggle Begins

A journey of a thousand miles
Begins with a single step.

September 25, 2000

As Dave is driving along I-29 south to Kansas City and from there east on I-70, his thoughts are naturally varied including the mother he will never see again and his immediate destination, Edison, Georgia. First, and for miles, all he can think about is how much he misses Gary, his companion of so many years; and for long minutes, maybe even hours, Dave hardly realizes he is talking to his mother, as if she were at his elbow:

"...and you know, Mom, I don't even know where we go from there."

Tears flow now as Dave is struck by the hard reality that he is alone. *Mom is gone.* Pulling over to the side of the road, he barely hears the horns of passing vehicles, but understands: *My God, I never signaled. I was in the outside lane, crossed two lanes and stopped suddenly right here without... It's a wonder I'm alive.*

"I've got to get a grip. But as I was saying, Mom, I don't know where I am going after I get to Edison and Calhoun County. Calhoun County, Calhoun."

Calhoun...John C. Calhoun. As a rose bud slowly forms from a barely discernible size, to that of the proportion of one's little finger nail, to the mass of a laboring man's thumb, and finally bursting forth with its blossom's birth, Dave slowly acknowledges he has a massive problem ahead of him. John C. Calhoun is Dave's Rorschach test; and at this very moment Dave knows he is failing the test. John C. Calhoun, for Dave, signifies the Confederacy, the very cause of the American Civil War, Slavery, and the Old South. Indeed, is there really a New South?

While he has always considered himself a political liberal, detested the Jim Crow laws, and all such segregation efforts to "keep those Niggers in their place," he never participated in the Civil Rights marches, sit-ins, or any such demonstration of his solidarity with the cause. Yet, that is precisely where his heart lies, and Dave seriously doubts there is in fact anything like a "New" South. *It has been only 46 years since Brown v. Board of Education, 32 years since George Wallace ran on a Segregationist ticket for President; and Strom Thurmond is still very much alive and kicking in the Senate; nor is the KKK just an historical anachronism. It will certainly not be a welcoming place for people like Gary and me.*

"What the hell am I doing this for? I am going to feel either like a fish out of water in red neck Georgia; or, worse yet, totally estranged from all the other fish." Moments later Dave recalls his mother's words: "They need to get things right...and so do you."

"That's what this is all about, Mom? My own personal purification? I thought this damned journey had to do with doing you a last favor, a fulfillment of a death bed request. I thought I was engaged in this for you, not for me. Shit! Well, I tell you what: I should be in Edison tomorrow afternoon. I'll drive the full length of Hartford Street, east and west. Then, this kid is turning right straight around and heading back to Omaha. That's what! Then, Gary and I can get on with our life."

In his heart Dave knows he is lying to his dead mother. Deep in his soul, as if written with an indelible pen, there resides a promise authored by his mother to whom he can never recall telling even a small fib—a covenant signed and sealed as if in his own blood. Dave has wriggled out of commitments many times in his life, but never, no not ever did he even think about wriggling out of a promise to this woman. And he knows with the certainty that he will draw another breath that he is going to see this thing through. Whatever is required, whatever the cost, he will go the route.

There is a force driving him: a force much bigger than himself, a force over which he has no control, a force that is mysterious, and somehow even spiritual, if not sensual. It is the force of love and the power of a loving relationship severed from its physical presence. Penny, the hospice social worker, he recalls, had warned him that his grieving would be profound because of his "special relationship" with Anna, "deeper than 99 out of 100 mother-son relationships," she said. "Grieving," Penny noted, "is a matter of relearning the world, relearning how to get around in this world without the one we love any longer being physically present."

This son who had done everything with his mom, shopping, movies, opera, symphony, often with Gary coming along as well, knows that this journey to Georgia is in part his exercise in relearning his world. But Dave had read somewhere that grieving is the "process of exhuming all that was, lovingly examining it, and carefully reburying it." Somehow he understands that he is definitely into the exhumation piece even now, with, as Ray Charles so often sang, "Georgia on (his) mind."

September 26, 2000

Having stopped at a café near Abbeville, Alabama, for lunch, Dave is faced once again with a feeling of antipathy. *What is it?* he wonders. *Is it the southern drawl of the waitresses? Is it the fact that the one and only Black took a table in the very rear of the room? No one appeared to have told him to go to the rear. No sign commanding: "Front Tables, Whites Only." The fact is a white man sat in the other rear corner, and the white waitress served them both; indeed, she treated the Black Fellow just as friendly as she treated anyone else in the place. I wonder, though, how would she treat me if she knew* what *I am?*

Moments later, Dave is crossing the Chattahoochee River at Fort Gaines, Georgia, and grabbing his attention, as if it were lit in neon, is the road sign informing him: **Edison 15**. This is a road sign no different than any other anywhere in any other state. To Dave, however, it means that in about 20 minutes he will be in a place he had never heard of until about a week ago. Edison is a town he would probably have never heard of, if it were not for his mother's dying, if it were not for the strange carryings on at her deathbed. What was that all about anyway?

Sure enough, within minutes Dave is rounding a curve past a convenience store and up ahead the sign welcoming him to Edison, Georgia, and just beyond that the first street sign informing him he is now on Hartford. "Well, Mom, here I am. Where the hell are you?"

Dave is enthralled with the attractive homes of varied architecture along the west end of town. These 1950s vintage houses are followed up by a 1920s-era downtown with quaint raised sidewalks along the way.

Then it happens—the sickening feeling of a front tire having gone flat. Pulling over to the curb, he gets out to inspect the damage and notices he is parked directly in front of the Public Library. Fortunately, they are open for business.

Entering the library he inquires of the woman at the desk where the nearest service station might be located. She is a pleasant, helpful and most friendly woman, attractive in a strangely familiar way—strangely familiar. She is very interested in Dave, where he is from and where he is going.

The first is easy: "Oh, I am from Omaha, Nebraska," Dave responds. "But I'm not at all sure where I'm going. Other than to change my tire and find an auto shop, after that everything just depends. It's all up for grabs, I guess."

"I see," the librarian replies as she turns to note the roar of a 18-wheeler passing through town.

As she does so, Dave is shocked by what he sees; or is it shocked by *who* he sees. It is as if he were looking at his mother in her younger years. The same round face, high forehead and full eyebrows; the dimple in her chin, brown eyes; and the clinchers: a very similar lilt to her voice and the blonde hair. He stands gripping the edge of the checkout counter for all he is worth, fearing he might lose his equilibrium. He has never been drunk in his life, except for one evening when he began to feel real woozy. He feels that way now.

"By the way what is your name?" she inquires.

"Dave...Dave Benson," he manages to respond.

"Well, I'm pleased to meet you Dave. I'm Annie Belle."

"No!" Dave gasps.

"What?" she retorts with a puzzled expression as if she cannot believe what she has just heard. Did she just hear a complete stranger deny the most basic of all truths—her very identity, her name, the very name she has lived with all these 25 years? What *is* this guy?

"No...I mean...it can't be. No, that's not it. What I mean is that...well, you see, my mother's name is Anna. I mean my late mother's name was Annie. And I am here in Edison because she told me, just before she died, that she would meet me on Hartford."

Dave's face is as red as the Confederate flag he noticed hanging from the front porch of a house just down the street. Never before in his life has he felt so out of control, so dumb-founded, so lacking in his ability to communicate with another person.

"Forgive me, I feel like a klutz. But just before you told me your name, I was already stunned by how similar you look to my mother, especially as she was in her twenties and thirties."

"Don't worry. I figured something was going on, but I am really interested in what you said—that your deceased mother told you she would meet you here in Edison? Right here on Hartford Street? Let's sit over here at that table by the microfilm machines, and you can tell me the details."

Dave finds a listening ear in this librarian, but an unnerving familiar countenance. Taking it all in, Annie Belle finally responds by asking, "Tell me Mr. Benson, what were the family names in your mother's background?"

"Please call me Dave. I think the most important link lies between her mother and the Wootens. I have done some genealogy research on the internet, and the best I could do, it seems important, was to find a David L. Wooten who was born here in Calhoun County in the 1830s I believe; and who died in the early 1900s in Morgan."

It is now this young librarian's turn to feel stunned. "Dave, there is a connection somehow between the Wootens and my family line, the Sheppards, but it will take my mother to help sort it out. She is gone…" Annie Belle hesitates in mid sentence, looks to the floor, and then continues by saying, "but I will talk with her tonight. I know there are many Wootens around this whole area. Why don't we meet in Morgan tomorrow around 8 at the café-convenience store across the square from the Courthouse? I will have some information for you."

Dave returns to his car. Before pulling away from the curb with his spare tire now in place, he glances again toward the library. What he sees startles him. The lights are off. The place appears to be closed and quite empty. "Whoa, that was quick. Why didn't she tell me to leave? I can take a hint."

September 27, 2000

It is a typical convenience store handling the "necessities" of life: motor oil, Twinkies, AA & AAA batteries, Windex; but an extra add-on is this 5-booth café. The folks are friendly and the food sure smells good. However, Dave is getting nervous. It is already 8:30 and no Annie Belle. Maybe it was just a dream. What are the chances that he could find someone so quickly in Edison who could so much as hint at being of help in his nebulous quest? What are the chances that such a person would look so much like his beloved mother? What, dear God, would the odds be that she would also carry the name Annie?

If you buy into Carl Jung's theory, and Dave made that purchase a long time ago, there is no such thing as coincidence. If something occurs by coincidence, then it has happened through accident, accidentally. No way does Dave see this Annie as an accidental occurrence in his life, far from it. No, this Annie, and the very fact that he had a flat tire in front of her library, are not accidentally dovetailed events. It is Jung's synchronicity at work. There is something going on here that defies explanation, something that goes beyond the pale of normal human events, something almost Other Worldly.

Just as Dave is about to give up and order his own breakfast, she walks in explaining that she was held up this morning; that he should go ahead and order; that she wants nothing, not even coffee; and that she will have to leave soon.

As Dave stands at the counter waiting for his food to be served up, he feels puzzled. Annie Belle seems strangely different this morning compared to her almost intimate friendliness the day before. She seems in a hurry, troubled, and evasive. Turning slightly to look at her, he notices her whole posture is that of a woman nearly despondent. Even her shoulder-length blonde hair has lost its sheen and she is idly yet intently staring out the window, gripping the edge of the table so firmly that her knuckles have turned a luminous white. Dave feels an inexplicable chill run through his entire body.

Just as he is about to lift the tray with his scrambled eggs, sausage, muffin and coffee upon it, he glances around at his destination only to experience a blurred vision of Annie. He places the tray back down, removes his glasses only to discover they are perfectly clean. He shakes his head at the thought that this blurred vision of Annie is very much like the Rothko painting of the girl with the turkeys—ghostlike and surreal, almost as if the girl is not there at all.

"If you don't mind. I mean…I hardly know you, Annie Belle, but you seem troubled. I mean it's really none of my business, and I do not mean to be intrusive." A half-smile breaks through glumness, but like the sun on an otherwise damp, dreary, cloud-shrouded day, the light disappears so quickly that Dave wonders if he really saw the familiar and much valued sign of wholeness and well-being.

"No, that's okay. I'm fine. Just not a morning person, I guess. But I do have some information for you. I talked with my mother, she thinks you should check out the cemetery here in Morgan. It is just the other side of the courthouse on the edge of town. You will find a large collection of Wootens there. You can't miss their section of the cemetery. By the way my mother wants you to know that David L. Wooten is a fine man.

"You also need to check out the records at the courthouse; but before you do that, go back to Edison. Across the street from the library is a Historical Center. They will let you see all the records you want."

Rising from the table, this young informant sadly and with a forced smile bids Dave a good day and walks away as he is in the process of finishing his meal. "Wait," Dave almost pleads, "will I see you again?"

45

Turning back now to face her interlocutor, Annie Belle appears ever more faded, a shadow has fallen upon her very presence and persona. "I…I don't know. But I must go now. It is time. Just one other thing, Dave. Stop in at the Salem Cemetery on this side of Edison right off this road. Perhaps we will meet again. What you are doing is so important, and you do need to get things right." Abruptly, she turns and walks out the door.

Dave panics: quickly swallowing his coffee and nearly choking, he rushes to the door. "Annie, I don't even know your last name, nor do I know your mother's name."

"Price," she responds. With that she disappears around the west side of the building.

Bewildered, as he has never been bewildered before, Dave closes the door, retrieves his cup and walks over to the coffeepots for a refill. The store clerk smiles at Dave and inquires, "You look puzzled sir. Can I help you?"

"Yes, by God, you sure can. Do you know that young woman who was here with me?"

The store clerk, a happy-go-lucky middle aged woman who reminds Dave of the TV Aunt Jemima he had seen as a kid, suddenly loses her fun-loving and jovial manner. It is as if Aunt Jemima's pancakes had flopped right there in front of millions of viewers. She turns strangely hesitant and puzzled. "Sir? Ah, I don't recall anyone being with you? Guess I just wasn't observant."

"What? Only seconds ago I rushed to the door and talked to her, and you were right over there by the door on the other side of the counter as you are now; and I recall you looking right at us."

"Yes, sir. I saw you at the door. I heard you talking to someone, but I never saw anyone other than you, Sir."

Shaking his head to clear his thoughts, Dave decides to take a cup to go, pays his bill, and walks out the door. Peering in the direction of Annie Belle's departure, Dave nearly loses his grip on the Styrofoam cup. There is no parking lot on the west side, just tall brush and a ditch. "What the hell!"

Turning left from the Convenience Store and driving around the square, Dave notices out of the corner of his eye a large monument off to the left. Since another car is tight behind him, he continues around the square a second time. This time knowing exactly where he is going, he has an earlier view of his destination. He wonders how he could not have seen it before. One of the monuments is so huge, he thinks, you would have to be blind not to see the cemetery from any location.

The large monument draws him to itself as if it were an industrial magnet and he a tiny metal peg. He is hardly prepared for what he discovers one hundred feet from the monument before him. Engraved in large letters is the word: **WOOTEN**. On the south side of the monument he finds:

David L. Wooten
Oct 4, 1839–Mar 31, 1909

"Okay," Dave explains to all of the Wootens beneath his feet, "now all I have to do is figure out how, or even if, you all have anything to do with my mother and her death bed visions." Turning back toward the convenience store Dave adds, "and you Annie Belle Price."

After taking careful note of all the engravings at the hardly inconspicuous Wooten plot, Dave heads toward the courthouse and begins the turn into a parking place. Suddenly he changes course. For the fourth time this morning, he drives the circuit around the Town Square. The car seems to be driving itself now, going west on Georgia Route 37 toward Edison.

She said she might see me again. What the hell does that mean? She works at the library, so anytime I stop in there, I will see her—if she's on duty of course. But, by God, I'm going to stop there first and find out when she is scheduled to work. "David L. Wooten is a fine man," she said. IS? She said that as if he is still alive!

"Hi, I'm Dave Benson from Omaha, Nebraska. I was in here yesterday afternoon. I had a soft tire right out front. Well, actually it was pretty flat by the time I left here. Anyway, Miss Price so kindly helped me out by telling me where I could get a tire repaired, as well as heading me in the right direction of finding some ancestral data. Could you tell me…?"

Dave stops in mid sentence as he realizes he must be speaking a language foreign to this librarian's ears. This woman, perhaps 25 years older than Annie Belle Price, and looking so distinguished, matronly even, when Dave first approached her, stands before him now with her mouth agape. She appears as puzzled as Dave felt after noticing there was no parking lot behind the Morgan convenience store.

"Sir, you must be mistaken. This library is not open on Mondays. Used to be, but we had to cut hours due to budget about a year ago. And, I'm very sorry, Sir, but there is no one by that name who works here; never was."

"Now wait a minute. I was in this library yesterday and yesterday was Monday, or at least it was on Omaha calendars. I met this young woman who was standing right where you are standing now. We went right over to that table near the microfilm machines and talked for quite some time—at her suggestion I might add. Only about an hour or so ago she and I met at the café in Morgan where she finally told me her last name. All I got yesterday was that her name was Annie Belle. And you're telling me now that no Annie Belle Price works here? No Annie Belle Price ever worked here? And the library I was in, *this* library, wasn't even open?"

"Well, Sir, I am truly sorry, but all I can tell you is that this building is not open on Mondays, it was not open yesterday, and yes Sir no person by that name has ever worked here."

"Okay. Play along with me here, please. I admit I may have simply assumed she was a librarian and that she worked here. She never, now that I think about it, came right out and said she worked here or that she is a librarian. Perhaps…perhaps, she was simply here with one of your staff who dropped by for some reason prior to my arrival? Perhaps Ms. Price is a member of the community, a library customer?"

"Again, Sir, all I can tell you is that there are only three people who have keys to this building: myself, the other librarian and her husband who is our custodian—and they have taken a long weekend to go to Atlanta to visit family. They will not be back until this evening. I know of no one in this county by that name; certainly no one who patronizes this library has such a name. This is a small county, this is a small town and we pretty much know who's who around here. In fact I make it my business to know folks because of the nature of my job."

Feeling like a whipped puppy, Dave ungraciously thanks the librarian and dejectedly walks out the door. While feeling disappointed and mostly abandoned as if by his last friend on earth, his attention is drawn to the sign just down the street: **Historical Center**.

Being totally consistent with Dave's "lucky" day, the Historical Center is open only Wednesdays and Fridays. So, he decides to head back to his motel room in Albany, but as he drives out of town he notices the cemetery at Salem Baptist Church which the mysterious Annie Belle mentioned. He pulls into the churchyard and parks.

The church sits back from the road facing south with a large grassed frontage and parking area accessible from a street off Route 37. A small burial ground on the north side and the much larger cemetery on the east complete the framing of this Norman Rockwell-like scene. The north lots are marked with simple gravestones; the eastern assemblage is remarkable with its sometimes-huge vaults, tombstones and statuary.

"Segregated unto death," Dave blurts out sarcastically. "But at least the ebonized were apparently allowed to worship at this pretty little church, as well as permitted to be buried on the grounds—even if out and away from the white folk."

Dave saunters off toward the north lots noting with saddened interest the engravings, etchings perhaps would be the more appropriate term: Eliza 1860, Elisha 1839–85..."And how many of you were slaves and servants of the folks over yonder," Dave asks the silenced ones beneath his gaze.

Wandering aimlessly around this graveyard, Dave finds himself entering the more ornate and documented cemetery, coming face-to-face with a large granite monument: **SHEPPARD**. Dave feels stunned, as if awakened suddenly from a dream; startled, really. He is taken back to the morning only a week or so ago when he found himself on the floor of his bedroom.

"Dang. My Miss Mysterious did say I needed to check on the Sheppard/ Wooten connection; and here be the Sheppards":

Sadie Ann Sheppard	**Augustus Eugene Sheppard**
Feb 2, 1870–Oct 31,1945	**Dec 1, 1859–Nov 28, 1909**
William Drayton Sheppard	**Martha S. Sheppard**
Sep 30, 1830–Apr 13, 1915	**Sep 30, 1833–Apr 13, 1915**

Dave mulls over the interesting coincidence of dates of birth and dates of death for William and Martha, and just as his mind wraps around Sadie's middle name, Ann, his eye falls upon a nearby marker.

Once in a while, not often, but once in a while events unfold in our lives, events outside of ourselves, which become a part of our on-going selfness, a major connecting thread to the fabric of our lives. For Dave, until this moment, while standing at the Sheppard plot at Salem Cemetery in Edison, Georgia, the only other such moments, encounters transformed into stories to be told and retold and told again included:

  • how he had, as an 18 year-old newly graduated high school senior, backed away from an ice cream stand at the Nebraska State Fair and knocked an ice cream cone from the hands of a cute well-proportioned, curly-headed hunk—his name was Gary;
  • how he even recalls the page number he was reading in

Parson's & Shills', **Toward a General Theory of Action**, when Gary came home to inform him of Kennedy's assassination.

He does not know it at this very moment, but he is about to have another story to share. A story that he will repeat over the years until he gets it right—the story of how he saw her: Yes, his eye froze on the marker:

Annie Belle Sheppard Price
Nov 19, 1888–Sep 16, 1912

But out of the depth of his soul Dave feels a presence; and out of the corner of his eye he observes something the rational mind would argue cannot be. At the edge and just behind the tombstone stands the smiling "Miss Mysterious Annie Belle Price."

Dave is speechless. Her soft and glowing blonde hair loses its sheen as if the sun has suddenly gone under cover; but there is not one cloud in the sky. Her smile evolves into the sadness he witnessed as this mysterious young woman disappeared earlier in the day back at Morgan. Suddenly, for the second time, she is gone from Dave's sight.

A Blackbird perched on a tombstone nearby cocks its head in apparent wonderment at the man sitting on the ground, his arm wrapped over one of those human-made stones. This bird does not understand why those humans do such things as haul large stones around and place them side-by-side in such places as this. This bird does understand, however, this man. The bird flies to a spot closer by, cocks her head to the left, to the right, forward and back. This bird, in a most primitive way understands the pain of loss. She has recently lost her mate.

With each sob from the forlorn human embracing the stone, a chirp is emitted from the observant Blackbird. Following each human sob with its subsequent bird chirp comes one of the mother bird's babies, each one taking its own perch, each one adding its own voice to a most beautiful but unobtrusive chorused requiem.

This caring bird, on the other hand, might be quite surprised if she could understand that this hurting man has no idea why he is crying. Dave wonders aloud in the sanctity of this private space: "Why am I so emotional? Is it simply the shock of not only seeing Annie Belle's tombstone, but also my imagining her standing here? Hell, that was no damned imagination. Or, was it seeing what I presume is Annie Belle Sheppard's mother's grave as well, Sadie Ann Sheppard? Or was it pure and simple grief over Mom's death. Most likely a combination of all the above, plus one. This Annie is a carbon copy of Sharon. Yes, I was attracted to this Annie. I have been (have been?), attracted to Sharon. But I know I can have neither one of them, any more than I can have my mother back. I have heard of complicated grief, mine is getting more and more complicated. I hate this shit!"

Chapter 4:
Eureka

...a work of art
[comes] from one place,
one time, and
one writer's personal circumstance
that manages nevertheless to reach
across five generations
to address accurately the general human condition.
Can there be a better definition of art?
(Edward O. Wilson, *The Future of Life*)

September 28, 2000

Dave and his unnoticed companions remained at the cemetery until the sun began its exit over the horizon beyond Edison. He then traveled back to Albany to his motel room where he journaled himself to sleep.

As he awakens the next morning with his journal at his side, he picks it up and reads:

✳ ✳ ✳

"Dear Journal,

"This really is too much. First my Mom's deadly illness. Then her death and her 'commission' to me to impart upon this damned journey! All the strange visions she had; all the strange things she said. But, and I have never admitted this to anyone, not even myself, or to you: I never saw the people she saw. I never talked with them as she did. But I did have a sense of their presence, especially the David she talked about. If there were such a thing as spectacles one could put on to peer into times past, lives lived, people and times gone from us, I know I could have seen what Mom saw. I could have heard what she heard. Alas, I could not; but now...

"Yes, now I wonder if that is not the cup that is granted to me. Why, if so, does it feel both like a blessing and a curse?

"My Mother, Anna Barnes Benson told me she would meet me on Hartford. I meet this most mysterious Annie Belle Price on Hartford. She looks so very much like my mother. She tells me she would perhaps see me again at Salem. I find Annie Belle Price's grave at Salem Cemetery, and I see her ever so briefly near the tombstone. Mom died on September 16, 2000. Annie Belle Sheppard Price died on September 16, 1912. Is there anything beyond the sheer coincidence of dates? I think so, but I know not what.

"Did I really see, meet, and talk to the Annie Belle who died 88 years ago? Was it my Mom? Or, dear God, was it both? Neither?

"There is more to this story. I am both eager as well as more than a little frightened to find out how the thing ends. Worse yet, what if there is no ending? In any event, there is no turning back now. I must go on. The Historical Center opens at 10 in the morning. I will be there.

"Dear God, you are certainly the God of Surprises. Be with me."

✷ ✷ ✷

At 10 A.M. sharp Dave is at the Historical Center right behind the person with the key. Mrs. Davidson is a kindly lady. She is interested in Dave, where he has come from, how she can help find the who and what he is looking for. But before Dave can really explain his needs, he learns this lady in her early seventies has lived her entire life right here in Calhoun County, right here in Edison, right here on Hartford Street. She has 6 children, 15 grandchildren, and 2 great grandchildren. She and most of her family are members of Salem Baptist...That is the opening Dave has been waiting for—he moves in as Mrs. Davidson takes a breath:

"Tell me, do you know of a young woman in her mid-twenties by the name of Annie Price, Annie Belle Price?"

Mrs. Davidson studies him carefully replying, "No I don't; and I'm reasonably sure Young Man, that no such person lives here in Edison; or in Morgan, Arlington, Leary, or anywhere else in this County for that matter—unless she moved here since yesterday. It's sort of my business to know who's who in these parts."

"And know everyone's business as well, I suspect."

"But, if you go up to the cemetery at Salem Baptist Church, you will find a marker for an Annie Price who died in the early 1900s. You will find her with the Sheppards. Her father Gene, mother Sadie, and her grandparents are all there."

Sensing that the better part of timesaving is the wisdom to know when to keep one's mouth shut, Dave chooses to say nothing more. It is already 10:30; time is a-wasting. On to the task: "I'm here hoping to track down some of my late mother's ancestors."

Dave is not yet used to speaking of his mother in the past tense, nor is he really comfortable using the adjective "late". He is a long way from being courageous enough to say, "My deceased mother." He feels a kind of disorientation just having admitted to Mrs. D that his mother is no longer living, that she is dead.

"Oh, I'm so sorry. How long ago did she pass, if I may inquire?"

Sensing immediate disaster here and anticipating that any encouragement at this point could mean another half-hour's delay in reaching his goal, Dave responds, "Nearly two weeks ago. It is mostly due to her last wish that I am here and I feel a great urgency to get on with the task she set for me."

At this point the way is made straight for Dave. He has a willing and open audience. Better yet, a living, breathing, encyclopedia of local historical trivia, a font of local genealogical wisdom, and a bottomless data bank. After explaining how it is that he has reason to believe there is some familial connection between his "late" mother and a David L. Wooten who once lived in or near Morgan, this comely, talkative, community busy-body, becomes transformed into a professional and scholarly archivist.

"Mr. Benson, I do believe you have come to the right place. I'm not at all sure how much information we have here, but I do happen to know we have more than a little, perhaps more than you really want. Follow me."

Doing as ordered, Dave trails along behind until she motions for him to take a seat at a small round table. Within seconds Dave is holding a folder labeled *Wooten*. Before he can bring himself to open the "Wooten File," however, Mrs. D. has placed two other folders in his care:

"A'm raasonably sarton y'all need to take a gander at those two as wayl," she informs Dave with her most authentic Southern drawl—a drawl that Dave is not only growing somewhat accustomed to, but even developing a kind of fondness for as "wayl".

"You see," she continues, "you mentioned Annie Belle Price. Well, she was a Sheppard and I think it was her sister who married a Wooten. Their mother, Sadie was a Manry. Those are the other two files. By the way, Dave, many folks think Wooten is a German name, but it is English and means a copse of trees. Please don't ask me how I know all this stuff. Grew up with it, I guess. My mother and her mother were, for a long time the town archive, 'cept it was all in their dear old heads; but my dearly departed husband always said there was 'nothen in their hayeds'. God rest their weary souls, all three of them."

* * *

The room has turned deadly quiet, and Dave is left with the folders debating which to open first. Finally, the Wootens win the toss. While he cannot find the proof of the theorem that his mother is related to the David L. Wooten line, he is sufficiently satisfied that this is the David who visited during her dying days.

Two Civil War documents concerning David L. Wooten and his brother Roach nearly jump out of the folder begging Dave's attention:

David L. Wooten
13th Regiment, Georgia Volunteer Infantry,
Evan's Brigade, Gordon's Division
Army of Northern Virginia,
Randolph & Terrell Counties
(Randolph Volunteers)
Enlisted 12 April 1861
Age 22
Roach Wooten
51st Regiment, Georgia Volunteer Infantry
Drayton's Brigade
Cuthbert Rifles
Randolph County
Enlisted 10 March 1861
Age 20
Surrendered 26 April 1865, Greensboro, NC

But when Dave opens the Manry File, the task before him begins at once to become clearer and daunting as well.

Sadie Ann Manry married Augustus Eugene "Gene" Sheppard. One of their daughters, Bessie, indeed married a William "Will" Wooten. Dave's attention, however, is drawn to another Civil War document apparently misfiled with the Manrys:

William Drayton Sheppard
32nd Regiment, Georgia Volunteer Infantry
Ramsey's Company E
Washington County
Enlisted 7 May 1862
Age 32
No Further Record

Dave ponders the significance of "No Further Record" for a few moments when three other War Records appear. It is Sadie Ann's uncles, her father's brothers, James Henry, Benjamin F. and John Bird:

James Henry Manry
51st Regiment, Georgia Volunteer Infantry
Company E, Pochitla Guards
Calhoun County
Enlisted 22 March 1862
Age 21

Benjamin F. Manry
51st Regiment, Company E, Pochitla Guards
Enlisted 22 March 1862
Age 19
Killed 14 September 1862, South Mountain, MD

John Bird Manry
51st Regiment, Company E, Pochitla Guards
Enlisted 22 March 1862
Age 17
Killed 14 September 1862, South Mountain, MD

Suddenly, Dave slams the palms of both hands on the top of the table before him: "My God, it's Ben and Johnny B. I don't believe it," he exclaims as if he wants the entire town of Edison and perhaps the whole county to know.

Just as suddenly, Mrs. Davidson appears with motherly expression painted upon her face: "Is everything all right in here?" she asks.

"Oh, yes. I'm quite okay," Dave stammers. "It's just that…Mrs. Davidson, do you have a few minutes? Could you sit down? I need to tell you what is really behind my visit and what I have just found."

"Well, Young Man, I do have a few minutes—in fact quite a few. My partner just came in, so she will be able to handle things for a while. But I would prefer that you call me Darlene."

For the next half-hour Dave details the entire account of his mother's dying days, as well as his experiences since arriving in Calhoun County. Mrs. Davidson sits uncharacteristically silent for a long moment, brushes her hair back away from her eyes carefully tucking the renegade strands of almost lucent gray back behind her ear. Finally, she leans forward, takes Dave's hand into the protective embrace of her own.

"Dave, if I may call you Dave rather than Mr. Benson, I have no more information that I can share with you from this great storeroom of wisdom up here," she says while tapping her head. "I do have something in another file that may well prove helpful to you. It is an old diary. Never read it myself, but as I recall it covers a considerable period of time. Sadie Manry kept it from the time she was about 10, I believe, until at least the early 1900s. You go get a cup of coffee and I'll locate that diary for you."

True to her word, the diary is an old one, over a hundred years old now. The pages are brittle and brown. Some of the writing is quite faded, sometimes written with pencil, most of the time in ink. A few pages appear missing, many are torn, folded, faded, or combinations of the three. The frontispiece in an immaculate and bold script proclaims,

This is the Diary of:
Sadie Ann Manry
Edison, Georgia

The first entry is dated 21 February 1880:

Grandma Manry gave me this diary to keep. Guess I'd better use it. But I just don't know what to say. Guess that's not really important. But I don't want nobody no how ever looking at what I write here. So, Diary, keep shut!!

The next several pages and entries are either illegible, missing, minor reports about the weather, or accounts of special family events, such as birthday celebrations:

3 June 1880:
Today is my brother Allie's birthday. He is 12. Wish I were that old. He knows a lot. Wish I was that smart. He's so strong. Wish I was that strong. Allie is a lover. He loves everybody and everybody loves him. Wish I could love like Allie does. Wish someone would love me.

4 July 1880:
Fireworks are banging & exploding & looking pretty downtown, but B. Pappa says we will never attend a 4th of July celebration until after the Lord Almighty takes Grandpa & Grandma Manry home. Grandpa says there is no way he would ever party with the North after "what they did to my boys."

It is her entry dated 14 September 1880 that glues Dave's eyes to the page:

Went to Grandma & Grandpa Manry's today. Wish I'd a stayed home. I forget how utterly glum they get on September 14th. Every year it be the same. Usually, like on September 13 and Sep 15, they are themselves. But, Law, the 14th is a time to stay away. I'd much rather go to a funral than walk between those two on this here day. B. Pappa says it has been this way ever since Uncle Ben & Uncle John Bird were killed up on that mountain up in Marilyn. Grandma isn't so bad, probably cuz B & JB weren't her kids. She doesn't even get worked up about her first husband being killed in the War. Maybe she didn't like him as much as she likes Grandpa. Wish I had known my other Grandma Manry! In fact, I wish I'd known Uncle Ben and Uncle John Bird.

Dave stares at the page. *So, Grandpa's boys, Ben & Johnny B, were killed by Union forces at South Mountain, wherever that may be in Maryland; but is there more to the story? Is there more behind the apparent depression, the hurt, the anger, and the on-going and obviously intense grief? Who knows? I probably won't ever know.*

15 September 1880:

That dream, it happened again! The same thing as before. It's not scary, but what does it mean? I think I have had it at least twice before: On top of a mountain stands this fox by an open well. The fox looks so sad. That's it; that's all there is to the dream!

12 October 1880:

It was such fun riding over to Albany, being at Cousin Hattie's for her birthday celebration. My, those folks know how to put it on! But Mamma says it just is not like it used to be. I don't know what it used to be. I get so sick of hearing that. Mamma says IT ain't what it used to be. B. Pappa and Grandpa always get to going on it: The help ain't what it used to be. The cotton ain't what it used to be. I don't think anything is what it used to be. I just wish they would shut up and enjoy something. It's as if they don't want a girl to enjoy anything.

21 February 1881:

So, so I'm eleven years old. So what? Nothing really changes. God, I wish something would change. Anything!!

1 March 1881:

This house is going to get crowded. Mamma is trying to be sly about it, but she can't fool me. She said, "What would you think about having a little brother or a little sister?" I said, "Are you telling me you're with child, Mama?" She says, "Just wondering, that's all." We'll see. I think she is just preparing me for the change. Maybe she's preparing herself.

10 April 1881:

Well, the theory of having a little brother or sister is becoming a proven fact. Mama can't hide it any longer.

14 September 1881:

Why, oh why didn't I tell Mama & B. Pappa that I was deathly sick & stayed home? That way I would have missed the awful scene. The visiting preacher's sermon was so boring. IT

59

made me sick. But then, I completely forgot that this is Gloomsday for Grandpa. After the worship service Grandpa insists, once again, that we all walk over to the cemetery. Once again, Grandpa goes morbid: "Why couldn't they have been buried here? Why? Why?"

The thing is I don't know where Uncle Ben & Uncle John Bird were buried; and no one will tell me. I asked Grandpa once and I'll NEVER do that again! I asked Grandma twice, but she just looks at the floor and says, "Its best a girl not know that." I hate being treated like a little kid. Mama & B. Pappa are no help either. They just walk away and say nothing. Maybe the Union Army took Uncle Ben & Uncle JB up North somewhere and put them in a museum or somebody's trophy case. I don't know and I give up asking!

15 September 1881:

Same dream as I've had before, but this time the fox looks off into the distance, then back to the well. I've never petted a fox, but I want to pet this one. He is so sad.

15 November 1881:

He's here! My little brother Theo Richmond was here when I got up this morning. B. Pappa said, "We didn't want to disturb you. Besides it is not really the place to be for a child." Well, I'm not a child. I'm almost a grown-up. Papa said, Dr. Wheeler & Eliza, Theo's Nanny, wouldn't let him in the room either. Well, B. Pappa is a man and men don't have babies. They only make 'em, somehow.

Dave thumbs through the pages that follow until his eyes land upon an entry for 7 February 1884:

Gene Sheppard dropped by today to ask B. Pappa if he would allow Gene to take me to the dance a week from tonight. BP agreed. He likes Gene. Gene is a pretty successful Planter. He is much older than me. He is quite handsome and so very polite. But I wish he had asked me first. And I wish BP had asked me before he agreed to the bargain! It makes me feel like a bale of cotton or a cow! Yet, I feel flattered.

A dance—whatever will I wear. Mama & I have to do some serious talking. Eliza is such an accomplished seamstress; she can fix me up in something new & beautiful in no time.

14 February 1884:

Eliza did it. The dress is beautiful. It fits as if it were made special for me! Well, it WAS! But I am so nervous. I hope I don't pass out when Mr. Sheppard (I mean Gene) comes for me.

15 February 1884:

Heaven: Yes, Diary, Heaven is where I am today. Last night was so much fun!! Gene is such a wonderful dancer. He is so gracious, and he makes me feel so important. He treats me like a real adult, like a woman, not a girl, not a teenager, but a Woman! I felt like the "Queen of the Ball." I was just about the youngest girl, I mean woman there; and Gene was probably the oldest man with a date, other than the married men with their wives. I think I love him.

18 February 1884:

My God, Gene stopped by tonight. He asked me to go with him to Albany on my birthday. He asked BP& Mamma for their permission after he asked me. I like that. I like him. I told him I wouldn't know what to wear and he said, "Wear the dress you wore the other night. You look so beautiful in it." My God, I thought I was going to faint!"

22 February 1884:

To Albany tonight with Gene for my birthday dinner at the most elegant hotel in the city…I'm so excited I can't think. I certainly cannot possibly write! I cannot sit still.

23 February 1884:

Becoming 14 is a birthday I shall never ever forget as long as I live! The ride to Albany was so marvelous. The dinner delicious as well as superb. I had no idea Gene's parents were going to be at the hotel as well, but they simply stopped by our table to chat for a few minutes. Mr. Sheppard (he asked me to call him WD) and Mrs. Sheppard are such decent people. Guess I'm supposed to call her Mrs. Sheppard. Maybe I'll call her Mrs. WD sometime and see how that goes over.

On the way home Gene asked me to marry him. He wants my permission to ask B. Pappa for my "hand". I sure hope he wants more than my *hand*! I told him I need a little time to think about it. He is so understanding: "Take as much time as you need," he said.

Well, I'm not telling him this, but I really needed only the time it takes for the carriage to turn its wheels once! As hard as it is, I will wait two weeks before I tell him I accept. I accept. I accept--- I can't believe this is happening to me!

24 February 1884:

Earlier today I remembered something that happened at the hotel the other night: Gene & I were talking at the table. His parents came by, took the other two chairs and ordered tea. We had a very cordial conversation until Gene's friend Hodge Wooten also came by. Hodge pulls over another chair and again the conversation was most delightful, until—and this is the Big Until:

Hodge (whose real name is Hodges T. and known to most as simply H.T. Wooten) said something about his uncle having been in the War & that his uncle had been a POW. I was sitting right directly across from Gene's parents. It seemed just as soon as HT brought up the subject of the War that Mr. & Mrs. S gave each other a look that I've seen Mama & Papa give each other. But this was the kind of look Allie gave me the day we had snuck onto the freight train over at Williamsburg, and realized the train was getting ready to depart. I don't think WD or Mrs. WD wanted to talk about the War. I think they wanted to get off the subject as much as Allie and I wanted to get off the train.

15 March 1884:

I did it. Oh Dear Jesus, I did it. I told Gene I would marry him. He was so happy. He jumped up out of his seat. Danced a little jig. Pulled me into his arms and swirled us around the middle of the room. Mamma & B. Pappa & Eliza & Theo & Allie came a-rushing in to see if the ceiling had fallen in or something. Gene went right to the task and asked BP for his consent to our marriage. BP, with that devilish twinkle in his eye, said he would have to think about it. He walked toward the study with his hand on his chin, took one or two steps, whirled around and said, "Sure."

Mamma agreed, somewhat reluctantly. She would have liked for me to complete one year of finishing school. She jumped in after BP consented to the general idea, and ordered that the wedding not be earlier than July of next year. She wants me to be clearly 15 going toward 16 before getting married.

BP wisely added another proviso, "And whatever you do, do not under any circumstances have this wedding on the 14th of September! Later on Gene asked me what that was all about. I just said it was a special day for Grandpa. Didn't want to get into that right then!

Everyone seems pleased, except for Allie. He thinks Gene is too old for me: "Look at it Sadie! Gene is almost twice your age. He will be only three years from being 30 and you will be 15." I set him straight. I told Allie that when Gene is 60 I will be 49 and nearly 50 and that when Gene is 80 I will be nearly 70. It makes no matter as long as two people love each other. But I don't think Allie goes along with my reasoning. He does agree that Gene is a fine man. Allie only wants the best for me.

14 September, 1884:

When am I ever going to learn? Gene and I went for a ride way over to Leary this afternoon. On the way we stopped by just to see how Grandpa & Grandma Manry were doing. Grandpa has not been doing too good of late. Why did I think he'd be doing any better today of all days? He was sadder than I have ever seen him. After we continued on to Leary, I explained the whole thing to Gene. He was truly saddened.

Our ride was a pleasant one except for all that—and then, we stopped over at the Sheppards. Again, they are such warm and hospitable people, but when Gene told them about Grandpa Manry's grieving over his two sons' death in the War—well, all

I can say is the room turned frigid. It was as if Gene had said nothing at all. I didn't say anything to Gene afterward, but he could not have helped but feel at least ignored. I felt annoyed, slighted, even offended. I do not want my Grandpa's pain diminished in any way.

One very exciting & happy thing came out of our ride this afternoon: We have set our wedding date for August 4th. That is only 11 months away. Only? Eleven months feels like an eternity.

15 September 1884:

My recurrent dream! Why does it keep coming back? But this time it was real different, I mean REALLY different: same mountain, same fox, same sad fox, same open well; but Gene's dad stands off to the side looking away from it all. This dream is not scary and never has been; but it is getting boring. Actually, it is not boring at all. It does seem to be going somewhere.

From here on Dave's interest in Sadie's journal entries diminishes; they have so much to do with wedding preparation. He is struck, however, by the timeworn experience of being a teenager, an adolescent. Sadie is clearly both at this time in her life, even as she prepares for the adult experience of marriage. Yet, there is never any journal entry concerning the wedding itself.

He is about to fold the time-weathered book shut when he notices Sadie's entry dated 20 June 1886:

My Dear Grandpa has passed. I cannot say that he is dead. He has passed the test of being a great man, great father, great husband to two wonderful women, great grandfather, and a great Christian. Dear Jesus welcome Grandpa Manry into your Heavenly Kingdom.

I shall never forget and shall forever value my presence at Grandpa's bedside, Lord, in his final hours with us. He wasn't real conscious of our presence, but he was quite aware of your presence. He reached out for or to you speaking your name as his Lord and Savior.

And then, oh then, he spoke as if B. Pappa's mother was

there: "Ann, oh Annie, you have come." I vowed right then and there that if I ever have a little girl her name shall be Annie.

But the miracles did not cease with Grandma Annie Manry coming for him. Their sons Ben and Johnny B came as well. Grandpa died weeping with joy and calling, "Ben, my son, John Bird, my boy, let us go home." Grandpa lay back down, and with the most beautiful smile I ever saw upon his face, Grandpa died. There I said it: Grandpa died. I can't write anymore. I am crying.

One hundred and fourteen years later someone else is weeping, and he knows what he has to do. As certain as day follows night and as sure as water flows down hill, Dave knows he must go to South Mountain. However, he thinks he knows one other vital fact: Hodge Wooten, Hodges T. Wooten, H.T. Wooten is most likely Hooten-Tooten Wooten, Dave's great-great grandfather.

Chapter 5:
A U-turn

Perhaps everything terrible
is
in its deepest being
something helpless
that wants help from us.
(Rainer Maria Rilke, *Letters to a Young Poet*)

September 29, 2000

Having located South Mountain as part of the Battle at Antietam near Sharpsburg, Maryland, Dave slept well through the night, confident now in where he is going and the goal to be obtained. All he need do is "go to the mountain" as the old adage puts it, the mission will be complete, and then back home to Gary (and Sharon?) and on with life.

However, life is rarely that simple. Goals to be achieved usually require delayed gratification. The greater goals bring with them greater costs. Dave has not yet reached the point of realizing his goal, to be reached, will require huge investments of time, energy, resources, and most of all self-understanding. He has not yet come to appreciate Rilke's caution and promise that on the other side of the challenges and terrors of life lie riches and rewards only the soul can value. It is probably just as well.

As Dave walks into the motel lobby, bags in hand, and tosses the room card-key on the counter, the desk clerk raises the rhetorical question: "Checking out, Sir?" It is at that very instant that Dave executes a U-turn in his mind and replies: "No, no, I'm not. I mean I thought I was, until you raised the question. Can I have that room back for at least another night?"

Having been granted a stay on his stay at the motel, Dave carries his bags back to the room and heads back toward Edison. It has occurred to him that there is much more he needs to know if he is to accomplish this mission. "If there is even a molecule of fact to be known about each of the people Mom mentioned, I need to milk Edison and Calhoun County dry before I go on. Mom said there is a need to 'get things right,' well I need to know more."

As Dave enters the Edison Public Library, the librarian asks (Dave believes in a knowing and cautiously sarcastic manner), "have you seen that young woman again?"

Somewhat defensively, Dave replies, "No, sure haven't. Not even sure I ever did?"

To Dave's surprise, the librarian walks around the counter to where he stands, looks him squarely in the eye and says, "As I recall you are Dave Benson, but I don't think I introduced myself. I am Hattie Colquitt; and I'm here to tell you, Young Man, never, ever, discount the kind of experience you claim to have had right here in this room and down the road at the cemetery and at the café in Morgan. You are talking to believers in this town. We know those things happen. Folks in this town are not going to come up to you on the street to spontaneously tell their story; but they all have such stories of encounters with those on the Other Side."

Dave, a bit nonplused by this unexpected but most welcome, affirmation and reassurance, can only say, "Thank you."

"Now, what can I do for you today, Mr. Benson?"

"Well, first of all, you have already done a great deal for me, believe me," Dave says with a sincerity emphasized by taking Hattie's hand in his and looking her directly in the eye. "Just call me, Dave, please. It has occurred to me that I need to know a whole lot more than I do about the Wootens, Sheppards, and now the Manrys as well. Do you have something in the stacks that can get me started?"

"Dave, I think I'm about to make your day. Right over here we have a volume entitled, *Against Oblivion: History of Calhoun County, Georgia.* I'm not at all sure it will answer all your questions, but it will give you a jump-start; I'm reasonably sure of that."

Beginning with Sheppard because of the intriguing Annie Belle link and the diary, Dave soon hits pay dirt.

WILLIAM DRAYTON SHEPPARD & MARTHA SHEPPARD, he types into his laptop:

"Though not related, both their fathers were named John Sheppard. Both were from Washington Co., Ga. William and Martha had the same birthday only three years apart, and both died on the same day, one in the morning and the other that night…Martha Sheppard Sheppard's father was a prosperous planter and slave owner in Washington Co. William, an ambitious young man, came to Calhoun County obviously looking for cotton land. He soon acquired much acreage and reared a large family."

Augustus Eugene Sheppard was one of the five children. Recognizing Augustus as the husband of the diarist and apparent father of Annie Belle Price, Dave hurriedly thumbs through the next few pages. His gaze freezes on the passage, "Eugene and Sadie's original home place is now the residence of Verna Sheppard. They had 11 children." Annie Belle Sheppard is one of those listed.

Wow, busy folks. I need to find this "original home place," if possible.

But it is the next paragraph that glues Dave's eye to the page:

"William and Martha m. on 12/13/1851 in Washington Co., Ga. William served as a private in the War Between the States in Cpt. E.P. Howell's Battery, Light Artillery, Steven's Brigade, Martin's Battalion in the state of Mississippi."

Dave sits back to absorb what he has found so far, noting it all on his laptop. There is something, or is it more than one, that troubles him, but what is it? *WD came to Calhoun County as an "ambitious young man." But he was 32 in 1862 when he enlisted. He would have been 35 when the war ended. In those days 35 was considered middle age. But this book was written nearly 30 years ago, over 100 years after the War, and perhaps the author was incorporating present day standards of age and aging into the stuff of history.*

Suddenly, the other item that causes him to wonder is the discrepancy, he thinks, between the information in this book and that which he found at the Historical Center regarding WD's service with the Confederacy. Paging through his notes he finds the information taken from the Center's files with the source indicated as *Roster of the Confederate Soldiers of Georgia*. What he has just found in *Against Oblivion* provides no source other than as written by a granddaughter, Eunice Lewis, Annie Belle Sheppard Price's sister.

Why? How? Dave wonders. *It certainly makes more sense that WD would have served with a Washington County regiment if he lived in Washington County at the outbreak of the War. Doesn't make much sense that he would have served with a Mississippi unit.*

He is about to move on to the Manry line, when his attention focuses on Gene Sheppard's date of death, November 28, 1909. Dave's internal computer goes to work. He is startled to realize that at age 39 Sadie was left with the plantation, plus a one-year-old and a three-year-old, as well as six other children. At least, three of her eleven children were grown and out on their own.

"That woman sure had her hands full," Dave says without realizing he has spoken aloud. Mrs. Colquitt, to his surprise is right at his elbow. "What's that?" she asks.

After explaining to her what he has learned, part of it by deduction, Mrs. Colquitt informs him that there are two or three places he might want to check out. Yes, from what little she recalls having heard, Sadie Sheppard certainly did not have it easy—especially after her husband died.

"From then on, I guess it was pretty much an uphill battle. Actually, she may have won a battle or two, but she did lose the war of keeping the plantation intact. There is no longer anyone alive who has even second hand knowledge of her. But I can tell you this Dave: Sadie Sheppard is a sort of legend in this town. She was a strong woman."

"Is there more you can tell me?" Dave asks.

"Not a whole lot, other than this: First, you might want to drive up the street here, and right where the church sits about two blocks up on this side of Hartford is where the original Sheppard Plantation sat. Secondly, the house that once sat right there is now just north and to the west of Morgan. I can give you directions, if you want. The house has been restored to look pretty much like it was 100 years ago."

Dave thanks Mrs. Colquitt for her helpfulness, and returns to the task of reading through the Manry and Wooten lines. Later, as he gets up from his perch at the table, which he now realizes has been a three-hour visit, Mrs. Colquitt is again at his side. "Before you go, Dave, I don't know why I'm telling you this. I have no idea what it means, or if it is important."

"Ah, how's about letting me be the judge?"

"All I can tell you, Dave, is that my parents and my grandparents, both sets by the way, said a number of times that the Sheppards were a fine family, but they were rather secretive. My Grandfather Culbreth once said, and I remember this real well, it was Thanksgiving when I was about five years old. Grandpa said something like 'The Sheppards have always been a family who would do anything for anybody in need. They will share all they have and all they know if they think it will help you. Yet, there is something there. There are some things that don't add up. As open as they are, you have the feeling that they are holding back some great wisdom from the rest of the world.' There, I told you; and now I wonder if I should have kept my mouth shut."

"Mrs. Colquitt, thank you. I don't know if it is important or not, either. But I do appreciate your candidness."

"Well, there is one other thing I would like to point out to you and I don't really know why I think I should." Taking the book, *Against Oblivion* into her hands, she pages through until she comes to the Sheppard section and places the book in front of Dave. "This Sheppard," she says as she points to the name, David Sheppard, "is a third generation descendant from Annie and Gene. He was a gifted artist. He studied in Paris. Worked in New York. Showed around the world."

"That is very interesting. My, ah, friend, Gary, is an artist. Perhaps he has heard of David Sheppard. I'll ask him. In fact I need to call him tonight. He is probably worried sick. I haven't called since I left home. Gary and I have been..." Dave catches himself and quickly adds, "but you have used the past tense with respect to this David Sheppard."

"Yes. Unfortunately, David died of AIDS about five years ago."

My God, she knows. She knows I am Gay. "That's too bad," is all Dave can muster to say.

Half way out the door, Dave steps back inside saying, "Mrs. Colquitt, again, thanks. Thanks for your help, and especially for your sensitivity. I would like to have Gary meet you someday. In any event, I am sure I will be coming back here before I return home. Something tells me you have not seen the last of me."

"Dave, I hope that is true; and, I would like to meet your special friend, Gary."

Oh, you would, would you? I wonder. I don't think so. Gary is probably not what you have in mind at all, Lady.

✳ ✳ ✳

Deciding to not take the time to check out the Turner Street house, Dave places his laptop in the car and walks up the street. As he closes in on the church he cannot help but notice the beautiful grounds and the surrounding wooded area. It is not difficult for him to imagine a large plantation being here. In fact his imagination places Tara from the movie *Gone with the Wind* right here where the church parking lot in back is located. In front of "Tara" and right where the church sits, Dave "sees" a large lawn and gardens with a circular drive.

"So, Sadie, you and Scarlet lost it all? How hard that must have been for

70

you and your family. Perhaps Durant had it right when he said it is 'almost a law of history that the same wealth that generates a civilization announces its decay.'"

Walking across the street to where the copse of woods stands guardian for the church and its community of faith, Dave says to those who once worked and played here, those who were born and died here, those who lived and loved, the Sadies and Genes, the WDs and Marthas and the Annie Belles: "Tell me a secret. I'll tell you mine: I am Gay. What is yours?"

* * *

Later that evening Dave takes out his journal in the quiet of his motel room and reflects on the day, reviewing what he now knows, noting what he thinks he needs to know, and how he feels:

Dear Journal,

I feel exhausted, yet exhilarated. I feel as if I am about to make a great discovery, yet it feels like a blind alley; worse, I sometimes feel as if I am blind.

I feel puzzled. There are some things that just don't fit, especially with William Drayton Sheppard (WD). Just sitting at the site of the old Sheppard Plantation, I felt uneasy. Reading Sadie's diary certainly provided a premonition that things were not right. I guess that's some of what Mom was talking about.

But speaking of Mom, it has just now occurred to me that all of the people she mentioned have "turned up" save two—Horace and Johnny G. All of those, other than H & JG, were Confederate soldiers. There have been no Horace or John G. Manrys, Sheppards or Wootens to show up from that era, as yet anyway. Right now my instinct says Horace and Johnny G are not to be found in Calhoun County. Indeed, I don't think they were in the Civil (whoa). I don't think they were in the Confederacy, but I do think they were in the Civil War.

What if...My God! What if they are the Barnes boys who were supposed to have been in the Union Army? All I ever heard was that there were two or three in the Barnes line who served. Need to call Gary and have him ship me that nutshell and ever so sketchy Barnes Family Tree Mom had.

One thing I know: I am not yet ready to go to South Mountain. I need to go to Washington County, Georgia, first. Maybe I can find WD there.

Another thing I know is that for some people, like Mrs. Colquitt, my sexuality appears written on my face, it's in my voice, it's who I am. The Mrs. Colquitts of this world see it. They see me for who I am and they accept me. I just need to learn to do the same.

I have more to say. I think. But am too tired to...

Around one o'clock in the morning Dave awakens with the journal still on his lap. Placing it on the nightstand, he turns the light off and is snoring within seconds.

Chapter 6:
Northward Bound

There is a day
when the road
neither
comes nor goes,
and the way
is not a way
but a place
("1997 VII," by Wendell Berry)

September 30, 2000

As Dave drives on Slappey Boulevard North heading out of Albany (trying to keep his eye peeled for the connection to Georgia Route 300 N), he unknowingly misses his turn at Oglethorpe. Dave's compass, if he had one, would tell him he is going due north, when in fact he should be cruising northeast. At about the same time he does realize the navigational error, he sees a sign indicating he is five miles from Leesburg and that he is on US 19. Pulling over to the side of the road, he grips the steering wheel with both hands, knuckles turning white with the anguish that is just now flowing to the surface from the deep recesses of a lonely, abandoned soul.

For the longest while he takes advantage of this time and space away from any living soul. No fear of a person in the rooms next door hearing a grown man weeping and wailing through the ever-thin motel walls; not even a mother bird and her family around to intrude, or so he thought.

This unintended "detour" is transformed from merely a way to get to where he is going to a place to be Dave—a place to be real, maybe even a place to heal. With no warning he is startled by a tapping sound at the driver's window. As he lifts his head toward the sound, he freezes at the sight in his side view mirror: flashing lights and standing just to the rear of the driver's door stands a Georgia State Patrolman.

"Sir, is everything okay?" asks this kindly looking police officer who instantly reminds Dave of his late Uncle Harry as he looked on the day of his retirement from the police force: same stocky build, pure white hair, nurturing demeanor; same cigar smell.

"Yes and no," admits Dave. You see my Mom just died, and today is her birthday, and I've gotten myself lost. Actually, I'm not so much lost as feeling lost."

"Yes, sir. I understand. I recall when my Mama died; that first day or two was pretty raw. When did your mother die, Son?"

"Over two weeks ago back home in Omaha."

"Two weeks ago?" Dave does not notice the expression of mild disbelief, but he does hear the sympathy in the officer's voice as he acknowledges the factor of annual reminders in one's grieving process. "And today being her birthday just kind of yanks the pain to the surface. Been there and done that myself, Fella."

Dave looks to the passenger side of the car marshalling the strength to say, "Yeah, all that plus the fact that I simply forgot today was her birthday. How could I do that, forget my own mother's birthday."

Then he notices someone standing at the passenger door. This man has a saddened, but friendly and beckoning look. His clothes are a bit ragged. He has all the appearances of a street person, dressed in faded and worn army clothing. No, those are not Vietnam era clothes. They are not even World War II army fatigues. His are military apparel, but from a more ancient vintage. These are Confederate army-cloth.

As Dave begins to speak to this stranger, the stranger turns his head toward and then away from Dave in a "come with me" manner and is suddenly gone. Turning now to the Patrolman, Dave hesitantly inquires, "Did you see that?"

"What?"

"Oh, I just thought I saw something over there," Dave gestures off to the right.

"Well, I don't know about you, Sir; but after my Mama died there was a long time there where I swear I was a-seeing her in the damnedest places. Learned to keep my mouth shut about it though. It does happen, Son; don't you worry about it."

74

No it wasn't Mom that I saw, but I think I'll take your advice and keep my mouth shut.

"Thanks, officer. Where am I anyway?"

"Well you're about five miles from Leesburg; and, as long as you asked: You have had the terrible luck of running into not just an officer of the law, but an old history buff to boot—one who is getting older and older by the hour, I might say. Anyway, this here little pullover area is approximately where there once was a depot on the Macon-Albany Railroad back in the 1850s and '60s. Yep, used to be known as Wooten Station. Don't for the life of me know why I'm a-telling you this, but don't cost ya no extry. Now you have a better day, Young Fella and drive safe."

Dave is stunned, "Wooten Station; and that was... This is absolutely insane, but that was David L. Wooten. I'm as sure of it as much as I know how greatly I miss my Mom. He wants me to follow him, but to where. Well he motioned northward and that's where this boy is heading anyway."

* * *

Later that day, around 1 P.M., Dave enters Sandersville on Georgia Route 24 and soon finds himself at the town square with the Washington County Courthouse in full view. It is a huge white Federal style building with a parking lot on the east side. The square is typical of so many towns Dave is familiar with such as David City, Nebraska, and Glenwood, Iowa, where the Town Square is literally a square with the courthouse in the center. Sandersville appears to be a prosperous town with every storefront beckoning walkers-by to stop in for a sandwich here, a book there, or a refill on a prescription.

Noticing a sign that says Washington County Genealogical Research Center, Dave allows the sign to lead him where he hopes he has to go. The Genealogy Center is straight across the square from the courthouse and is housed in a white-frame building most likely a family home at one time.

Noretta, a matronly woman with a welcoming manner that almost literally sucks Dave through the door as if he were precious gold dust and she a giant Hoover seeking such treasure. "What can ah do fer you, Sir?" she asks.

Dave explains that he hopes to find information concerning William Drayton Sheppard, especially, plus WD's wife Martha, their parents, and where their plantations may have been located. "And, I particularly want to verify William Drayton Sheppard's Civil War service record. So far I'm stumped."

Noretta orients Dave to the resources available and points out that the Center closes at 5 P.M. While it will not officially be open tomorrow, she will open the facility to him and him alone for as long as he wants tomorrow at 10 A.M.

Dave and Noretta are able to turn up only a meager amount of helpful data. They are able to verify Martha's parents as John Sheppard and Ava Brittan Sheppard, but there is nothing on record here concerning the identity of WD's parentage.

Noretta finally suggests that they walk over to the Courthouse to see what they can find. As they cross the square, she explains to Dave that Civil War era records for Washington County "tend to be an endangered species since many public records were burned and pillaged as Sherman's March to the Sea slashed its way right through here, you know."

Noretta introduces Dave to the staff at the Probate Office and turns him loose in the mustiness of history. Again, the fruits of research hang like that of a drought-ridden orchard; only a couple of items are worth plucking:

> • The certificate of marriage between WD and Martha verifies they were in fact married in Sandersville.
> • Beyond that, nothing—until Dave scans through old newspapers most of which threaten to crumble at the touch. He's not even sure why he saw them, such inconspicuous news items:
>> –NOTICE: Martha Sheppard's name along with that of a few other Sandersville residents: as of January 1, 1863 Martha S. Sheppard had not picked up her mail for three months.
>> –OBITUARY: "Friday, May 22, 1874: In Sumter County, GA., little William Robert Sheppard, on the morning of 29th of April 1874, aged 10 years, after an illness of 14 days of pneumonia, son of William D. and Martha Sheppard, formerly of Washington County."

Why, Dave wonders, *would the Sheppard mail go unclaimed for that length of time at that date?* Until then, he assumed that WD & Martha Sheppard most likely migrated south to Calhoun County around the time of Sherman's March to the Sea in the Fall of 1864, or later. *Instead, is it possible that Martha may have abandoned or sold their property near Sandersville as much as nearly two years before? At a time when the war yet seemed winnable by the Confederacy? How can it be that a Confederate soldier, at a time when few were getting passes to leave their units, could have been home to sire a baby anytime in 1863–64?*

Returning now to the Research Center, Dave thanks Noretta for her help. In addition he informs her he is still stymied by the shortage of information, especially regarding WD's Civil War service.

She smiles and responds, "You know we folks here in the South generally prefer to speak of that war as the War Between the States or the War of the Rebellion. You see our ancestors never saw anything civil about it. It was our ancestors right here in Sandersville who felt the torch. While the civilians here may not have been shot or stabbed in the body, they were stabbed in the heart as they witnessed all that they had worked for go up in flames or carted-off. Our folks lived through Sherman's Hell, and seven generations later we have not forgotten. In fact the ghosts still cry in the streets, in the woods, and on the land at night.

"As bad as it was here, on the scale of things, certainly compared to Atlanta, we were spared Sherman's wrath and the depravity of his men. Our great-grandmothers gathered in this very square to plead with Sherman to spare the courthouse. By the gods, he ordered his men to put their torches down. But if you traveled here from Albany, you may have come through Milledgeville, the Georgia State Capital at that time. No amount of pleading would have saved them. They were doomed as soon as Atlanta fell. The legends are rife over there of the ghosts crying out at night, walking the streets; lights going on, lights going off for no apparent reason.

"Sorry, sometimes when I get going, my husband says I don't know enough to stop. Just one other thing and then I will shut up. It sounds to me like you have about exhausted the resources at places like Edison and Sandersville. If you've got the time, I would suggest you go to Richmond and spend some time at the Museum of the Confederacy's Library. In fact if you want I can call them right now and you can set up an appointment."

✳ ✳ ✳

Instead of heading directly for Richmond, Dave decides to return to Milledgeville and spend the night there. After calling Gary, and then Sharon, he becomes enfolded in a shroud of exhaustion. No ghosts in the streets of Milledgeville could possibly disturb this man's need for bodily repair. But the dream:

Not long after closing his eyes Dave is on a train for Milledgeville. It is an ancient train more than full of people. There is a couple with a little boy who draws Dave's attention. The boy, whom his parents call AE, appears to be about 4 or 5 years old. His mother is an attractive woman who seems more protective of her husband than of her son. The boy's father is in a Confederate uniform. Dave notices as they board the train that the soldier walks with a cane. Nothing unusual occurs in the dream until the train suddenly comes to a stop. The soldier jumps out of his seat and runs down the aisle, but does so without his cane; and, without even so much as a limp.

In the land of dreams Dave has found WD Sheppard, Martha, and their son Gene. He is as sure of it as he is that his mother is dead, that Gary loves him, that he loves Gary, that Sharon loves him, that he, well, likes Sharon. The dream is all Dave can think about for the rest of the night. But how do you talk about this with anyone?

Dave knows Gary will listen. He is sure Gary would find the content of the dream interesting. However, Gary is sure to ask, "So, Good Buddy, what the hell do ya make of it?" Dave fears his interpretation of this dream will only produce an air of disbelief, at best, or quite possibly a diagnosis of, "Hey, don't you think you are loading your own stuff onto this dream, like you're dreaming what you want to dream, Man!" And Sharon just wouldn't get it, period. But then, you just never know with Gary. He just might understand completely. Most of the time Gary's insights are superior.

Shit, I wish Gary were here. With that thought Dave finally drifts back to sleep.

Chapter 7:
On to Richmond

...under the pavements, trembling like a pulse,
under the buildings trembling like a cry,
under the waste of time,
under the hoof of the beast above the broken bones of cities,
there will be something growing like a flower
something bursting from the earth again,
forever deathless,
faithful coming into life again...
(Thomas Wolfe, You Can't Go Home Again)

October 1, 2000

Driving north out of Milledgeville on Georgia Route 22 Dave notes the "Welcome to Sparta" sign at the edge of town. It is then that the dream comes back. He first recalls someone on the train saying something about boarding at Sparta, wanting to make it to Macon and on south to "Wooten Station near Albany where it is safe," and then there was something about "chewing" or was it "going to" gum?

"Such is the fickle nature of dreams," Dave tries to convince himself. "But that was such a real dream; and all four of us walked right into that hotel where I stayed last night, right along with a young girl, Eliza what's her name. She told me but I cannot recall it now. Here they all were in 1860s garb and me with my 21st Century Dockers, Birkenstocks, and Polo Shirt. Weird, but oh so real."

As he closes in on I-20, Dave's passageway north to Richmond, he comes to Warrenton, Georgia, and something in the back of his mind clicks: the girl Eliza said something about how hard it was for her and her party to get to

Warrenton. "This is so strange." *Actually, I think I'm dreaming with my eyes open.* Dave shakes his head and lowers the window for a little fresh air.

Just to the west of Augusta, Dave pulls off at a Rest Area, parks, and picks up his cell phone:

"Gary, look, every time I have called you, I've told you things are going fine. Well, frankly, it has all been a big-assed lie. Things are going, but I have no idea where they are going. Sometimes, like right now I think I'm going loony. I'm heading for Richmond, Virginia, and will be there tomorrow. I have an appointment at a library there for two days of research. I may be in Richmond for several days, actually. It has occurred to me that I need to do a helluva lotta research on the Civ...I mean the War Between the States."

"Boy, those Southern Crackers have gotten to you. You are even beginning to drawl," Gary breaks in jokingly.

"Yeah, I think they are getting to me, and it's not all bad. What I'm calling for is to ask a big favor. I need, Gary. Can you work things out to hop a plane and meet me in Richmond, for a day or two? I will be staying at the Richmond Inn in south Richmond."

"Dave, are you sure? I thought we agreed at the outset that this was a journey you needed to make totally and exclusively on your own? I do not in any way want to interfere with you and your Mom. She was intimidating enough in life. I don't want to piss her ghost off."

"Gary, I'm not asking you to complete this confounding journey with me. I just need to talk with you for a few hours." Your presence on the phone is important and I so appreciate your loving concern; but, Gary, I need your presence with flesh on it. I need you."

"Okay, Buddy, I'll try to work that out and I'll be in touch. Stay with it, Bud. I love you."

"Gary, you're a doll, I mean a Hunkuva-Doll. One other thing, would you bring with you the file folder labeled, 'Family Tree?' Don't know why I didn't bring it with me in the first place."

October 2, 2000

As Dave approaches Exit 69 for south Richmond, traffic comes to a complete halt. Police cars, fire trucks and ambulances ahead inform him of the unmistakable fact that a serious accident has occurred and that he may be stuck here for a while. Nothing is moving, except for another ambulance which he sees in his rear view mirror, slowly threading its way through the bumper to bumper traffic; nothing, that is, except for a man Dave realizes is heading his way up the side of the hill off to the right.

At first he thinks this is a street person coming out from his hideaway heading to a shelter for an evening meal, maybe even a semi-comfortable bed for the night. Maybe so, but this fellow is heading straight for Dave's car. *Looking for a hand out. Well, up with the windows, on with the AC, doors locked. Sorry, Fella.*

Suddenly, a chill runs the full length of Dave's body. The vagrant is not a vagrant. The "vagrant" is the same person, the same apparition Dave observed back at Wooten Station, the same man in a Confederate uniform motioning at Dave to follow him.

"David?" Dave hears himself saying.

The man in weathered Gray, smiles, and is gone.

✳ ✳ ✳

An hour later Dave walks up to the registration desk at the motel. The clerk informs him he has a message on the voice mail in his room. He asks the clerk, Jerome, to recommend a restaurant. Jerome, a tall and well-built fellow with broad shoulders, smiles and tells him that there are several very good cafés and restaurants in downtown Richmond, especially along Cary Street. Smiling, he adds invitingly, "and CJ's Brewery is where all the guys hang out. I'll be going there after I get off here in a few hours."

"Yeah, well, thanks; but I am really tired and will be putting-in early tonight." *People may not know who I am, but they sure do know what I am.*

The message is conveyed in Gary's voice: "Just letting you know I will be in Richmond tomorrow early evening. Don't worry about picking me up at the airport. I'll find my way to the motel and will wait for you there. Hey, Guy; just let the motel folks know I'm coming. I don't cotton to getting there, and some Southern Cracker turned motel clerk telling this Nigger to go back to the Plantation. Later."

Dave chuckles, sighs a sigh of relief, calls down to the Reservations Desk to inform Jerome, "A Gary Lee will be arriving tomorrow—late afternoon/ early evening to share this room. If I am not here sign him in, give him a key, and adjust my bill as needed."

"Sure. Will do, Mr. Benson. That explains it. I understand, Mr. Benson."

"That explains it?" What the hell? Oh, yeah, I get it. Well, you can keep on thinking you understand, you Dumbshit.

October 3, 2000

At about 10 A.M. Dave enters I-95 recalling the vision of DL Wooten at this very same spot yesterday, and for a moment wondering why of all places DLW should "show up" right there. It is a thought and a question that linger for only a brief moment. Other thoughts take over, such as making sure he takes the correct exit.

The beauty of downtown Richmond and the entire cityscape strike Dave immediately as something he would like to share with Gary. As he awaits a light change at Broad Street, he says to the light, "Gary will love this city." Minutes later, after parking his car in the parking garage at the Medical College of Virginia Hospital just across the street, Dave is walking up to the Museum of the Confederacy right next door to the Confederate White House. *Great Gobs of Goose Shit, I feel like a Yankee Spy.*

The Museum is a more modern building, but the Confederate White House is literally white, as is the Museum's quarters. The White House is of the Federal Style architecture with large white marble columns holding up the front portico to a large square house. As Dave walks up the pathway to the Museum he notices a beautiful courtyard between the Museum and the White House. While he would like to go sit awhile in the courtyard, he is drawn even more to what awaits him in the Museum's library.

"May I help you, Sir?" some distant voice asks. Dave's attention is welded to the huge portraits of Jefferson Davis, Robert E. Lee, the plethora of Confederate flags. The songs of Dixie playing over the sound system, and all that he sees, have acted as a catalyst to transport this "Yankee in King Robert E's Court" as if he were Dorothy no longer in Kansas, but at the door to the Emerald City. The colors here, however, are hardly emerald, but mostly red.

"Uh, yes, yes. I'm sorry, just got a little distracted by the immensity of the place," Dave lies. "I have an appointment to do some research at the library here."

Shortly thereafter Dave is escorted upstairs to an out-of-the-way world of books and files. "If you can't find it here, it may well never have existed in the first place," Karen, the research librarian half-jokingly says to Dave. "I have pulled out some files to get you started, based on our conversation the other day. You will undoubtedly discover a need for more, which we may or may not have. You just let me know. This table is reserved for your use for today and tomorrow."

Starting with the index to the *Rosters of Georgia Confederate Soldiers*, Dave begins with a search for William Drayton Sheppard. The search yields several possibilities. Finally, WD shows up:

WD Sheppard
Enlisted Company E
Ramsey's 32nd Regiment,
Georgia Volunteer Infantry,
Army of the Tennessee
Washington County, GA
(Lawton-Gordon-Evans Brigade)
Age 32
7 May 1862
Listed as Deserter, 30 September 1862

Dave sits and stares at the page. "Whoa."

A young man of apparent African-American heritage, perhaps in his thirties is seated at the next table. He looks up and smiles. Dave returns the smile to this rather handsome Gary look-alike. He is broad shouldered with a very similar twinkle in his eyes. Karen comes directly over. "Found something already?"

"Well, I think so. We'll see."

I'm not ready to talk about it, if it's all the same with you. A deserter. That explains a lot. Wonder if Sadie ever figured that out. I must get back to the copy of her journal that Mrs. Davidson ran off for me. Explains the secretiveness. Shoot, it may even explain some of that dream I had the other night in Milledgeville.

"If you've found *anything* worth exclaiming about, you're doing far better than this here 'Freed Slave', and I have been here for two days," laments the young man. "By the way I am A'Jamal and I am trying to trace some relatives of mine who were slaves and who, if you can believe this, turned right around and fought FOR the Confederacy. Man, I just want to know why they went and did that. Makes no damned sense to me. It apparently made no sense to my daddy either, nor his daddy before him. Dad and Grand Pappy, they never really wanted to talk about it. Damn!"

"Yeah, well, sounds like you and I are on similar missions—trying to trace answers to questions that our families never wanted to talk about," Dave responds. But as he does so he is nearly mesmerized by this Younger Gary. A'Jamal is simply twenty years younger than Gary is now, but nearly a carbon copy of Gary when Gary was that age. Dave laughs as he sees the ironic humor in his thought—*a carbon copy? Whatever other kind of copy* could *it be?*

"Yeah, Man, I know what you mean. Seems like family secrets know no boundaries according to race, color, nationality, or any such shit."

Dave simply nods his head all the while thinking to himself, *A'Jamal, you are so right for the wrong reason.* Instead of carrying this conversation on any further, Dave proceeds with his research. His mind keeps coming back to, "Listed as Deserter, 30 September 1862" and "No Further Record." *A deserter for Pete's sake. I have never been a supporter of the Confederacy's cause, but by God when you say you believe in something strong enough to enlist; well, damn it, stay with it—don't jump ship. How do I tell Mom her great grandfather was a deserter?*

"That's stupid; I don't have to. She's..."

A'Jamal looks up once again. Dave smiles apologetically and resumes his search, feeling a bit like the proverbial kid caught with his hand in the cookie jar.

While it is a laborious task, Dave's daylong research efforts pay off with the dividend of verifying the service records for David & Roach Wooten; as well as James, Ben & John Bird Manry. In addition he locates the information regarding all of the battles in which these combatants' regiments were engaged, including WD's brigade. Dave is now determined to plot each of these men's battlefield presence individually and collectively. However, he knows that is another day's work, at least.

The verification process reveals facts, beyond WD's apparent desertion.

- James Manry had been taken prisoner at Gettysburg on 2 July 1864.
- David Wooten became a POW on 19 September 1864 at the Battle of Winchester, Virginia.
- Both were taken to Point Lookout POW camp somewhere in Maryland.
- David Wooten, the records say, was "Paroled from Point Lookout and transferred to Aiken's Landing for exchange, 15

March 1865"; and "Received at Boulware & Cox's Wharves, James River, 18 March 1865."

So, Mom, you just heard it wrong: Not Lookout Point, but Point Lookout. You were always getting things backward, you and your dyslexic view of the world.

"Hell, you went for a long time calling Gary, Lee," Dave laughs as he remembers.

Again, A'Jamal peers over a book smiling expectantly at the laughter's source. Again, Karen is at his elbow, but this time with the news that it is quitting time.

Dave will return tomorrow for another day of research. Karen will have a file on Point Lookout ready for his inspection, plus some other material, which she thinks, might be helpful.

"By the way Karen, do you know where Point Lookout POW camp was located; and Aiken's Landing or Boulware & Cox's Wharves?'

"If you hang on a moment, I think I have a couple of maps, which will be of help to you. The sites will be identified on contemporary maps."

Moments later, as she hands the maps to him, Karen admits, "I must say I got a kick out of hearing you laugh a few minutes ago."

"Oh, I'm kind of embarrassed about that. It had little to do with anything found today, but a great deal to do with my Mom. You see, for a long time, she kept confusing my friend Gary's last name with his first. She does that a lot. Good Lord, I have to get a move on—Gary may be at the motel already. Thanks for the maps and all your help today. See you tomorrow."

* * *

As soon as Dave opens the door to his room, a giant of a man grabs him. He is in the embrace of the one person now left in this, Dave's world, who Dave loves with nearly every fiber in his heart. His longing for this very moment has become so palpable that he can fairly taste it. This has been the longest period of separation they have had to endure since being assigned to separate Air Force bases years ago.

Dave is crying, and to his surprise cannot stop. Gary holds him in his massive arms saying nothing to interrupt the flow of tears. Finally, after perhaps ten minutes of a time when words are no longer necessary, nor adequate in conveying the depth of love between two human beings, Dave squeezes out the words "I miss you, Gary. I love you."

Gary's big brown eyes begin to fill. Soon, the twin reservoirs begin to overflow and the rivulets turn into a cascading flood of human emotion pouring down an ebony embankment, suddenly transformed into a hurricane force as Gary thunders, "Me too." It is Dave's turn to console a hurting lover.

* * *

Later that evening, if a University of Richmond Sociology major were looking for the two happiest people in Richmond, and he or she were to walk into CJ's just off Cary Street in the Old Town section; there would have been no question: "The two guys in the back-booth, the good-looking blonde and his Black Hunk." They have just finished their meal, enjoying a variety of beers from CJ's Brewery, talking animatedly, and occasionally intimately.

The place is subdued with indirect and soft lighting; the walls are of a dark-paneled quality. They absorb both the light and the secrets shared here. The dark panels also protect the secrets and pain known only by the brick and mortar behind them—the trauma of a city devastated by war. If these walls could speak, they would inform the world of the utter folly of war out there; they could also catalog the vast variety of wars waged in the souls who have walked into this sanctuary.

These same walls provided sanctuary 135 years ago to those pursued by the "enemy". The "enemy", however, changed by the minute or hour. Sometimes it was a man in blue, minutes later it could be a man in gray; or perhaps a woman disguised as a man in blue or gray. No matter who it was these walls remained impartial. It is the same this evening. These walls are party to another war being waged—a war that seeks understanding as its booty. Dave and Gary are merely the most recent refugees to enter here.

"Well, Man, what brings me to Richmond?"

"My insecurities, and me I guess."

"As in?"

"As in…Well, for starters, as you know I came here, to the South, to pay off on a promise to my dying mother. I really thought it would be a simple matter. Hell, at one point I fully intended to drive up and down the main drag in Edison, Georgia, and head right back to Omaha. But I had a flat tire."

"A flat tire? Great Jumpin' Jackrabbits, Man. I've had lots of flat tires and not one took two weeks to fix," Gary interjects with his typical humor.

"Yeah, well, you see I notice the library is open. So I go in to find out where I can get the tire repaired; and, there she stands, a young woman who not only looks like my mother at that age, but her name is Annie Belle, as well. Annie is very helpful as far as the tire issue is concerned, and she promises to meet me for breakfast the next morning with the further promise to bring with her info pertinent to this quest I am upon."

"Damn, you sure do move fast, Stud," Gary says as he snorts in his beer.

"Shut your mouth, Black Boy," Dave retorts laughing with the first hearty laughter in weeks. "I didn't move fast enough, Gary. She disappeared on me; literally, she disappeared. And then I return to the library to find out when she is scheduled to work, only to be told no one by the name of Annie Belle works there or has ever worked there. Furthermore, I'm told I wasn't even in the library because it was closed the day of my flat tire."

"Just show's ya: Never, ever, get a flat-tire. Seriously, Guy; I mean this is heavy stuff."

"Gary, it gets worse. I saw that same young woman again, standing right at her gravestone."

"What!?!"

"You heard me. Sometimes I think I'm going nuts, or that I am living in a dream, or both. Sometimes I even question if what I have told you really happened. Did I really see and talk to Annie Belle Price who died 88 years ago? Was it my mother? Neither? Both?

"I have had good luck tracking down most of the folks Mom talked about. For example, the David she so frequently mentioned; it turns out he is David L. Wooten, survivor of numerous battles as well as a prison camp. In fact, Gary, you are really going to think I have gone off the deep end; but I have met him. Not to talk to like with Annie Belle, but twice now while stopped along the highway in my car, he has approached me—both times in faded Confederate Gray; and both times motioning me to follow him."

"Okay, Man. Tell me more about this David Dude, and this Annie-Come-Lately. Are they really relatives of yours; I mean like ancestors or something like that?"

"Gary, all I can say at this point is that I think David is my Mom's great grandfather—haven't proven it as yet. But as far as I am concerned I have beyond doubt proven he is the David Mom was talking to and about before she died. And Annie Belle? Well, I'm not sure exactly where she fits into my Mom's lineage. But I know she does."

"And so, David was a Confederate hero?"

As far as I am concerned, he was...is, but that's an issue I need to discuss with you later. All I have had time to look at so far is a huge list of battles, David was present for, and the fact that he was a POW at someplace called Point Lookout. If you remember, Mom talked about Lookout Point."

"Hell, that figures. To this day I think she still thinks I'm, Lee Gary."

Dave laughs to remember, but as he does so he takes the folder with his research findings which has been sitting all this time on the bench next to him, and taking the maps Karen had given to him spreads them out onto the table. "I didn't take the time to look at these. The research librarian at the Museum of the Confederacy gave these to me as I was in a hurry to get back to the motel. See here, she has circled Point Lookout. Hey it is not real far from here, just out on the tip of this peninsula over here in Maryland."

"Do you plan on going there?"

"Not sure, yet; but probably," Dave replies as he casually glances at the other map. "Holy Shit, Gary. Look at this. Karen has indicated here what at one time, during the 1850–70 period anyway, was Aiken's Landing and Cox's & Boulware's Wharves."

"Yes, Sir, by gum that's what it says; imagine that. I would never have guessed this could happen. Wait just a minute while I call my whole family. Maybe they will care about this. They don't seem to give a flying fart about me, or us."

"No, Gary, what I mean is this. Those are staging areas where David Wooten was given his freedom toward the end of the War. See where she has noted the Landing & the wharves? Now look directly to the west. What is the first thing that you see?"

"Well, I see I-95. Hey, I get it: DW hitchhiked home to Georgia by hopping onto a Dixieland Transport Truck that just happened to be going to, what's the name of the place, Westinghouse, Georgia?"

Nearly everyone at CJ's is looking toward the corner booth at two guys having the time of their life. The White Guy is bent over in laughter. The Black one is wiping the tears from his face.

"Okay, Smart-Ass, open your blood shot eyes and look again. Wide now. Note the exit number, 69. That is the exit for our motel. Just to the south of that exit the other day as I was driving here from points south, there was an accident that stopped traffic for some time. I was less than a quarter of a mile from the exit, when this man in Confederate Gray walked from this area where the Landing and Wharves were in the 1860s toward my car. I spoke to him. 'David,' I said. Actually, what I said was, 'David?' He smiled and motioned for me to follow him."

Moments, minutes pass with no verbal exchange between these two men who have been so busily engaged all evening. Several people are observing them again, wondering at the sound of silence ringing so resonantly from the corner booth.

"Listen, Dave, all kidding aside. I have no doubts whatever about what you are telling me here. You're talkin' to a Brother with a strange mix of African and Cherokee blood. Both of them folks are strong believers in visions and the existence of the Spirit World. Sounds to me like you are hot on the trail—of what, I'm not sure.

"But let me tell you something: Not everyone in this world would have seen what you have seen. You have followed your intuitions. That is one of the blessings of who we are, maybe one of the curses as well. Some would say the blessing and curses of *what* we are.

"I think we are more than a *what*. We are not things; we are people who have a special intuitive feel for the extra-ordinary. Look at Bernstein, Copland and Tchaikovsky to name a few. I am convinced we would not have such beautiful music, if it were not for their special sensitivity coming out of their sexual orientation. Peter T went with his intuitive nudging and out came "Swan Lake". You have gone with your intuitive nudgings; and out from history, out of Aiken's Landing has come the one and only, David L. Wooten, the one and perhaps many Annie Belles."

"Gary, you don't know how much I needed that. I am trying to be open to whomever I meet and to whatever I find. You know, Gary, Will Durant once wrote in the context of studying Egyptian history that, 'We cannot understand the Egyptian or man—until we study his gods.' I am trying, as difficult as it may be at times, to remain faithful to the spirit of Durant's premise. I am trying to understand what drove these folks. This trip is being as much a search for myself as it is a search for…God knows what. In fact I'm not sure God does know what it is that I am in search of, frankly.

"You know, I thought I had completely, once and for all, settled the issue within my soul that I am Gay. But I have had my moments on this trip when I have questioned the whole thing. And the thing is, Gary, not once, since I left Omaha, have I even sensed a prejudice toward me because I'm Gay. Of course, I have never tied a banner around me that says, 'Gay Man Walking.' Yet, it is as if…well, no offense, but I might just as well be Black, because my being Gay seems as obvious to at least some people apparently."

"Well, Ol' Buddy, that may be the difference between you and me. I've experienced nothing but prejudice all my life, just because I'm Black. Trying to explain that I'm Cherokee, never helped much either. So, being Gay just added a little extra. Now, I must say being Gay in the Black community, doesn't exactly put you to the top of the run-of-the-mill folks' popularity chart. You're a White Boy, Man, you really don't know what prejudice is like. Look around this place: except for that one over there, the Elvis wannabe with the Judy's Tanning Salon get-up-and-go, hell I'm the only Black here. If you could read their minds, 9 out of 10 are asking themselves, "what is that White Boy hanging around with that Nigger for? Thirty years ago, if I had tried to come in here, I would have been thrown out on my ass and probably beaten up for even turning the doorknob."

Suddenly, Gary's jokingly tough bravado turns to something else entirely. "The fact is, Dave, I struggle with who I am as well. How many times have I cried alone in the night wondering why I could not be 'normal'? Whatever the hell that is. But by God I am who I am; and I mean that literally. It was God who made me. I did not choose to be Gay. I didn't take lessons, you know: 'Joe Gay's 12 Steps to Becoming a Homo' with a money-back guarantee. My Mama didn't raise me to be the only Queer on the block. You and me and all the folks in here are products of God's magnificent work. It's just that we are different than a lot of folks out there—at least different than many of them think they are. One day many of them will wake up and realize they too are Gay and have been all their Pretend-lives."

"One other thing is going on, Gary. I began this stupid journey with full knowledge that I was prejudiced against the South, the Confederacy, and the whole works. But I have experienced nothing but the kindest hospitality. Now you get that shit-eating grin off your face. I know your experience of Southern hospitality would be different. All I'm trying to say is that MY prejudice is being severely tested."

"And all I can say Good Buddy is, you're on your own on that score. Don't count on any help from this kid. You see my Black ancestors were either sold on the slave block or flogged on the block, or both. Later on they were redlined out of the damned block. My Cherokee ancestors were driven from their land and set out on a forced march—all of it happened right here in the land of cotton, tobacco and Jimmie Crow.

"One thing I do know is this, and I suppose you might be real interested in this. The Lees in my family were slaves on some damned plantation right here in Virginia. They were, I suppose, like all slaves—overworked, underfed, and just plain brutalized. There. I've told you all I know; probably more than I know, actually."

"I hear you, Gary. I wish you didn't have to leave in the morning, but I so appreciate the sacrifice you made to come here, right smack-dab to the very capital of the Confederacy, just to be with me. Seriously, I not only appreciate you, but I need you and love you."

"Well, I can't tell you how excited I was when you asked me to come. I admire what you are doing, and I think you should consider writing a book entitled something like Dave Benson's Odyssey."

"Yeah, sure," Dave laughs. "Tell me, do you happen to know the names of your slave ancestors, the Lees?"

"Well, my Granny used to say, 'They was Amanda and Jacob Lee.' That's all I know."

Gary then looks around the room and back to the table becoming uncharacteristically silent and pensive, staring into the very depths of the stein of Guinness held in his two-fisted grasp. His mood has shifted radically from the lighthearted remark about "Dave Benson's Odyssey" to that of a troubled man. Dave watches him carefully, waiting for his partner to speak, to make another wisecrack, at first thinking the appearance of glumness is but a prelude to another Gary-ism.

He soon realizes that Gary is not playing around. His mood is prelude all right, but Dave knows him well enough to understand that this is Prelude to Serious Shit. This is the Gary who on another occasion at a different bar back in Omaha came down from the clouds surrounding Care Free City, landing as if he had parachuted in through those clouds only to find he had landed in the wrong place. It was then that Gary had shared the wrenching news that his family had not only refused to meet Dave, they showed Gary the door with the admonition to "never-ever darken the door again."

"What's happening, Gary?"

"Well, Dave, I don't know. You tell me."

"Huh? What you talk about Black Boy?"

"Look, White Boy, I'm serious. There is something we need to get worked out. It concerns Sharon, as we talked about on the phone a while back. But it is more than Sharon. It is you and I. Mainly it is you, Dave Benson, and who he thinks he is. Who he thinks he wants to be. What he is. You talk about studying the Egyptian and Southern Gods in order to understand Egyptian and Confederate civilization, well I ask you Dave, who the fuck is your God? What is driving you? Maybe I should ask it this way. What is holding you back from admitting to yourself and admitting to the world just who the fuck you are? Look, I talked with Sharon just before I left Omaha. You have some decisions to make."

Dave's face has become an outward sign of that which has gripped his heart. His face has gone from being relaxed with glittering eyes, laughter pouring from his lips to a tightness as if he were a puppet and the puppeteer had managed to cause his face to almost wither like a prune in the noon day sun. Inside, he wants to flee, call it an evening, go home. But this is one situation he can see no escape from. Tonight there is no way to escape Gary's sometimes-brutal honesty. Dave is trapped.

Yes, trapped, like the kid on the playground many years ago. Dave was a high school senior that day on his way home. He found himself walking by the public elementary school just at the moment when he heard a cry for help followed by raucous laughter.

Over in the corner of the playground were five boys beating on another boy. There was no escape for the victim. They had him in a corner with his tormentors preventing any opportunity to flee on two sides and a hurricane fence completing the entrapment.

"Faggot, Faggot, Faggot. Say I'm a Faggot, you Faggot. Say it," they screamed. Dave ran onto the playground and drove the bullies away. He only wishes someone would return the favor at this moment.

"Gary, I really don't know what you're talking about," Dave says as he looks over Gary's shoulder at nothing in particular.

"To hell you don't. You just don't want to look at it. You don't want to admit it."

"Okay, Gary. Obviously you know me better than anyone, especially me. What is it I don't want to look at? What is it I do not want to admit?"

Gary rolls his eyes and motions to the waitress. "Would you bring us another round of drinks? And by the way make that a boilermaker for my partner here."

"Hey, I don't even like boilermakers."

Gary smiles for the first time in minutes, but does so only for the waitress's benefit saying, "Never mind this White Boy here, he sometimes just doesn't know what's good for him. He doesn't know it yet, but he's going to need at least one shot and a beer before this evening is over."

With the waitress now gone, Gary leans across the table with a ferocious look on his face making Dave think of how Cassius Clay aka Mohammad Ali must have looked to his opponents just as he delivered the final blow. In this case instead of a roundhouse punch being delivered, Dave's "opponent" reaches over and takes both of his hands.

"Dave listen to me. I know you're Gay. You know you're Gay. But I also know that you are still struggling with the fact; yet, I also know that you think there's no problem, that you have totally accepted the fact of being on the edge of this homophobic world of ours. I also believe Sharon has the sense that you're Gay. I am pretty damned sure she knows I'm Gay. But Brother listen to me and listen close. Sharon loves you. I'm not going to try comparing her love for you with mine. All I know is that she loves you even with her suspicion that you're Gay. She is holding onto the hope that you will 'give it up' or 'decide not to be Gay'; you know, 'decide to be straight.'

"Damn it, Dave, I love Sharon too. Oh, not like you I'm sure; and it's not a sexual love either. I respect her as a person, a sincere, compassionate, caring, loving person. Sharon is a powerhouse of a woman. I just don't want to see her being hurt."

"Jesus, Gary, how is Sharon being hurt. I hear you saying that I'm hurting her right now. Where the hell are you coming from?"

Dave's face has turned a raw red. There is anger in his voice and pain in his eyes. Mohammad Ali has scored a hit, not just one but serial blows; and the judges are busy making note of it all.

"Dave all I'm saying, all I'm asking, is that you think about it. You owe it to yourself. You owe it to Sharon; you owe it to your mom. Damn it, I think you owe it to me. Maybe, just maybe, you also owe it to your God. And perhaps, Old Buddy, you might just owe it to those folks you are tracking down on this journey of yours. I'm no historian, but I do know this about history: There is much to be found in history that we want to deny, ignore, or rework until it all comes out meeting our prejudices, wants and desires. I don't think you can possibly be fair to the secrets of History with the capital H, if you are not willing to face into the secrets of your own history, Man. No way. I just don't. That's all. I'm done. Said what I needed to say."

As the waitress heads back toward the table with the big Black Guy and the fair complexioned but troubled looking White Guy, she notices how the white one has suddenly become even more troubled, in fact he is crying. As soon as she sits the drinks down before these two men, the white one quickly guzzles down the beer with hardly a breath and instantly follows the beer up with a lightning-like grab for the shot glass and downs the whiskey. "Not bad for someone who doesn't like a boilermaker," she thinks to herself.

Moments later the two men have paid their bill and the waitress watches as they walk toward the door holding hands.

October 4, 2000

Today's trek to the Museum's library proves to be a cache of potential riches. Diaries, service records, and battles fought by each regiment. Some of the material that Dave glances at he decides is potentially useful, and requests a copy to take with him—such as: *The War-Time Journal of a Georgia Girl, 1864-65 by Eliza Frances Andrews* and *Prison Life at Point Lookout.*

At lunch time when the Library staff lock up for a noon-time break, Dave wanders down to Cary Street wishing with all his heart that Gary could be with him. *How wonderful it would be to have lunch with him. Oh, but how wonderful it was to have him for those few short hours. I love that guy. He loves me enough to risk the confrontation of last night. It was painful, but Gary is right. I need to do something about my relationship with Sharon.*

Spotting the café/computer shop he had seen the night before, Dave orders lunch and signs-on for computer time. Going on the hunch that Horace and Johnny G. were Barnes boys, Dave goes to Ancestry.com's Civil War page and types in HORACE BARNES, NY. To his total amazement, yet infinite pleasure, the monitor informs him:

> **Horace Barnes**
> **Enlisted as a Private on 02 October 1861 in Ogdensburg, NY at the age of 21.**
> **Enlisted in Company D, 60th Infantry Regiment, New York on 30 October 1861**
> **Killed on 16 June 1864 in Golgotha, GA.**

Dave moves quickly now to type **JOHN G. BARNES** in the search box, hits enter, and instantly up comes:

> **John G. Barnes**
> **Enlisted as a Private on 27 August 1864 in New York City, NY at the age of 18.**
> **Enlisted in Company I, 184th Infantry Regiment, New York on 16 September 1864**
> **Mustered out on 29 June 1865 in City Point, VA**

For Dave, that is enough evidence to prove that the Horace and Johnny G. his mother talked about were in fact her great uncles, his own great-great uncles from the Barnes limb of the family tree. Now, he knows for sure that the War Between the States was also a war between families, his family.

The balance of the day is spent back at the Museum's library organizing a chronological list of battles and who was where. It is all very interesting, some of it revelatory and stunning. It is not until he gets to the Battle of Antietam, as the Union called it, or the Battle of Sharpsburg as known by the Confederacy, that Dave experiences one of the "ah-ha" moments of life. Noting that the Battle of South Mountain occurred on 14 September 1862, the day the Manry boys were killed, Dave becomes mesmerized by the additional fact that there were three battles at South Mountain, one for each of three gaps: Crompton's, Turner's, and FOX'S.

Dave just sits staring so intently, that if his vision were powered by laser beam he would have been able to observe beyond the library wall, through the Confederate White House next door into Jefferson Davis' study where a dozen tourists now stand marveling at the wall papered effects. Instead, all Dave sees are the words "Fox's Gap". All he hears is his mother saying something about a Fox and a Gap; and then Sadie's diary-noted dream concerning the fox, the sad fox.

There are moments in our life when we know beyond all knowing what we must do. That moment has come for Dave. Even as he sits in this chair, he is already on his way to South Mountain. *Fox Gap here I come.*

But there is one other thing Dave knows he must do and that is to write a book as Gary suggested. However, while he does not yet know the title of the book, he does know the title will NOT be *Dave Benson's Odyssey.* Gary's other "suggestion"? Well, that's another matter.

Chapter 8:
The War Between Families

Those poor, arthritically swollen knees
Of my mother in an absent country...
A reading from the Gospel according to Mark
About a little girl to whom He said: 'Talitha cumi!'
This is for me.
To make me rise from the dead
And repeat the hope of those who lived before me...
Be with me, I say to her, my time has been short.
Your words are now mine, deep inside me:
'It all seems now to have been a dream.'
("With Her," by Czeslaw Milosz)

10 December 2002

Dave's editor, Bill, has the manuscript before him. He has decided this is the night to spend with Dave's work if it takes him all weekend. The trip to Chicago was, thankfully, canceled. The entire weekend at home is his to do with as he pleases. While there are a few other things he can think of to do, things he would like to do (like nothing) he feels a need to read Dave's stuff.

Bill sits by the fire, flames crackling, while snow falls lazily in huge fluffy flakes outside his window. Wrapped in his maroon housecoat, feet propped up on the brown leather ottoman, he flips open the manuscript entitled:

The War Between Families
By
Dave Benson

A FINE LINE OF DISTINCTION:
IN SEARCH OF ROOTS

Introduction:

This book is history. It is fiction but as faithful to the facts as possible. This book examines the Civil War from the perspective of one very extended family—a family who, at the time, did not know they were family.

This book relates some of the bloody events of the War Between the States, but it is not a military history. This book focuses on those who have gone before us, yet it raises the question of whether in fact they are really gone. This book tries to make sense out of that which is known, as well as that, which must, regretfully, remain beyond the reach of recorded history.

This book examines the battleground we are all a part of, whether we realize it or not—the battle to understand ourselves through the skirmishes of seeking understanding of the motives and values of others, as well as our own.

This is a book of short stories and vignettes, but it is hoped that the whole will be much greater than its parts. The reader may well find that one of the battlegrounds related herein best describes his or her own world.

The story told here is a story of stories. Those stories appear, first of all, because many of the people featured herein appeared to my dying mother. She made me promise that I would search them out after she died. It seems they visited my mother for a purpose. I believe they wanted their stories told. Given the bizarre events that led me to these people, I came to believe that I was meant to follow the trail. Given all of that, and not wanting to appear presumptuous, I believe those who read this meager account are in some mysterious way meant to do so.

This is an historical fiction piece, which seeks to maintain the integrity of the historical facts. While the writer was able to uncover many treasures explaining the lives of the people here, no trunk in any obscure attic ever turned up with its lid open and luminescent lights flashing upon diaries and letters detailing every thought and emotion of every character. Instead, the author takes off from what he knows and does the best he can at immersing himself in the life and times of one extended family from 1830 to the early 1900s.

Will Durant claims in his eleven volume series, The Story of Civilization, that an historical understanding of a people's virtues must "lie in the interpretation of the time." I hope to accomplish some measure of that level of understanding of a people and their times so very distant from my own lived experience.

Chapter One: If Mountains Could Speak

From the observation tower at Antietam Battlefield near Sharpsburg, Maryland, one has a panoramic view of the mountain to the south, simply known as South Mountain. From here we see a broad expanse of land dotted with countless numbers of four to seven-foot-tall cedar trees.

Today, these trees seem to be standing sentry guarding this beautiful land made fertile by the blood of nearly 23,000 men on that fateful day, 17 September 1862. The trees seem to be charged with the responsibility of preventing any more bloodshed. If you listen really close as the wind rushes across this valley and through the ranks of the cedar, a chorus sings "No More War, No More War, No More War, No More... No... "

South Mountain appears from here to be a series of three bread loaves lined up with one loaf sitting slightly to the west of the other two. On closer inspection the bare eye reveals three gaps: Turner's Gap to the north, Crampton's Gap to the south, and Fox's Gap in the middle.

This mountain stood as a witness to the carnage that occurred along the banks of Antietam Creek on the 17th, but on Sunday, the 14th of September this mountain was among the victims: over 4600 human deaths, plus a plundered desecrated mountain. No one tabulated the number of four-leggeds or winged ones that were slaughtered through no fault of their own. In modern war parlance the animals and the birds, the mountain itself, were simply "collateral damage."

Sunday morning dawned with David Wooten positioned on the north side of Crampton's Gap along with his 13th Georgia Infantry Regiment. David's brother James (better known as Roach) was on the opposite side with his 51st Georgia Infantry Regiment, Company F (better known as the Cuthbert Rifles). About a mile away at Fox's Gap the Manry brothers, Ben, John Bird, and James greeted the day along with their Company E of the Georgia 51st.

David Wooten enlisted with the 13th Georgia a little more than 16 months before at the age of twenty-two. Within four months of his enlistment, David had seen battle at Sewell's Mountain, Virginia, twice, and Cotton Hill, Virginia. By September 14, 1862 David will have been in a total of nine conflicts. He will have witnessed fields running red with the blood of at least 62,351 men, 30,983 of them his fellow Confederates. Beginning within minutes after sunrise on this beautiful Sunday and ending late in the day the following Saturday, 20 September, David will have witnessed another 27,979 bodies. This time the dead will be lying like cordwood in the cornfields between this Gap and Sharpsburg, as well as in the streets of Shepherdstown only four miles distant from the Tower where I stand gazing into history.

David's brother, Roach, enlisted with the Cuthbert Rifles six months prior to this particular Sunday at the age of twenty. While Roach had been in the service of the Confederacy 10 months less than David, he had already observed more than a little of the inhumanity human beings can render unto one another. As part of Brig. General Thomas F. Drayton's Brigade, Drayton's Division, Roach had been present at the Seven Days' Battle as well as Second Manassas. His introduction to carnage came quickly and on a grand scale. By the morning of 14 September 1862, he had stepped over more than his share of 53, 916 bodies. It would have been little comfort to know that he had seen over 3000 more Union dead than Confederate.

The Manry brothers, at Fox's Gap, had all three of them enlisted with the 51st Georgia on the same date a bit less than six months ago. John Bird was 17, Ben 19, and James 21. They had gone to bed at night with the same scenes in their heads that Roach could not shake. While they were in a different company than James Wooten, they were, all four of them, in the same Drayton Division.

It would be another 46 years before the Wooten and Manry boys would be considered family by those who were in 1862 yet to come into the world; but on this day, 14 September 1862, the Wooten and Manry boys were already family. Three of these young men (with an average age of 20) would see the sunrise on Monday, September 15—two would not. It would be another 138 years before someone would stand atop this Observation Tower, and say to no one in particular: "Five of my uncles fought on that mountain and two died."

For all I know, it has taken the 138 years for anyone in my family to finally discover what really happened to Ben and Johnny B. I do know, however, that my family has been haunted by what they have known. That which they have not known, but only guessed at, has haunted them as well. I also know that many a soul in my family has been unable to rest even after death. I am here atop this observation deck with my partner Hope—the hope that finally, after 138 years my family writ large may find peace. That is my hope for me as well.

September 1862

Unknown to any of these uncles of mine, or even General Robert E. Lee, General McClellan, commander of the Union Army, had come into possession of Lee's campaign plans the day before. Knowing for certain that

Lee intended to control the passes at South Mountain and to send General Jackson's forces to Harper's Ferry, McClellan ordered massive deployment to South Mountain under the cover of darkness. Lee's Special Order No. 191, had become McClellan's special opportunity to attack and take control of all three mountain passes—a golden opportunity to end the war.

C.S.A. General Daniel H. Hill says in his recollection of the events of this day that: early in the morning he climbed "...the lookout station (and saw) the vast army of McClellan spread out before me...It was a grand and glorious spectacle, and it was impossible to look at it without admiration. I had never seen so tremendous an army before, and I did not see one like it afterward...The sight inspired more satisfaction than discomfort...

There would have been little comfort or inspiration for the Wootens and Manrys as they may have looked down on this army of 87,000 men poised to attack them and their 18,000 confederates. At least David and Roach saw it coming. While they were in separate deployment locations, they could see from their respective perches above Crampton's Gap that they were grossly outnumbered. It was clear to them that if this mountain was to be held in Confederate control, they would need to fight a run-and-shoot-shoot-and-hide battle. Seventy-five years later it would be known as guerrilla warfare. Eventually, the strategy changed to simple delay and run. Before the day was over Crampton's Gap would be in Union possession.

Ben & John Bird Manry, however, never knew what hit them. At about 9 A.M. it was all over. Ben at age 19 and JB at age 17 were dead. Their older brother James was among the few at and around the Wise Family Farm to escape with their lives or avoid capture in the initial attack by the Union's IX Corps.

James saw his brothers gunned down. They were across the way from him at the time. He was posted behind a stonewall to defend the wooded hillcrest west of the farmstead. Ben and JB were posted to protect the farm, the Wise Family, and the all-important well. The fuselage was intense and sustained. He saw his brothers lying by the well. He saw the Wise family fleeing toward Sharpsburg. But there was nothing, absolutely nothing he could do. James and the entire 51st Georgia would be retreating and counter-attacking all day long. The Union would not take Fox's Gap until later that evening when General Lee would order a retreat.

Night had fallen and so had two brothers. A third would carry the unreasonable but very real guilt the rest of his life that he had not protected his brothers.

* * *

I stand here now at the east edge of Fox's Gap. I wonder what this view was like on the evening of 13 September 1862. I can imagine both Ben and JB standing here enthralled by the serenity of this pastoral setting. A broad and fertile valley lay before them, and beyond in the distance the hazy outline of the Catoctin Mountains.

Did their view that evening of the rich land remind them of home? Would they not have sat down on the nearest rock and wondered if the soil in this valley could support the growing of cotton, tobacco, peanuts, and maybe even pecan trees doing so well back home in Calhoun County? Would they not have discussed the fine features of their girlfriends back in Edison? Would they not have looked forward to tomorrow as a badly needed day of rest? After all, it would be the Sabbath. Would they not have fondly given thought to being at home for Sunday worship at Salem Baptist Church? Sure, there was always the risk of a boring sermon, but it would be worth the price of boredom to be with the girls of their dreams.

As I walk to the west and up the rise along Reno Road, I see Ben and JB, now joined by their brother. The three are arm in arm, laughing and joking—pleased that for once their Companies are posted so very near each other. James' Company had just arrived from the west. He has not yet seen the rich valley his brother's are talking about. James decides he will be up at daybreak to see the sunrise on the much talked-about valley to the east. The brothers bid each other a good night. They promise to get together before the day is over tomorrow—a promise never to be fulfilled.

I stand here now, at the well. I wonder at the wantonness of that day. On the Sabbath lives were savaged. Corpses and the wounded left unattended. God's creation violated: trees shelled to shreds; the earth ripped and gouged with canon-balls; horses with gaping holes in their bellies. At least Mr. Wise's cows were taken for their milk and meat; perhaps a better fate than the homestead endured with its ransacking and burning once the Union took control sometime after 10 P.M. on the night of 14 September.

But what was it that prompted these three young men from southwest Georgia to enlist in the Confederate cause? What has drawn them to this spot nearly 1000 long torturous marching miles from the serene security of the Manry Plantation in Calhoun County?

Was it the fear that a way of life was at stake? For decades the issue of slavery had been a hotly contested one. Or, was it loyalty to the Family Legend?

Summer 1847

All three boys remember their Grandpa Henry Manry. John Bird's recollection comes mainly from the stories that make up the family lore: the Legend of HM. John Bird was, after all, only two when HM died. The stories heard so often over the years formed a "picture" in his head—an image based on an infantile subconscious memory that flashes before him just as the bullets strike.

Ben's image of "Grampy" is much more vivid. Grampy holding him in his lap while seated in the old rocker made of twigs—about the only thing Ben can recall that HM brought with him when he moved in with the family. It was the stories Grampy told that mesmerized this four-year-old, especially those stories of the War of 1812. The only thing was that Ben never really understood why some of those stories didn't make much sense. If it was the War of 1812, what was Grampy doing fighting a battle at some place called Fort Oswego in 1814?

One Sunday afternoon, HM and Ben are rocking away on the front porch and HM predictably launches into another of his exploits in the War of 1812, but this one really happened in 1812.

"Yes sir, by gum, we had taken all we were going to take from England and her uppity ways. We declared war and I jumped right up to the line and said, 'Sign me up, boys.' Of course, some of them boys thought I was an old man at 29.

"Hell, I mean Heavens, before I knew it, I was a riding like the dickens with a whole troop of men from Sussex, Virginny, heading down toward this here neck of the woods. You see, Young Man, there was this huge British arsenal up in Louisville, Kentucky, and the US troops had already taken control of that prize. They had moved the whole thing, every rifle, canon, pistol, yep, every grain of gunpowder down here to Milledgeville. My job was to draw claim to some of that war treasure for our Virginny troops. We loaded up wagons full of ammunition and weaponry and hurried right back home. We wuz 'fraid those sea faring folk would invade the shores of Virginny 'fore we could get back. Lucky for us all, they were too stunned to act there fer awhile. Sometimes, Young Feller, a man has to be a man. War ain't fun, but sometimes there's no alternative. Sure hope you don't ever have to go to war, but if you do...Well, Ben my *boy, I can tell; you would make one brave soldier man."*

James, being the oldest of the three, has the more extensive memory. HM moved in with the family right after James was born. He kind of grew up under Grampy's watchful care and tutelage. James heard much the same stories as did Ben, but more. It was, among other things, the stories of change and the need to take a stand that James remembered most.

One day when James was about five years old, Grampy Manry took him along to the Cotton Gin. "You may find this hard to believe, James, My Boy, but when I was your age, there was no such thing as a cotton gin; and you can't imagine life around here without this beast being around, can you now?"

James and his brothers had soon learned that Grampy's questions never waited for answers. Saved time and energy that way. "Well, let me tell you," HM continued, "the beast has made all the difference. Since then, we have been able to produce more and better cotton at less cost per bale. Some folks way up in the North think it's possible now for us to provide them with their cotton finery without having the help of our slaves. Well, those folks don't have a brain in their head. Never did. Never will, and that's what worries me.

"One day, I'm afraid, we...well, not me, but perhaps you and your brothers will have to go to war to protect not only our way of life here in the South, but even the North's way of life—a way of life dependent on our cotton. Those Northerners are too dumb to see it."

HM takes out his old seaman's pipe, stuffs in a couple pinches of tobacco and lights it with a swift scratch of the match against James' behind: "This pipe my Granddaddy Manry brought over on the boat. My Daddy always said it was a French pipe. Said that's what his daddy always said it was. Never could understand that one. The Manrys came from England, Sussex, England, in fact. That's why when they landed in Virginny, they named the area where they settled, Sussex. But Manrys are crafty people. I bet some of those Manrys swum the channel to France on a French Pipe Hunt one day.

"But back to what I was sayin'. Thought I was a goin' to have to go to war another time, by the gods. There I was 39 years old back in '22; your Daddy was born two years afore that. We was livin' up there in Darlington, South Carolinny, when a bunch of slaves revolted against their owners who had treated them real good, far as I know. This Nigga by the name of Denmark Vesey was the ringleader. They not only escaped from their plantations, but they set the torch to Charleston. But, like in 1811 in New Orleans when the Andry slaves revolted, the Federal troops stepped in and took care of the

situation. Over 80 of them slaves was killed in '11. Eleven years later 36 more were killed for stepping over the line.

"If it hadn't been for the Government, we'd a had ta take up arms again. I was already too old for that kind of carrying on, but I would have. Yessiree, I would have. Sometimes a man has to do what a man has to do. Your Grandma Jane & I worked too hard to lose it all to some persnickety rabid slaves.

"Then, then it was less than ten years after that, when that there Vesey almost burned down a whole city, that another one by the name of Nat Turner not only led a revolt, but killed 60 white folk. These have been hard times these past 60 years that I have seen. I pray the times will be better for you and your brothers. But I just don't know. I prayed real hard that none of my boys would ever have to go to war. Those prayers have been answered. Your Daddy, my son William was too young at 12 for the Black Hawk War in '32. I just hope he is too old for the war I see coming with Mexico."

* * *

HM died the next year. James was seven when he stood at his Grampy's grave. Being the elder, having learned so much more from and about his Grandfather Manry, James took much more of HM with him to the Confederate Recruitment office 14 years later. However, neither Ben nor John Bird would forget the example of their beloved Grampy who smoked his "French" pipe whenever he felt like it, and took a stand as a fighting man when he felt the time and the issue had come.

Grampy's prophecy held true. The United States went to war with Mexico one year after he died. His prayers seem to have been answered. His son William was 28 and married with four sons. He was, therefore, exempted from having to serve.

Even though the Mexican-American War was short-lived, Grampy's other premonitions of what the future would hold for his grandsons would, in hindsight, seem to condemn them to signing the enlistment papers fourteen short years later. The issue of slavery continued to divide the Nation. While the South won the battle in Congress in 1850 known as the Fugitive Slave Act, it only inflamed public opinion in the North. Just when Northern consternation seemed about to die down, out came the publication of Uncle Tom's Cabin in 1852. Then, the whole issue of slavery reached a near-boiling point with passage of the so-called Personal Liberty Laws enacted by several

Southern State legislatures. Mob riots raged in Northern cities protesting Northern enforcement of what was viewed as unjust and mean-spirited Southern laws.

In 1859 when James is 18, the picture blackens with only a slight ray of hope. John Brown and his fellow troublemakers raid Harper's Ferry. The dastardly raid is put down, and the unspeakable fellow is hung. His hanging, however, only seems to anger the North even more. The prospects for more and more bold efforts to free the slaves threaten the horizon of the future, like a black cloud looming just beyond a mountaintop.

The strap that cinches the saddle for the War-Horses of the South is the election the very next year of Abraham Lincoln as President. Within three months of Lincoln's election South Carolina and Georgia have seceded from the Union and the Confederate States of America has formed. Then, on April 12, 1861 Fort Sumter is fired upon by the Confederacy, and the War is on.

The Manry Plantation, 1861–62

While the attack upon Sumter and the Confederacy's capture of it, spurs much pride and hope throughout the South, the glorious victory comes not without cost. Human casualties may have been minimal for the Confederate States of America; however, the economy of the South took a direct hit—an injury that would slowly drain the lifeblood from the Southern way of life.

As a young man of twenty, James understood by May, only one month after Sumter that the Confederacy had to win it all or lose it all. There could be no middle ground. The handwriting was on the wall of the shops in downtown Edison: A shirt that cost $2 in March at Lewis General Store was now listed at $2.20.

Toward the end of July news came of the Confederacy's victory at Manassas. The news brought with it an outpouring of excitement. Manassas was the talk of the town.

Two weeks later James is at the store looking again at that brightly colored shirt. What an impression it would make on Mary Sue, if he were to pick her up for the dance Saturday night all decked out in that there shirt! Deciding the time has come to put his money where he wants this shirt to be, James pulls the coveted cotton piece from the rack and takes it to the counter.

His heart is already beating an extra half-dozen beats per minute, when Mr. Lewis says, "Jim Boy, you have had your eye on this shirt 'bout as long as you've had your eye on little Mary Sue. I've seen both of those eyes of yours goin' this way and that over both of those fine pieces of cloth. I can sell you the one, but not both. That'll be $2.30, Jimmie."

James is stunned. First of all he had no idea Mr. Lewis had ever seen him examining that shirt. He certainly had no idea Mr. Lewis had ever even seen him with Mary Sue. But Mr. Lewis' price is the real shocker. "What? Are you sure Mr. Lewis? I mean I was in here just a week or so ago and I know the price was $2.20. I really didn't look at the price tag today, I just assumed..."

"Well, Jim Boy, I'm afraid the days of assuming from day to day are over. As I'm sure you know that same shirt, I was a charging only $2 not many months ago. I don't mean to pressure you, Son, but if you want it, you better buy now. The price is going to do nothing but go up and up, I'm afraid. I hate to do it, but I have to make a wage. I can't afford to become Lewis Public Handout Company, you know. I shudder when I think about what's going to happen."

"I am going to have to wait, Mr. Lewis. All I got right now is the $2.20."

Later that evening, James, Ben, and John Bird are sitting around the table with their father, William, and mother, Ann, and brothers Billy, Irvin Bird, Joey and Simmie, along with Penny, their little sister. The discussion comes around to the costs of maintaining the family and running the plantation. Seems like that has become the table topic more and more recently. James finds an opening to lament the rising prices at Lewis General Store, especially the cost of shirts.

"I know, Jimmie," William affirms. "We have had to change currency to Confederate dollars. I figured when we fired that shot up at Sumter that we were going to see some dramatic changes. It didn't surprise me in the least that we would have to come up with our own currency. Guess I was too optimistic thinking we would have brought those Yankees to their knees by the 4th of July. Guess I was too dumb to realize it would mean harder times for us all. Right now I do not think this war is going to be over any time soon. I do believe the times are going to be tougher. Mr. Lewis is right, Jim, if you want that shirt, you better get down there."

"Well, I'm going to wait a bit. The price won't change much. Actually, I think I'll play Mr. Lewis' game. I'm going to wait until right after Christmas. He always lowers his prices for a few days the day after New Years. I'll be there first thing in the morning. Bet I get it for the $2 price he had on it in March."

"Don't count on it," William says to his son, as he lights the French pipe by scratching the match across the seat of six-year-old Simmie's pants as the boy rushes by in hot pursuit of his older brother Joey. Eight-year-old Joey, *the family poet, quickly runs back into the room standing at a safe distance from James saying:*

> *Shirt, shirt, shirt, shirt, shirt*
> *James Henry buys two*
> *Both are for Mary Sue*
> *Tomorrow a skirt*

"You," James shouts in pseudo anger and jumping to his feet as if he were to chase his poetically mocking brother. "You, like that shirt, were worth $2 in March, but now your value is down to two cents—and that's overpriced," laughs James.

* * *

January 2, 1862
James arrives at Lewis General Store on his trusty stead, Ranger. Dismounting and tying the Palomino at the rail, James almost runs into the store, catching himself as he approaches the door and slows to a walking pace. "Good morning, James," a voice from nowhere greets him. Finally, James finds Mr. Lewis behind a huge pile of clothing.

"You scared me, Mr. Lewis. I didn't see you and even after you spoke, I couldn't find you there for a while."

"Just trying to sort through this shipment. Somehow it made it through the embargo all the way from Baltimore. This is the end though. We can expect nothing getting here from Baltimore ever again, at least until the War ends. Do you realize, Jimmie, that most of the goods I have carried are manufactured up North? Most of it from Baltimore as a matter of fact. Now how can I help you this morning?"

"Well, Mr. Lewis, you know that shirt I've been looking at for some time? I've decided to buy it, finally! 'Tis a nice way to begin the New Year, it is." As James speaks his eyes survey the store. The smile disappears as he notices his shirt is no longer hanging in its accustomed spot. A low-grade panic seizes him as he blurts out, "You've sold it!"

Mr. Lewis smiles and reaches out to touch James reassuringly on the shoulder, "No, Jimmie, I knew you were going to come in here one day to buy it. So, I just set it aside for you. But, I still must charge the market price, you know."

James, the elder of the Manrys has always prided himself on being more mature than his siblings; indeed, James valued the opinion held by his teachers and others in the community that he was more mature than any of his peers. He experiences a sinking feeling in his gut like the time when his teacher Mrs. Powers reprimanded him for using a cuss word on the playground. Besides it was so very embarrassing; and James is embarrassed now, but also relieved.

"Oh, Mr. Lewis. Thank you for doing that for me. I really appreciate it. You are so kind."

"Well, Jimmie you may not think so highly of this old man when I tell you the really bad news."

"What do you mean?"

"The price. I have to charge you $2.50."

"$2.50!" James is dumbfounded. His first thought is that he wishes the shirt had in fact been bought. But then he couldn't stand the thought that someone else would be wearing it around town, especially at the dances. "$2.50 did you say, or $1.50? I thought you would have things marked down today."

"No, James, my boy, no markdowns. I can't afford to mark down a thing anymore. In fact, the way things are going I should be marking up everything in this store by the hour. I'm losing my shirt, as they say, even by selling this one to you at that price. I'm truly sorry, but I have to stick to the $2.50."

James has mixed emotions as he walks into the house carrying his long coveted new shirt. It is his now and he looks forward to the dance next Saturday night, and he can't wait for Mary Sue's reaction when he arrives to pick her up for the trip over to Gum. But, the fact is that he is nearly broke. Everything he buys lately has cost more. They have even raised the price of tickets to the dances. His dad said just last week that maybe dancing would be the only thing with a stable price: "I do believe what you are paying to dance today is exactly what I paid at your age to take Annie to the dances." His dad's comment may have been the kiss of death to the "antique" of a stable price.

James displays the shirt for his mother's approval as he tells her the story of Mr. Lewis putting the shirt aside, and the sadder story of the cost. Annie expresses her pleasure over her son's acquisition that she knows he has longed to possess. Yet, James cannot help noticing the reserve in his mother's voice, the sadness in her eyes.

"What is it, Mother?" Annie knew both by James' tone, but most

especially by referring to her as "Mother", that her face had done it again. William, her parents Henry and Nancy Bird, anyone who really knew her, could tell how she was feeling just by looking at her face. Her Grandfather Peter Bird once said, "That child's face is an open book." Now, even her children were known to glance at her once and proclaim, "The book is open." James did not say that just now, but he might just as well have shouted it from the top of the Pecan Grove.

"James, your shirt is a small ball of cotton compared to the expense of running this plantation. Everything, not just shirts at Lewis's, is becoming so expensive. Your father and I do not know how much longer we can last. We have no idea if we will even be able to sell our cotton this year. If we can, we expect to get so very little for it. We may have to let some of our slaves go. We cannot sell them. They are worthless on today's market. If we let them go, God knows what that will mean. If we let two go, will all the rest revolt and leave us? We can't let them all go. We need them. Without them there is no harvest. If we let any of them go free, what in heaven's name are the poor creatures going to do? All they know is cotton, and the future for cotton right now doesn't look real bright."

"Mama, I know what you're saying. I have given all that some thought. It scares me, Mother. That's why we need to win this war and win it soon. I think I'm going to have to sign up. I can't leave it to the other guys my age. I have to help. Besides, Grampy would want me to. 'Sometimes a man has to take a stand and fight,' he used to say. 'Sometimes a man has to do what a man has to do.'"

"Oh, James, I pray this war will end today, that you will not be required by conscience or otherwise to pull a trigger on our own countrymen. The North, you know, are people too, our people. They are us. They, not all, but many just have a different view of the world than we do here in the South. No, James Henry Manry, I do not want you to enlist. But, if you must, then you must I suppose."

"Well, I'm not doing it today; and won't," James hesitates for effect, "until I get to wear this shirt once for Mary Sue." Annie laughs a half-hearted laugh. James notices the absence of the telltale twinkle in her eyes that normally comes with her laughter.

As he heads for his bedroom, he suddenly stops, turns around saying, "Mama, you made a good point about the slaves; but you forget one important thing."

"What's that?"

"We have taught many of them to read and write. They are going to have an advantage over most slaves here in Calhoun County, or anywhere else."

"That may be true, Son. But just remember, the time is not yet right for us to advertise we have been learnin' those poor creatures."

"I know, Mama, but a while back I heard a man who rode in from North Carolina telling Mr. Lewis that even General Lee has been teaching his slaves to read and write. I say if General Robert E. Lee can do that, we can too. Besides, it makes me feel better knowing that when we sold Amanda and Peter to that trader from Virginia that he was actually representing General Lee. I think my efforts to teach Amanda and Peter have not gone for naught. I bet General Lee has kept up their education. They were so eager to learn. I bet they get married one of these days."

"Okay, James," Annie responds along with her familiar full-blown smile, "but just remember this: General Lee has a whole army to defend him."

James is relieved at seeing the vintage smile on his mother's face, but not completely. He has noticed the absence of her reassuring, "all's right with the world" smile. He is well aware of her worries and concerns as they have just now discussed. He knows she is worried about the future of her children. But intuitively, James knows there is more.

"Mother?"

"Yes, James?"

"Are you okay? I mean the war aside and all; are you okay?"

"Oh, I get tired a lot lately. Just all the worry, I guess," Annie replies as she looks at the floor. Her son knows she is lying, but he decides to leave the issue alone. He knows one thing very clearly and definitely: James does NOT want to know what it is that has wiped away his beloved mother's perpetual smile.

March 2, 1862

James, Ben, and John Bird have taken a long ride up to Morgan, enjoying this early spring day. The conversation, as usual, swirls around horses and girls, dances and picnics, hunting and fishing, dreams and fantasies of their futures. Riding into Morgan, they decide to stop at the Morgan Café on the westside of the Courthouse.

The waitress, a cute brunette about JB's age, takes their orders. "Hey, I don't recall seeing you before, do you live here in Morgan?" John Bird asks.

"Maybe you haven't seen me, but I have seen you. I'm Sally Wooten. My mom and dad are Simon and Elizabeth Wooten."

"Oh, ah, I'm John Bird Manry, and these are my brothers, Ben and James."

As Sally walks away, James is about to burst. "'Maybe you haven't seen me, but I have seen you. I'm Sally Wooten,' she says. Well, little brother how are you going to handle this, if I may ask?" Ben and James are doubled over in laughter. John has an acute case of red-faced embarrassment.

A long moment of silence follows as the brothers notice Sally coming back toward their table. In the midst of their silence, three men at a corner table are talking animatedly. "I tell you true. Conscription is a comin' fellas. I heard the Judge say this morning that Mobile is about to pass the bill. Jefferson Davis is clamoring fer it, so it will happen," the Older One says with all the assurance and authority of a Moses coming down off the mountain with the Tablet in hand.

"Then I'm signin' up tomorrow. If that bill passes, I want to make sure I make my own options," the Younger One asserts.

"Did you hear that?" Ben asks.

"Yeah," says James. "The Ugly One makes a good point. If conscription is going to happen, then I too would like to join up with the unit of my choice. Rather than having other people do my pickin' for me."

"Me too," agrees Ben.

"You got that right," echoes John Bird.

March 20, 1862

Within the next three weeks, John Bird and Sally had gone to a dance in Arlington. Sally had introduced Ben to her best friend Lizzie, and on Saturday March 20 the three Manry brothers escorted the girls of their dreams to a picnic and dance over to Gum. It was a fun day, great food, wonderful music, and not one opportunity to dance missed.

The near perfect day is brought to a halt, however, by the Ugly One who the Manry boys had seen at the Morgan Café nearly three weeks before. As the music ends between dances, the Ugly One shouts out the news that storm clouds are moving in from the northeast.

"We've got to go," James warns. "It's a long way to Morgan and Edison."

No one really minds leaving early. They still have the time to be together getting back home. However, somewhere between Leary and Morgan, James draws back on the reins, "Whoa, Molly. Whoa Maggie. Whoa, girls."

"Why are we stopping?" Sally asks.

"Shh," whispers Lizzie. "Just wait and see."

"Well," James replies, "we have something we need to tell you."

"Yeah, you see we were wanting to tell you sooner," stammers Ben.

"We are enlisting Monday morning," John Bird informs the passengers, "and we really don't know when we will see you girls again. But we sure hope y'all be around when we get back.".

Mary Sue grabs James by the hand. Tears are running down her cheeks, "You know I'll be here James Henry Manry."

✳ ✳ ✳

The three Manry brothers enlist in Company E, 51st Georgia Infantry, early in the morning of March 22, 1862. Their mom and dad, William and Annie, their siblings, several other relatives, plus Mary Sue, Sally and Lizzie are there to send them off.

On the way home William expresses to Annie how it is that, "I just don't feel good about this." She points out to him that few parents have ever felt real good about sending their sons off to war.

"It's more than that, Annie. I can't explain it, but the future looks so black to me. It looks as black as looking down a deep well—nothing there."

✳ ✳ ✳

Three weeks after their enlistment, on April 14th the Confederate Congress passed enabling legislation for military conscription, and two months after their enlistment, the Manry brothers were engaged in what was to become known as the Seven Days Battle. Six weeks later the 51st Georgia would be at Second Manassas. Two weeks after Manassas Ben and John Bird would be dead at Fox's Gap, South Mountain, Sharpsburg, Maryland.

And, I, Dave Benson, know now what really happened to my great-great uncles at Fox's Gap. I know now the haunting anger that seeped for generations throughout one of the Southern branches of my family. I know this now in part because Sadie Ann Manry Sheppard has told me; and recently discovered government records verify her story.

But first let me tell you about Sadie. No, I have never met her. She died in 1945, three years before I was born. Besides I never knew she even existed until about two years ago as I began following up on leads my dying mother shared with me. These "leads" were at first mystifying and mysterious. In fact I thought my mother was just plain losing it, that the medication was causing hallucination, but the fact is that she was on very little medication, none of which would cause any hallucination. Eventually, I learned that her visions, and the things her visitors invisible to me were telling her, were much more than a dying woman's fantasies. This was real. It was real to Mom, and it has become so very real to me.

You see, my mother and I had a very close relationship, always did, but especially close after Dad died. I don't remember what I'm about to tell you action-in-progress wise, but "recall" it only from a photo I found one day while playing in the attic at home. My childhood home was a farmhouse. Four wooden columns supported a large white wood frame building with a long front porch. It was an imposing structure complimented by a large red wooden frame storage barn, a smaller metal roofed fiber boarded cattle barn with the two barns anchored by a white cement silo topped by a red wooden roof. Twenty yards from the barns was a small red chicken house, and twenty yards toward the house was a large red wooden framed garage. Between the garage and the house was a small wood framed milk house.

My bedroom was upstairs and just off from my bedroom was a crawl space into a large unfinished attic. Well, it was a crawl space for my parents, for me it required only a slight bend. The attic was my own personal world. It was here that I fantasized about becoming a Texas Ranger, a fighter pilot, a cowboy, a sheriff, a state trooper, a ballet dancer, hair stylist, and even a nurse. There were always plenty of wonderful things to investigate and explore from up there, including an old Victrola and several old scratchy records. I would crank up the Victrola, put on one of the records and sit for long hours enjoying the music—music Mom had given up when she married Dad. I could not understand the words, but I loved the rhythm and the feel. This is where I learned to love opera.

One day when I was about five years old, I jimmied open an old trunk. Must say I had worked at that sucker for a long time over the course of many months, but on this particular day I managed to pry it open. At first there appeared to be nothing out of the ordinary. Some old clothes, mostly women's or girls', but I was strangely attracted to a few of them. I tried on a woman's hat, a shawl. There were two girls' dresses. One fit me real well, so I left it on. The dress felt comfortable. I liked it. From that day on whenever I went to My World, I would dress up with some of the treasures in that trunk.

And then I found it. In the very bottom of the trunk, in a small tin box about the size of a cigar box, were a few photos. One of the photos was that of a small box covered with flowers and a young woman who looked strangely like my mother. In another photo stood a very young girl, maybe two or three years old. She was wearing the smaller dress I had found in the trunk.

My curiosity could not take it any longer. Despite the risk I feared I was about to take, I pulled off the dress, ran out of the attic and downstairs to my mother. I found Mom in her very familiar posture—standing at the kitchen sink gripping the side of the counter and starring out the window mumbling something like "Why did you call me Anna?"

I was really far too preoccupied with my discoveries and my questions to make much note of Mom's own question. With the eagerness of a five-year-old who has just discovered the greatest thing since Santa Claus, I held out the photo of the young woman by the small box and blurted out: "Look Mom, see what I found. Do you know who this is?"

At first I thought she had not heard me, but when I looked up into Mom's face I knew she heard me. I will never forget that moment. It was as if Mom had seen a ghost. I never had seen my mother express any fear. She seemed to be afraid of nothing and no one, but at that moment I knew Mom was frightened. "Where did you get this David!" I'll never forget that moment in part because it was one of the few times in my life that she ever called me David.

At that point I knew I was in over my head, but I confessed. She didn't say a thing for a long time. Well, it seemed long to a five-year-old who was convinced his life was about over. Finally, Mom composed herself and asked, "You mean the woman?"

"Yes," I said hesitantly.

"Well, Dave, that's me."

"Wow, Mom, you look so young, and so pretty. But you sure do look sad. Why were you sad?"

"I was sad because your sister was in the box, Dave."

Well I never heard of having a sister. I got really excited and handed Mom the other photo saying, "but she got out of the box. Here, see. Where is she now?"

That was it. Mom went back to her window. She stood there for a long, long time and then I thought she was beginning to laugh. Her shoulders began to heave like when she would be ready to burst forth with one of her vintage and boisterous laughs. My Dad had always said that the giggles which first attracted him to her grew into volcanic explosions as she got older. What was to come on this day was certainly an explosion, but it had nothing to do with laughter and merriment. It had everything to do with pent up grief, mourning, and downright pain.

Mom began to sag. It was as if she were Icarus flying into the sun, melting away. Slowly, she fell to the floor and wept. I felt so powerless, confused and afraid. I didn't know what to do. I headed for the door saying, "I'll get Dad."

"NO," she screamed. "I'll be okay, just sit here with your mother."

So, I sat with her. She held me so tight I thought I was going to faint. Finally, she loosened her grip, turned me around, and said, "Dave, the person in the dress is you."

"Me? Me in a dress? Why was I in a dress? I'm a boy."

I was dumbfounded. I couldn't believe it. But, the me that I thought was a sister did look pretty. It was not a bad photo. I did look pretty.

"Dave, all I can tell you is that that was you. Please don't ask me again. Okay?"

"Okay, Mom, but why was my sister in the box?"

"That, Dave, is called a casket. It is something they put dead people in. Your sister died soon after birth. That was her casket. That was taken at her funeral."

"What was her name, Mom?"

"Annie, but please do not ask me any more questions about her, and PLEASE do not mention any of this to your father, okay? Promise?"

I agreed to the bargain, took the photos back to the attic, placed them in the tin box, and tenderly put the tin box back into the bottom of the trunk. I never so much as looked at the funeral picture again. But nearly every time I went to the attic from that day forward for years I would open the trunk, dig down for the tin box, open it, take out the picture of the "little girl" and tenderly hold it to my heart.

Why am I telling you this story? Some 47 years later, that is two years ago and only weeks after my mother's death, I found what appeared to be the same young woman in that photo with my sister Annie's casket standing before me in a library in Edison, Georgia. My mother's friends knew Mom as Annie. My sister's name was Annie. The young woman in the Edison library was also Annie.

Annie Belle Price was her name: Annie Belle Sheppard Price. The next day I returned to that library to inquire when she would next be on duty. I was then informed that there was no librarian by the name of Annie Belle Price, nor was there anyone in Edison or Calhoun County by that name.

Furthermore, I was told the library had been closed the day before, that there was no way I could have even been in the building to say nothing about meeting anyone within its walls.

However, the more I dug around in the historical records, the more I came to understand that in some most mysterious way I had in fact encountered the "risen" Annie Belle. She had told me that she looked very much like her mother. While I never did find a photo of Annie Sheppard Price's mother, a local history buff and longtime resident of Edison confirmed that she had heard her parents remark how similar daughter and mother looked. Annie Belle's mother was Sadie Ann Manry Sheppard.

While I was in Edison I spent a great deal of time at the local Historical Center where I was given a copy of Sadie's diary. As I read her diary her face was ever before me. It was Annie Price's face; it was my mother's face. It was as if my mother were talking to me. How can I make real to you the joy of encountering my mother alive in the dead who were somehow more alive than dead?

Before Mom died she told me she would see me on Hartford, and there I was sitting in a Historical Center on Hartford Street, Edison, Georgia. Mom had provided more clues than that, however. She had mentioned Ben and Johnny B and how it was that I needed to find them. There was something about a fox and a gap relative to Ben and Johnny B. So, there I was on Hartford going through old records, ultimately finding information that confirmed Ben & Johnny B as Manrys who were in fact ancestors of my mother's. Then this kindly librarian places Sadie's diary in my hand.

In Sadie's diary she puzzled as a young girl and young woman over the mystery of her uncles' deaths. She agonized over the pain their deaths caused her Grandfather Manry. She, like me, had tried to get some answers. She had asked about the disposition of her uncles' bodies only to be met with stone wall silence or the admonition to not talk about it again. She too, like my mother, mentioned something about a fox and a gap. It had come to Sadie in a dream and to my mother through a conversation with David who was a frequent visitor in her dying days visible only to Mom. Sadie wrote of her dream that the fox she had seen was a very sad fox.

I had read Sadie's account of the dream at a time when I was pursuing a number of other leads. It was not until much later that I returned to her journal to continue getting to know Sadie, but mostly with the desire to hear and to see my Mom one more time. May I share some of Sadie's later journal entries with you now?

November 19, 1888

I can feel her coming! Her? Yes, I know this baby is going to be a girl. How do I know that to be true? Well, journal, for now it is just between you & me. Last night I was sound asleep. No kicking, no movement of the baby at all. I felt so relaxed, but tired, exhausted with trying to keep this family fed, clothed and washed. Don't know what I would do if I had anymore to worry about than Gene, CA and myself. Well, guess I will find out with this new one.

Anyway, there I was sound asleep when Grandpa Manry appears at my bedside. I had never once dreamed of Grandpa since he died two years ago. Last night I sure did. There he was just as real. In fact, Journal, and you keep this to yourself, he was more than real; I mean more than a dream. Grandpa reminded me of my resolution a long time ago to name my first daughter Annie after my Grandma Manry.

"Remember," he said, "this child must be Annie." That's all he said, and with that he was gone. But I remember my resolution and I'm going to find it and rewrite it right here in honor of this little one, Annie Sheppard. Come little one. Come Annie Belle. Come.

Here it is: 20 June 1886. My Dear Grandpa has passed. I cannot say that he is dead. He has passed the test of being a great man, great father, great husband to two wonderful women, great grandfather, and a great Christian. Dear Jesus welcome Grandpa Manry into your Heavenly Kingdom.

I shall never forget and shall forever value my presence at Grandpa's bedside, Lord, in his final hours with us. He wasn't real conscious of our presence, but he was quite conscious of your presence. He reached out for or to you speaking your name as his Lord and Savior.

And then, oh then, he spoke as if B. Pappa's mother was there: "Ann, oh Annie, you have come." I vowed right then and there that I shall insist on people calling me Annie from now on; and, if I ever have a little girl her name shall be Annie.

But the miracles did not cease with Grandma Annie Manry coming for him. Their sons Ben and Johnny B came as well.

Grandpa died weeping with joy and calling, "Ben, my son, John Bird, my boy, let us go home. Grandpa lay back down, and with the most beautiful smile I ever saw upon his face, Grandpa died. There I said it: Grandpa died. I can't write anymore. I am crying.

So, you see. No, I'm sure you do not really see. I'm not sure I really see; but as I read Sadie's entry, I felt a certain feeling of "coming home." Yet, it was more than that. It was a feeling of being held like that child long ago on the kitchen floor in his mother's arms. In fact I felt as if I was going to faint. The child of five who had become a man of 52, ten times older than the little boy who had come down from the attic, the man-child who had lost his mother had now found her. I could literally see Sadie because I had seen her daughter; and in seeing them I had seen my mother.

Oh, but I digress here, it seems, but not really. What does all of this have to do with knowing what really happened to Ben & Johnny B? What does it all have to do with the boy in the Attic? Well, that too becomes clear in a further reading of Sadie's journal.

As it happened I was carrying Sadie's journal with me the very day I was prowling around Fox's Gap. For some reason I had felt for several days that I needed to carry Sadie with me. So, every once in a while I would open it up to read further. Sadie often had meals with me. While waiting for my order to come at whatever restaurant or café I was at, Sadie would keep me company. But on this day at Fox's Gap on South Mountain after trekking around the site of the old Wise Family farm where Ben & Johnny B had been killed, I went over to the site of the farm's well and sat. I was imagining the horror that transpired there and the helplessness James Manry must have felt in seeing his brothers lying by the very well where I was now seated.

It was an October day when I was there. The foliage was breathtaking in its depth and variety of color. I imagined how pretty the mountain might have been in the middle of September when Ben, Johnny, and James were there. Were they also struck by the magnificence of God's palette, or were they consumed by premonitions and fears of that which was to come? I sat there wondering about what those young men may have been feeling when I consulted Sadie one more time.

November 20, 1888
   Oh, Praise God, little Annie Sheppard, Annie Belle, has

arrived. Grandpa Manry would be proud. Would be? I KNOW
he is. Grandpa came to me in a dream last night, and again it
was soooo real!!! He said to me, "Sadie, Sadie Ann, your
Grandma Annie is so happy for you."

Dumb me, and so how did I respond? Well, I never even
acknowledged the baby, I blurted out: "Grandpa, you never
told me what happened to my uncles?" Grandpa looked so sad
and all he said was "Sadie, they dumped Ben & Johnny into a
well. That's all we know."

When B. Pappa came to see the baby and me this afternoon,
I fibbed to him. I couldn't tell him about seeing Grandpa at my
bedside. Instead, I said, "Pappa, one day before Grandpa died
he told me that Uncle Ben & Uncle Johnny were killed and
dumped in a well. Is that true?"

BP turned white, stammered, and asked, "Why are we
talking about this? Shouldn't we be talking about your little
girl?"

"I don't know," I fibbed again. "Is it true? Were their bodies
dumped in a well like a load of useless trash?"

"Yes, Sadie, yes." And Pappa walked out of the room.

It was at that moment when I said to no one in particular, since no one else
was even present, but mainly to the mountain, "If only you could speak."

Yes, if mountains could speak, South Mountain would surely speak the
truth. Yet, perhaps the truth is more brutal than even a mountain can endure.

The Truth at Fox's Gap: September 14, 1862

At about 9:00 a.m. Union General Jacob Cox's Kanawha Division of
General Reno's IX Corps attacked Confederate General Samuel Garland's
brigade in the south field of the Wise Farm. This battle was one of the very few
Union-Confederate engagements where hand to hand combat occurred.
General Garland was killed and future U.S. President Rutherford B. Hayes
was wounded. Later that morning the fighting centered on the vicinity around
the Wise farmhouse. It is here that Ben and Johnny B were killed, left lying by
the well.

By around 4 p.m. the Union forces commenced their final assault upon the
remaining Confederates who were entrenched in the Sunken Road across
from the field where the day's battle had begun. This was Confederate
Brigadier General Thomas F. Drayton's Brigade. Drayton's Brigade

advanced toward the south end of Wise's field only to be outflanked and grossly outnumbered. Drayton's forces suffered a 50% casualty rate. The fighting ended around 11 p.m. and all turned quiet.

When the day began the Wise Family Farm would have taken on a relatively pastoral view. The small wood framed house was protected from the elements by a vertical wood fence, a stockade in construction and appearance. A tree hugged the east side of the house and another stood vigil maybe thirty feet away to the west. The pasture across from the house was encased by horizontal fencing and lined by trees in various stages of fall foliage.

By the end of the day the Wise Farm was the scene of utter devastation. The ground was scarred by the impact of cannon. The Wise Family home was abandoned. Ben and Johnny B, plus 56 of their companions' bodies were still lying near the well on the north side of the house.

Any war, any battle, any conflict that results in the taking of human life may defensibly be defined as an atrocity, an affront to God and humanity. Certainly the engagement of September 14, 1862 could be so defined with the loss of over 4600 lives. However, all that transpired between 9 a.m. and 11 p.m. that day pale into relative insignificance compared to what was to occur in the next few hours after the fighting ceased.

Union troops on, we presume, someone's order dragged Ben & Johnny B's bodies and the bodies of 56 other Confederate soldiers littered about the Wise Family farm and in the immediate vicinity of the family's well to the well. One by one Ben and Johnny and their 56 friends were thrown down into the well. The intent of this action appears to have been not just that of desecrating the dead enemy, but to punish the Wise family for simply being there.

Ultimately, when the fighting had finished and the Wises returned home, they found nothing but ruin, including their water well filled with corpses. The Wise family, in turn, was blamed for the atrocity. According to the Union Army, Farmer Wise interred the dead soldiers in the family well in order to place blame upon the Union. Eventually the Wises were exonerated, but the Union forces were the victors and to them were bequeathed the spoils of war, which includes, in this case, avoidance of responsibility and proportionate punishment. I am reminded of a comment Will Durant makes in the context of an historical assessment of the relationship between climate and power with special focus upon the foundations of India:

A FINE LINE OF DISTINCTION:
IN SEARCH OF ROOTS

Forever the north produces rulers and warriors,
the south produces artists and saints,
and the meek inherit heaven.

Durant, it seemed to me that day at Fox's Gap, was speaking very directly to the North vs. the South in the America of the 1860s. Yet, I also wondered if Durant was entirely accurate. The South, I doubt was entirely composed of artists. I certainly doubt they were all saints. While Christian scripture and the writings of such people as Saint Augustine condoned slavery, history's reverence for either God's word or Augustine never hinged on such approbation of slavery.

Whatever the case, wherever the truth lies, the fact is Ben & Johnny B's bodies were dumped as trash into that well. By the time the bodies were discovered and brought out to daylight there was no way to identify the bodies. They now rest in a Confederate cemetery as Unknown Soldiers in nearby Shepherdstown.

The knowledge of Ben & Johnny B's fate had the same effect upon their family as rape often has upon the woman defiled. The family was mortified and angry as if it were themselves for generations who were defiled and violated of all human dignity. The wages of war bring no dividends to the losers, but even the winners lose in such cases of wanton disregard and hatred.

After reading Sadie's journal entry, I sat and hugged her journal until, if the journal were human it would have fainted. And I wondered: Who were the Gods of the North? Who were the Gods of the South? Who was God to Ben and Johnny B? As I sat near the well that swallowed the Manry brothers, I even wondered aloud, "God, were you even here? Are you here now? Did James ever find meaning in his brothers' lives? Could he assign a meaning to their deaths? Was there meaning to his own sacrifices?"

Over the course of the next few days I would have reason to raise the latter two questions repeatedly as I walked the battlefield at Antietam and the streets of Sharpsburg and Shepherdstown. A few answers came sooner than expected served up in part at a strange café by a familiar stranger.

Chapter 9:
The Ruse

...and the king of Israel said to Jehoshaphat,
"I will go into battle disguised, but you put on
your own clothes." So the king of Israel disguised
himself and then entered the fray. Meanwhile, the
king of Aram had given his chariot commanders
the order, "Fight with no one, small or great,
except the king of Israel."
(2 Chronicles 19: 29-30)

Burnside's Café is a quaint little shop on a side street off Main in Sharpsburg. The town itself has obviously come back to life after the devastation caused by the bloodiest single-day conflict in American military history. Many a town would simply have packed itself up and headed out. After all, blood flowed down the hills of the battlefield into the streets. Blood flowed out of the churches, homes and other buildings that were pressed into service as makeshift hospitals. The Mumma, Poffenberger, Smith and most other farms had become killing fields and butcher shops. Sharpsburg received the carcasses—dead ones, dying ones, maimed and wounded ones. In fact, Sharpsburg has taken advantage of their pivotal, though bloody, moment in history to bring new life out of a cauldron of unprecedented death. Burnside's Café is my most immediate example.

It is a small, but interesting café. No more than eight tables, plus a small eating bar constitute the accommodations for customers. Oh, but the ambiance and the menu! The walls are nearly papered with a multitude of photos and drawings, sketches and paintings of the Lower Bridge over Antietam Creek. There are numerous photos of General Ambrose Burnside, photos taken before, after and during the engagement at Antietam. There are photos of Burnside's signature on a variety of documents, and photos of his family. In addition, there is a well-lit display case. In it are relics of the battle for control of what became known as Burnside's Bridge.

The menu? Well, let me tell you about the menu. It includes a full page, full-blown background photo of the good general on the front cover. The back cover provides a short biographical sketch of the man, and a short summary of his role in the war. In a highlighted box at the bottom the reader's attention is fixed upon the notice that Burnside memorabilia, books and postcards are available at the checkout counter.

One can order a Burnside Burger or a Burnside Bridge Buffalo Burger. For dessert the delectable Ambrose Apple Pie. For those with a hearty appetite there is the General, a 16-oz tenderloin steak. I decided on the Ambrosia Reuben.

When the waitress took my order, I asked, "Now what distinguishes the Ambrosia Reuben from the Omaha Reuben?" (Expecting her to respond with something profound like, "Huh?") Until this inquiry was laid out there, this 40ish brunette of serious demeanor seemed to be doing her job in a near-robotic manner. To my total surprise, she bursts into a wild laugh—a laugh that reminded me of a hen house full of chickens early in the morning announcing in unison their accomplishment for the day and demanding to be given their just reward.

"Sir," she finally forces some composure to say, while hitching up her short skirt that had fallen with the rising of her hilarity, "there ain't no comparison, well not much, some I guess. But you are the first person I have ever served who seems to know the origin of the Reuben."

Trying to illustrate my own font of knowledge, I responded, "Yes, I not only know it originated in Omaha, but that it was a man by the name of Reuben who invented it. In fact, Reuben was the chef at the Blackstone Hotel. The Blackstone at the time was one of the finest restaurants in Omaha and was on the top floor of the Blackstone Building."

"Precisely," she shouts for all to hear. Then, for the second total surprise in as many minutes, Sheila announces, "Ladies and Gentlemen, we have with us today an authority on the Omaha Reuben. I am willing to bet he is from Omaha. He is also an authority on the Ambrosia Reuben, but he does not, I bet, know why."

Playing along with the game Sheila has put before me, I reply, "Yes, by the God of Ambrose Burnside, I am indeed from the great city of Omaha,

Nebraska. 'Tis the home of Girls & Boys Town, ConAgra, Mutual of Omaha, Fred Astaire, Henry and (and for a while) Jane and Peter Fonda, Gayle Sayers, Bob Gibson, AND the Reuben."

Surprise Number Three: Everyone claps, except for one young man sitting alone at a corner table. He looks vaguely familiar, probably something about him that reminds me of someone I know. My attention on him is quickly diverted by Sheila's immediate intervention. "But do you know why you do not know why you are also an expert on our very own home grown Ambrosia Reuben?"

"No I do not know why I do not know why. Something tells me, however, that you DO know why I do not know why. You have me in such suspense; I can hardly stand it."

Then, a voice from behind me says, "Christ, Sheila, besides, the man's starving to death. Get him his goddamned Reuben, will ya?"

The room bursts into laughter once again. One young man is slapping his thigh, his partner, an older fellow, is wiping the tears from his eyes. Everyone is having a good time, and so am I. Well, everyone except for the serious looking strangely familiar one in the corner. He simply nods his head this time in my direction—a nod with a sideways and downward motion. Again, he seems not only distant from the festivities going on around him, but so damned familiar for a stranger.

"Well," Sheila says with her very slight Southern drawl, "I'll tell ya why and then I'll get your 'goddamned Reuben', I will."

The fellow who was slapping his thigh is now slapping the table in front of him. I am, along with Sheila, the best act in town, methinks.

Sheila has put her order pad in her skirt pocket and stands with her hands on her hips waiting for the commotion to die down. Finally, she warns the crowd, "Now y'all shush, 'cause y'all need to hear this. The Ambrosia Reuben did indeed get its original inspiration from the one and only Omaha Reuben. Yep, we serve it the same way; up to a point that is. It's corned beef and sauerkraut on rye or pumpernickel with Thousand Island's Dressing, just like the original. The difference is this, we have named ours after General Ambrose Burnside, obviously—Ambrosia, right? Plus, recognizing that the original came out of Omaha's **BLACKSTONE** Hotel, AND recognizing that Ambrose himself sported big **BLACK SIDE-BURNS**, we put side-**BURNS** on our Ambrosia Reubens by singeing them on all four sides with a Cajun-rub letting them simmer for two to three minutes on a **BLACKSTONE** purchased several years ago in, guess where?"

"Let me take a wild guess," I interject. "It couldn't possibly be Omaha, could it?"

The place is alive once again with laughter, and this time clapping from all corners, except one. The Serious One soon gets up to leave. As he walks by me there is another nod of the head seeming to motion to me to follow him. He doesn't say anything. He just heads toward the door. At that very moment Sheila arrives with some coffee and I lose sight of Joe Serious.

Later, as I am paying my bill, I ask Sheila if she knows the young man who was sitting in the corner. Surprise Number Four: "Sir, there was no one at that table. At least not since you came in; and there is no one there now." Sheila is looking at me as if I had just arrived on a UFO.

"Why? Did he make a pass at you?"

Shit, there it is again. I cannot get away from it. If She knows, everyone in this café knows that I am Gay.

"Probably even General Burnside knows too," I blurted out.

"What?" Sheila asked.

"Oh, nothing," I responded with embarrassment.

Recovering some presence of mind, I tried again, "He was probably in his early twenties wearing light brown leather boots, and light gray..."

I chose not to finish my description. In fact, could not, for I knew. The non-verbal was the same today, as it had been before.

Entertaining the possibility that maybe I am going nuts, and at the same time thinking that maybe I am simply imagining things, I step out to the street expecting him to be there. He is not. I walk slowly back to the car expecting him to show up. He does not. I open the door slowly, looking all around as I gradually lower myself into the seat. Placing the key in the ignition while surveying the street for him to show up somehow, I turn the key. It is then that I see what my eyes at first tell me is a mirage. A note sits behind the steering wheel propped up against the dashboard in front of the speedometer.

There are times in one's life when the receipt of a letter causes one to take a deep breath and proceed with utmost caution despite competing feelings of trepidation and the excitement of curiosity, This was one of those moments. It was similar to receiving a letter from the IRS and being at once afraid it will be the notice of an audit as well as hoping it will be a check. I unfolded the note, held my breath and read:

Return to the Catoctin side of S. Mtn. Listen to General Cox.

Not being sure who General Cox was, I figured the best and easiest way would be to discuss the issue with a Ranger at the Antietam Visitor Center.

The answer was quick in coming. General Jacob Cox was a Union General. He had fought at South Mountain. The Ranger looked at me with a grin from ear to ear and said, "Are you in luck today. We have a report by Cox that I saw just the other day. Give me a minute and I'll make a copy for you. It is a report of events leading up to and during his Division's engagement at South Mountain."

* * *

Instead of sitting down to read the document, I sensed that what I should do is take the mysterious note's advice and head for the Catoctin side of South Mountain. Traveling north out of Sharpsburg on Route 34, I soon find myself in Boonsboro looking for Alternate US 40, the Old National Pike. Boonsboro is considerably larger than Sharpsburg, but very similar in layout of the town and style of public architecture. The route I am taking leads southeast up the north side of South Mountain through Turner's Gap, a winding tree-lined route beyond description in its beauty. Once I am through the gap a wide valley lies before me and off to the far east is another mountain range, the Catoctin Mountains.

Pulling off to the side of the road I decide to just let the beauty of this gorgeous valley soak in. I am struck by the serenity of the place. Small farms dot the valley on either side of the creek running through it, Catoctin Creek. Then, I realize I am parked near the intersection of the Old National Pike and Fox Gap Road. This is a gravel road that parallels the valley, running by a few private homes and always affording a panoramic view. Again I wonder if the Manry boys had been able to fully appreciate the magnificence of this valley while they were here. Of course, at that time it may not have been so serene and eye pleasing with the valley full of the enemy's killing machines.

About a hundred yards from the next intersection with Reno Monument Road which will take me back up to Fox's Gap and the Wise Farm, I decide to pull over and read General Jacob Cox's report. It is an interesting document entitled "Forcing Fox's Gap and Turner's Gap." Cox's narrative, at the start, summarizes his division's movements beginning on September 5, 1862, heading toward Sharpsburg. At first his account barely interests me, but when he gets to September 13th my interest is heightened as I read:

About noon of the 13th, I was ordered to march with my division to Middletown, on the National road leading to Hagerstown ... My own camp for the night was pitched on the western side of the village of Middletown.

126

The Catoctin or Middletown valley is beautifully included between Catoctin Mountain and South Mountain, two ranges of the Blue Ridge, running north-east and south-east. The valley is 6 or 8 miles wide, and the National road, as it goes north-westward, crosses South Mountain at a depression called Turner's Gap. The old Sharpsburg road leaves the turnpike a little west of Middletown, turns to the left and crosses the mountain at Fox's Gap, about a mile from Turner's.

Here I am having just traveled the "National road" through Turner's Gap, with a view of the Catoctin Mountain to my left and off in the distance a slight view of present-day Middletown and only a hundred yards from the "old Sharpsburg road". In a few moments I will be taking that road through Fox's Gap. It is beginning to feel as if I am living history.

General Cox continues on with his account noting his receipt of orders to march on Crampton's Gap with little expectation of any significant Confederate resistance. His orders were to begin the march at 6 a.m. in the morning of September 14th. Soon after moving out with Col E. P. Scammon's brigade,

...just as we crossed Catoctin Creek, I was surprised to see Colonel Moor (who had been captured by the Confederacy on the 12th near Frederick City) *standing at the roadside. With astonishment, I rode to him and asked how he came there. He said he had been taken as prisoner beyond the mountain, but had been paroled the evening before, and was now finding his way back to us on foot.*

"But where are you going?" said he.

I answered that Scammon's brigade was going to support Pleasanton in a reconnaissance into the gap.

Moor made an involuntary start, saying, "My God! be careful": then, checking himself, said, "But I am paroled!" and turned away.

From that moment on the Union commanders, including General McClellan who was always and ever convinced there were more Confederate troops opposing him than there ever were, became convinced that South Mountain was crawling with the Army of Northern Virginia. Battle plans were redesigned and caution became the major strategy.

At the time of my reading of Cox's report, I was merely impressed with the fact that I was probably near the very spot where Cox and Scammon came upon the paroled Moor. Just off to my left, to the east, stood a large red barn with a black roof. Further to the east stood a long line of trees that seem to outline the flow of the Catoctin Creek. Right in there would have been the rendezvous of Cox, Scammon & Moor.

I was also impressed with Moor's integrity and the rules of war that he took so seriously. In exchange for his freedom, he was not going to provide any information about the enemy that he had been privy to, even to his own commander and to his own cause. Such rules of war died, I believe, with the end of the American Civil War.

The Ranger, I discovered, included a photo with the Cox report. It was a photo of at least seven badly bloated bodies near a stone wall. The caption states:

Confederate Dead At The Crossroads By Wise's House At Fox's Gap
From A Sketch Made The Day After The Battle

Facial features were absent, but I could not help thinking that Ben and John Manry could well have been among the corpses the unnamed artist used as models for his historic sketch. That did it. I knew I had to go back to the site of the well. Yet, as I drove the short distance, I also wondered aloud, "Okay, David L. Wooten, so I have been to the Catoctin side of South Mountain. I have read the Cox report. So what?" I was soon to find out what was what.

Sitting again at the ill fated and abominable well site, it occurs to me that not many hours before I had sat here with Sadie's journal and discovered the foundation to a long-held family secret. "Perhaps Sadie holds some more answers," I said to the well and to myself.

Reaching into my briefcase I pull out Sadie's voluminous record of her life, thinking all the while that I should really take the time to read through her journal from beginning to the end. However, reading Sadie's Journal is like reading *War and Peace* in terms of its length. Picking up where I had left off while at this very same geographic spot the day before, I began to read.

For nearly 10 years and many pages of mostly chronicling day-by-day events and issues of raising by that time three children and assisting in the management of a large plantation, Sadie's journal entries were pretty common place jottings. Indeed, the births of her next two children, Bessie and Roy, were noted not at the time, but only in passing as she mentioned their names from time to time.

It was not until I came to the entry for September 14, 1898, that my attention became riveted to the page. She began her notation for that day by mentioning how she had gone to the cemetery to place flowers at her Grandfather Manry's grave, and that as she was about to leave:

Uncle James Manry suddenly showed up. I didn't see him coming.

I had no idea he was within miles of me. He startled me so that I nearly fell backwards. In his typical mannerly way, he apologized repeatedly for "intruding" on my "conversation" with Grandpa Manry. Uncle James, in preventing me from toppling over, then held me in his arms for a long moment. This was the first time I recall Uncle James showing me any real affection, or anyone for that matter!

Finally, he says to me, "Sadie, I heard what you said to my father, your grandfather, just moments ago. I heard you say something about your Uncle Ben and Uncle Johnny being treated so inhumanely by the Union at Fox's Gap; and wondering if there was any real purpose to their lives.

"You may or may not know that I was there. I have kept my experiences in the War very much to myself. I have wanted to forget. I have not even told my wonderful wife what I am about to tell you, Sadie."

This was the first time in my life that I was having a real conversation with Uncle James. I was not about to say a word at that point. I did not want to spoil the magic of the moment. Uncle James went on to recount how he witnessed Ben and John being killed and the helplessness he felt.

"Annie," he says to me (Uncle James never before referred to me as Annie, so I knew this was really getting serious!). "Annie, I have been haunted all my life by the fact that I did not risk everything and go to my brothers when I saw them hit. Many of my comrades at the time reassured me there was nothing I could have done, and that I would have faced certain death myself. All of that may be true, but I have felt enormous guilt all my life since that day.

"But you know, Annie, I'm glad I happened to come along just now, hearing you raise that question about my brothers and whether there was any real purpose to their lives. Yes, their lives may have been short ones, but they sure did have purpose. They brought much joy to my mother and father, as well as the girls they were courting when they went off to enlist. They were good soldiers, damned good soldiers. They were so good that they may have prevented the Union from winning the war right there at South Mountain."

Guess I looked a bit skeptical for Uncle James placed his hands on my shoulders and looked me square in the eye:

"Annie, I don't think I have shared this with more than your grandpa and grandma. Your two uncles played a large role in perhaps the greatest military ruse ever. You see it was about two days before the battle at South Mountain when our cavalry captured a Yankee officer by the name of Moor, Colonel Moor. I don't know whose idea it was. It could have been General Longstreet himself. All I know is that our commander, Lt. Col. William MacRae called a bunch of us together and spelled out the plan.

"The plan was this: We were to dupe this Yankee into thinking that our

military presence on that there mountain was far greater than it was. There was myself, Ben & Johnny and Roach Wooten from over in Morgan and a few others who were assigned guard duty over Col. Moor. Col. MacRae had a script all worked out for us where Col. Moor would 'accidentally' overhear us talking military strategies for the coming day or two.

"We would 'accidentally' divulge unit numbers, personnel strength, types and numbers of weaponry, as well as tens of thousands of reinforcements only hours away. None of it was true. Of course, we were directed to never divulge anything that was true. MacRae or maybe Longstreet orchestrated an ongoing parade of troops right in full view of our 'guest'. He didn't know that he was seeing the same soldiers, horses, canon, cavalry, artillery, and infantry over and over again.

"We let him go later that night. The four of us Ben, Johnny, Roach, and myself were the ones who set him free. We took him to the crest of the old Sharpsburg Road, wished him well and watched him as he walked down the mountain toward the immense line of Union troops that we had seen earlier in the day massing in the valley.

"As Col. Moor disappeared into the dark, we had ourselves a good laugh. It was the last time Ben and John ever laughed. I'm sure of that. Indeed years went by fast and furious before I ever laughed again.

"Now I'm not saying the Yankees were a pushover, or that we won the battle. Obviously, we were forced to let the mountain go. Obviously Ben & Johnny died up on that mountain. Now that's losing the battle. But, listen to me Annie. If it had not been for that little ruse, 30,000 Union troops would have come right on ahead over that mountain and crushed our measly 9,000. Chances are I wouldn't be here telling you all this. I too would be down that damned well.

"On the other hand, Annie, I never really knew how effective the ruse had been, or even IF it had worked to any degree at all, until a few years ago when the 51st Georgia had a reunion in Albany. I have a copy of a report General D. H. Hill wrote—a report that was much discussed at our gathering in Albany. I'll dig it out and bring it over to you tomorrow. You can judge for yourself if your Uncles' lives had any purpose."

I have been as faithful as I can be to what Uncle James said to me at the cemetery today, in part because he said more to me today than in all of my life put together.

I sure hope he remembers to bring that report to me.

I think Uncle James has lived with a lot of hurt. He has certainly lived with an immense amount of death.

A FINE LINE OF DISTINCTION:
IN SEARCH OF ROOTS

September 15, 1898

Uncle James remembered. I have read General Hill's account of the Battle of South Mountain. I know now that Uncle Ben's, Uncle Johnny's, AND Uncle James' lives definitely had purpose. While the role they played in the military ruse was deadly serious, it is also hilariously funny. They really fooled the guy, Col. Moor. He fell for it completely and he did exactly what they hoped he would do, that he would warn the Union of the Confederate horde. They in turn believed him. The already cautious Union Army became ever more so and we bought more time.

I would sure like to hear more of Uncle James' war experiences.

$$* \quad * \quad *$$

As I read Sadie's remarks I was struck by the enormity of it all. Yesterday, I had raised the question of meaning. Today I find the answer in Sadie's journal. Perhaps I would have found it eventually, but I had a lot of help. Perhaps it is as Mom said before she died, that I needed to get things right. Why do I feel as if I have no control over my own life?

One other thing: inserted within Sadie's journal was the copy of General Hill's report. His remarks certainly cinch the argument that her uncles' lives made a difference, an historical difference. Early on in his analysis he claims: "The battle of South Mountain was one of extraordinary illusions and delusions...the Confederates deluded the Federals into the belief that the whole mountain was swarming with rebels...."

In conclusion Hill observes:

...from whatever standpoint it may be looked at, the battle of South Mountain must be of interest to the military reader as showing the effect of hallucination in enabling 9,000 men to hold 30,000 at bay for so many hours, in robbing victory of its fruits, and in inspiring the victors with such caution that a simple ruse turned them back in their triumphal career.

As I was closing up Sadie's journal, a small map fell out, "A Map of the Positions at Fox's and Turner's Gap—Battle of South Mountain, Sept. 14, 1862." Indicated on the map at Turner's Gap was the location of Evan's Brigade, David Wooten's brigade, and as I was to learn later, William Drayton Sheppard's brigade as well.

Now I had a little better idea why it was important to the stranger in the corner at Burnside's Café that I go to the Catoctin side of South Mountain.

Chapter 10:
The Gathering at Antietam: The Morning

Though you may have been driven to the furthest
corner of the world, even from there will the LORD,
your God, gather you; even from there will he bring
you back. (Deuteronomy 30: 4)

* * *

Therefore, they shall be like a morning cloud
or like the dew that early passes away,
Like the chaff storm—driven from the threshing floor
or like smoke out of the window.
(Hosea 13: 3)

By the time I was ready to traverse the battleground at Antietam, I had established a number of facts concerning the course of the fighting on September 17, 1862. I had a rough idea of the position each of my ancestors occupied that day. I also possessed variable information about each one. What I did not know, of course, is what their experiences were really like here at Antietam.

I knew that Ben and Johnny Manry never made it to Sharpsburg. Their bodies were stuffed in that well by the time the fighting began along Antietam Creek. While they died, their brigade lived on. Their brother James lived to fight another day, many days. He lived to tell some of the story eventually, after 36 years, to his niece Sadie.

On the morning of September 17th, James's brigade, Drayton's Brigade, composed in part of the 51st Georgia, Company E., was spread out on the edge of a cornfield just to the southeast corner of the village of Sharpsburg. Roach Wooten, David's brother, was also a member of the same brigade. Beginning at about 6 a.m. they would have heard the fight raging to the north of them as Union General Hooker's First Corps made its advance upon the northern entrance to Sharpsburg along the Hagerstown Road.

Hooker was aiming to take control of the high ground where the Dunker Church sat; and where I now sit. As I rest here on the front steps of this pretty white framed church nicely trimmed with black shutters on the south and north sides, I am struck by the irony of what I am about. Inside this building the pews and lectern are all set up for worship. This community of faith has always been a peace church, a denomination that has historically practiced non-violent resistance, a pacifist church. Yet, the Dunker Church that day in 1862 became the first focal point of unprecedented violence. The church that preached and worked for "peace on earth and good will to all," became the center of all hell breaking loose.

If these hallowed walls could talk, they would share untold secrets of the agonies and terrors of war. They would be able to confide in me what three of my ancestors experienced that day, for they were here. David and WD may have even sat on this very step. Yes, if only these walls could talk, I am ready to listen.

The problem for Hooker was that General Stonewall Jackson's Confederate Army was entrenched right here. David and WD lay in wait with their companions, all members of Lawton's Brigade, Ewell's Division of Jackson's Corps composed of the 13th Georgia and Company E of Ramsey's 32nd Georgia. The former being David's regiment, the latter being WD's unit.

At about the same time of Hooker's attack, Union General Joseph K.F. Mansfield's 12th Corps began its advance through the wooded area to Hooker's left sweeping toward the same strategic spot—the Dunker Church. With Mansfield's Corps was General George Greene's 2nd Division. In the 3rd Brigade of this division, led by Lt. Col. Charles Brundage, was Horace Barnes.

Thus it was that on this battlefield that day were four of my Confederate great, great uncles fighting my Union great, great uncle. The family, so to speak, had gathered 138 years before any of us realized we were family—a pre-reunion.

James had the traumatic experience of seeing not only his two brothers killed three days before, but also losing 50% of his comrades in the general vicinity of the Wise Farm only seven miles away. James was 21 years old.

Roach and David were 20 and 22 years old respectively. Horace Barnes was 21. WD was the old man of the bunch, 32. Only WD and Horace were married, both with one son. WD, however, had an additional worry back home. His father was in very poor health. WD would be the only one of these two married men who would return home to his family.

As these five men greeted the dawn of this new day, they most likely would have cursed the weather, for it had rained during the night. In fact the previous couple of days had been full of rain and fog. As a result General McClellan delayed his plans for engaging General Lee in battle approximately two full days. This morning was no different, except perhaps being foggier than ever. A shroud of fog hung over Sharpsburg and the surrounding area as perhaps a premonition of what was to come.

Anyone walking along Sharpsburg's Main Street at, let us say, 5:45 that Wednesday morning, would have seen the fog rolling down the hill from the southwest filling up the street and inundating the leaves and branches of the trees along the way. It would have seemed that the fog was being blown into the vacuum of the valley by some giant machine. Not a Deus Ex Machina this, but a machine of pending evil.

The dirt street was indistinguishable from the pall of the fog. Even the six-foot incline roadside along the front of the Lutheran Church was filling in with this aura of foreboding. Sharpsburg would still be asleep at this hour, or so it would have appeared. Few lamps would be lit. All of the windows of the wood frame houses along the street would have been dark. In another fifteen minutes on a normal day, windows would begin lighting up as town folk would rouse themselves from bed, build fires in their fireplaces and stoves, light their lamps preparing to venture forth into the damp and chilly early morn of a new day. Today would be different, very different.

At 6 o'clock no one in Sharpsburg roused himself or herself from bed. From the north came the unmistakable roar of cannon, the sharp blasts of rifles, the staccato of pistols, and the heavy roar of hundreds of horses and wagons pounding the earth. The fog coming in from the south would soon be joined by smoke from the north.

Before the day would end, wayward shells would scar the church. Instead of fog filling the street, it would be the walking wounded seeking help, litter bearers bringing in the maimed—the white of fog being replaced by the red of blood. The Lutheran Church and many other buildings in and around town would become hospitals and morgues. This was not a normal day. At the click of General Hooker's pocket watch, this day became like few others in history. Like Pearl Harbor 79 years into the future, September 17, 1862 would be a "day that will live in infamy."

✳ ✳ ✳

Horace's 3rd Brigade of the 2nd Division, 12th Corps, had marched most of the night through rain. They had crossed the Upper Bridge of the Antietam around midnight. He had enlisted with the 60th New York nearly one year before. He knew what rain is like. Edwards, New York, his home, received much rain and considerable snow each year. Being wet and cold was not a new experience for him. But up until October, 1861 he could always return home to his parents (Harvey and Ruth), his siblings (William, Mariette, Henry and John); but best of all in recent years he could come in out of the cold to his beautiful wife, Caroline, and their son Leonard, age two. He will never get to see his second son, Horace, Jr., born soon after he left home with the 60th New York.

It had been a long dreary march across the valley. The only positive of the day was first seeing the bridge, the Upper Antietam Bridge, and realizing they would be able to cross the creek without having to ford through the rising waters. Then, seeing the farmhouses on the western side of the bridge, he laughed as he noticed the wash hanging from the line to the east and south of the house on the south side of the road. "Wonder how long that wash has been drying," he said to Frank, an old friend from Edwards.

"Yeah, do you think it will ever get dry? If she don't haul in that line by tomorrow night her clothes will be full of bullet holes, I'm 'fraid."

Just when they thought they had reached their destination, thinking they would bivouac right there at the western side of the creek, orders were shouted out to bear right. Col. Brundage rode along the line of troops informing them, "You only have about another mile to go men." It was 2 a.m. when they arrived at the Poffenberger farm, their home for the remainder of the night.

There would have been little or no sleep for the rest of the night (or morning as it were), given the cold and wet conditions, but particularly so given what every man knew the breaking of dawn would mean for them. It was common knowledge that the six o'clock hour would bring the sound of Hooker's Army moving on the enemy off to their right. As soon as that engagement was resounding throughout these farmlands, Mansfield's Army would be moving out as well, allowing only enough time to elapse to deceive the Confederates into thinking all they needed to worry about was Hooker along the Hagerstown Road.

While Horace lay in his somewhat soggy bedroll he was thinking of three major issues alternately, or even on occasion all three at once: First and foremost there was Caroline and their little boys Leonard and Horace at home. He had asked his younger brother, Johnny, to watch after Caroline and the boys, and he knew Johnny well enough to be a most responsible 15-year-old who would take *his* favorite brother's request seriously.

Indeed, so often since that day, November 4, 1861, when he boarded the train in Ogdensburg headed for Washington, D. C., with the 1st St. Lawrence Regiment to join the 60th NY, Horace retained one special memory:

As he watched from the window of the train, his family seemed to pull away from *him*. They were all there to see him off with the expectation that he would be back soon. It was sure to be a short war. Yet, each one carried a not well-hidden worry. Mom, like all moms in history, felt a pang of dread at seeing her son go off to war. After all Horace was the third one to go. William, her oldest, signed on soon after Fort Sumter in April and Harvey, her husband, left soon after. Everyone thought then that the war would be over by now.

William had left his wife Anna and their two children feeling the need to fight for the Union. Anna looked the most haggard, perhaps because she had received only one short letter since William left six months ago.

Horace wondered, perhaps prophetically, "is Anna feeling like a war widow already? Is Mother? Is that what Caroline feels like?" There was Caroline surrounded by his family: Maryette, his 18-year-old sister who could definitely relate to 19-year-old Caroline and 17-year-old Anna. Maryette's fiancé, David, had enlisted with William. In addition, there was his older brother Henry, age 23 and his wife Martha. Johnny was taking the big brother at home responsibility seriously. Johnny stood with one arm around Maryette and the other around Caroline.

While, Horace felt proud of Johnny being a man, he could not help but feel some strong competitive emotions as well. He would give anything to have remained on that platform and wave goodbye to someone else (preferably not another family member). "God, how I want to be back there with Caroline and ride home with her, to hold her in my own arms, damn it. Am I jealous? Yes, I am jealous. I want her in MY arms.

"But why did I ever enlist in this damned awful war in the first place?" he mumbled to himself in the inner sanctum of his bedroll. Well, part of it was wanting to call his own shots. He knew conscription was on the horizon and he wanted to do his own choosing.

Perhaps equally important was the temptation of "easy" money. Horace, like thousands of young men, both North and South, found the billboard notices and newspaper advertisements more than appealing:

A Great Rush
to Join the
1st St. Lawrence,
60th NY Regiment
NY Volunteers
9 Months
Don't wait to be drafted!
Married Men $366 Bounty
Rally Boys for the Old Flag
NOW IS THE TIME
to Rally Round the
FLAG OF THE COUNTRY
United States pays, in addition to the above,
$100 Bounty
Every man enlisting receives in cash,
upon the mustering in of his Regiment
$88
EVERY MAN TO HIS POST
AND VICTORY IS OURS!

For Horace, a young husband and father with one child and another on the way, plus the "promise" that this was to be a short war, a short commitment on his part, the more immediate promise of $554 just for signing on the line were matters beyond temptation. It was a near no-brainer. Besides, for a young man of his age, personal mortality tends to be a rather remote concept. He had plans for the future, his own farm, a large family, and the desire to grow old with Caroline and their grandchildren. The $554 could go a long way in enabling the dreams to become real.

Another explanation for his voluntary enlistment (and most likely William's, as well), was the family military legacy. Horace felt a certain need to carry on the living legend of a family that always held up its end of the bargain of being a citizen. "Sometimes a man has to fight for the land that he loves," is what Horace's grandfather James Barnes had always said. Not that Grandpa Barnes had ever done it himself, but his daddy, Jonathan Barnes, had served in the Revolutionary War as a drummer in a Connecticut regiment.

Horace's mother, Ruth, often spoke with pride about her great, great grandfather, Eleazer Peck, who had also served in the same war. And Grandma Sally Garrett spoke with profound pride as well about her father, John, who fought with a Connecticut militia against the British. The tradition needed to be continued.

Having enlisted for all of these reasons, the need for control of his own destiny, easy money, patriotism, and sense of obligation to family tradition and pride, there was one other very closely related concern and motivational force pulsating within Horace's conscience on the morning of September 17, 1862. He had just learned that his namesake Uncle Horace Barnes had died on June 6th in a military hospital in Washington, DC.

There was only one Union casualty recorded in that engagement at Fort Pulaski, Georgia, on April 10–11, 1862, but this Horace Barnes had been severely wounded and died two months later. He was 46 years old. Horace wept as he remembered his uncle, and he wept with projected grief as he thought of how his father would be taking the loss of his brother. *Pappy and Uncle Horace were so close. Damn, wish I could be there now for Pappy. Better yet, I just wish I were home rather than in this hellhole.*

But Horace knew as well that this was his chance to avenge the death of his favorite uncle. "I will get me a few Rebels today for you Uncle Horace," he thought to himself. At that moment he heard the thunder off to the right, and he knew his chance for revenge was near. Within minutes the 60th NY and the 3rd Brigade was moving out and into the East Woods toward the Mumma Farm—destination, the Dunker Church.

✳ ✳ ✳

As I sit here on the steps of that very church, I can hear them coming. Ten thousand 12th Corps infantrymen on the attack, buttressing Hooker's 1st Corps. Mansfield's 1st Division taking control of the North Woods well off to my left, while Horace's division heads straight toward me, as the other two brigades rush to take the East Woods which I can see very clearly from here.

It was in the East Woods that General Mansfield met his fate. The news of his death spread quickly, from tree to tree, man to man; then across the cornfield, despite the inferno of death transpiring there. As if the smoke of the burning Mumma farm buildings carried the news, it filtered through the West Wood's cauldron of death to reach the 3rd Brigade and the ears of Horace Barnes.

At first, for Horace, and nearly every man of the 12th Corps, the news of the loss of their leader brings feelings of fear and doubt. Are they now like a ship at sea in the night battered by high waves that have just swallowed their captain? By this time Horace and his brigade are deep into Confederate territory. They have created a wedge by which the Rebel army may be divided and destroyed with a little bit of help from back-up Union troops; or, be wiped out should the help not come.

General Greene sent a courier to General McClellan informing him of the strategic position won by the 3rd Brigade, pleading for immediate reinforcements. Those reinforcements never came, were never ordered, never sent. A chance to win the Battle of Antietam was lost early in the day, but it would not be the last time for that to happen today.

Meanwhile, the 3rd Brigade held their position for approximately two hours. They had the Dunker Church nearly surrounded. Horace's personal position was to stay close to the Brigade's flag bearer to provide him and the flag with as much maximum protection as possible. Running through his mind at one point was the thought of how his great grandfather, Jonathan Barnes, was a drummer boy in the Revolution. "If Great Grandpa Barnes had not been protected as I'm trying to do here, I wouldn't be in this world at all."

But there was little time for thought. The only time one had was to react. The sun had burned off the fog of the morning. The fog, however, was replaced by the smoke from the Mumma farm having been intentionally set fire, as well as from the smoke of gunpowder. Even though Horace was but fifty feet from where I sit, he could hardly see the building due to the thickness of the smoke and the burning of the eyes.

At one point Horace heard an intense volley coming from his right. He saw the concentration of rifle fire aimed right at his position from the Rebel line at the wooden fence less than 30 feet away. He could even see the faces of those who pulled the triggers.

He had never been that close to a Southerner before. He had certainly never been that close to someone who was trying to kill him. Nor had he ever been so close to someone he was trying to kill. "Shit, why are we doing this to each other?" Horace screams.

At that moment, however, no one ever heard Horace's scream. His agony is overwhelmed by the agony all around him. He looks around to see six comrades down. He recognizes all but one; that one is unrecognizable. His face is blown off.

Then, he hears Frank's voice. Frank is to Horace's right, beckoning those behind him to follow him in a charge on the fence-line Confederates. Frank has lost his cap, but certainly not his courage. He is angry and determined, as he and a dozen others charge toward the fence. Horace realizes Frank's intent. Frank is heading straight for the Confederate flag bearer.

David Wooten suddenly notices a blue mass heading for him, but he knows that the aim is not to get him so much as it is to capture the Confederate Colors. He has been responsible for protecting that boy and those colors through 20 battles so far, and he is not going to let either the boy or the flag fall to any Yankee today. He lets loose his version of the Rebel Yell which draws attention to David as he points out the coming Blue Flank.

Now the Rebel Yell of one man has become the heart-stopping, soul-piercing battle cry of fifty enraged Georgians. The yelling is, in a way, even more frightening than the weapons' fire. To a casual observer it might even appear that the Georgians yelled the New Yorkers to death; for it seemed that as the Rebel Yell increased in intensity and ferocity, the more Union men fell to the ground. Frank and his comrades lie now like cordwood a yard high along the fence line.

Horace finds himself in the midst of intense Confederate musket fire. Shells are as thick as fleas on a mangy dog, and it continues for what seems like hours. The shelling stops only because the 27th North Carolina is suddenly upon the 60th NY and its allies with close-in fighting. Then, the 49th North Carolina closes in to encircle the Union position. With a sinking heart Horace witnesses the 13th New Jersey, 28th Maryland, 111th and 28th Pennsylvania regiments panicking.

"My God," Horace screams, "they are deserting us. Those bastards."

WD saw it all. He heard the young Yankee urge his compatriots toward the Southern flag. He heard David initiate the Rebel Cry. But he had seen more than that. Earlier he witnessed the chaplain for Lawton's Brigade bless him and his comrades, that God be with them, and that the Yankees be smitten. Then, WD watched and listened just before all hell broke loose as the Yankee chaplain gave the New Yorkers absolution, with the accompanying prayer that God be with them, too.

WD, of course, had not counted the dead and wounded, but from the general vicinity of the Dunker Church, it would have been obvious that the sacrifice of human lives and health was immense. Over 43,000 men had met in an area within eyesight of this desecrated place of worship, and nearly 13,000 had fallen. Anyone, but perhaps especially a man like WD, a man raised in a long family and community tradition of Baptist faith, would ask, "How can the one God be with both of us? God, this is crazy. Am I crazy? Maybe, God, you are the one who is crazy."

Perhaps, God was with the Georgians and the North Carolinians at that moment for it was then that the Rebel Cry went up again all along the Hagerstown Road, all around Dunker Church and throughout the West Woods as the Yankees fell back in retreat. As WD observed the ground around him after the firing ceased four and a half hours after it had started—ground not just littered with dead and wounded, but piled high with bodies and pieces of bodies—he stood alone with his thoughts. "There either is no God, or God has abandoned us all. ALL of us, Yankee and Southerner alike. What is this all about anyway?"

WD had also heard the cry, the anguished cry, the angry cry of some Union soldier near the 60th New York's flag, "My God, they are deserting us." However, what WD really "heard" was the anguished cry of someone else echoing across time nearly 1830 years before, "My God, my God, why have you deserted me?"

To describe the end of the fighting here at Dunker Church as the end of fighting would be a gross misnomer. Sporadic weapons' fire continued for some time. Perhaps, lull is the best word to use. Then, nearly as soon as the lull broke out here, a most horrendous outbreak of destruction commenced straight over to the east from where I sit—the battle of the Sunken Road or Bloody Lane as it came to be known.

In the meantime, Horace's 3rd Brigade, along about 1:30 p.m. was ordered to retreat to the East Woods where they finally were able to rest and regroup. Sitting with his back to a tree, he took out his canteen, gulped the first water he had been able to consume in at least seven hours. The hardtack he had pulled out of his backpack tasted as good to him as Thanksgiving dinner at home. He was famished. It had been nearly 24 hours since he had consumed anything solid.

He closed his eyes trying to get some rest knowing it would not last long. But how does one sleep with thousands of weapons being fired less than a mile away? How does one rest when there is always the threat of the enemy breaking through your best defenses? How do you trust yourself to keep more than one eye shut, when you know the enemy's sharp-shooters could be behind the next tree? How does one find comfort, when your best friend's body is still behind enemy lines?

Yet, Horace managed to doze off, perhaps only for a second. When he heard the rustling of leaves, he awoke with a start. He felt like he had been asleep for hours. His body felt so heavy, his eyes crusted not so much from the depths of sleep as from the tears and sweat joining together like cement.

As he awoke, he noticed a young man with a sketchpad. Horace was immediately interested in what this civilian artist was drawing. The artist slowly moved closer and closer to his subjects, and Horace came to understand the focal point of this sketch. The artist inched his way to a maple tree off to Horace's left where two men lay in Confederate uniforms.

Horace's first thought was to put the men out of their misery. "No, God no, what if Frank lies wounded up at that church? No, God, don't let some fool like me but in Confederate garb go up to Frank and put him out of his suffering. Give him a chance, dear God."

Horace then heard the young Confederate on the left beg the artist to give him some water. The artist apparently had none to give. Then the same Rebel asked the artist to pull his friend off from him. His friend was dead. Finally, the Rebel pleaded with the artist to carry him out of the woods saying, "My regiment will be right along to take me home."

A few minutes passed, as the artist tried to comfort the fallen Rebel, when Horace heard the Southerner yell out for all to hear: "Oh, praise God, here is my train now. It's time for me to go." With that outburst the young Georgian collapsed. The artist pulled out his own handkerchief and draped it over a Georgian face. *Guess his train came in for him,* thought Horace. Less than two years later the "train" would come for Horace.

Then, the artist commenced another sketch focusing on another young Georgian kneeling at the head of an older Confederate. The younger Georgian speaks to the artist saying, "please pray for him; he's my pappy." The artist says something that Horace cannot hear. The artist then kneels down in a prayerful posture. The younger Confederate is now weeping as the artist pulls off the bandana around his own neck and shrouds the second Georgian face in almost as many minutes.

Meanwhile, David is standing guard on the north side of Dunker church when he notices a civilian approaching him from across the pike. He is tall and lanky, long hair, mustache, and carrying a notebook. David snaps to attention and raises his rifle.

"Halt, what is your business?"

"I am Charles Coffin, Army Correspondent, Sir. I am..."

"I reckon you are well-named, Mr. Coffin, for what you see before you here," David breaks in with the kind of so-called gallows humor, in this case battlefield-humor, killing field humor that helps one to cope with the horror that permeates the very air one breathes. It is the kind of humor a person draws on when the only alternative is to cry out with utter despair.

"Yes, well, you're not the first Yankee or Rebel who has observed the absurdity of my name in a place such as this. As I was saying, I am unarmed as you can see. I am not a spy for the North, just trying to let folks back home know what war is all about. Most of them don't think much about their own being killed, like..."

Coffin, hesitates and chokes back the tears spurred by all that he sees around him, mostly a sea of blue. "My God, look at them. Were you involved in this battle?" he asks with a sound of incomprehension.

"Yep, sure was. Those Yankees came at us in waves. They were brave men, Sir. You from New York? That's where many of these are from, or Ohio, the best I can figure out."

"No, neither. I'm from Philadelphia. Would you mind if I look around? If I'm going to give the folks anything like a real picture of things here, I need to immerse myself in even the goriest of gore. I'm personally sick of what I read in the papers, so-called reporters giving nothing but glory to the goriness of war."

"No, go right ahead, but stay in my line of vision. If you don't, there could be trouble, if you know what I mean?"

"No, I don't. What DO you mean?"

"Well, Sir, let me put it this way: if you start t' move out of my line of sight, I will have to shoot you and ask questions later. How's that? Is that clear?"

"Sure is, soldier."

Correspondent Coffin heads toward the fence where the blue clothed bodies are piled deep. Soon David notices the correspondent leaning forward. David heads toward him.

As David is within a few feet of the reporter, he notices that Coffin is taking a book out of a corpse's coat pocket. David raises his rifle. *What the hell? Is this guy robbing the dead? What kind of reporter is he? I should shoot the sonofabitch.*

Coffin then sits down by the dead soldier and begins to read from the book. It's the Bible. Coffin reads the 23rd Psalm, and looks up acknowledging David's presence. "Just noticed this Bible sticking out from his coat. It sort of rested right there on his chest."

David instantly recognizes the New Yorker as the one who led the charge on the 51st Georgia Color Bearer. Coffin reaches out to David for help in getting back up. As they walk away a weak voice says, "thanks." David and Coffin spin around to find the young Yankee's eyes fluttering.

"My God, he's still alive," bellows the unbelieving reporter. "You aren't going to kill him are you?"

"No, I'm not, though it may have been my bullet that got him. Of all the Yankees here, he is one I recognize. He led a charge on our Flag Bearer. He was like a madman and he had at least a dozen madmen with him. They seemed to have gone nuts, insane, trying to charge through and over that fence to get one flag. Nuts!"

"Please," the bloodied Yankee whispers, "60th New York. Horace...My friend...Tell him.... goodbye. Peter. Lover. Tell...Peter...I...love...him." With that, he breathed his last breath.

"Did you hear that Soldier?"

"Yeah. You know a few hours ago he intended to kill me—and all of my friends here. I may have been the one responsible for his death. I hated him then. He hated me. And now, I just wish I could find his friend Horace. Is that crazy, or what?"

Coffin, looks directly into David's face and asks, "How about his lover, Peter?"

David looks down at the body, blood still oozing from the ground beneath him, "Yeah, wish I could find his lover alive. This man was a brave soldier; I don't give a damn what else he may have been."

Coffin grins, nods his head and murmurs, "I agree."

"Wonder who he is?" David inquires.

"Well, the Bible has just his first name, 'Frank,'" responds Coffin, "and I don't see any other forms of identification on him."

"Listen, Mr. Correspondent, if you ever find out his family's name; and if you ever have the occasion to speak to his family, either directly or in print would you do one thing for me, for him, yeah for his lover Peter too?"

"What's that soldier?"

"Tell them this Rebel regrets having been responsible for killing a good man, a real hero."

Coffin reaches out to take David's hand saying, "Soldier, it's a deal."

Unknown to either Charles Coffin or David Wooten, WD is standing on the front steps of the church observing all that was going on, and deeply moved by the scene unfolding before his eyes. Here was a brave, tenacious Confederate praying (lamenting?) the death of an enemy.

"Dear God, this whole thing is making less and less sense. It is a horrible dream. Wake me up, Lord. How can I get home? How I want to be home, now. Lord, open the door. Let me out of this. Take me home to Martha, Little Gene, Mom and Dad. Stop this insanity. Lord. IF you even exist, DO SOMETHING."

WD is startled by his own voice, realizing he has yelled out, "DO SOMETHING." Instantly, he notices David and the civilian with the notebook pivoting around, looking his way.

"What do you want us to do?" shouts David.

WD is now about as embarrassed as he has ever been in his life, but no more embarrassed than he will be many times in the future. "Oh, don't mind me. I was just talking to a God that I'm not even sure exists, a God I'm pretty sure doesn't give a shit, frankly."

David and Coffin simply nod their assent to this assessment of things. Coffin returns to his horse, tips Frank's Bible first toward Frank's body, then to David, finally to WD, and heads toward the Sunken Road. Suddenly, he wheels his big Roan around and angles directly toward the church where WD and David are both standing on the steps—where I am now sitting.

"Hey, get a load of this: From the flyleaf of this here Bible: 'I hope and pray that you may be permitted by a kind Providence, after the war is over, to return to me. Love, Peter.'"

"Wonder who Peter is?" WD asks casually expecting no real answer.

"His Lover," responds David who walks off to the south side of the church.

* * *

I stand here today before this plaque at the Dunker Church, and I shake my head at the pathos of the words and the tragedy of what happened here. Let me share those words with you:

I am the Church of the bloodiest battlefield in all American history. I had my conception in the minds of a group of pious, zealous folks, who were among the first settlers to make their homes on the banks of the Antietam.

They called themselves Brethren because brotherhood was the main objective of their devotion. Their associates in the neighborhood called them Dunkers or Dunkards, a corruption of the German word tunker which means plunger or the word tunken, to dip. Immersion was their form of baptism.

Early before daylight, on the 17th of September 1862, the bloodiest single day battle of all American history began, I was the objective of the Federal forces.

I was pierced with cannon balls and bullets—my rafters studded with metal. I was used first as a bulwark for both armies. Then I became a hospital.

I heard shrieks, moans, groans, and cries that stayed with me all my life. My furniture was all splattered with blood.

I still exist as the little white church of the Antietam Battlefield. I live in the hearts of all who ever knew me. I am still a symbol of peace and brotherhood.

Antietam was the battle that emancipated the slaves. I am a symbol of spiritual emancipation. I represent unity, the Brotherhood of Man under the Fatherhood of a loving, kind God.

Chapter 11:
The Gathering at Antietam: The Afternoon

Now in Caesarea was a centurion named Cornelius
of the Roman cohort Italica, who was religious and
God-fearing...One afternoon at about three he had
a vision in which he clearly saw a messenger of
God coming to him and calling 'Cornelius'!
(Acts 10: 1, 3)

As Coffin rode off to the east toward the fighting at the Sunken Road, WD slowly realized a whole new battle was underway. Coffin was heading for the Sunken Road. If he thought the loss of human life was impressive in the vicinity of Dunker Church, the Cornfield, and the East & West Woods, he would be appalled at what he was about to discover at the Sunken Road, a place forevermore to be known as Bloody Lane. While there were 12,600 casualties in the former battle, there were by comparison far fewer in Bloody Lane. However, the early morning battle left bodies distributed throughout a larger geographic space. At Bloody Lane, Coffin would find 5500 bodies in what would appear to be a mass grave.

* * *

As I walk this lane today I imagine, in more modern times, the conquering army bringing in bulldozers to level off this ditch leaving the 5500 bodies beneath the soil. I picture the scenes of Nazi death camps, uncovering ditches such as this with the skeletons of 5500 people. I picture similar scenes in Iraq and Serbia with 5500 corpses of Kurds and Moslems in Iraqi and Serbian ditches such as this one here only yards away from the sleepy town of Sharpsburg, Maryland, USA.

The circumstances are, of course, quite different between Antietam and Hitler's, Hussein's or Milosevic's efforts at ethnic cleansing. At least each side here at Bloody Lane had a fighting chance in that at least each side was armed. Here at the Sunken Road, as well as at Dunker Church, it was not so much a matter of legitimized murder in the name of War, as it was a matter of suicide—enemy-assisted suicide. Thousands of men on each side squaring off and aiming at the hearts of thousands of men only a few yards away, firing muskets, rifles, pistols, cannon and howitzers.

One hundred and twenty years later, the engagement at Bloody Lane could, with some justification, be classified as an early example of Mutually Assured Destruction. In the 1980s and 1990s Mutually Assured Destruction was perceived to be a deterrent to war. In 1862 the tactics of war nearly guaranteed mutual destruction, but it hardly avoided war.

$$* * *$$

WD had heard the fighting at Bloody Lane and the frequent reports as scouts rode back and forth from the front reporting to General Jackson. What he heard now was different. Somewhere between 10 and 10:30 the unmistakable sounds of engagement seemed to be coming from a point further to the southeast. David heard it as well. For WD it was interesting. For David it was alarming. He knew a battle was brewing in the general vicinity where his brother Roach was waiting with the 51st Georgia.

"Lawd, spare Roach from this battle. He and the 51st have had enough," David prayed aloud.

Unknown to him, WD had just walked around the corner of the church and heard David's prayer. "Excuse me, Private, but I couldn't halp hearin' yaw plea to the Lawd. I join ya in that prayer, young man. I also agree that the 51st has had enough, but then haven't we all?"

"That's for sure soldier. By the way, I'm David Wooten from Morgan, down in Calhoun County."

"Yes, guess it's time that we officially met. I'm William Sheppard, William Drayton Sheppard. You can call me WD. I hail from Sandersville up in Washington County. You know David, I look at all of the death around us here and all the death the roar off to the east and now off there to the southeast represent, I'm sure; and, well, I'm not sure any of us really know what the hell this is all about. I think about my family back in Sandersville, the plantation, my Pappa who may even be dead by now, my wife and the boy. I think about our enemy out there, and I'm sure they think about their homes in NY and Pennsylvania, their families, their wives and sweethearts, Mammas and Pappas. Do any of us really know why we are trying to kill each other? Couldn't thar have been a betta way to settle our differences?"

"Well, WD, I got into this thing not to protect my family's plantation. I got into it because I didn't want any Yankee telling me what to do. I didn't want the North telling us Southerners what to do or where to go. But I'll tell ya'll something: most of the time these days I'm no longer sure why I'm here. Now we have Jeff Davis telling us what to do and where to go. It gets real confusin'. I mean I got a brother down there with the 51st. His friend just lost two brothers up on South Mountain the other day. I have no damned desire to lose my kin here or anywhere."

"I understand," WD says rubbing his chin. "You know it would somehow be easier if these Yankees spoke a different language; or better yet if they were from some foreign country, or some planet other than ours. But they're not; they'all just like us."

All this while David has been looking back and forth, first to face WD then toward the location where he imagines his brother to be. WD is not even sure David has been listening to him.

"Ya'll ever think about walking away from it?" David whispers.

"No," WD lied. But there it was, someone else had spoken the unspeakable. Walk away from it. Walk away. *Run away is more like it,* he thought to himself. "Desert, " he heard himself saying; but WD was not the only one to hear it.

"Yep, desert, sure as hell is the name fer it. Can't say I haven't thought about it. You know, Soldier, I have been in 17 battles. Well, today makes 18. Eighteen battles since I enlisted in April of last year. Eighteen battles since the first one nearly 12 months ago. According to General Garnett last night..."

David stops in mid-sentence, smiles, and then continues, "I mean, no general ever confides in me. I just heard him talking to a scout that the 13th Georgia has witnessed, according to his best calculations, at least 40,000 deaths since we were mustered into service. There is some comfort, I reckon, in knowin' that less than half was our men. Garnett mentioned 16–17,000. Frankly, I don't take much comfort from those statistics. The fact is the next bullet could be mine to keep."

"So, are you saying you may take the walk?"

"No, I didn't say nothin' of the kind. I just don't think I have the guts to do that. I don't want to be shot or hung as a traitor, branded, whipped, or otherwise disgraced for life. And let's not forget those bounty hunters who I hear are even more brutal than them Yankees.

"Besides, it's one helluva long walk to Morgan from here. Bet it's at least 700 miles if you could go as the crow flies. And speaking of crows, I haven't seen any crows or birds of any feather in days. Them winged ones are a mite smarter than you'n me. They just stay the hell away from here.

"But ya'll know I've pretty much walked the distance gettin' here, and that was a real roundabout. First to Sewall's Mountain over in Virginny, back to Georgia, then back to Virginny and Richmond, to Malvern Hill, to Richmond again, to Bristoe Station, then Manassas followed by South Mountain a few days ago and now here we are. Despite it all, WD, I just don't ever see myself abandoning the cause. Yet, I'm losing sight of what the cause was supposed to be. You?"

WD is staring off toward the sounds of battle to the south. His eyes take him not to the battle raging for control of the Lower Bridge, but far further south to Sandersville, Georgia. "Well, David, I'm just a young'n when it comes to this war. I just enlisted four months ago. This is my first battle, and there for a few minutes thought it was going to be my last. Who knows, 'fore the day is over it may well be my last."

"And if it isn't?"

"What?"

"If there is a tomorrow, and you're part of it, what then? If you had the chance to just disappear, would you?"

"Don't know. I just don't know. Probably not, but, well, maybe. I feel traitorous for even saying 'I just don't know' and 'maybe'."

"Naw, ya'll just bein' human, that's all. Besides after today we'll probably never see each other again with you up in Sandersville and me way down in Morgan. All I can say is I think under the circumstances it takes about as much courage to cut and run as it does to stay and fight these ever-incessant battles."

At that moment both David and WD are jolted out of the depths of their revealing conversation by the deafening sound of infantry and artillery to the south. "I'm sure my brother is in the middle of all that," David mumbles. "Sure wish he would get away from it and go home."

Suddenly, bugles blared. Officers scurried to rally their ranks. Ewell's Division was heading south.

David L. Wooten and William Drayton Sheppard would never see each other again—as in really see, as in acknowledging each other as fellow Confederate soldiers.

* * *

As David had guessed his brother Roach and Roach's friend, James Manry were indeed in the thick of the battle to hold possession of the Lower Antietam Creek Bridge. Around 10 a.m. the 51st Georgia had been flung into battle holding a position overlooking the bridge. Drayton's Brigade was charged with bolstering Toomb's Brigade down in the vicinity of the western entrance to the bridge with Drayton's Brigade fortifying the ridge above.

In an odd, but fateful alignment of numbers, similar to the sometimes unusual alignment of the stars and planets, Union General McClellan ordered the 51st NY and the 51st Pennsylvania to flank to the left and right respectively up the hill from the bridge. Consequently the 51st NY and 51st Pennsylvania were to engage the Toombs and Drayton Brigades of the 51st Georgia.

At first the fighting was but a minor skirmish since the Union forces under the direct command of General Ambrose Burnside were necessarily cautious. They were in an unfavorable position having to cross the bridge, or ford their way through a creek of uncertain depth. In addition, assuming they could take command of the bridge, they were still saddled with the unenviable task of fighting their way up the hill. The Confederates were in the controlling position of being able to fire down upon the invading army, a position akin to shooting clay pigeons. It was going to require massive firepower to counteract the Confederate Army's commanding hold.

After a few hours of skirmishing with the Union inching their way closer and closer into possession of the bridge, Union General Crook ordered the deployment of a weapon that would soon make the difference. The Union had previously captured a battery of Confederate howitzers. These powerful guns were brought into place and fired with double charges directly at Toomb's and Drayton's Brigades with devastating effect.

"What the hell? Where did those howitzers come from?" screams Roach as a shell lands behind him. Shaking the dust from his face, James screams back a reply. "I think they got them from us, Roach. Keep your head down."

As James says this he notices with great relief, yet some trepidation as well, the filing in of a massive number of troops to his right. At first he does not recognize who they are until he spies the 13th Georgia flag. Roach apparently sees the flag as well. "James, look over yonder. There's my brother's brigade and General Garnett's entire Division! They are here now to back us up."

James turns his head to see what Roach is talking about only to witness the explosion of multiple howitzer shells directly in front of the 13th Georgia flag. "No," Roach shouts. "No, go back. David, David," he cries.

James rushes over to Roach and wraps his arms around the distraught soldier, thinking, praying, "God, spare these two brothers. My parents have lost two sons, spare the Wootens that same fate."

Roach then catches sight of David way off to the right, not far from a house on the outer edge of Sharpsburg. James notices how Roach relaxes, and relaxes himself, only to have the calm shattered by a merciless fuselage of howitzers. The air is as thick with shells, as the woods are full of gnats south of the gnat line in the worst of gnat seasons. The dust from the bombardment has created a smokescreen between the 51st and 13th Georgia Regiments. The 13th Georgia's flag is no longer visible.

Now the shells are no longer landing between the two regiments; all living hell is breaking loose directly in front of Drayton's Brigade. Calhoun County men are falling left and right around both James and Roach. The order is given to fall back into the orchard to their rear, but the shelling keeps pace with their retreat. It is bad enough to have to suffer barrage after barrage of howitzer shelling, but now even the orchard has turned on the Confederacy. As the howitzers zero in on the orchard, the apple trees fire their fruits upon the heads of the men from Georgia.

Not long thereafter another order is issued to retreat into Sharpsburg. As soon as they reach the near vicinity of the town, the bombardment ceases. It is now a little after 4 p.m. It has been a long day that will soon get longer, especially for the Union.

David takes advantage of the lull in fighting to look around for his new acquaintance, the fellow from Sandersville. WD is nowhere in sight, but that is not unusual. In the confusion of the repeated retreats, anyone could be almost anywhere. "The most important issue is where is my brother?" David said to his soul.

It is then that he sees the 51st Georgia color bearer. He scans the front line and recognizes Roach's slouch. Next to him is Roach's best friend these days,

James Manry. "Praise God," proclaims David as if he were a Baptist minister inspiring his flock to holiness.

Rushing over to speak to his brother, David comes upon him as Roach is worrying to James, "I just wish I could find David. I want to know that he is okay, that's all. I pray he is safe."

"Well, I'll let you in on a secret," James smiles knowingly. "I was praying just a bit ago that both you and your brother will get through this insanity without injury. Your parents and family do not need to go through what my parents will be going through. Do you realize my momma and pappa most likely still do not know that they have lost two sons? There's no way the news could have gotten to them as of yet."

"Well, I'll let you both in on a secret," David says as he walks up behind them and puts an arm around each of their shoulders. "Your prayers really work; either that or I'm dead and don't know it."

The first few minutes of the brotherly reunion are spent recounting the events of the day, but David suddenly switches the topic of conversation. "I met this older fellow with the 32nd Georgia, WD is his name, William, believe it or not, William Drayton Sheppard. Don't know if he is any relation to your General Thomas Drayton. Frankly, I'm a bit concerned about WD."

Turning now to David, James asks, "Did you say this WD fella is from Calhoun County?"

"No, he's from Sandersville in Washington County, not far from the state capitol in Milledgeville. He's a fine man. Considerably older than we are. I think he said he's in his early thirties. Has a wife and small son; plus his father is in very poor health, maybe even dead by now. Just 'tween you and me I wouldn't be surprised if he decides to leave all this behind him tonight. Would I blame him? Hell, no. Would I do it myself? Hell, no. I'm too chicken. I'm in this for the long haul, but WD's war I believe is much closer to Sandersville than to Sharpsburg."

As David is talking, Roach's attention is drawn to the cornfield off to the south of them. "Wow, look at that will ya? That's A.P. Hills's Division in that cornfield, but they're all decked out in Union uniforms. Now that's clever as hell. Watch them. They're movin' out closer and closer, small steps at a time, movin' in on Burnside's flanks. They're goin' t'burn Burnside; you just watch. This should be fun."

At that very moment, as if General A.P. Hill had intuitively discerned that the ruse was about to be discovered, he ordered his division to attack with a fury. The 51st and 13th Georgia bugles were sounded and those who had rested were suddenly back in the fray of battle.

The surprise move by A.P. Hill arriving from Harper's Ferry in the guise of a Union division, plus the inspirited Confederate forces in the vicinity resulted in a near rout of Burnside's army. Pushed back now to the bridge, Burnside steeled himself against an anticipated even heavier onslaught—an onslaught that never came. General Lee knew he did not have the power to retake the bridge. From that afternoon onward through history, the Lower Antietam Bridge would be known as Burnside's Bridge.

Soon the fighting ceased. Night fell. McClellan prepared for Lee's expected counter attack to begin early the next morning. WD, David, James and Roach already knew there would be no Confederate assault. They were all on the gradual move by cover of dark withdrawing to the south.

✳ ✳ ✳

WD, David, James, Roach, and Horace smelled the same smells, smells that knew no boundaries between the Blue and the Gray. These were the sickening smells of death, the putrid, nauseating smell of already rotting corpses, the acrid smell of gunpowder, the somewhat sweeter aroma of rotting apples, and the near intoxicating smell of cornstalks and corncobs ground into a mealy mash fermenting in the fields and mixed with human blood—truly a devil's brew.

WD, David, James, Roach, and Horace heard the same sounds, sounds that neither Confederate nor Union flags could flutter away. These were the sounds of the "unbroken moans of dying men" coming from all directions and from one end of the battlefield to the other. The sound of a dying man was the same whether it came from the Lower Bridge, the Middle Bridge or the Upper Bridge. The anguish had the same tone and timbre whether it came from the West Woods, the East Woods, the Mumma or the Smith Farms. The cries of pain and lost dreams were as horrifying to hear in the dark of night whether they came from the depths of the Sunken Road or the heights overlooking Burnside's Bridge. The nightmare was the same for the North as it was for the South.

WD, David, James, Roach, and Horace saw it all and they saw it all the same. They saw the bodies, in some places three or four or five deep. As they each moved out that afternoon and evening, none of the five could have walked anywhere without trampling upon bodies of the fallen. They saw the devastation of the land, the Mumma farm buildings, the town buildings, indeed the desecration of the Dunker Church. They shared the vision of innocent horses, having been driven into battle, dead and dying throughout this once fertile and life-giving farmland.

WD, David, James, Roach, and Horace felt the same kinds of feelings. They felt the despair of seeing so many of their friends dead, dying and fiendishly wounded; many maimed for life. They felt the hopelessness coming from the dashed hope earlier in the day that this would be the battle to end the war; knowing now that the war would go on. They felt the numbing exhaustion that comes from endless nights without sleep, endless days of marching and fighting, never-ending worry about loved ones back home, and ever-lurking doubts about what it all means. They felt the fear that tonight or tomorrow would be the time when the enemy would prevail. They felt the feeling of unfeeling, the sensation of already being dead.

WD, David, James, Roach, and Horace smelled, heard, saw, and felt it all. However, no one senses it all like WD.

* * *

Stepping as carefully as he can to avoid walking upon a corpse and realizing there is no way to avoid the sickening feeling of walking on once-living-breathing beings, WD hears himself reciting the 23rd Psalm. "The Lord is my shepherd; I shall not want. He maketh me to lie down in green pastures…" He cuts off the prayer in mid-sentence, spins around, lifts his arms toward the heavens exclaiming, "Bullshit, Lawd. This is no green pasture; it is red with blood. I used to believe, but today I think you are as much of a myth as any Greek mythological god. On the other hand maybe you do exist and if so then I want nothin' to do with you. You are a Bullshit God." Lifting the haversack from his left shoulder, WD wipes the tears from his eyes.

The bodies on the ground have all the appearances of being bags of potatoes in a field after a bountiful harvest. However, these are what are left of human beings with hands and feet, faces, hearts, hopes and dreams. Despite WD's anger at God, he recites from Psalm 115:

> *They have mouths, but they speak not;*
> *eyes have they, but they see not;*

They have ears, but they hear not;
noses have they, but they smell not;
They have hands, but they handle not;
feet have they, but they walk not;
neither speak they through their throat...

And the haversack nearly on its own account rises to wipe the tears once again.

Later that evening WD awakens from a light sleep. He is not even certain that he was asleep. Indeed he is most certain that he is living a nightmare that seems designated to haunt him into perpetuity; yes, even beyond his own grave. Rolling out of his blanket, he decides to take a short walk. "Well, it will be a short walk," he informs his inner self. "I am not going to walk on any more bodies tonight." Then, he is struck by the growing stench of death and decay.

He had recently thumbed through a Bible loaned to him by a Catholic friend. He was fascinated by the books of scripture found there, but not included in his own Protestant version. He was especially intrigued with the Book of Tobit. It was the only portion of that Catholic book of scripture that he had the time to read before giving it back to its owner. With the stench around him tonight WD is reminded of a verse from Tobit:

As soon as the demon smells the odor...
he will flee and never again show himself...

"Oh, if only this war, this battle would produce that odor, the odor that would keep the demon of war eternally away from us."

However, being a man of the Bible WD considers the context of the Tobit remark. It was Tobiah's sister Raphael giving him advice concerning his desire to marry Sarah, as well as telling him what he should do prior to having sexual intercourse with her. It is this thought that sends WD into a spasm of grief over being away from his beloved Martha.

It does not help one whit that this same verse brings to mind WD's favorite sister-in-law, Martha's sister Sarah, as well as his own 8-year-old sister by the same name.

But what would Martha think of him if he deserted? What would his father and mother say? What would Sandersville think? How would friends and acquaintances receive him? What would Sarah the elder think of him? For that matter how would he even make the trek home? It would mean walking the entire way, hiding out, disguising himself, hopping rides and hoping no one discovers who he is, or what he is—a deserter, a traitor. It would mean, if discovered or caught, certain disgrace and most likely physical punishment including the possibility of death.

WD had witnessed what happens to a deserter. The poor fellow had apparently attempted to run away from the fight above the Lower Bridge. First, he was marched in full view of his former friends in the 28th North Carolina. They had shaved one side of his head, stripped him bare and dressed him in a barrel, the "wooden overcoat." He had heard the story of another deserter being shot by his best friends in the 1st Georgia. They were so distressed they could not perform the task efficiently. He was shot repeatedly before he died, and did so in excruciating physical and emotional pain.

WD was not quite sure how his mother, Phanelty, or his father, John, would receive him if he did desert. John, a deacon at New Bethel Baptist Church, held strong views about the legitimacy of slavery. "All under the yoke of slavery must regard their masters as worthy of full respect," John would often quote from the first verse of 1 Timothy 6."Let as many servants as are under the yoke count their own masters worthy of all honor...that the name of God and his doctrine be not blasphemed."

However, WD had often been troubled by the ninth verse, Chapter 34 of the Book of Jeremiah where it is said that, "Everyone was to free his Hebrew slaves, male and female, so that no one should hold a man of Judah, his brother, in slavery." After all, every one of the slaves on the Sheppard plantation is Baptist, baptized by WD's father, brothers and sisters in Christ, as it were.

By the same token Martha's family's one and only slave is also a Baptist. That brings up another issue. How are Martha's parents and siblings going to react if he decides to walk off from this war? "Sarah has strong opinions about everything. She will probably disown me. It's probably a good thing I didn't marry her, even though she is much closer to my age, older by three years, in fact."

Then there were Martha's two older brothers, Charles and Johnnie. Charlie enlisted before WD did, and Johnnie has probably run off and lied his way into enlistment by now. Hudson at 12 years old idolizes his brothers and WD as well. "But that will end when he hears that I have deserted," WD exclaims silently to himself. "But I haven't deserted—yet."

And there are his own brothers, Patrick at 22, Augusta at 16 and 6-year-old Charles. Patrick was so eager to go off to war, Augusta will be next, and Charles so proud to have his big brothers fighting the Yankees.

Despite his father's decided opinions about the natural order of slavery; his last words were disturbing. Not in a frantic way, but in a manner that forced WD to think about it every day since. Those words spoken from his father's bed echo in WD's ears every moment, silenced not at all by the tumult of battle. In fact it seems to WD that his father's words became even louder, the louder the fighting became.

"Son, remember this. As Ecclesiastes says in Chapter 3:

There is an appointed time for everything...
A time to be born and a time to die...

"I know Son that I am as ill as I have ever been in my entire 51 years of life. I hate to send you off to war like this, but I know that I may never see you again. I pray every day that I can get through this illness. Lord willing, I will. But I don't want to kid you, Son. I really think this is my last battle. And I send you off to battle with unceasing prayers that you will be safe."

John was finding it more and more difficult to breathe. He stopped, wiped his brow, took a deep breath, and continued. "William, you know as well as I do that Ecclesiastes also says in that same place that there is,

A time to seek, and a time to lose;
A time to keep, and a time to cast away.

"I think, Son that the historical time is here when we have to lose and cast away. Our way of life here in the South is going to be cast away even if we win this war. It is over, William. It is over."

WD said goodbye to his father with an ache he had never experienced before. He turned to leave the room only to hear his father saying one last word of fatherly advice. "Son, and remember this too. I think it is in Chapter 9 of Ecclesiastes where it is said that, 'Wisdom is better than force.' You just remember that, Son. Wisdom is better than force."

Returning to his bedroll, Allen Smith, a longtime friend, neighbor and fellow member of New Bethel, whispers to WD, "The word is that we move out before sunrise. We are heading for Shepherdstown."

WD had never heard of Shepherdstown before. He wonders if this is some kind of sign or omen. Shepherdstown is spelled differently than his family name, Sheppard, but they both derive from the same root, those who raise and care for sheep. Yes, this must be a sign from the Lord God himself. Is it a sign that Shepherdstown will be the last battle, the battle that will end this war, one way or the other? Or is it that Shepherdstown will be the place of sanctuary, where perhaps no battle at all will be fought? Could it be that somehow Shepherdstown would be the magic place where he can be mysteriously and swiftly transported to that other "Sheppardstown"—Sandersville and the Sheppard Plantation?

Yesterday, the 16th, he had received the first letter from home since his enlistment. Martha had written,

> *Dearest William,*
>
> *I wish I had better news to report, but you need to know that John is not at all good. After you left, it seems that he has given up. I fear he will be not long with us. He does not seem to be in pain, just pain of the heart. He seems convinced that our whole way of life is ending. He believes the South is about to lose the war.*
>
> *Dearest, your father may be right. Indeed, I fear he may be more right than even he imagines. Our slaves have left. So now it is up to me and Phanny to keep the place going. There will be no cotton crop next year. So it is just as well that the slaves have left. We could not provide for them anyway.*
>
> *Gene seems to be very sickly lately. For the past week he has been coughing, wheezing and so without energy, but with most energetic fevers.*
>
> *The only goods news I can think of is that I miss you, William. I pray every moment of every day that God will shield you from all harm and return you to me soon.*
>
> *I know how slow the mail is going to be. I write this to you on the 30th of August. It will probably be a month or more getting to you. So, despite our upside down world I wish for you a happy birthday on our birthday date of September 30th. That we were both born on the same day of the month I treasure greatly. But what I treasure most is your presence at my side.*
>
> *Your Loving and Lonely Wife,*
> *Martha*

The thought of the Plantation going to rot was difficult to conceive. Everything was in fine shape when he left only a few months ago, but now… Well, he had to face into it. The Plantation may not even exist by the time he returns home. The very thought of Martha and his mother having to keep everything together stabs WD to the heart. The possibility that his father has already died provides a deeper stab. But it is the desperation, the loneliness and longing, the love expressed by Martha for him that sends him to his knees.

Out here in the dark of night WD feels as if he is in a cave and he "hears" the words of Elijah, the prophet who sought refuge in a real cave. This is the Elijah who had put so many to the sword, feared now for his own life and despaired over all of the lives he had taken. In the dark night of his soul, Elijah wailed, "It is enough, O LORD." In the dark of WD's night, he "sees" the image of Elijah walking off from his war for forty days and forty nights.

✳ ✳ ✳

I sit here now on the ridge overlooking Burnside's Bridge wondering what kind of men they were who thought they could take possession of this beautiful structure against all odds. I also wonder at the insanity behind such a thought. Today the bridge presents itself as one of the most serene objects in the world. In fact this whole place is a picture of peacefulness. I can almost hear Beethoven's Pastoral Symphony.

Those very waters duplicate this white stone bridge with its three portals allowing the waters to pass through. The creek sits ever so still allowing a near perfect reflection of the bridge. Indeed, from where I sit it appears that there is an exact inverted replica of Burnside's prize acting as its foundation.

I wonder too, if Sadie has any insights to share on the events of that day September 17, 1862.

Chapter 12:
The God of Surprises

Do not be surprised, beloved,
that a trial by fire is occurring
in your midst.
It is a test for you,
but it should not catch you off guard.
(1 Peter 4:12)

September 14, 1906

I have heard God referred to as "The God of Surprises." If that is the nature of God, guess I should stop being surprised. Today, however, was just plain loaded with surprises. But why SHOULD I be surprised about anything on this date? For as long as I can remember, September 14 has always been a date to remember. Wish I had been keeping a running account of all the September 14s in my life.

First thing this morning Gene and I packed up Birdie June, Ida Gene, Emmie Sadie and Bonnie Lucille and off we went to the cemetery.

I'm not sure Gene really understands the deep significance of this date to my family. Not that he hasn't heard it numerous times. He appears to not really care. Nothing seems to move him. It's as if the Civil War never happened as far as he is concerned. Well, guess it didn't happen as far as his family was concerned. Seems like everyone I have ever known had some family member in the war. Most folks I know lost at least one. But the Sheppards seem to have miraculously escaped all that. I say "seem to", because one of the biggest surprises today was a revelation that explains so much about the secretiveness of Gene's family.

But first, Journal, let me say that another "surprise" today was coming face-to-face with the reality of how my family is growing up, up and away from us. It just suddenly hit me this morning, as I was getting the children ready to go. Our family has already changed dramatically and will only continue to do so at even greater speed. C.A. is 20 and pretty much on his own. Annie Bell is 18 and seems to be real serious about John Price. Bessie is 15 and so infatuated with that Will Wooten; it's getting worrisome. Willie Eunice is 13, going on 30. Roy is only 11, but he thinks he knows it all. He tells me, "If anything should happen to Father" not to worry because he would take care of the plantation and me. (Where do tell does that come from?)

Birdie June is 9, Ida Gene is 7, Emmie Sadie is 4, Bonnie Lucille is 2 and here I am pregnant and about to give birth to another. I am getting tired, but I also worry. My God, I have had 9 children, number 10 is almost here, and it has all happened in only 21 years of marriage. No wonder I'm tired.

What really troubles me, though, is Roy's innocent comment, "if anything should happen to Father." Why would an 11-year-old even think such a thing? It was, after all, nothing more than an innocent child's innocent comment. So why does it bother me? Bother me? It doesn't bother me; it scares me. Am I being superstitious or just plain stupid? Maybe it's the pregnancy.

In any event we arrived at the cemetery to find Uncle James there with Auntie. We talked for awhile and I picked up the sense that Uncle James needed to talk. It was such a beautiful day, a perfect fall day so warm and smelling that sweet aroma of fall when you can almost smell the pecans roasting on the trees. Uncle and I agreed that we would just walk back home. Gene agreed, even volunteered, to take the children home. Just when I think I have that man figured out, he goes and does something like that! Auntie agreed to meet us at our place. I think Uncle and Auntie had that all worked out before they even arrived at the cemetery.

As Uncle James and I walked the cemetery together, it was light conversation at first. Soon, however, we began going deeper and deeper. Guess I started it by saying, "How have you done it Uncle Jim? I mean how have you and Auntie handled 14 children? My nine, by comparison, seems grossly insignificant. I am exhausted most days, yet you two have always seemed so energized and alive."

He didn't offer any real insight. He just said something like he was sure I am feeling exhausted because of the pregnancy. But I pushed on. "Uncle James, you and Auntie seem to raise your family together. Most of the time I feel absolutely alone. Gene is a good man, don't get me wrong; but, God, he might just as well be a circuit rider when it comes to parenting. Taking the children home just now has to be a monumental effort for him. In fact I'm puzzled by how ready he was to do that."

UJ's response to the Gene-as-parent issue was clothed in another surprisingly relevant issue. "Sadie," he said, "I have also noticed that Gene is really quite uncomfortable with the War as a topic of conversation, maybe more uncomfortable with that than with being a parent. As a parent he IS much older than you. Here you are at age 36 and he is 47. When you reach 47 you will appreciate Gene's lack of energy."

All of a sudden I felt defensive, "Well, Uncle, let me tell you this. Gene is no different now than when he was 27 at the arrival of our first, C.A., or at 29 with Annie Belle, or 32 when Bessie came on the scene. The children have, from the beginning, been MY children!"

UJ claimed he understood. There was a long moment of silence between us. Then I broke it by asking him to say more about Gene's discomfort with the War as a topic of discussion, noting that I too had observed the same thing and that it seemed to be especially true for Gene's Mom and Dad.

Uncle appeared to be having second thoughts about saying any more. He probably regretted having said what little he had already offered. Finally (miraculously I kept my mouth shut waiting and waiting for him to get it out there), he said, "Sadie, this is strictly between you and me. What I'm about to tell you could be dynamite in this town."

Then, as only Uncle James can do, he got that wonderful twinkle in his eye and said, "So if Edison blows up some night, I will be forever grateful that we chose to move to Randolph." We laughed together, and that was fun; but I really had no idea what I was laughing about.

"You see, Sadie, your father-in-law deserted the cause."

I felt as if a bolt of lightning had hit me. I was numb. "How do you know that?" I blurted out.

He went on to explain an encounter between himself, his best friend prior to, during and after the war, Roach Wooten, and Roach's brother David while they were at Sharpsburg. UJ says David Wooten and WD fought together at Sharpsburg near the old Dunker Church and that they got to know each other fairly well, briefly. UJ recalls that David suggested WD was ready to desert, or at least David was not going to be surprised if he did. Then, it was many months later that UJ learned WD had in fact deserted that very night, or at least he had come up missing as of the next morning, September 18, 1862.

I told UJ that WD had never so much as hinted he was in the war. In fact there was normally the unspoken understanding that he was, perhaps, too old or that he had been exempted. There was certainly no way to engage WD or Martha in a discussion about the war.

But I was still puzzled. How does UJ really know with certainty that WD deserted? Could he not have been injured, captured, or simply become so exhausted that he fell behind his regiment—a straggler I think they called such men. They weren't deserters. They weren't casualties, as such. It just took them much longer to keep up. After all most of those men had no shoes and minimal clothing. Illness was rampant. Exhaustion seemed to be rationed out much more plentifully than food. A Straggler is all that WD would have been. He probably caught the "disease" from his son who is always a straggler when it comes to the duties of parenthood!

UJ just looked at me. Finally, he said, "Sadie, it is a fact. WD did desert. As you may know, I was captured at Gettysburg on July 2nd of '64. David was captured in September of that year. We never saw each other from the afternoon of September 17, 1862 until we met up with each other at the same Prisoner of War Camp at Point Lookout, Maryland. Once we reconnected he and I became at least as good friends as his brother Roach and I had been."

While he was saying this about David Wooten, I must admit I may have missed some things he might have said. All I could think about was Bessie and Will—and Gene.

It bothers Gene, much more than me, that Bessie seems so dead set upon dating Will. I mean he is seven years older than Bessie, but who are we to say that is too much of a gap?

Gene wants Bessie to go to finishing school. I have agreed to his bargain, but I just don't know. I agree she should look at all options for her life. She is such a gifted young woman. But Gene is so dead set against her marrying Will that at times it just plain mystifies me. He claims Will's father is "just a teacher" and that Bessie can do better. I am regretting my being party to Gene's strategy and offer to Bessie—Finishing School with all expenses paid and the opportunity to live in either Atlanta or Augusta versus no support for her wedding to Will.

Yes, I want Bessie to do something with her life. Yes, I know it is a different world our children will be living in. Yes, I know the Old South is dying (or is it dead already?). Yes, I know all this. What I do not understand is why Gene is so adamant about Bessie and Will when he seems less concerned about

*Annie and John, and I do not see any difference in family roots between Will
and John.*

*I just lied. I think I am coming to understand Gene's bull headed stand on
Bessie and Will's relationship. Is Gene covering for his father? Has he been
doing that ever since I went to that dance with him all those many years ago?
Was he lying to me way back then when he claimed he did not understand his
parents' behavior whenever the topic of the War came up? Has he been
anything but an innocent in the family secret?*

*If Bessie marries David Wooten's son, is that getting too close to the
truth? I think Gene has been a co-conspirator for years. I bet he was let in on
the Sheppard Skeleton-in-the-Closet from about the time he began dating
girls whose families had someone in the Confederate Army.*

*It just makes me so angry. I am good enough to have his children; good
enough to maintain his home; good enough to virtually run the plantation.
But am I good enough to be told the truth? No! No! No!*

*I have never felt so betrayed!!!!! It is as if the father's desertion has begot
another. And Martha, so sweet and loving toward me. "You are just like a
daughter to me," she has said if once then a million times. Maybe all I have
ever been is just another one of their slaves!*

*I cannot write anymore tonight. I just feel beat, beaten down, defeated,
and downcast.*

September 15, 1906
*It is 2 a.m. Couldn't sleep. So many thoughts going through my head—
Gene and his parents not being honest with me; Gene & Bessie, Bessie &
Will, Annie Belle & John, Finishing School for Bessie, our full intent to
"buy" her away from Will, and why?*

*Gene's dislike of the Wootens has nothing to do with social status. It has
everything to do with fear. Gene knows what UJ knows, and UJ knows what
David Wooten knows. They all know what WD knows and WD knows he
deserted the cause.*

*I cannot sleep until I get this all down and stop this endless cover up, this
endless lie, by sharing it with you Dear Journal.*

*Uncle J went on to say this morning at the cemetery, "one night as we
were sitting around roasting a rat..." I thought I misunderstood him, but he
quickly added, "you see, Sadie, at Point Lookout many were they who
considered themselves lucky if they could catch a rat. It meant at least one
meal a day. Anyway, as we were roasting one of them critters this one night,*

this new prisoner came along, sat down opposite of me at the campfire. We recognized each other at about the same time. It was David Wooten. Now keep in mind I had only met him once before and that was on a battlefield, but we must have made a lasting impression on each other. He did on me, I know."

I asked Uncle how it was that David made such an impression on him. Of course, I asked this question for more than one reason. I wanted to know why Gene is so opposed to the Wootens becoming part of our family. I can't remember all that UJ said, but he sure changed my impression of the Wootens.

UJ said that David fought in more battles than any man he had ever met. David was in the war from the near beginning and made it to the near end. He said that David was about as tough as they come; yet, as gentle and sensitive as any person he had ever encountered, man or woman:

"David Wooten has seen more death, more corpses, more hardship, more miles of trekking through all kinds of conditions, weather and terrain, and witnessed more friends killed; yet, he was so understanding and forgiving even before WD deserted. You know what he said right there at Sharpsburg? He said something like, 'it takes at least as much courage to walk off as it does to stay the course.' The other thing David said was that WD had told him about his worries concerning his small son, his wife and the plantation, his parents, and the fact that he feared his father might even have died already. Said his father was in very poor health. Now that is one helluva man who can fight like a mad dog for a cause and forgive someone who needs to walk away from it."

I again asked Uncle J how he really knew WD had deserted. He replied that he did not know it to be a fact until the "Night of the Rat." When David showed up, they got to talking. UJ had been curious to know if the soldier David had talked about that afternoon at Sharpsburg had actually walked off as David had suspected he would do. David told him he had never seen WD ever again.

*Then, right after the battle at Deep Bottom, Virginia, and before the fateful battle of Winchester in September 1864 when DW was captured, there had been nearly a month long break from the fighting for the 13th Georgia. Somewhere in there David's talent for book keeping was recognized by his commander and he was assigned the task of organizing division records. It was then that David saw the notation for **September 30, 1862: William Drayton Sheppard—deserted.***

Uncle went on to explain that because stragglers were such a common problem, if a soldier did not report at roll call on a given morning, allowances were made. Often times a man would not show up for days. Not because he had run off, but because he simply could not keep up. So, it was common to allow as much as two weeks before declaring a missing soldier as a deserter. David figured WD had been allowed about 12 days.

My dilemma is what do I do with all this? Do I confront Gene? Do I confront WD and Martha? Or, do I keep my mouth shut? Do I continue the conspiracy of silence and deception? I surely am not going to divulge this knowledge to the whole town of Edison or the County of Calhoun! Nor am I going to sit all the children down and tell them their grandfather was a traitor to the Southern cause! Beyond that I just don't know what to do, or not to do.

Well, all of that was "one" of the surprises from God yesterday. Actually, seems more like a curse than a blessing.

The other surprise came from Annie Belle. She just informed me last night that she and John are planning on getting married in March. I mean she told me this in the same matter-of-fact way that she might have told me she was going to wear her multi-colored shawl to town rather than her beige one. Now, I don't understand this but Gene seems to be far more tolerant of John than of Will. Frankly, I would trust Will with my life when I wouldn't trust John with telling me the correct time of day. There is something about him that seems shifty. Personally, I think John is the kind of man who would steal from his own mother.

Anyway, seems it's up to me to inform Gene of Annie's intent. I think I know how this all goes. I tell Gene. He gets angry, momentarily. Then, he cools off. He calls Annie Belle into the sitting room. John is with her. Everything is wonderful. If it were Bessie and Will, it would be hell let out for noon. By the time Gene would be done with Bessie and Will, Sherman's March would look like a Sunday school picnic!

* * *

September 16, 1906
Annie Belle had come home later than usual last night having been out with John over to Gum for a dance. She appeared to have had a good time. She was bright and cheery as they came through the door. John left and she suddenly became very quiet. I asked her if something was bothering her. "Not really," she said. Then after awhile she said, "Mamma, I had the strangest

dream the other night. I keep thinking about it. It won't go away. In fact I have had that same dream before. It's just that this one was sharper and clearer than the rest."

The one part of her dream that concerns her is where she is at the Salem Cemetery—and she is standing at her own grave! Dear Journal, that would scare me too. In fact it does frighten me. What does it really mean?

✻ ✻ ✻

At this point I want to give up and go home to Gary, but at the same time I have this overwhelming desire to talk with Sadie, Annie Belle, David, WD, and Sadie's Uncle James. That is not possible of course. The only thing that does seem possible is to sit here and experience fully the chills that are running up and down my spine.

My mother in her dying days had dreams that were "more than a dream," she said. Those "dreams" or visions, or whatever the hell they were, included "David" who turns out to be David Wooten and WD, both of whom turn out to be my great grandfathers.

I'm not sure I'm on for continuing with this "odyssey," as Gary put it. Yet, I can't not do it. I have to see this to the end. Just hope it is not my end.

Sometimes we find ourselves into something that we want to toss out of the window of our lives, but just cannot let go. The full intent is to pitch it, be done with it, to hell with it; yet, like flypaper, we cannot get it off our hands. In my case it is partly conscience. I cannot in good conscience leave Annie Bell, so to speak, standing in the cemetery at her own grave without further pursuit of the truth.

What truth, pray tell? Why *must* I go on? I've accomplished my goal have I not? I've spent months chasing a dream and the dream has caught up with me. No, the dream has caught me. I am in its grip and I cannot escape. Do I want to?

Here I was ready to go to Point Lookout primarily for curiosity's sake; don't really *need* to. Yet, there seems so much undone, unknown.

In fact Sadie's journal draws me like sailors drawn by the mythical sirens of ancient Greece. I pick it up once again and am soon riveted to Sadie's notation of:

March 3, 1907

Well, she's done it. Annie Belle, my first born daughter, has married John today. Oh, it was a lovely wedding. She is so happy. Gene seems pleased. And I am feeling so bleak, as bleak as this dreary rainy day is dark. Don't know when I've been so down. Why?

I'll tell you why, Dearest Journal:

1) It is my oldest and first daughter to be married. People tell me that is the hardest for a mother.

2) I still have this very basic and deep distrust of the man she has married. All the while they were at the altar, I had this image of a devious man up to deviousness with my beloved little girl.

3) Then, there was Deacon Turner's remark a few days before the wedding, "Sadie, do you think this marriage is wise?" But what could I do? We've already had one blow-up over daughter's choice of husbands. Brother Henry Turner has known John since John was born. Henry does not think this is a wise match at all!

4) Worse yet, a picture flashed through my head of Annie Belle and John standing up there at the altar with her tombstone right there between them. I nearly cried out. "Stop! Stop!"

5) Then, I noticed all day long that while Gene was being cheery, I caught him several times looking almost frightened, pale, and seeming to gasp for breath. Of course he wouldn't talk about it!

July 15, 1908

It is done. Bessie and Will were married today. Will Wooten is our son-in-law to Gene's great dismay. I just hope it will work out for them, that Bessie will be happy. Most of all I pray that Gene can just let go of it. He barely acknowledged Will's father, David.

Personally, I find David to be a most delightful man. He is serious, courteous, and witty. What you see is what you get with this man. If Will turns out like his father, Bessie has a real man. In fact I wish Annie could have caught half the man. Instead...Oh well, I need to let go of it.

I do need to say here, Journal, that Brother Turner said to me privately just before the ceremony, "Something is not right here. It's none of my business, I suppose, but I am officiating here. What is it? I sense that Gene does not approve of Will. Sadie, I know Will and his father. They are fine men. Bessie has a good man here."

Then, the real surprise: Deacon Turner went on to say, "Sadie, there is much more to Gene's disliking Will Wooten. I probably should not say this to you, but I feel the Christian thing to do is to tell you. Clara, my dear wife, was born and raised in Washington County, near Sandersville. She knew WD and Martha's families mostly by reputation. David Wooten, as you know is a war hero. WD is said to have deserted the cause. I believe somehow that explains the Sheppard dislike for the Wootens."

I wish now that I could have gotten Henry to talk to Gene. I wish Henry could have talked some sense into Annie Belle.

Uncle James whispered to me at the reception that he wants to meet me at the cemetery tomorrow. I agreed to meet him there around 10. He will stop by on his way to Morgan. I do not have the slightest idea what this is all about. I do hope all is well with him.

I also hope with the excitement of today and lack of rest that I will be able to get there on time. This pregnancy is perhaps the worst one yet. I just never thought this would happen to me. Eleven children in 23 years! If Annie Belle had gotten pregnant right after they were married, she could have a child older than this one which is to come! This is it. No more! I am going to name this one, boy or girl, The End!!

Dear Lord, I am so worried about Gene. He won't listen to me. He refuses to go to the doctor. I know he is not well. He knows it too, but he won't admit it to me. If he goes and dies on me.... Loving God, I can't believe I just wrote that! Gene may not help much with the children, and sometimes I get so angry with him; but I love him. Furthermore, if I'm honest with myself and you Lord, and you Journal, my greatest fear is being left to raise these 8 children all by myself.

July 16, 1908

Well, Gene may have ignored David Wooten at Bessie's wedding, but Uncle James sure didn't! That's what he wanted to talk to me about. UJ is getting old. His body is getting weaker, but his mind is as sharp as a sharpshooter's aim. He had three issues he needed to talk to me about.

1)As it turns out Uncle also has had deep reservations about Annie Belle's marriage to John. He said he didn't want to interfere and decided to say nothing before the wedding. Now he regrets having been a "silent witness," as he puts it, especially since he has talked at length with Brother Turner.

Uncle says there is no better judge of character than Brother Henry Turner. He not only thinks John is devious, but he fears for Annie's health. Uncle J said what I have refused to admit to myself. Annie is not well. She is just like her father in denying the obvious. UJ wonders what has happened to the young woman who had always been full of fun, alive and vital, full of energy and wit. He sees her now after only 16 months of marriage as an old woman becoming ill of body and feeble of spirit. UJ has spoken what I have been refusing to see; or at least acknowledge. But what can I do?

2) He is equally concerned about Gene's health, and

3) While the reception was going on UJ and David took a walk down Hartford, up Turner and back through the woods to our place. David told Uncle of an incident at Point Lookout that he had never shared before.

If I've got it right, it goes like this. David had gotten to know a friendly young Northern Guard at PLO by the name of Johnny, Johnny Barnes from New York State. David had great respect for the way the 60th NY fought at Dunker Church in the Battle of Sharpsburg, and said so. This Johnny appreciated David's remarks. His brother had been there. His brother's regiment was that very same regiment, the 60th NY. As time wore on Johnny expressed more and more curiosity about what had really happened to his brother's regiment from David's viewpoint.

David had very little to share about the 60th of NY, beyond being aware that the 60th NY after Sharpsburg was present at Chancellorsville in May of '63 and at Gettysburg in July of the same year. David had no recollection of having faced the 60th in direct combat after Sharpsburg. But he did mention to Johnny the charge launched at Dunker Church by a New Yorker named Frank and how Frank's dying words were something to the effect of "Please tell Peter I love him," and "Tell Horace goodbye."

This Northern Guard nearly fell to his knees. "Oh, my God! Horace is my brother and Frank was Horace's friend since being toddlers. Peter was Frank's best friend in a most unusual way, if you know what I mean?"

"His lover, is that what you mean?" inquired David.

David went on to emphasize to Johnny that Frank may have been "a bit funny, if you know what I mean"; but he was "one helluva brave man."

Uncle James says David told this Johnny that if the Union had had more men like Frank they would have won the war sooner.

Johnny informed David that his brother Horace had died at Kennesaw Mountain up near Atlanta in June of '64. In late August, as soon as Johnny turned 18, he enlisted with the 184th NY. His sister Elizabeth claimed a red-

hot cannon ball encircled their home one night. She knew right then that Horace was dead.

A few days later a chaplain and an officer came to their home in Edwards, NY, somewhere near the St. Lawrence River, with the unwelcome news. The chaplain handed Johnny's mother a letter written months before by Horace. It was addressed to his mom and dad, and was dated June 15, 1864. Horace died June 16th near Golgotha Church.

One other thing, Journal: When I told Uncle what Annie had said about her seeing herself standing at her own tombstone... Well, Uncle James sagged. It was as if he suddenly aged right before my eyes. He appeared to be at least 100 years old. He said he needed to get right home. I tried to talk him into coming to our place for a bite to eat. He declined and headed for Randolph. As he drove off I shouted, "but I thought you were going to Morgan?" He didn't hear me, or didn't want to.

May 15, 1909

The good news is Bessie's baby is a healthy beautiful little girl. The not so good news is that Will is having trouble finding full-time work. I have to talk Gene into hiring Will. I think an ideal position for him would be to manage our farm over in Williamsburg. He could do a job that needs to be done. They would not have to pay rent to anyone. We could just make the house over there part of the deal. Little Louise would have plenty of room to play and grow in. But it won't be easy to sell Gene on the idea.

Come to think of it there is one other piece of good news. At least my youngest is older than my first grandchild. Seven months is not much, but it counts! Thank God for small favors.

May 16, 1909

Well, that idea didn't go anywhere. Gene got so angry that I "would even suggest such a thing." The more we talked the madder he became. Then I got stubborn. There for awhile my goal was to prod Gene into getting angrier and angrier. I was so angry and it felt so good to be that angry.

Then, I became so frightened. Gene was so mad he could not breathe. He collapsed right into the sofa. I yelled for Roy to go fetch the doctor. Gene refused. "I'll be okay," he said. "Just got too excited."

He worries me. Something is wrong. I think this whole thing with Will and Bessie is eating him up. I would like to talk with Gene about the whole thing with Will, David Wooten, and WD's desertion, but I'm afraid to. If Gene gets as emotional again as he was today... Well, I really do not want to be a widow.

November 26, 1909 (Thanksgiving)
   It was good to have everyone here for Thanksgiving, but it sure is a houseful—18 of us. There were a few downers however. John just came in time to eat and then left Annie Belle here by herself. Gene, of course, would not speak at all to Will. Later, Gene could hardly talk. Says he thinks he has laryngitis, but he seems to be out of breath a lot, wheezing and getting so very red in the face. I am worried. At least he has agreed to see Dr. Colquitt tomorrow.

November 27, 1909
   Guess Gene knows what's wrong as well as doctors. Laryngitis according to Dr. C is the problem. Lots of bed rest and plenty of fluids. Bed rest? Right! Keeping Gene down is like trying to keep a runaway freight train in place. It will never work. I tell him we have everything covered and all he needs to do is get well. He says okay, but I know he doesn't mean it.

November 28, 1909
   Out of the blue, Gene says, "You know I've been thinking that we should ask Will & Bessie to take over management of our farm over in Williamsburg. I think we can work out a deal where we pay him some wages, plus a certain percentage of the crop income, and use of the house on the property. What do you think?"
   I was flabbergasted, excited, pleased. But I could have hit him. In fact I wanted to hit him right where it would hurt the most, and would have if it hadn't been for him being sick. I mean he presented this great idea as if it was his own original, bonafide, and patented, copyrighted idea! But I sure was not about to make a fuss over the fact that he had stolen MY idea. I wasn't about to make a real big deal about it either for fear he would reconsider and back down if I got too excited. So I simply said, "that's a good idea, Gene."
   I don't think he is getting any better. He seems to be in a lot of pain and I just do not know how that has anything to do with laryngitis. Sometimes lately he says things that just make no sense at all. Just a little bit ago as I was tucking him in for the night he said to me, "Grandpa and Grandma Sheppard were just here."
   I asked him, "Do you mean WD's or Martha's?"

Then, out he came with that wonderful grin of his and said, "Both."

I reminded him all four are dead. He simply said, "I know that, Sadie. All four of them told me it's time to straighten it out."

"Straighten what out?" I asked. Of course Gene had no idea. Or if he does, he is not telling me.

Frankly, Journal, this is getting spooky. Yes, I am afraid, terrified, because I think I know what this is all about!

November 28, 1909

My greatest fear has been realized. I am a widow with 8 children to raise by myself! Thank God, I really appreciate that. Right now, Lord, I am really angry with you; but I am so angry with Gene that I could scream. If I were alone I would scream. The first chance I get I'm going to drive over to Wayback or someplace really remote and scream my head off. No, I will scream my heart out.

I knew he couldn't handle being confined to bed. So, first thing this morning, while we were all still in bed, he goes out to the barn. I heard a strange sound downstairs and there he was on the floor halfway in and halfway out of the door. Roy and I got him into the sitting room spread out on the sofa. Willie Eunice ran for Dr. Colquitt. Gene passed out as Willie went out the door. When Dr. C got here he took one look at Gene, wrapped his arms around me and said, "He's gone Sadie. Gene's gone."

Little Bonnie Lucille was sitting in her little rocker over in the corner of the room with a full view of her daddy. She jumped right up out of her chair and ran over to Dr. C saying, "Doctor, are you blind? My daddy hasn't gone. He's right there in front of you!"

Doctor C was embarrassed. Good God, I laughed. Doc must think I am an awful wife and widow that I could stand there and laugh. I mean I laughed until I thought I might pass out and join Gene in wherever he's gone.

Dear Journal, you are the only one I can say this to, but Gene has taken the easy way out. It even seems like he did it on purpose.

Well, I hope Gene is at peace. I hope he is with Uncle Ben and Uncle Johnny. They too died on a Sunday. On the other hand maybe Gene will stay away from them for fear they would want to talk about the Civil War and ask why his daddy deserted. Gene I am so mad at you. If you came back from the dead right now, I'd kill you!!

Chapter 13:
Seeing Beyond the Point

(M)an cannot cut himself off from the one great pool of all life itself without losing all that he has gained. Periodically he must return to the depths of his archaic past in the fathomless unconscious: to be renewed by the underground waters of life welling from the nouminal source; to glimpse at the Beginning a vision of the End of his mysterious search.
(Frank Waters, *Pumpkin Seed Point: Being with the Hopi*)

It has been a pleasant trip here this morning from Fredericksburg, Virginia. As I approach the Governor Vance Memorial Bridge, the sunrise reminds me of the breathtaking sunrises and sunsets of Nebraska. I really want to stop in the middle of the bridge, over the Potomac, get out and gawk. However, that long line of cars behind me, even at this early hour, will not appreciate it. I surely do not desire precipitating any road rage, to say nothing of inciting bridge rage! Nor do I have any wish to become Maryland road kill.

The trip for David Wooten and James Manry would not have been so pleasant. Instead of driving a car over a modern bridge, they too were driven, but driven like cattle off a boat laden with prisoners like themselves. I know as I cross this magnificent bridge that I will return by nightfall to Richmond. They had no idea if they would ever see Richmond again.

It is a leisurely journey down the Chesapeake Peninsula. Very little traffic. Small towns from La Plata, Maryland string along Maryland Routes 6, 5, and 235: such as New Market, Hollywood and California. It is ironic and difficult to even imagine that only 24 miles north of La Plata lies the confused noise of the Washington Beltway. At this very hour there are thousands of cars speeding along that highway, while I see no automobile in either my rear view mirror or ahead of me, similar in that sense to driving in Western Nebraska.

Perhaps it is the psychological influence of having studied the map; but as I travel this route, I feel a strange sensation. It is like being drawn into a vortex. Or is it the sensation of being sucked into a funnel? In fact, even my breathing is becoming more labored. Yes, I'm sure the knowledge that the land is becoming constricted on both sides, as this peninsula's tip draws me to itself, has something to do with my vortex experience.

Breathing should be easier at this elevation. By the time I converge on Point Lookout I will be only about 5 feet above sea level. Yet, my breathing is as belabored right now as if I was driving to an altitude of 8000 feet. This, I know, is not just a geographical vortex that I am caught in; this is beginning to feel like the vortex of my life. I feel as if I am going to the depths of hell. Yes, I'm scared. I want to turn around and go home to Gary.

But I cannot do that. This is my war, a war I do not fully understand. I have to do this. There is no going back.

Stopping at this small diner, Captain Pat's, in Lexington Park, and enjoying my lunch, I can not help but wonder about David and James. How long did they go before having anything to eat, anything at all, between the time they were taken prisoner (at Winchester and Gettysburg) and their arrival at Point Lookout? For me, Point Lookout is but one of many destinations. For them Point Lookout would have promised only one thing— a terminal, the final point in their life's journey.

I sit here now having traveled the nearly 20 miles from Lexington Park over to St. Mary's to Ridge, Scotland and Scotland Beach. The final few miles took me through a pretty wooded area to the Confederate Memorial Monument where the names of those who died in captivity are verifiably inscribed. This obelisk that looms before me honors all of the 14,000+ men and women who died here. However, only 3,384 or approximately 24% of those who never walked out of this POW camp have been officially verified. Record keeping was not a particularly well advanced art, especially when it came to the fortunes of the Confederate prisoners held at the tented city here.

Here? Well, I am slowly building up the courage to drive the last mile to where "here" was for those who died, the scene of the North's Andersonville. When so many died at Point Lookout, how is it that both David and James survived? Will I ever know? These men are my ancestors. Is there something they can teach me about survival? After all, they were different too. Like me in a sense, they were outcasts, different than those who held them captive.

They were enemies of their captors and probably seen as enemy by many households on this peninsula at the time.

This is Point Lookout State Park where I am now, but it was hardly a Fun Park for the 52,000+ Confederate Soldiers held here at one time or another from July 1863 to June 1865. James was one of the first Sons of the South to live here right after the Battle at Gettysburg. David arrived from the Battle at Winchester nearly 14 months later. David was here for about seven months, James for twenty-one months.

As I sit here now in my car in the parking area, I see a very desolate tip of an otherwise luscious peninsular landscape. There is only one small tree, an apparent newcomer to this rocky beach. It stands like a solitary guard watching over a two-story square building which now houses a Naval Weather Station, two smaller rectangular structures between itself and a tall five-story radar unit mounted on a metal frame with ladders winding their way to the sphere at the top. This is what I see.

David and James would have seen something very different. The two-story building in 1863–65 was a lighthouse. The top roof, as well as the westside entrance's porch roof, was attractively trimmed with decorative wooden scallops. These scallops were only a ludicrous symbol of the plentiful food lying just off-shore surrounding this prison, but unavailable to those who lived here as Prisoners of War.

It is doubtful that many POWs would have gotten this far down the point. David and James, as enlisted men were quartered further up the peninsula on the Chesapeake side. The "Pen" was a rectangular fort-like enclosure with 12-foot-high walls and sentry platforms on the outside. Inside the "Pen" were rows upon rows of Sibley Tents and seven rectangular cookhouses on the west end. David and James happened to reside on Pennsylvania Avenue, the main "street" in the "Pen".

This house was the Headquarters building where Brigadier-General James Barnes, no relation to Horace, held sway over operations. General Barnes and his nephew, Captain Barnes, Assistant Provost Marshall, were generally considered kind and considerate human beings by most of the prisoners here. However, a prisoner would have had little opportunity to view the Headquarters Building. General Barnes seemed to have made it a point to remain secluded within his Headquarters Building; therefore generally unaware of what was happening in the "Pen".

Lucky were they who could catch a crab, cook it over an open fire and share it with others as a meager supplement to the food that often failed to

177

come out of the Prisoners' Cookhouse (a building that looked much like the present-day rectangular buildings).

Adjacent to the "Pen" to the south was a smaller rectangular holding pen for Confederate officers. To the south of the officers' POW camp were a number of barracks housing the "Contraband," i.e., quarters for the Negro guards, plus horse stables. Just to the south of these facilities stood a copse of woods. On the southeast corner of the woods stood an imposing house with features very similar to the present day U.S. Naval Station building.

The meager and boringly repetitive portions of food doled out daily was but one-third of that which could sustain life. This was not a function of wartime scarcity, but a conscious policy of both General Barnes's superior and inferior. War Secretary Stanton refused to order basic amenities for POWs. Provost Marshall Major Brady, effectively the officer in charge of Point Lookout as far as the POWs and day-to-day operations were concerned, made sure that life was miserable for the internees.

Fortunate were they who could run down, stone, or otherwise capture a rat for an evening meal. Fortunate not because of the scarcity of such rodents, but because the prisoners' means for such capture were severely limited. Nearly unheard of were those who had their own blanket to shield them from the bitter cold of winter. More common were those who shared a blanket with four to six others. Not unusual were those who shared a tattered blanket with as many as sixteen other men.

As I sit out here on the very tip of the peninsula my eyes travel to the east across the Bay where I can spot land, an island, known as Smith Island or Martin Wildlife Refuge, approximately 15 miles away. To the west I can see the mainland. Hull Neck, Virginia is only 7 miles distant.

It may have been tempting for David, James, and many more to figure out a way to swim the distance. But even if they could survive the "Dead Zone," that stretch of land between their Union Army reject-tented City and the posted guards, without being shot by the ever watchful sharpshooters, the swim (if they could swim) would be extremely risky. How far could a malnourished body go? How far could even the most healthy make it before being picked up by the ever present patrol craft?

Even if one were to survive the Dead Zone and the ordeal of the swim across to the mainland, the Union Shore Patrols would diminish the odds of escape to approximately one in a million. The longer swim to Smith Island perhaps would decrease the odds of being picked up by patrols, the larger body of water making observation and discovery more difficult. However, the odds of surviving the more exhausting trip would be cut by more than the half represented by twice the distance to the mainland.

What would a successful escape to Smith Island mean? Well, it would present the need to eventually make another risky five-mile swim to James Island (now James Island State Park) and then a shorter swim to the DelMar Peninsula. All of it subject to Union patrols by land and by sea.

The options for escape were so limited only 50 were recorded in the history of this POW Camp; that is less than one one-hundredths of one percent of the total number of prisoners held here. Perhaps David and James considered it, but decided the odds were more in their favor to wait out the war in this hellhole. Perhaps witnessing the punishment of one failed escapee was enough deterrence. Being hung by the thumbs from a pole was neither a pleasant scene, nor a healthy experience for the one being hung.

One advantage Point Lookout offered to them was this: A pair of shoes. As a Union prisoner each Confederate soldier was requisitioned a pair of shoes—a benefit the Confederacy rarely conferred upon their own army beyond original muster.

But I still wonder. How did David & James survive? Perhaps some clue lies within the Point Lookout Museum.

✻ ✻ ✻

The museum staff is just as helpful here as the staff were at the Museum of the Confederacy in Richmond. Cherrye made it clear that their records are very sketchy, and that nine out of ten times the researcher never finds anything he or she hopes to find. However, Cherrye is aware of a small file on the prisoners from the 13th Georgia.

The file she brings to me is an accordion-type folder. One tab says "Notes." As I carefully page through the "Notes," which includes pieces of diaries, letters in various states of repair and legibility, I come across a small diary-type book with a leather cover. In the upper right hand corner I can barely make out the initials: DLW. My heart stops.

The suspense is killing me. Yet, I hesitate to even turn the cover. I am at once savoring the suspense and damned fearful that there will be nothing relevant within; worse, is the thought that literally nothing will appear. Just blank pages. Or, maybe even worse than that, pages and pages of writings made completely illegible due to the weathering of age hastened on by the harsh living and weather conditions in Tent City.

Finally, with my heart in my mouth, I draw the cover open and to my total amazement the frontispiece proclaims in a very bold hand:

The Prison Diary
of
David L. Wooten
(13th Georgia)

September 30, 1864
> *Arrived Point Lookout 26 Sept.*
> *Have never seen anything like this.*
> *Hope to never see anything like it again.*
> *Food horrible.*

> *Very cold, specially at night. Can feel change in weather already. I pray we can get outta here before winter sets in. This war is over not only for me but for the Confederacy. We are done. Just a matter of time. But how much time?*

> *Can I survive this? Got off the steamer, came ashore and saw hundreds of caskets waiting for us to die. Is that what this place is? Are we brought here to die? Is that official Union policy? Well, if so then this soldier will be the last to go. I will do the North no favor by dying!!*

> *Met one chap in particular who I think we can become friends. He has been here awhile. Malachi Bowden is his name—2nd Georgia.*

October 1, 1864
> *What a cold and rainy day this is! Nothing but mud. I'd give anything to be in warm wonderful S.W. Georgia! Even the gnats would be welcome!*

> *Such a surprise to find James Manry here. Seems like decades ago since we met in battle at Sharpsburg. J. is looking good for all that he has been through in the last two years. He has been here for well over a year and has a pretty good sense of the place. He tells me he figures about 40–60 die here each day. Well, if that is true, then the odds are not real good for walking out of here.*

> *I'll go with the high estimate of 60 deaths/dy. That's 1800 deaths/month. Heard our guard, Pvt. Barnes, say they have been bringing in 1500 new prisoners/month. J. said he figures there are about 10,000 of us here. Best I can calculate more than a third of us are going to die here, just assuming everyone is equal. But many of the men here are less equal than others. Many*

have wounds both of the body and spirit. Some are refusing to eat or are simply unable to eat what little nourishment comes their way. For them the rate of death is going to be more like 99%. I figure I need to eat everything and anything they bring to me; plus, if I can supplement their atrocious fare with even a rat my chances of going home whole will be greater. I think all of the men here have families to return to, as do I; some have a girlfriend or wife. I have Elizabeth to live for. I figure my chances of survival are somewhere in the neighborhood of 99%.

I can calculate and figure, rationalize and analyze, compute and formulate all I want. The fact is if I come out of here alive, it will not be because I figured it all out in my head. It will be a matter of the heart—my love for Elizabeth and her love for me. If more than a month passes after I return home before Elizabeth Colley and I get hitched, I will be a very disappointed man!!!!!!

November 7, 1864

James says there was only about 140 prisoners here when he arrived in August of '63, but he came with nearly 1700. Private Barnes says there's nearly 9000 here now, especially with the 1600 who arrived recently.

Got acquainted with C.W. Hutt of Westmoreland, Virginny today. He is a very interesting man. He loves to read and he gets lots of books sent to him by family. I haven't even got so much as a letter from anybody. Anyway, he tells me about the book he has just read, The Respected Wife. *CW offered me the book. I hesitated to take it. Do I really want to read something that will make me more depressed than I am already? Something that will make me long for Elizabeth more than I would without reading about a wonderful woman?*

November 25, 1864

Pvt. Barnes says the War is as good as over. Says Sherman took Atlanta about two weeks before Winchester. Probably just as well we didn't know that then or maybe Sheridan would have had an easier time routing us. Barnes says Sherman is marching toward Savannah. Don't think there will be much stopping him now. Barnes says Governor Brown of Georgia sent his State Militia home just a few days after Atlanta. If that is true (and I have no reason to doubt Barnes), then this war IS over.

Very interesting fellow came in today; Sidney Lanier is his name. Lanier is a playing his flute every chance he gets. Someone said he's a poet. Don't know about his poetry, but his fluting is a real joy.

November 26, 1864

CW and I went to the Confederate Minstrel Show this evening. He seems very blue. In fact, he tells me he feels so lonely even in the midst of 15, 000 men. He longs to be home. We have been going to the Prisoner of War Camp School. As CW says, "It gives me hope." I am hoping to become a teacher when I get out of here. Get out of here I will!!

November 30, 1864

Georgia has fallen!

That's it. Far as I am concerned the war is over. Done.

Some new "recruits" came in yesterday all of them captured in the midst of Sherman's so-called March to the Sea. Savannah is gone, and with it Georgia and the whole dream of the Southern Confederacy. Dream? Feels more like a nightmare.

Joe from Macon says he was taken at Sandersville on Thanksgiving Day. Not much thanks in that! Says it was a bunch of women who talked Sherman out of sacking the whole town.

SANDERSVILLE? That was the place that fellow, William Sheppard, was from. Wonder where he is now? Wonder if the patrols got him? Did he make it back to Sandersville? Did he get run off his plantation by the Federals? Or by his own neighbors? I'll never forget him. Some would say he was a coward. I say he was one fine man. Maybe I should have cut and run right along with him that night at Sharpsburg.

December 3, 1864

CW and I went to the Camp's Variety Show. It was fun and amusing. In fact, it was downright hilarious. But I just feel so very blue. The Show reminded me of the minstrel Liz and I went to in Gum. God, that seems so long ago! Another lifetime even!

December 15, 1864

Gave The Respected Wife *back to CW. It was not so bad, but it did cause me to dream more and more about Elizabeth and our future together. I mean I sure hope we still have a future together!! CW gave me* Red Jack *to read.*

December 19, 1864

CW gave me Night and Morning *to read. I haven't finished* Red Jack *yet. CW must read night and morning, 24 hours a day!! Maybe he's figured out a way to read while he's sleeping. I can't keep up with him. Maybe he doesn't even read. Maybe he just passes books around.*

December 21, 1864
Damn that CW! I finished Red Jack *this morning and he gives me* The Outcast *this afternoon. Now I have 2 books to read.*

December 25, 1864
Christmas. Well, it's not a joyful one, but at least it has been a beautiful warm day. Haven't had a joyful Christmas in a long time, at least three years. But this sure was different. Union Guards and their Confederate prisoners singing Christmas carols to each other. There has been a significant change in atmosphere here. Even the Nigger Guards are friendlier toward us.

Pvt. Barnes sat down with James and me and we talked battles. When he found out we were at Sharpsburg, he asked if that was anywhere near Antietam. Told him it was one and the same, he became very quiet. Then he asked if we had seen anything of the 60th NY.

Told him we sure had. That the 60th NY and the 13th Georgia had squared off at Dunker Church. Said his brother Horace was there. Liked to knock me over. Told him about the charge led by Horace's friend and how the friend mentioned Horace in his very last words. What a small world!! Makes the war feel really dumb and stupid. I have forgotten why I thought it was a good idea. Must admit to feeling low-spirited today. All I can think of is Elizabeth.

My Christmas present to myself is my new "mattress." Picked me a bed of "sea feathers" today while the weather was nice. Never thought sleeping on stones could be such a luxury.

December 26, 1864
Pvt. Barnes came by again on his regular patrol. He wanted to talk about his brother. In fact for the first time a Union Guard has told us his first name. John Barnes is his name. Says his brother Horace was killed in June of this year in Georgia, someplace near Atlanta in the Battle for Kennesaw Mountain. Says his brother left a wife and two children. J. asked him what will happen to the widow. Pvt. Barnes says, "I'm going to marry her when I get home." Well, that's brotherly love, I guess.

December 31, 1864
Took most of my meager savings and splurged by going to "The Eating

House." Had myself a real feast of coffee, biscuits, potato pie and hash. Some chaps go there every time it's open. Poor folk like me can't afford it as daily fare.

January 1, 1865

Pvt. Barnes came to me while I was eating the gruel this noon. Saw me sitting alone. I need to be alone every once in a while. He asked if I knew that his brother's friend was "Funny." Said I figured that out from his dying words, but that don't matter none to me.

What matters to me is that the man was one brave soul. I admire that in a man whether he is white or black, Confederate or Union, "Funny" or whatever. Man or woman for that matter. "Funny" Frank fought with as much bravery against us, as any man I ever fought beside. Molly Perkins just had a baby here a few weeks ago. I never fought beside her, but I hear she was as brave as any man and braver than a lot of them.

But why did Pvt. Barnes raise that question? Thought he knew I knew.

Finished Night and Morning. *Gave it back to CW. He is slowing down. He did not give me another book. 'Tis a near miracle!*

January 2, 1865

Pvt. Barnes asked me the strangest question this morning. He comes up to me and with no greeting or any kind of comment says, "Do you think my brother was Funny?"

I may have angered him. Without thinking much about it at all, I said: "How should I know? I never met your brother. Never laid eyes on him for all I know? All I know is he had a friend, apparently a very good friend. All I know about your brother's friend is this: 1) His name was Frank. 2) Frank was a brave man and a good soldier. 3) Frank apparently was Funny and had another very close friend other than your brother. 4) Frank's other very close friend apparently was Funny too. 5) Your brother has a younger brother who cares a great deal about him and is grieving his death. And 6) your brother left a widow and two young sons who will be well taken care of as soon as you get back to New York."

Never thought I would see a Union Prison Camp Guard cry, but I did today.

A FINE LINE OF DISTINCTION:
IN SEARCH OF ROOTS

January 3, 1865

Pvt. Barnes left me a note at mail call today. All it said was "Thanks, Pvt. John Barnes."

I have been here four months and that is the first "mail" I have yet to receive. Sure hope Elizabeth has not given up on me. I'd give anything to see her, to hold her, to hear her voice, to be in receipt of a letter from her.

February 24, 1865

The word circulating around here is that the Union burned Columbia, South Carolina, to the ground a few days ago. How much longer can General Lee hold out? Not much longer, I'm sure of that. We fought the "good fight" as the Good Book says. It just wasn't good enough.

February 23, 1865

I would much rather be home, but I must say there have been two redeeming graces of being here: 1) the books CW has kept putting into my hands, and 2) the PWC School. Alonzo Morgen, the superintendent, and HJ Carter who have been teaching my English Grammar and Math classes are excellent teachers. I think I can do that too.

February 25, 1865

For the 10th time since I have been here they have asked me to sign the Pledge of Loyalty in exchange for my freedom. Now even Pvt. Barnes has broached it with me. I have been holding out because I do not want to betray the cause. I am holding out until the cause seems to be whipped. Well, we're getting real close. Besides, I really do not hanker to stay here much longer. Since I have been here five men from the 13th Georgia have gone out in one of them wooden caskets (Tucker, Pettigrew, Grier, Cain, and Colzer). I have no intention of riding outta here the same way as they did.

March 1, 1865

Pvt. Barnes came to say goodbye. Says he's heading out for a new guard assignment over to City Point, Virginia. He's a good kid. He has had hardly any battle experience, but that's just as well if his brother's wife and nephews are going to be taken care of. When he turned to go, he said to me: "Wooten, just sign the damned paper!"

185

March 5, 1865

    Well, Lincoln has been inaugurated for another term as President of the Union. That is like one more nail in the coffin for the Confederacy. Major Brady, the Pompous Fool, was a gloatin' this afternoon when he announced Lincoln's inaugural. He said the Confederacy is as good as dead, that the Confederacy is like a man who is dying. Might have one good breath left, but it will be the last one. As much as I hate the man, I must admit I agree with him. It is over.

March 7, 1865

    Well, to use Pvt. Barnes's words, I signed the damned paper.
    James says he's not signing until General Lee says it's over.

March 14, 1865

    I leave tomorrow. Paroled. We will board a steamer destined, I'm told, for City Point, Virginia. I will miss James and Malachi and CW. Malachi will be leaving the 17th. I just don't know about James. I tried one last time to get him to "swallow the oath." He is as dead set against it now as he was 8 months ago. This time he hands me a poem that has been sneaked over to us from the Confederate Officers' Pen. Major Randolph's poem makes it clear where James stands. Think I'll copy it down:

THE GOOD OLD REBEL
Oh, I'm a good old Rebel,
Now that's just what I am;
For this "fair land of freedom"
I do not care a damn.
I'm glad I fit against it—
I only wish we'd won.
And I don't want no pardon
For anything I've done.
I hates the Constitution,
This great Republic, too;
I hates the Freedman's Bureau,
In uniforms of blue.
I hates the nasty eagle,
With all his brag and fuss;
But the lying', thievin' Yankees,

I hates 'em wuss and wuss.
I hates the Yankee nation,
And everything they do;
I hates the Declaration
Of Independence, too;
I hates the glorious Union,
'Tis dripping with our blood;
And I hates the striped banner—
I fit it all I could.
I followed old Mars' Robert
For four year, near about,
Got wounded in three places,
And starved at Pint Lookout.
I cotch the roomatism
A-campin' in the snow,
But I killed a chance of Yankees—
And I'd like to kill some mo'.
Three hundred thousand Yankees
Is stiff in Southern dust;
We got three hundred thousand
Befo' they conquered us.
They died of southern fever
And southern steel and shot;
And I wish it was three millions
Instead of what we got.
I can't take up my musket
And fight 'em now no mo',
But I ain't a-goin' to love 'em,
Now this is sartin sho';
And I don't want no pardon
For what I was and am;
And I won't be reconstructed,
And I don't care a damn.
by Major James Randolph of J.E.B. Stuart's staff

It has been a heavy day. Reading through David's journal has been an exercise in taking on someone else's pain, assuming another's burden. But it has also been a day of liberation.

Liberation? What do I mean by that? Hell, I'm not even sure. All I know is that I feel liberated somehow.

As I sit out here on this pier looking back to where the Tent City was, imagining David, James and their Union friend Pvt. Barnes walking this same turf, I am overwhelmed by the coming together. Right here at this POW camp, three men whose families were at the time very much three separate families, came together in a precursive sort of way for what would not officially occur for 20–30 years.

These were my ancestors. These men were fighting not just the war that political leaders started; they were fighting their own personal wars as well.

All three of these men were prisoners. From the outside looking in James and David were the real prisoners and John was their guard. The fact is none of the three could leave here until they were released.

David was a prisoner beyond being a Northern captive; he was imprisoned by his sense of loyalty to a cause that he knew was dead, if not buried. He even wondered why he did not leave with William Drayton Sheppard that night at Sharpsburg. He was imprisoned (albeit in a gentler more comfortable way) by his love for Elizabeth. He even wondered if she would still be there for him after being gone for three long years.

James was in a situation very similar to David's. However, James's political imprisonment was measurably greater than David's confinement. James would not consider leaving the confines of this military prison until the cause was not only dead, but buried. It was after General Lee's surrender at Appomattox Courthouse on April 9, 1865 that James agreed to sign the Loyalty Pledge.

Of the three men Pvt. John Barnes was perhaps the most imprisoned of all. At the age of 15 he had made a commitment to his brother to take care of Horace's wife and child. It seemed innocent enough, easy enough. She was a strong woman, an independent woman who didn't seem to require any taking care of at all. After all the war was going to be a short one.

Then, another baby came along and Carolyn needed more help. One day in late June of '64 word came that Horace had been killed and John is torn between staying home to fulfill his commitment to Horace, and to volunteer for the Union Army. In the end he opted for both, or hoped that would be true. He would join the war effort to avenge his brother's death and then return home to care for Carolyn and the boys. But John was trapped into two roles he otherwise would not have chosen.

John was imprisoned by Horace's death, the very grief of it. Horace was far too young to die. He and Carolyn were as much in love as anyone John had ever known. John witnessed first hand the terrible grief Carolyn experienced upon learning of Horace's death. Her sister-in-law, Mariette said she had a "dream that wasn't a dream" that informed her beyond doubt that Horace was dead. It was a fireball that circled the house, as it turned out, the very day Horace was killed. Carolyn and Maryette were inseparable from that day on.

John felt a bit jealous as he saw Maryette and Carolyn becoming closer and closer. Maryette was taking charge of caring for Carolyn and the boys. John was playing a diminishing role in this business. Finally, a little over two months after Horace's death, he made the decision to sign up as a volunteer with the 184th NY Infantry Regiment in the hope that when he returned home Carolyn would love him as she loved Horace. But would Carolyn be the one he would otherwise have picked to live his life with? John was not at all sure. He was as much a prisoner of circumstance as was James and David.

John was also feeling imprisoned by the questions arising from Horace's friendship with Frank who was "Funny." Did that mean Horace was "Funny" as well? Could Horace have been leading a double life? John remembered the many times Horace and Frank had gone somewhere with each other, even after Horace and Carolyn were married. Yet, it was nearly impossible to get a straight answer from either Frank or Horace about where they had been, or what they had done together. Carolyn never seemed to notice, but Mom and Dad did. John heard them talking to each other one night, wondering and worrying why it was that Horace was spending so much time with Frank. After all the whole town of Edwards knew Frank was "Funny."

John was trapped between an overpowering love for his brother, bitter grief over Horace's death, and an anxiety over whether his brother might have been "Funny" too.

For me, nearly 150 years later, and for once in my life, I am beginning to feel as if I can breathe once more. I am beginning to feel a sense of freedom in being who I am. Why? How?

I think it is because I have come to see in David Wooten, a war hero if I do say so myself, a man who could look at what others would see as a traitor and see a man of courage. David could look at a man whom he knew was a homosexual and see a man of great strength and courage. As far as David was concerned it was okay to be Gay. If it was okay by David Wooten way back then… Well, then, it should be okay with me.

Furthermore, I doubt that Horace Barnes was Gay. Rather, I think he was simply faithful to his close friend who just happened to be Gay. If, that was okay for Horace, then it should be okay for Dave Benson, Horace's great-great nephew. It should be okay for me to admit to the world that I am Gay, and be proud of it.

For once, being a student of history is paying off for me, right here, today, at this very moment. I am thinking of all the homosexuals in history who have left a mark (both good and bad, but a definite mark): Gays who did not just shrivel up and die, or crawl into a hole like a gopher. These Gays refused to remain in the closet or cower in the shadows of their time and cultures.

I think of Astyages, the ruler of Media; Darius III, the ruler of Persia and Alexander's dearest friend; Socrates and his apparent lover Alcibiades; Sophocles, the great Greek dramatist; as well as Alexander and his other very dearest friend, the fair and brave youth Hephaestion.

Then there are those in more recent history: Leonard Bernstein, Samuel Barber, Igor Tschaikovsky, Aaron Copland, and so many others who have contributed so much to the world by celebrating life, love, and the beauty of creation through the medium of their music. Then, there is Senator Barney Frank who has the courage to confess his Gayness in front of God and country.

So, why have I been so reluctant to really admit to my world that I am Gay? I know I have to admit my homosexuality to Sharon, but why have I been so unwilling to do so?

Part of it is fearing the loss of her friendship, but the biggest issue is that Sharon is kind of my Icon for the world. I have been afraid that if I were to lose her as a friend, I would lose the world. Yet, Gary is the world to me. It is his love that fills my senses. When I think of growing old and one day being on my deathbed, who do I most want at my side? Gary, of course!

✳ ✳ ✳

The sun is beginning to set over the Virginia horizon just beyond Hull Neck. The island to the east of this peninsula is turning an orange color. A solitary figure walks slowly down the pier. As he reaches the depression in the land just to the north of the Naval Station and near the public restroom, he begins to run. He runs down into the depression made by the excavated mass graves of Confederate dead, and as he reaches the crest begins to laugh. His laughter increases in intensity and hilarity.

He rushes by a young mother and her little boy. Her son looks up to his mother and asks, "What's wrong with that man, Mommy?"

"Oh, I think he is just terribly happy, Tommy."

"Why is he so happy, Mommy?"

"I really don't know," she responds, as mother and son stand transfixed watching as the man reaches the very tip of the beach and shouts, "Yes, God I am Gay. I am Gay!!"

Chapter 14:
Close Encounters

We are all visionaries,
and what we see is our soul in things.
(Henri Amiel [1821–1881])

March 2, 1865

*Pvt. Johnny Barnes shipped out from Point Lookout early in the morning aboard the New York, appropriately enough. The New York was a large steam-powered paddleboat with two tall smokestacks and an attractive protective housing for the paddle wheel with **NEW YORK** embossed upon its side. The ship had been pressed into service as a prisoner exchange craft from nearly the beginning of the war. Johnny was likewise pressed into service as a guard on this, for him, a one-way excursion.*

Thirteen small windows on each side of the lower deck afforded the men from the South a limited view of the journey to freedom unfolding beneath their feet, beneath the hold of their vessel to liberty. The upper deck afforded a better view with nearly 30 windows twice the size of those below. Of course this was the deck reserved for Union soldiers and dignitaries. The very best view, naturally and essentially, was that of the captain's—a small command post with large windows on all four sides at the very top and front of the New York.

Johnny had an easy assignment here. No one was about to jump ship or otherwise attempt an escape. All of these Confederates had already taken the Loyalty Pledge; they were officially paroled. All they had to do now was get off the ship when told to do so and wait in line for their processing out to freedom.

They would be given an allowance in Confederate dollars and off they *would go to return home. Their allowance, however, would not get them far, since $1.00 in Union currency was the equivalent of 60–70 Confederate dollars. The shirt that could have been purchased by James Manry three years earlier for $2 Union would now cost $120-$140 Confederate; and the value of Confederate currency was sliding downward like an avalanche.*

Johnny had much time to reflect on his future, as well as on where he had been. This was a 220 mile journey from Point Lookout (or Camp Hoffman as it was officially known by the Union) down the Chesapeake Bay hugging the Virginia shoreline and skirting Smith Point, Chesapeake Beach, Fox Wells and Windmill Point to the mouth of the Rappahannock River. Plying ever southward from the Rappahannock past Deltaville, Gwynn, New Point and Bavron, the New York steamed its way to the outer perimeter of Fort Monroe. While Johnny was standing transfixed at the sight of the famous fort he nearly lost touch with the fact that the New York was veering westward and then north into the James River.

This journey would end at a place called City Point, Virginia. Johnny had heard that City Point was hardly a city. In fact before the war it was nearly abandoned. However, now it was General Grant's Headquarters. Being the spot on the James where the waterway narrowed as one traveled north, as well as the convergence with the Appomattox River, City Point had become a most strategic location for Command Headquarters and a major transfer point for the exchange of prisoners.

Johnny wondered what it was like for the Sons of the South on this ship knowing they were about to be set free. He thought of the two Confederates he had befriended back at Point Lookout, James and David. One day they too would be on this very ship, perhaps, heading for the same destination, City Point.

He thought of himself. It had been only eight months since he enlisted. At the moment he was having a hard time remembering why he had signed up, why it sounded like such a good idea back then. Oh, he knew why. He wanted revenge on those who killed his brother. But since then he has found two Confederate friends.

When he enlisted a Confederate was the same thing as Satan. Besides, the enemy was a faceless entity. Then, he volunteered, when asked, to transfer from the 184th NY for temporary assignment with the 1st U.S. Volunteers for guard duty at Point Lookout. That's when his prejudices against the South took a serious shaking. Now the ignominious and anonymous icon for legitimate war-making had taken on real flesh and bones in the form of human relationship. Now it is that Johnny is wondering what it all means.

David and James had been in the fray for three years. They had been through far more than he had; and they were on the losing side to boot. Why then did he, Johnny Barnes, feel like he had lost the war?

There was no joy for Johnny. He felt as if his heart had been surgically removed. Numbness had taken over his entire body. Watching the Chesapeake and now the James shorelines pass by, Johnny felt as if his entire life was passing him by. He just did not care that he could see Norfolk or Newport News off the starboard side. He just wanted to go home.

"Home? Really? Am I really ready for that? Home, will no longer be the same. Horace is gone. I'm only 18 and when I go home I will have a wife and two boys to look after. I like Carolyn, but do I love her? Do I really want to get married? What I most want to do is go to wherever Horace is buried. That's what I want to do. Will that happen? Naw, I doubt it.

"First of all, no one will probably have any idea where Horace's body is located. Furthermore, who will even know where he was actually killed? The fact is when this war is officially over and they tell me I can leave, everyone back home will expect me to hightail it for Edwards. God, these men in Gray have more freedom than I do; and I'm on the winning side.

"Sometimes I feel as if I am that mysterious old man I met that night back at Point Lookout. There I was just doing my duty of patrolling the perimeter when I saw him coming towards me. He was an old sailor, I thought, or maybe just plain worn out. But what was he doing here? I hurried over in his path ordering him to halt, but he kept coming right at me. I held my rifle out straight away from me to bar him from coming any further. It was as if he did not hear me or see me. He looked so harmless that I never even thought of threatening to shoot him. Instead, I took several paces forward and aimed my rifle crossways to his chest intending to stop him or knock him over if need be. But he kept coming and walked right by me.

"By me? No, he did not walk by me. He walked right straight through me. I mean, when I shoved my rifle into his chest there was nothing there. His eyes were so hollow; I could not really see any eyes, just sockets. He not only walked through me; he looked through me as well. And his breath! My God his breath was like death itself. I turned to watch him after he passed by, I mean through, me; but he was gone, and I never saw him again. Well, that's not really true; I see him nearly every time I even doze off.

"My dreams of that old sailor are like living nightmares for I see myself in that old mysterious sailor. I am feeling as hollow inside as that ghost of a

man, or man of a ghost, looked to me as he approached me. Yes, sometimes, like right now, I feel dead inside.

"I told Captain Barnes about my encounter with that sailor and he told me I am one of the few who have seen the old man before. The theory is that he was the victim of a ship wreck about 60 years ago, got washed up on shore and keeps wanting to return to his ship. Seems like he is always found by someone like me in the same spot, and he always disappears heading for the Point, presumably destined for his ship out in the Bay."

These are the thoughts that preoccupied Johnny as the New York inched its way to City Point (Hopewell, Virginia, as it is known today). Regardless of the rumors he had heard about his destination, Johnny nevertheless expected a city considerably larger than what he had grown accustomed to at Camp Hoffman. In a way he was not to be disappointed.

March 3, 1865

As the New York made its way to the waterfront in search of a docking, Johnny was entranced at the sight of so many ships. There were at least twenty boats; about half were sail craft and the others paddlewheels similar to the New York. All were loaded, he presumed, with provisions either for the Union Army or for the citizenry. As far as he could see there was no room at all for the New York to dock, but the captain seemed intent on heading straight for the wharf. Just then, Johnny noticed a ship backing out and away from its moorings apparently making room for the New York's precious cargo of Johnny Rebs.

It was then that he could see beyond the ships at the wharf and the covered wagons lined up loading and unloading cargo. Beyond the covered wagons, Johnny noticed a number of small wooden hutches around which there appeared to be a number of women in long skirts. It occurred to him that he had not seen that many women even at a distance, in a very long time. He chocked at the thought that Carolyn would be waiting anxiously for him to return home. Or would she? Perhaps she has no interest in getting married again. Perhaps she has found someone else to care for her in his absence.

"That would be okay with me," he thought to himself. "But I did promise Horace, and I do like her. I just don't know. I thought I had it all together in my head when I left home, but..."

Johnny could not help but notice that the ship pulling away from the wharf making room for the New York was the Silver Star, nearly a replica of the New York. This paddlewheel most likely would be destined to retrace the New

York's route to bring more repatriated Rebels from Camp Hoffman at Point Lookout to this very wharf in a few days.

As his ship pulled up to the wharf, Johnny looked fore and aft. All he could see up and down the riverfront were the masts of countless schooners, some with sails furled, others lowering their sails, yet others raising their sails skyward, but most sitting listlessly anchored off and away from the docks. From the wharf he had a closer view of the city to the west of the dock. From his elevated view on the upper deck of the ship, all he could see were rooftops of hastily built wooden sheds and storage buildings, railroad cars, tents, and stockpiles of foodstuffs. Off in the distance he could make out the tell tale configuration of munitions stockpiles.

Everywhere Johnny looked up and down the wharf, and later as he walked the obnoxiously smelling dirt streets, the only laborers he saw were Negro men. He wondered, "I thought we fought this war in part at least to end slavery. They may be getting paid, but they are doing the same work they were forced to do before the War!"

To the west of the dock Johnny could see Old Glory waving in the wind. Just below the flag was a small wooden building with a single window on its north and south sides, fireplace chimney on the west end, and an outhouse on its west side. This was General Grant's Headquarters.

Johnny is told to report to the Headquarters building to receive his duty assignment. As he threads his way through the covered wagons, hundreds of soldiers like himself, horses, cattle, sheep, and excrement deposited in the so-called streets, he comes face-to-face with the women he had seen from a distance. Each one standing or sitting in front of a crib, offering to ply her trade at reasonable rates.

In less than two weeks David Wooten would be making similar observations. City Point would be the site for life changing events for both David and Johnny, if not the nation.

March 15, 1865

0700 hours: Pvt. John Barnes receives a new set of orders. He is to re-board the New York when it returns to City Point from Camp Hoffman on March 17. He is to accompany the cargo of paroled Rebs to Aiken's Landing further up the James and to remain there indefinitely to oversee the exchange of prisoners.

"It can't be any worse up there than it is here in this pigsty," Johnny thinks to himself. "However, it is much closer to Richmond. Richmond, I

hear, is really a mess; and will become a ruins when we take it. And it take we shall. At least Aikens will be a change for me."

0730 hours: David Wooten is escorted to the wharf at Point Lookout and finds himself boarding a sleek paddlewheel named the New York. Destination: City Point, Virginia.

"Finally," he muses to himself, "I am on my way back to Elizabeth. Don't know how I will get there, but I will get there as fast as I can. When these Yanks let go of me, I'm off and running for Morgan, Georgia!"

March 17, 1865

0600 hours: General Grant is informed by special courier that President Lincoln, his wife Mary, and son Todd will be arriving at City Point on March 24th via the ship, the River Queen. General Grant is to secure housing for and protection of the Presidential party.

0800 hours: The New York pulls into sight. Pvt. Johnny Barnes is at the wharf awaiting the docking of his next assignment.

0830 hours: The New York's passengers begin to disembark. Johnny stands idly leaning up against a wharf pole when he glimpses a familiar sight—one of the Rebs he had become familiar with at Camp Hoffman, David Wooten.

"Wooten! Thought we'd never see each other again. So, you signed the damned paper after all. Good for you, soldier."

"Barnes! So you are here. Going to wait out the War here?"

"No, I'm not. I'm going with you as a matter of fact."

"What?"

"Well, you see, everyone on this ship will be getting back on in about an hour, and I will be going with you. The orders are that this batch of New York prisoners will go on up to Aiken's Landing for official transfer and then on over to Boulware and Cox's Wharves for actual turnover to the Confederate Army. So, your journey is not quite over, but it is only about 20 some miles up river from here. It won't be long now."

"Well, I'm ready to get back aboard ship right now. I can hardly wait to actually head south."

"Yeah, I can understand that. I should be feeling that way myself, about heading north, I mean."

"You mean you don't? You aren't anxious about returning home to your family when this thing is officially over? Seems like that is going to happen real soon."

Johnny proceeds to tell David the circumstances of his life: How he feels trapped in his relationship with Caroline; his driving urge to visit Horace's gravesite, but the realistic sense that the urge will be an unrequited one. Not an urge, even, more of a compelling need.

"You see, David, Horace and I have always been extremely close. He saved me from more than a few life-threatening incidents. One day when I was about five years old I was standin in the front of one of our work wagons. Papa was driving the horses. Horace was in back of me. The wagon hit a bump and I began to fall forward. Horace tackled me and I flew free of the wagon wheels; Horace, however, broke his ankle. Another time, I just happened to walk into the pasture as our bull was getting ready to do his thing with one of our heifers. The bull turned on me. I thought I was a goner. I panicked and could not move. Suddenly, Horace was between me and the bull. He smacked that old bull right between the eyes with a mall. The bull stopped right in his tracks and went down on his knees. Horace grabbed me and carried me to safety.

"One night when we were alone and recalling all of our adventures together, Horace said to me, 'Johnny, I love you. I hope we never ever get separated. Maybe when we both find us each a good woman to marry we can live close by, have wives who love each other like we do, help raise each other's kids, and keep our special relationship alive until death do us part.' Need I say more?"

"Good God, no, Barnes. You and your brother had a most unusual thing going. Don't take me wrong, but you sound more imprisoned than me. At least I have a pile of decisions ahead of me; you seem to have had so many taken away from ya."

Johnny turns his face from David and looks toward the flag fluttering in the breeze.

David turns to observe what it is Johnny is looking at when he notices a great amount of activity around the flagpole.

"What's going on up there?"

"Well, I'm not real sure but... That, Johnny Reb, is General Useless Grant's headquarters. I hear tell through the rumor mill that the Good General got word this mornin' that President Lincoln is comin' to pay a royal visit a week from today. So, I guess that means a great deal of gittin' ready. Glad I'm gittin out of here."

1700 hours: The New York pulls up to the wharf at Aiken's Landing located about one mile down river from Varina, less than 10 miles south of Richmond.

A FINE LINE OF DISTINCTION:
IN SEARCH OF ROOTS

It is a relatively small landing for such a large ship. Straight up from the landing at the top of a gentle slope is a large two-story square-shaped brick home, the residence of A.M. Aiken and his family. There are five windows on the top floor facing toward the James. Skirting the eaves are the ornately carved scallops that remind Johnny of the Headquarters building back at Point Lookout's Camp Hoffman. The Aiken home sports four windows in the front at ground level with the front door spaced exactly in the center. A white-pillared front porch with six wooden columns supporting the porch roof makes this home seem inviting; yet a melancholy reminder of that which was left behind by the men in Blue as well as the men in Gray.

Between the Aiken home and Aiken's Mill (a three story brick building with five windows on each of the top two floors, four windows on the bottom with the front door in the middle, and two windows on each floor at the ends), stands a Purple Martin hotel about twelve feet high. It has three floors with six open doors on each level on all four sides, accommodating 72 Martins at a time.

David stands before the magnificent Martin house, amazed at the busyness of the birds preparing their nests, and is reminded of a passage from scripture:

> *Look at the birds in the sky. They do not sow or reap,*
> *they gather nothing into barns; yet your heavenly*
> *Father feeds them.*

He is stunned as he realizes, perhaps for the very first time since leaving home, that he has no idea what home will be like for him. He has no idea what home is like for those he left behind. Is home even there? What will he find? Does Morgan even exist anymore? What are the chances that Elizabeth is still to be found on the old Colley place? Perhaps he and all those he loves would be grateful to have a place as elegant as the Purple Martins at Aiken's Landing.

Suddenly, David hears a bugle blast and a loud-mouthed sergeant ordering all Georgians to line up with Pvt Barnes for a march from Aiken's Landing to Cox's Landing for the official turnover to the Army of the Confederacy. This shall be the last step to freedom, albeit a mighty long step. It is nearly a mile and one-half march to Cox's Wharf at the south edge of Fort Brady.

While this march is a most welcome hike, David experiences a sudden feeling of anxiety. Not only does he have grave doubts and concerns about what he will find back home, he freezes inside at the thought that he has no idea how to return to Morgan. Just as quickly as the anxieties arrive, David pushes them aside with the thought that being free he would surely figure it all out. With Elizabeth as the goal, there would be no stopping him. He would be like the birds of the sky and fly directly to Elizabeth's nest.

"Tenhut," barked Pvt. Barnes. "It is your choice gentlemen. Do you wish a normal pace for this mile-to-two mile march, or do you want to do double-time?"

A long moment of silence followed, as the paroled Confederate prisoners needed time to let the question sink into their consciousness. They had never experienced such a question. Neither Confederate nor Union authorities had ever given them a choice about anything, anywhere. Then, as if by some archetypal force, the men spoke with one voice: "Double-Time, Sir!"

For David it was at once the longest and shortest march in his military life. It seemed as if they would never get there, simply because they had no idea where there was. Furthermore, being out of shape, David and most of the men were out of breath when Pvt. Barnes called a halt at Cox's Wharf. David was out of breath, but he had not run out of all the things he was running through in his mind—things he wanted to say to Elizabeth. In fact he felt a little annoyed when Barnes ordered them to stop; there was so much more he needed to think about, to talk about with the woman of his life.

"But what if she has given up waiting for me? I can understand why she might have decided to move on with someone else. I guess I could handle that. I just need to know. If only I could be like those Martins and fly a straight line home."

It was then that David observed the small contingent of smartly dressed Confederate officers standing on a platform with an equal number of smartly dressed Union Army personnel. His heart missed a beat, and his head felt a bit woozy.

1900 hours: After a very brief Exchange of Prisoners ceremony, the Confederate officers instruct their new charges to line up for a de-briefing. As David breaks from Pvt. Barnes's formation to queue up at one of three de-briefing stations, he hears Johnny's voice: "Wooten!"

Spinning around, he sees Johnny hurrying toward him. Johnny reaches out to shake David's hand and as he does so says, "David, I have no right to ask this of you, but..."

"But what?" David inquires as he notes Johnny's dejected manner. The

young in-charge man whom David had known no longer appeared in charge of anything, himself included.

"Look, I don't know where you have to go to get home. I have no idea what I'm really asking of you, as far as the burden it may be to you."

"Ah, Private, I mean Johnny, what is it? Just tell me."

"David, there is only one thing I really want to do with my life when I'm released from this army. I want to go to my brother's grave, or the place where he was killed. I have no idea where he may be buried. All I know is that he was killed at someplace called Golgotha in one of the Kennesaw Mountain battles, near Atlanta."

"I sure can understand your need to do that. I'd do the same if my brother were killed. But what does this have to do with me?"

"All I'm asking is that if Kennesaw Mountain is anywhere near your way home. Would you give some consideration to going there fer me? Just go to Golgotha. Lay your eyes on it and sometime send me a short note describing what you saw there. Here's my address and a little somethin' to help with your expenses."

"Well, Johnny, Kennesaw isn't exactly on my way home to Morgan, and I never heard of Golgotha. However, I do know Atlanta is directly north of Morgan, so it would not be a great out-of-the-way trip to make. But why don't you go there yourself? The War will be over soon and as a Northern soldier you will have more clout getting around than I will as a defeated Confederate."

"My family is already sending me messages to hurry home. They are all anxious to see me, but they seem to really think that I need to get right back to take care of my brother's wife."

"Well, I'm sure ma family wants me to hurry back as well. But unlike you I have not heard from anyone in at least a year, even the girl I intend to marry."

"I know. I feel foolish for having asked ya to do this."

"Listen, Johnny. I realize that if you were to go from here to Atlanta before returning home, it would add at least 1000 extra and out-of-your-way miles and weeks of extra travel—even if you could travel in a straight line. I cannot promise a thing, except that I will try."

"Thanks, Soldier. I hope to hear from you sometime. I realize it may be a longtime before I do. I also realize it may never happen. I just wish we could have met under better circumstances."

"Me too, Johnny. Me too."

March 24, 1865

The de-briefing was much more of an ordeal than David expected. Mistakenly, he assumed that there would be a few questions and then he would be sent on his way back to Morgan (or Kennesaw?). However, each interview lasted for hours and there were only three officers available to meet with nearly 300 parolees.

The questions had to do with each of the battles David had fought in; knowledge, if any, of any men on a long list of missing in action including suspected deserters. The interrogation concerning Point Lookout seemed interminable. Because those interviewed were called alphabetically, David was one of the very last to be de-briefed and that occurred late in the day on March 20th.

On the 21st he was required to lineup for another wait. This one was for a medical exam. The wait was long, but the exam was short and extremely cursory. Later, he was often heard saying that the Confederate medics confirmed that he was able to breathe and was, therefore, declared healthy. Again, he had to await the exhaustion of the alphabetical list, with frequent interruptions due to medical emergencies that called the examining medics away from these serial and less than serious examinations.

On the 23rd David was finally sent on his way south. Having only the benefit of a regional map posted on a board at Cox's Wharf, David sketched out his route to freedom. It is thus that he set forth back down the James River walking its shores and arriving on the 24th back at City Point.

From the crest of a hill overlooking the James and City Point, David observed a brightly polished paddle wheeler at the very spot where the New York had docked one week before. This, however, was the River Queen. Union flags were flying everywhere, from dozens of poles on the ship, all the way along the landing and up the street to Grant's Headquarters. David knew what it all meant. President Lincoln had arrived.

Just then he saw the door open to Grant's Headquarters and out stepped a very tall man with black top hat, long black coat, black pants, and matching black beard. Behind him came another man in military clothing and with a fuller beard. David knew at an instant that this was Abe Lincoln and the commanding general of his army, General Grant. A minute or two after Lincoln and Grant stepped from Grant's quarters in full view of hundreds of Union soldiers, the President and his General clasped hands and stood solemnly as the Union Military Band struck up the "Star Spangled Banner." It was then that David noticed a woman and small boy standing in the doorway—Mrs. Lincoln and son Todd.

Later that evening David wove his way into camp. While he possessed identification that he was a parolee, he did not want to attract any attention to himself. Being an identifiable Southerner in President Lincoln's court could be problematic, and David wanted to avoid problems at all cost. On the other hand he was experiencing hunger pains.

At the edge of a long line of cribs belonging to the ladies now known by the last name of a Union General, Hookers, stood a food cart operated by an elderly woman and her 10-year-old grandson. David orders a turkey leg and coffee. Taking a bite out of the tasty turkey, David senses someone standing directly behind him. As he turns to see who it is, a deep baritone timbered voice says, "You on your way back home, Son?" It is the President with his wife and little boy, plus four armed bodyguards.

"Yes, Sir," stutters David. "Just paroled and on ma way back to Georgia, Sir."

"Anywhere near Atlanta and Kennesaw Mountain, Son?"

"Yes Sir, I mean no Sir, stammers David "I mean, Sir, that my home is many miles south of Atlanta; but I was thinking of going that way.

"Well, let me tell you something, Soldier. Back in June of last year I had a dream that this huge mountain right in the middle of the city of Atlanta collapsed. Moments later I was awakened with the news that the Army of the Republic had taken Kennesaw Mountain and that Atlanta could not possibly be defended by Lee's Army. I knew then that this damnable war was over. And, Young Man, I credit the Great State of Georgia for bringing this war to an end. Go home, Son, to your great state with my blessings."

"Thank you, Mr. President; and may God bless you, Mrs. Lincoln, and your son, Sir."

"Thank you, Son. I think I can use all the prayers I can get. I had another dream last night. Can't believe I'm telling a Confederate Soldier this, but.. I dreamt that I was in the White House rather than on the River Queen, and let me tell you Son being in the White House is a nightmare in itself. Anyway, there I was in the White House and I walked in on a group of folks mourning someone's death. I walked up to a soldier and inquired who had died. 'The President,' he said. Now, son, I'm not sure why I'm telling you this, unless it is to ask you to pray for me. Can you find it in your heart to do that?"

David is thunderstruck. The very man whom he had come to hate, the symbol of all that was evil about the North, the Union, and the Army of the Republic, had just now shared something so very personal with him. He felt as if he was having his own improbable dream. As if he was deep in a dream state, David heard himself saying: "Yes Sir, Mr. President. I will pray for you. I will, Sir."

"Thank you, Son. By the way what is your name? Where in Georgia are you from?"

"David L. Wooten, Sir. Morgan, Calhoun County. Not far from Albany, Sir."

"Yes, my old nemesis, John C. Calhoun loaned his questionable name to a good county. Carved it right out of Early and Baker counties. Am I right? John C. was always a little half-baked. Wouldn't you agree, Son?"

"Yes Sir."

"Then," grinned the President, "David L. Wooten, I shall pray that you make a safe trip back to your family, and an early arrival to that part of the late-Early County, and memorial to my dedicated opponent, good old John C."

With that, Abraham Lincoln was gone with his entourage, having disappeared from David's sight as quickly as he had appeared. Gone from sight, perhaps, but certainly not gone from David's life. The decision is made. David is heading for Kennesaw Mountain.

Chapter 15:
The Circle Is Unbroken

Everything that happens to us, properly understood,
leads us back to ourselves... (C. G. Jung)

November 1, 2000—Edison, Georgia

Dave is back in Edison, in a sense back to the beginning, and driving directly to the Edison Historical Center. This time he knows exactly what he is looking for. The Center is open, and is Dave ever in luck! Darlene Davidson is on duty.

"Mrs. Davidson, I don't know if you remem...?"

"Of course I remember you, Mr. Benson. It hasn't been that long since you were here!"

"Well, in some ways it seems like 150 years," Dave smiles in reply.

"What can I do for you today?"

"You have done so much for me already that I feel guilty asking you even for the time of day..."

"But? Listen Dave you just go right ahead and ask away. That's what I'm here for. Understand?"

"Okay. I've got it. Sure hope you've got it."

"Got what? Let's stop beating around the bush and get down to business. Shall we?"

"When I was here before, you most generously ran off a massive number of pages from Sadie Ann Manry Sheppard's diary. I cannot express in words how helpful all of that was in coming to understand the history and trials of my ancestors who once lived here in Calhoun and early Early Counties. However, you indicated at the time that there might be more letters, or whatever, to be found somewhere amidst your files here. Could I ask you to loo..?"

"Don't need to look, Dave," she interrupts, "since you were here, I have hardly been able to sleep. I've been thinkin' and ponderin' day and night where I might find more records on Annie. Finally, one morning as I was about to get out of bed, I had this inspiration come to me. 'Prisoners of War,' was what came to mind. I knew that a number of men from this area were captured. So I even came in early that morning. I went to the POW file, but didn't find much, EXCEPT a note that said 'See City Point.' Lo and behold, we had a large file on City Point. I think you need to take a look at that one."

"City Point! I don't believe it," Dave exclaims incredulously. "I just came from there. You see, since I saw you last, I've been to Sandersville, Georgia, Richmond, South Mountain, Sharpsburg and Point Lookout in Maryland, and then to City Point. I've done a great deal of research, a massive amount of driving, quite a bit of walking, observing and dreaming. But I have done more soul searching since then than ever before in my life.

"This whole trip began, I thought, as nothing more than honoring my dying mother's wishes, a hunt for whatever family history I might succeed in finding. But it has turned into more than that, Mrs. Davidson. It has become a hunt for the real Dave Benson. There are some things I need to know from the past that I hope will help me figure out who I am."

"Whoa!" Darlene breathes out as if she was blowing into a balloon. "I'm not sure we have a file on 'Dave Benson,' nor do I believe we have any folders entitled 'Soul Searches.' However, you just tell me what you need. If we got it, it's yours to peruse."

"Well, that file on City Point will do for starters."

"Yes, I'm certain it will, Dave. There's a letter in there written by David Wooten."

City Point, Virginia
March 25, 1865

Dearest Elizabeth,
I have no idea if this will ever get to you, no more than do I know if any of my previous letters have found their way into your soft warm hands. One thing I do know is that none of the letters I am sure you have posted to me have ever fought their way to my longing hands. But I MUST write this one last letter to you in case something should happen to me.
It is not just my hands that long to hold your letters, my arms ache to hold you, and my heart pines to have my eyes feast upon your beauty. I have been

engaged in so many battles since I last held you that my brain no longer remembers the number. I have seen so much brutal death and destruction that my mind really wants to forget. I have been a prisoner of war in what must be the North's most gruesome camp. The memory of you, the times we have had together, the prospect of returning to you and your embrace, the promise we made to each other to marry as soon as I would return from the War, seeing your face in my dreams every night, all of this and more has kept me alive.

But I must tell you something that you will find incomprehensible, I suppose. I met a Union guard, a most compassionate fellow, at Point Lookout. His name is Pvt. Johnny Barnes. We became friends. If you could understand the nature of Point Lookout, you would be shaking your head in disbelief. This is a camp where from time-to-time POW's would be picked at random in the middle of the night, taken out and shot. Just for the sport of it. Let me tell you of just one event with several incidents.

One night the guards came crashing into our tents, ordering us all outside and forced us to undress. While we were shivering in the cold, they then proceeded to ransack our tents and personal belongings. Said they were looking for weapons and instruments of escape. As if this was not enough, they took Malachi's pet spider (Shelly the Spider he called her, and stomped on her. Have you ever seen a man cry over the death of a spider, Elizabeth?) It just tells you how desperate a man can get to have something to love.

Then, one of the guards found Baron Trenk's pet mouse. Corporal Crumrine said later, "Baron brought his soul to that mouse." They brought that mouse (Mike the Mouse, Baron called him) out by the tail. One of the guards threw Mike into the air and another guard shot him. Have you ever seen a man grieve over the death of a common, ordinary mouse? It is what happens when a man is deprived of intimacy.

Private Hensley had been nurturing a blade of grass on the south side of our tent. He watered it, talked to it, protected it, and took such pride in it. A guard pulled up the precious blade and ate it. Have you ever seen a man weep over a blade of grass, Liz? It is what happens when hope is nearly destroyed.

You may know the Manry family. Well, James Manry, Johnny the Guard, and I, have become friends. For all I know James is still at PLO. He refuses to swallow the loyalty oath, and I respect him immensely for that. James has kept a running account of the number of men from his Regiment, the 51st Georgia, who have died there. When I left he said the count was 19, including 2 from his company. I know of at least 10 from my own Regiment, the 13th

Georgia, who also died at that hell hole—and that includes Jimmie Warren, a musician, mind you!

Johnny left PLO a few weeks before I did. We met up again at City Point, Virginia, and from there he was the guard for those of us taken on up to a place near Richmond where I was given my freedom. It was then that Johnny asked me to do him a favor. He has asked me to go to Kennesaw Mountain near Atlanta where his brother Horace was killed. Can you believe a Yankee asking a favor of a Confederate? Furthermore, can you imagine a Confederate doing a favor, especially this kind of a favor, for a Yankee?

Well, my Dearest Elizabeth, this Confederate is doing that Yankee his requested favor.

I hope to see you real soon, Elizabeth; and perhaps I will return before you even receive this letter. However, I do know the risks. I am going directly back into Union territory with a lame-brained excuse. I do have a letter from Johnny explaining my mission, but that letter probably will have little weight with any mean-spirited Yankee soldier.

No matter what happens, Dear Elizabeth, please know that I love you with all my heart. Please try to understand that this is something I have to do.

I've run out of paper, but not out of love for you.

David

David's letter to Elizabeth is the only relevant item to Dave's quest. Darlene suggests that he might go back to Morgan and visit the courthouse. Perhaps something might turn up at the Probate Office. Dave agrees it is worth a shot.

* * *

Alisha, the Probate Court Officer is a Black lady, congenial and extremely helpful. She seats Dave at a large table and a comfortable padded leather captain's chair. She points out the location of the probate records and invites Dave to help himself to them as well as the coffee in her outer office.

As she leaves Dave to himself and the ancient archives surrounding him, he laughs a muted laugh. He has done enough research on Calhoun County to know, first of all, that the County was in fact named after Senator John C. Calhoun in 1854, just four years after his death. It was no accident that the County was so named. The white citizens of the area not only were aware of

Calhoun's staunch defense of and belief in the righteousness of slavery, they agreed with him to the nth degree.

The irony, and the reason for Dave's amusement, is that the Calhoun County of 1854, a bastion for the defense of slavery and a citadel warding off all attacks on the "peculiar institution" and the Southern way of life, has certainly changed. Even 100 years after Calhoun County was carved out of Early and Baker counties, providing a political slap in the face to the Abolitionists and their sympathizers, no Black man, Black woman, nor Black child would have been allowed to drink at the courthouse fountain, nor use the same restroom as the whites. Now, the Probate Court Officer is Black, and a woman at that.

Nearly 61% of the people in Calhoun County today are Black. Dave muses further that that was probably about the proportion in 1854 as well. There would have been a few plantation families and many more slaves. In fact Dave had found that in 1860 there were approximately 20,000 slaves within a 20-mile radius of Edison. He also notes with interest that while home ownership in Calhoun County exceeds the state average (72% vs. 68%), the median value of those homes is nearly one-third the median state value ($48,200 vs. $111,200); and the percent of Calhoun County's population living below the poverty line is double that of the state (27% vs. 13%).

Dave sits for a few minutes pondering the dichotomy he has wandered into. This is one of the smallest counties in Georgia geographically (280 square miles) and in terms of density of population (23 people per square mile); yet, it was one of the biggest supporters of slavery and the South's Rebellion. Calhoun County had a large number of African-American slaves in the 19th Century, and it has one of the highest proportion of Blacks to Whites of all counties in Georgia today. Calhoun has a large percentage of people living in poverty; yet, it also has twice the state average rate of minority-owned firms (32% vs. 16%).

"This is a county with a strange and strained history," Dave says to the walls. "But things are happening here. Somehow I feel at home. Maybe it's the fact that Calhoun County has lived a life of dichotomies, as have I."

It is at that moment when Dave's eyes fall upon the Probate Records section labeled "W", and notices a box with a time worn notation, "Wooten."

He finds a number of interesting items in this box:

*The deeding of 250 acres of land to David Wooten by his father Simon Wooten: "for and in consideration of the natural love and affection which he has for his grandchildren..." (Recorded, October 17, 1885).

*A collection of newspaper articles (obituaries and wedding announcements) dating back to 1901, most with no dates whatsoever. But as Dave reads on he is able to decipher who each of David Wooten's daughters (Alice, Mamie, and Annie) married: Alice married Preston Addison. Mamie married L. B. Clark. However, it is in Mamie's obituary where Dave is thunderstruck when he reads:

"The deceased leaves…two sisters, Mrs. P. B. Addison, of Leary, and Mrs. John Price, of Williamsburg…" (No Date)

"John Price," Dave almost shouts. "John Price was Annie Belle Sheppard's husband. My God, he turned right around and married another Annie, Annie Wooten! The guy must have had an addiction to Annies. But then I guess I do too, now that you mention it!"

Moments later, Dave finds the obituary for David L. Wooten, and further evidence of the John C. Price/Annie Wooten connection:

"David L. Wooten was one of the most prominent citizens of Calhoun County, and his death is greatly deplored…One of his daughters, Annie, married…Mr. John C. Price, of Williamsburg." (No Date)

"It is coming full circle," Dave shouts, just as Alisha opens the door.

"What is a circle?" she asks with a most puzzled expression on her face. "Is there something I can help you with?"

"Well, I don't think so. I just don't know. It's just that all of a sudden and all over again I'm finding a most mysterious coming together of my ancestors. More to the point I have this strange sense that finally, after my 50 years of life, that I'm coming together.

"You know, Alisha, it amazes me that you make these records so very available to just anyone who comes by. Most places, it seems to me, put the actual records off limits, set restrictions to their use, or microfilm the documents. Not that I'm complaining, you understand."

"I hear you, Mr. Benson, but we really have few people coming in to do as you are doing. Secondly, most of the records pertain to white folk and most white folk have left this county. Thirdly, and most important, microfilming costs money and this county has so very little of that commodity."

"I get your point. Just driving around this area one can readily see Calhoun County is hardly among the most affluent."

"You got that right, Sir."

"Just call me Dave, please?"

"Okay, Dave. I just came in to tell you I am going to lunch. You can stay right here, I'll be back in less than an hour. But when you want something to eat, the food over across at the convenience store is good at a reasonable price."

"Yes, I know. I've eaten there." *Not sure I want to go back there.*

Moments later Dave continues digging through the Wooten Box and unearths another letter dated seven days prior to David Wooten's death.

March 24, 1909
Morgan, Georgia

TO WHOM IT MAY CONCERN:

As I write this, I know that I do not have long to reside upon this earth. The good doctor denies this, but I know. Whether I live another week, another month, or another year, I am attaching this note to my Last Will & Testament, and I FULLY EXPECT my beloved wife, Elizabeth, or whoever may be in the position to fulfill my wishes, to honor this request as if it were a corporate part of my Will.

A Brief Background to My Final Request as Noted Below:

It was 44 years ago today that I was given my freedom from being a Confederate Prisoner of War in the Union POW camp at Point Lookout, Maryland—also known as Camp Hoffman. It was on that day that I agreed to do a favor for a fine young man who was one of our guards.

I shall not go into detail, only to say that I respected him a great deal. He was kind and we became friends. His name was Pvt. John G. Barnes. His brother, Horace, had fought at Sharpsburg in '62. In fact Johnny's brother fought Will's father-in-law's father, WD Sheppard and me almost, you might say, face-to-face at Dunker Church (although Horace did not know us, or we him).

At Point Lookout Johnny and I came to the realization that James Manry and I had perhaps even laid eyes upon his brother. I certainly came to realize that Horace's good friend Frank's dying words were directed right at Horace; and, I might add, expressions of love for Frank's VERY SPECIAL friend as well. You see, WD and I were present as Frank took his last breath. He was one of the bravest men I have ever seen. I say this even though a few hours earlier he had led a charge designed to kill us all. I say this even though Frank's way of relating to men was, as they say, Funny.

Horace was killed at Kennesaw Mountain in June of '64. Johnny wanted more than anything to visit Horace's gravesite before returning home to most likely marry his brother's widow. You see he had pledged to his brother that if Horace did not return

Johnny would take care of his wife. Because of family pressure to return home immediately after the War, he could see no way to make the trip to Kennesaw. He asked me to go in his stead. I agreed, and I tried, up to a point.

My longing to be with Elizabeth took over my promise to Pvt. Barnes. I got as far as Athens. It would not have been a great way for me to go to honor my promise; but I was so overcome with desire for Elizabeth. I told myself that I could keep the bargain later. Later never came. I have felt great guilt these last 44 years.

MY REQUEST IS THIS:

That someone from my family promise to visit the grave of Pvt. Horace Barnes. That's all, just visit his grave. If anything else seems important to do after that, well that will be up to whoever makes the visit. All I know is that Pvt. H. Barnes was killed at a place called Golgotha somewhere near Kennesaw Mountain.

I pray to God that someone whom I call family will do what I never got around to do. I pray that you, whoever you are, will sign below and agree to do what you can to wipe away an old man's guilt.

The letter is signed, David L. Wooten. A few spaces below his signature a line is drawn and underneath the line in brackets are the words (Your Signature); and right under that the words, THANK YOU! The line, however, is blank.

Attached to the back of the letter with an old rusty paper clip is an old envelope addressed to "John G. Barnes, Edwards, New York."

Alisha finds Dave right where she left him, except he is talking on his cell phone: Backing away she wishes not to intrude, but waits for the conversation to end.

"No one ever went there. The envelope was never sent, Gary. So, guess what? I have one more stop to make before returning to Omaha. But I will be home real soon, perhaps by the end of the week. I have just a little more to do here in Morgan, then I'm off for Kennesaw Mountain and that is directly on the way to Omaha... I miss you too, Gary.

"Oh, Gary, before you hang up. I read in the *Atlanta Journal* the other day that a minister at First United Methodist in Omaha is officiating at Gay/Lesbian marriages. Yes, Gary, I want to do it. Can you get in touch with the minister there and set up a time for us to meet with him? I'm ready. I hope you still are. I love you, Gary."

As Dave folds his phone he notices Alisha. "Oh, Alisha, that's fine, come right in. I was just talking to my friend back in Omaha. I can't wait to see him again. It has been a long time. We aren't used to being apart this long."

"Dave, I didn't mean to eavesdrop or anything."

"No, you certainly were not eavesdropping. After all I am in your office, remember?"

"Well, I did hear something about Gay/Lesbian marriage," Alisha responds haltingly. "I just want you to know that my brother and his partner would give anything to have their union officially recognized. I just wish my job were across the hall where I would do all in my power to grant my brother that wish. Maybe someday."

"Guess it will be a long time coming before the State of Georgia grants anything like that, eh?"

"Probably. But look at me: Less than 40 years ago no one would have imagined that the Probate Office in Calhoun County would be headed up by a Black woman. Anyway, how are you doing?"

"Well, I'm about done here, I think. Just a few more files to take a gander at. Then I'm outta here; but I do need to see if you have anything here pertaining to the Sheppards. I have exhausted the Wooten file."

"You just sit right there, Dave. I'll check it out. I'm certain we do. I'll bring it to you."

The Sheppard File is voluminous, three boxes full of documents. The first thing Dave notices is the large number of land transactions, all of them acquisitions by Gene Sheppard up to the very year of his death. On December 20, 1902 Gene bought two acres of land along Hartford Street from J. F. Roberts and on Feb 1, 1908 another parcel of land along Hartford. Things seem to have been going well, but 1908 was, perhaps, Gene Sheppard's apex. One year later and he would be dead.

It was that very same year, 1909, that cotton production in the South reached its apex. From then on the economics of the South plunged ever southward. In 1910 there were 6,627 plantations in the South; thirty years later there would only be 1840 left.

For Sadie Sheppard, the downhill slide began the day Gene died. It was enough that she should be left with a large brood of children to raise on her own. Complicating the equation was the fact that the economy of the entire world was traveling headlong toward depression. Cotton had seen its glory days, never to return for the South, certainly never to return for Calhoun County. Within five years of Gene's death an economic depression was officially declared and World War I had begun for the U.S.

For Sadie Sheppard there was a war of a different kind. In 1915 her son-in-law John C. Price takes her to court suing her for his share of the late Annie Belle's inheritance—the same John C. Price who would later marry Annie Wooten. Also in 1915 an apparent conniving lawyer bought 325 acres of Sadie's land at a sheriff's sale auction for only $3000. Ten years before Gene paid $2000 for most of the same land transaction. In 1925 another sheriff's sale, and on January 3, 1927 yet another sheriff's sale to pay off debts and at the same time terminating the Sheppard Plantation—the final humiliation of a proud woman.

Dave sits staring at the documents before him detailing the demise of a way of life when he notices something white stuck down at the very bottom of a Sheppard file box. It is an envelope and inside a letter.

September 14, 1945
Edison, Georgia

TO NO ONE IN PARTICULAR (I just have to say this for the record)
I realize my days are limited. I will most likely not see Christmas this year. I am sticking this letter in my Will in hopes that those left after I go may understand some things which I cannot say in any other way.
I write this on the "Day of Days"—the 83rd anniversary of my Uncles' deaths at South Mountain. It was always a most difficult day for my Grandfather Manry and therefore a most difficult day for the entire family for years. Part of the difficulty was that Uncle Johnny and Uncle Ben's bodies were thrown down a well. But the real difficulty was that no one would talk about it. It was a secret; something our family was too humiliated to discuss. I regret that I never had the time, or took the time, to even try to find Uncle Johnny and Uncle Ben. I hope someone will do that for me after I am gone.
My Uncles' fate has been but one of many secrets in my family. I need to open the window of secrecy. I have been worn out with keeping secrets.
Perhaps the biggest and best-kept secret is that my wonderful father-in-law, W. D. Sheppard, deserted the Confederate Army after the Battle of Sharpsburg. I suspected it for some time, but it was not until the day he died that he admitted it to me. He simply wanted me (or maybe just someone) to know. He was so tired keeping it secret for all those years. Mama Sheppard died the same day as Papa Sheppard. I think she could not face living without him; but I think she also could not face living with the possibility that "The

Secret" would be divulged further than my ears.

Papa Sheppard, for some reason, wanted to tell me about his ordeal after leaving the Army. He expressed such deep gratitude of those anti-war folks up in North Georgia. It was the Peace Society who protected him and arranged for Mama Sheppard and little Gene to meet him at Sparta. He said his "North Georgian Saviors" told him he would be killed if he continued on home to Sandersville. They told him he needed to head south. They would have arranged for him to go to Alabama where the Peace Society was especially strong. But he wanted to stay in Georgia. He said he probably would have been captured and executed as a traitor, if it were not for those Peace Society people. He said he didn't agree with everything they stood for, but they took good care of him. They saved his life and they saved his family.

He also made a special point of sharing a story of an incident while the three of them (Papa, Mama, and Gene) were on the train from Sparta to Macon. He was dressed as a Confederate officer and was faking an injury.

Do I blame Papa Sheppard for deserting? No. But I do blame him for keeping it a secret for so long. I believe if it had not been for that one Big Secret in the Sheppard family, many other smaller secrets would never have taken root. Maybe, just maybe, Gene and I could have had a more open marriage. But then, my own Manry family had its secrets as well. Thus, I came well prepared to the Sheppard family knowing how to keep secrets. I am done with that.

That one Big Secret has had the effect of poisoning lives. WD was so afraid of being found out in this community that he would have nothing to do with David Wooten. Yet, he liked David. He admired and respected David. He was simply afraid David would let the skunk out of the bag. WD knew David knew. According to Papa, they got to know each other and liked each other at Sharpsburg. Papa even went in disguise to David's wedding. He intended to somehow let David know he was there. But when he heard David offer a prayer for two brave Yankee brothers, WD decided that if David could forgive the enemy he probably would have little forgiveness left for a deserter.

From that day forward there was an unwritten Sheppard Family Rule—Stay Away From the Wootens. It was a seed that germinated into a vicious weed. Gene, I believe, breathed in the pollen and became allergic in a very irrational way to anything known as a Wooten. When Bessie started seeing David's son, Will, there was no reasoning with Gene. One of my biggest regrets is that I, too, became a party to it all. The end result has been the *creation of a wall of separation between Bessie & Will and myself.*

BESSIE: Please forgive me for being part of the bribery you bravely and rightly rejected. Yes, you did not go to Finishing School as your Father and I tried so hard to lure you into doing. The fact is you have "attended" the most difficult "finishing school" of all, the school of life, the school of hard knocks, and the school of making your own decisions and living by them. I am proud of you Bessie. And, Bessie, please forgive your Father. He really loved you and wanted what was best for you. Please forgive your Grandfather and Grandmother Sheppard for the Big Secret that set everything else into a disastrous course—secrets and lies that will probably infect the health of our family for at least another generation. Try, Bessie, to do what you can to stop the Cycle of Secrecy.

WILL: Please forgive Gene and I and his parents for the unrelenting punishment of you for something your good father did not do. You and your father were ostracized for what might *have happened and never did and never would have happened because of the goodness of the man, David L. Wooten. If I could go back and change it all, stop it from ever getting started, I would; but I cannot and could not. No, I simply did not. I sensed there was something terribly wrong even before I married Bessie's father, but I took the easy way out. I kept my mouth shut. You and Bessie have paid the price. I am terribly sorry.*

MY DEAR GRANDCHILDREN (Louise, Florine, Annie Will, David Linton, Eunice)

Please forgive a grandmother you have seen so little of. We had a few years together while you (Louise, Florine, Annie and David) were small and living nearby in Williamsburg. But only you Louise, Florine and Annie may have any real memory of me. David, you were only two years old when your Mama and Papa moved away. Eunice, you probably know me like I know you. We know each other only by reputation. For that, children, I am heartily sorry.

I WONDER,

1) Can you all forgive me, Gene, William and Martha?

2) Will someone go to South Mountain for me, for my father and my Grandpa Manry?

If these things can be done, I believe my soul will rest after I am gone. But I believe the souls of my Uncle Ben, Uncle Johnny, Grandpa Manry, Gene and his parents will also rest in the embrace of a caring and forgiving God.

* * *

Sadie died six weeks later on October 31, 1945, but there is no evidence at all that anyone followed her bidding to go to South Mountain. Dave is satisfied, however, that someone did go. It took 55 years, but he, Dave Benson aka Dave Manry Sheppard Wooten Benson, went not only to the Mountain, but also to the Well.

No evidence at all, of course, that anyone did the forgiving she so sorely needed to rest her soul. "But I forgive you, Sadie; and I forgive you Gene, WD, Martha. I accept you all as family. I hope you can accept me."

As Alisha comes to the door, she steps quickly back. It does not appear to her to be smart to intrude on a man's pain. She gives Dave the space he needs now to cry a river of tears, finally released after a century and a half. An extended family had worked together all those years, often without knowing why or what, to dam the flow. One person, unlike Hans Brinker Anderson's little hero who dammed the dike staunching the flow of life-threatening water, opens the dike of pent-up family history and pain allowing the flow of life-giving water.

* * *

"Gary. It's me. I'm still in Morgan. I've just done some incredible research at the Calhoun County Courthouse. I will fill you in later, but right now I want you to know that I am basically on my way back to Omaha.

"I'm sitting in my car at the Morgan cemetery. I have been here before. It just seems appropriate that I make one last stop before I hit the road. In a few minutes I'll be on my way north to the Atlanta area to make a visit to Kennesaw Mountain. I feel as if I have taken an oath to make that stop. I'll explain all of this when I see you in a few days.

"Wish I could talk with you, rather than with a machine, but I love the sound of your voice, no matter what."

Dave gets out of his car and heads directly toward the large Wooten monument visible from almost anywhere in town. At the top of the monument is a life-size sculpture of a young woman seated with her right elbow resting upon her upper leg. Her fist supports her head as she leans forward looking despondently toward the ground. Her gown provides an attractive cover for an attractive woman. Her hair is neatly curled and parted in the middle of her head. A bouquet is held in her left hand with the flowers resting on her side. This is the monument to Berta C. Wooten born Dec 4, 1889, died Mar 31, 1914.

"At least she did not have to endure the troublesome war period," Dave says to himself; or so he thought. Suddenly, he realizes he is not alone. Standing just beyond a tree at the edge of Berta's monument is a young woman leaning up against another monument, an obelisk. Her back is turned, but she, like the sculptured young woman, seems to be leaning her head upon her fist, with her right elbow resting upon the ledge of the obelisk's upper base.

Dave wonders momentarily, "Where did she come from? I just walked by there moments ago." While he does not want to intrude, he has a sense that he knows this young woman. Where had they met? Perhaps she was one of the clerks at the Courthouse.

Dave's blood chills, his spine tingles, his head, his entire body goes numb as she straightens up and turns toward him. She brings her hand to her mouth looking sad, first to the ground, then to Dave. She seems to speak, but Dave can not hear.

Moving now around Berta's monument, Dave stubs his toe slightly on its lower edge monument momentarily losing his equilibrium. His left arm instinctively reaches out for support from the sturdy monument. He then speaks to the young woman, "Hi, do I....?

She is gone.

Dave runs toward the monument where she had stood. It is then that he knows why the young woman had been there. This monument reads, "Annie Wooten Price." And Dave knows he will never, ever, see Annie Belle again. It is done.

✳ ✳ ✳

Driving north from Morgan on Georgia Route 45 heading toward Albany, Dave notices a swampy area coming up on him. He is impressed with the primitive beauty of the place. Moss covered trees with burnt orange berries make this a sight Dave associates with Florida. Slowing down he observes a large stand of cattails, the kind his mother often talked about from her days of living in Central New York. "Mom said one of her favorite memories was that of going with her mother to the pond in the back pasture to pick cattails in the fall and cowslips and pussy willows in the spring."

Pulling over to park, Dave proceeds to get out and navigates his way carefully to the water's edge. He picks a bouquet of cattails and a few of the burnt orange sprigs, hoping there is no law in Georgia prohibiting such an acquisition. Quickly, he opens the trunk of the car and tosses his treasure inside. As he lowers the trunk lid, he notices a sign at the east edge of the bridge. There are no markings on his side of the sign, so he walks across the bridge in order to read the sign:

Ichawaynochaway Creek

Creek Indian for Buck Sleeping Place

And Dave remembers something else: *The Plantation. I was there. It amazes me that you do not see it yourself, Dave. It's right over there; I can see it so clearly. Not far from Knockaway...Knockaway...Knock...*

The memory awakened, somehow, seems less a memory and more of a presence. "But it wasn't Knockaway, was it Mom? It was Ichawaynochaway. Right Mom? Mom?"

Just then Dave hears a most beautiful melody, very much remindful of his mother singing a lullaby to him when he was young. His mother would hold him and rock him and sing to him for hours on end it seemed. How he loved that time in his life, often wishing upon wish that he could return to those safe and serene days.

"Mom? Is that you? Mom?"

No response to a loving son's entreaty, except for what Dave sees.

The source of the melody sits on one of the unpicked cattails at the edge of Ichawaynochaway Creek. It is a handsome Brown Thrush. No, there are two of them. The other, only a few feet away, is swaying on a branch of one of the dead trees. They seem to be serenading each other. In a flash, it is all over, and the two fly off together.

Dave knows he will never hear his mother's voice again; and it is okay. For in a most interesting way, Dave realizes that the Brown Thrush is signaling to him to let go. This is the bird that often lingers for mild winters even as far north as New York, but normally comes south at this time of the year.

Dave, too, must be on his way.

Chapter 16:
Kennesaw to Gettysburg and Back

All situations are passing memory.
(Tibetan Buddhist Teaching)

November 3, 2000

Traveling northwest out of Atlanta on US 41, the Cobb Parkway, Dave soon catches a glimpse of a mountain off to the left. As mountains go, this one at an elevation of 1,809 feet pales into insignificance in terms of height or natural beauty when compared to the Grand Tetons of Wyoming. But this mountain with its smaller companions looms most high when viewed as a mountain that shaped American history.

The North lost 5000 men (including Horace Barnes) at Kennesaw, while the South lost only 1000. However, the Confederacy lost the battle and this mountain. With the loss of Kennesaw the Confederate States of America effectively lost Atlanta and the War.

As Dave drives up to the Kennesaw Mountain Visitor Center the first thing he notices is the cars and the crowd. There are people all over the grounds—tourists like himself and picnickers, serious students of history and casual gawkers. It is not easy finding a parking place; nor is it a simple task picking his way through the crowd. Finally he finds what he is looking for, a Park Ranger.

"Sir, I wonder if you could help me?"

"Well, I'll try. What do you need?" the Ranger responds. He is a short stocky fellow dressed in the tell tale signature uniform of all Park Rangers, light brown shirt with US Park Service logo on the shoulder, and dark brown pants.

"Can you tell me, by any chance, where Golgotha is, or was, at the time of the battle here?"

"Well now that is the easiest question anyone could possibly ask me, but it is also a question I rarely hear. It wasn't a real big battle over there. But, it is literally in my backyard. If you will stop in and feed my dogs," he smiles, "I'll sketch out a map for you. It is only about five minutes from here. But why do you ask?"

Dave proceeds to tell the Ranger the story of how he is trying to track down one of his ancestors who fought for the Union and died at Golgotha. He learns from the Ranger that Golgotha Church was also known as Gilgal Church. He also learns that the Center has some records from the battles at Kennesaw available for inspection, if he would want to peruse them.

Dave thanks the Ranger saying, "I may be back later to paw through your archive," knowing he will not. At this point he is intolerably eager to do two things: He wants to lay eyes on the area where Horace was killed; and he wants to head out for Omaha and Gary.

Driving west on Stilesboro Road to Kennesaw/Due West Road, he turns left for a couple of miles until he meets up with Acworth/DW Road and turns right; and there is the Kirkwood Presbyterian Church where the Ranger directed him to pull in to park. The Ranger's directions are impeccable. Dave gets out of his car and walks up the street and there is the fenced in yard with the Ranger's dogs barking at him; although Dave cannot see the dogs due to the thick vegetation surrounding the house and fence.

"Go past three houses," the Ranger had directed, "and when you see a big oak with an orange sign on it; well, there you are. Behind that tree and down the hill a few yards is where the church was and where your great-great uncle would have been killed. Just be careful," said the Ranger. "It is a heavily wooded area full of poison ivy; was then, is now. The future President, Benjamin Harrison's 70th Indiana was pinned down right there for close to two hours by heavy Confederate fire. When Harrison finally got off the ground, he had himself a royal case of poison ivy. You might say," the Ranger grins with an impish smile, "Harrison had an itch for the Confederacy!"

Dave steps up to the embankment and walks into the woods for perhaps ten yards until he spies a thick undergrowth of poison ivy. "That's far enough," he says to himself and to the trees surrounding him. As he turns to go back to the street, he has a strange sensation come over him. It is as if he were being watched.

Taking another couple of steps Dave notices something (or someone) is moving off to his right. It is someone dressed in gray, Confederate Gray. He smiles, salutes Dave, and disappears.

Dave knows somehow in his bones that he has just had his last encounter with David Wooten. Looking around, he spots a tree stump almost beckoning to him to sit awhile. It is from here that Dave glimpses into the past.

* * *

It had been a long journey from Antietam to Golgotha Church. Not just in miles, but in the ordeals of war. It had been a painful journey from one maelstrom to another. It had also culminated in a strange vortex of humanity, a family vortex.

Oh, prior to Antietam, it must be admitted that Horace's piece of the war was terminally boring. In fact it was so non-eventful that desertion was common not for fear of being killed in combat, but from thinking one was going to die from absolute boredom. Until September 1862 and the engagement at Antietam, there were at least three desertions. For Baptist minister Richard Eddy, Chaplain to the 60th NY, the chief worry coming out of the legion's lethargy was the temptation such circumstances present for wide-ranging "moral depravity".

Less than nine months before the Battle of Antietam Chaplain Eddy felt compelled to report to Col. George S. Greene regarding his grave concern for the moral welfare of his men. Their propensity toward profanity and gambling was running rampant. Thus, his prescription for the malady:

> *I suggest that since profanity is such an inexcusable and yet heinous sin, that those who use it shall be subjected to the penalty prescribed in the Articles of War..."*

For a time after Antietam the 60th NY went back into a period of relative inactivity as far as fighting was concerned. Then in late April of '63 Horace found himself engaged in the ferocious battle of Chancellorsville, Virginia, where two of his friends, Sylvester Tupper and Wesley Oliver, were killed. He did not know it at the time, nor would he have cared, that David Wooten and James Manry were also at Chancellorsville. The battle stations for the three of them were far apart, but their fortunes were soon destined to merge in a sleepy little Pennsylvania town known as Gettysburg.

On June 3rd the 60th NY was camped on the southside of Aquia Creek in Virginia just eight miles from the Potomac River. Five miles to the south James Manry of the 51st Georgia was busy with his spy glass observing the

60th NY's movements and reporting to Brigadier General Paul Semmes's aide. This was the 1st Army Corps, Longstreet's Corps, Major General Lafayette McLaw's Division.

From the 3rd of June to the 17th the 60th NY moved camp a total of nearly 28 miles to Middleburg, and the 51st Georgia had moved 35 miles to Fairfax. They were now approximately 12 miles apart. By the 28th of June both forces had moved a total of nearly 50 miles to within six miles of Gettysburg.

Four days later the 60th NY would be encamped at Gettysburg's Rock Creek, less than two miles from the center of town and about the same distance from the 51st Georgia resting up at the Peach Orchard.

At approximately 3:30 that afternoon (July 2nd) the 51st was overwhelmed and James Manry was taken prisoner. At about the same hour Horace Barnes was wounded in the hand, a relatively minor injury but enough to take him out of combat for the rest of the day. However, as soon as the medical corps tended to him an order reached him to report for temporary guard duty. He was to escort Confederate prisoners back behind the lines to the Potomac for transfer to a place called Point Lookout, Maryland.

As Horace was parading the prisoners toward the goal of an awaiting ship, he made the acquaintance with one of the unfortunates, a fellow by the name of Manry. They talked briefly about where they came from (Southwest Georgia and Northern New York), and the battles they had been in. It was to be another ten months before James would put it together that the Yankee by the name of Horace that David Wooten talked about that day at Antietam and Pvt. Barnes's bereaved brother were one and the same. Nor did he know until the same period of time had passed that David Wooten and the 13th Georgia were only about three miles north at a battle station just beyond Gettysburg's town square.

By November 24th the 60th NY and the 20th Army Corps had marched to southern Tennessee and soundly defeated one of the two major Confederate divisions. Chattanooga was now in Union hands along with the equally important Lookout Mountain. The Union Army smelled ultimate victory. Horace was about to make a fatal decision.

On December 14, 1863 anyone who had served in the Union Army for two years or more was entitled to be released with home as his destination. However, the Federal Government offered a bounty of $400 and the opportunity to take a 30-day furlough to all troops re-enlisting.

The morale was so high, the prospects for closure to the interminable war so clear, and the money so attractive that Horace and most others in his regiment decided to stay on, taking their furlough in Chattanooga. While it was tempting for Horace to go home, to see Caroline and the son he had never yet seen, his family, and peaceful Edwards, he decided the 2400 mile round trip would hardly be worth the bother and the heartache. It would take him 10 to 12 days each way, leaving him only 6-10 days (if he were lucky) to be at home. But would the pain of having to leave so soon be more excruciating than simply to stay in Chattanooga? He decided the answer was Yes.

Horace simply wanted to end the thing. Of course the government's propagandistic rally cry also swayed the decisions of an exuberant group of brave men:

> *While we rally round the flag, boys, rally once again,*
> *shouting the battle-cry of freedom.*

The perception was that with the fall of Chattanooga and Knoxville, indeed all of Tennessee, only a few weeks more and the Rebels would give it up. The reality was that another 16 months of fighting would ensue. The bitter reality for Horace was that he would not live to see the end. Six months more and he would be one more Union casualty.

By the time he arrived at Kennesaw Mountain, Horace had witnessed 132,856 casualties in the battles of Antietam in Maryland, Chancellorsville in Virginia, Gettysburg in Pennsylvania, Chattanooga in Tennessee, as well as Ringgold, Resaca, and Dallas in Georgia. By the time his body would be removed from the makeshift grave at what would remain of Golgotha Church, the War would indeed be over.

Between May 25th and May 28th Horace found himself in the midst of several skirmishes at New Hope Church, Pickett's Hill, and Dallas. By this time combat had become almost commonplace in Horace's life. After all being present at the death of over 132,000 men makes one fairly accustomed to the roar of cannon, the screeching of projectiles through the air above one's head, the blasting of rifles, the chattering of pistol fire, the shattering of giant trees by canon balls; yes, even the cries of men and horses mortally wounded. However, it would get worse, and along with that a premonition of his death on the 25th at, of all the unlikely named places, New Hope.

The terrain around New Hope was exceedingly rough and dangerous. Small ravines were everywhere and they were camouflaged with dense thickets of woods and incredible tangles of underbrush. It was nearly impossible to see any great distance, and with that the risk of stumbling upon a Confederate rifle pit having taken careful aim at your very heart long before you would realize they were there.

It was not a good day to be a Union soldier. General Hooker would report the loss of nearly 1700 men that day. Horace came close to being among that number. He thought the fighting had ended. General Hood's troops were seen to have retreated. Horace stood up to observe the terrain before him when a shell came buzzing by his ear. It was then that he observed a Georgia flag and the raucous cry of a Rebel, "Turner, I think you got yourself a Yank! We'll notch thatun up fer the 25th Georgia. Great shot Joey!"

Suddenly, it struck Horace that this war is not just a matter of the North and South attempting to destroy each other. It is not just the Union and the Confederacy trying to defeat the other. It is not just the 60th NY and the 25th Georgia set upon bringing defeat to the other. It is some Rebel by the name of Joey Turner aiming to kill an Edwards boy by the name of Horace Barnes. Until then, Horace had been able to detach himself from the 132,000 dead and the hundreds of thousands living soldiers all set to destroy whatever and whomever they needed to annihilate. Yes, if Horace Barnes needs to be killed, then someone will do it. "Maybe it will be Joey Turner; but maybe I have to kill him," thought Horace.

He had heard more than a few shells and canon balls buzz by his head since Antietam. But never, no not ever, did he come close to seeing whom it was that sent the death-dealing missile his way. Never, in all his experience did he know the name of his assailant. Never, that is, until now.

This incident became something more than a realization. It developed into an awakening, certainly, but much more than that. For Horace it was the beginning of a living nightmare—a premonition that his life now stood at the edge of an abyss. The gods of war and of nature, nor the God of Love, did little to relieve Horace's anxiety.

Within a few days the clouds gathered and it would be nearly two weeks before the sun would ever be seen again. The mountains would roar with cannon. The hills and valleys would repeat and magnify the frightening sounds to a deafening concussion. Then, the thunder and lightning from multiple storms added to the inferno of fire and noise to the point where it seemed that the earth was coming to an end. "It is like waging war inside of an active volcano," screamed Horace to no one in particular.

On June 14th the sun finally broke through the clouds to the wide approval of men on both sides of the winding battle lines. It was an opportunity to wash and dry muddied and bloodied uniforms and blankets. By this time the 60th

NY was bivouacked between Pine and Lost Mountains overlooking a small church, Gilgal Church. Horace happened to be standing not far from General Sherman when he heard Sherman's order for the artillery to fire three volleys upon a group of Confederates observed up on Pine Mountain with spy glasses trained upon Sherman's party.

At the very same moment 21-year-old Private Joseph Turner of the 25th Georgia and son of the future Deacon Henry Turner was standing about 50 yards from Generals Johnston, Hardee, and Polk. Joey saw three puffs of smoke from down in the valley and seconds later the sound of the artillery producing the smoke. Suddenly, there was a commotion behind him. General Johnston was holding General Polk in his arms. Leonidas Polk was dead. Joey vowed to seek revenge by killing any and all Yankees gathered around that little church.

Later that evening General Johnston ordered the abandonment of Pine Mountain taking a new position by daybreak on the 15th near Gilgal Church. By noon the 60th NY under the command of Brigadier General John Geary's 2nd Division of the 20th Corps of the Army of the Potomac attacked the center of the Confederate line near the church. While the 20th Corps prevailed, so did Joey obtain his revenge. Pvt. Horace Barnes was mortally wounded. He died the next morning and was buried near the smoldering church.

Three days later Pvt. Joseph Turner was captured near Lost Mountain and was transported to Point Lookout Prisoner of War Camp where he remained for three months before being taken to Camp Morton, Indiana, where he was exchanged on February 26, 1865 returning home to Edison, Georgia.

✳ ✳ ✳

Dave has been in this spot only 20 minutes, at most. Yet, to him it seems as if he has been glued to this stump for hours, maybe even days; in some sense it seems to have been a century that has passed by since he left his car less than a block down the road. He would claim in later years that it was as if he could hear the roar of cannon and the cries of the dying, smell the acrid fumes of a burning church, and hear Horace's last words, "Caroline, Johnny!"

As much as he wants to return to his car and take I-75 North, he realizes there is no way he can do that now. The Ranger indicated that those who died here were buried in either the National Cemetery or Confederate Cemetery in

Marietta. Dave has a gnawing need now to visit Horace's grave, if in fact they were able to identify his body back then.

Most of the markers for the bodies buried at the scene of battle were makeshift. By the time bodies were taken up from such places as Golgotha, Lost Mountain, Pine Mountain, or anywhere else, the markers were illegible. Many, of course were they who were so decayed or mutilated that identification was impossible. It was not uncommon for bodies to lie untended for a week or more. In the heat and humidity of a Georgia June, the process of putrification occurred quickly.

Dave returns to the Visitor Center only to be disappointed that the Ranger he had talked to earlier was not there. However, he explains his need to another Ranger, a handsome young man around 35 years old. He stands tall, well-built, Black, a deep voice, slender hands and long fingers—so very Gary-like when Gary was that age.

"Yes, Sir, we do have the records here of who is buried where over in Marietta. You have a name for this ancestor of yours?"

"Horace Barnes, died June 16, 1864 at Golgotha or Gilgal."

"Okay, by any chance do you know what regiment he was with?"

"The 60th NY Infantry Regiment."

"Wow, this will not be hard at all. Just give me a minute."

In less than a minute the Ranger returns with a map in hand. "Sir, you're in luck. All you need do is go into Marietta to the National Cemetery at Washington and Cole Streets, swing into the entrance off Washington and near Cole. As you go up the hill you will come to section S immediately on your right. Within a few feet you will see Section A on your left and I on your right. Keep going straight up and soon you will see Section H. Pvt. Horace Barnes is somewhere in H, marker 8396."

"Thanks, Ranger. You've been very helpful."

"Oh, no problem It's my job. But tell you what. I will be getting off duty here in just a few minutes. If you'd like you could follow me. I'm going into Marietta anyway. I could take you right to the spot, and if you'd like we could go somewhere for dinner. There are several fine restaurants in the Square, especially The Flamingo where I usually go. It's our special hangout, you know."

Oh I know, all right, Dave thinks to himself. "I appreciate the offer, but this is something I really need to do totally on my own. As soon as I am done at the cemetery, I must be on my way back home to Omaha and Gary, my lover," Dave informs the Ranger with the same intentionality that Sherman must have used when he ordered the volleys that blew Polk off his horse.

"Hey that's fine, Man. Just thought I'd offer."

✳ ✳ ✳

It is a beautiful cemetery. Rich green lawn. Well kept. White markers. Each one with the soldier's name and marker number. Some have just the state initial. Others have the regiment name and number. Yet others have the company number as well.

Driving ever so slowly along looking for 8396, Dave decides he must get out and walk around. There seems to be thousands in each section." It`s going to be almost like looking for a needle in a ...."

It is then that he sees the marker right at the edge of the road, plumb in front of him:

8396
HORACE BARNES
NY

Quickly shutting off the engine, and flinging open the car door, Dave sticks one leg out and stops. He sits there as if mesmerized. He cannot bring the rest of his body to move, to respond. However, the fact is his brain has failed to communicate with the rest of his body. Dave is frozen in place.

For a long moment flashing before him are all the other major moments on this fate-filled trip when he came to a place of consequence: the Edison library, the café in Morgan, "Wooten Station" outside of Albany, the traffic jam outside of Richmond, Burnside's Café in Sharpsburg, Ichawaynochaway Creek and hearing the birdsong.

So well conditioned is he that he half expects to see Annie Belle or David. Yet, Dave is reasonably certain that he has seen the last of both. But there is something here. He senses that if he were to take one more step he would become engulfed in something so strange and mysterious, so inescapable.

Finally, standing in front of the marker he begins to speak. "Well Uncle Horace, I seem to be here as a proxy 135 years late for your brother Johnny and his Confederate prisoner friend, also an ancestor of mine. Johnny wanted so much to come here, but it was just too much for him to do at the time. I'm sure you understand. I'm also certain that you know Johnny did fulfill his promise to take care of Caroline. He married her, you know, raised your two boys; and then they had two boys and a girl of their own. Johnny died at 87 and Caroline at 70. They lived a good and long life, Horace—much longer than your short 25 years."

Dave then sits down on the ground and wraps his arm around the marker. His mind wanders and wonders at the mystery of it all.

Chapter 17:
The Book Signing

September 14, 2003

The leaves are already turning on this warm and humid afternoon. The parking lot at the shopping mall is full, and people all seem to be heading toward the bookstore, Dave among them. His heart skips a beat as he observes the large posters in each of the eight windows at Combs Bookstore:

A War Between Families
by
David A. Benson
(Local Omaha Author)
Book Signing
Sunday, Sept 14th
2-4 PM
Lecture at 2

Even having observed so many people entering the bookstore, Dave is taken back by the numbers. All of the chairs are taken. Many are sitting on the floor while others are finding places to lean. "Maybe the risk was well taken," TJ, the owner says quietly to Dave.

Dave had bargained long and hard with TJ. He wanted to have his initial signing on this date for a very important reason; and he did not care if the 14th of September *was* on a Sunday. "Not many bookstores even try to have such events on a Sunday. I fear no one will show," insisted TJ.

It was TJ's fear that prevented anything like a good night's sleep for Dave. "What if TJ is right?" Dave asked himself that question all night long. But there was much more to his restlessness than crowd considerations. In fact, given what he intended to say to whoever might show up, perhaps the smaller the turnout the better.

Gary, being his usual punctual self, has taken one of the best seats in the house—front and center. With him are Sharon and Peter.

After a short introduction by TJ, Dave takes the podium and begins:

I thank you all for coming on this beautiful Sunday afternoon. I'm sure you have plenty of other things you could be doing. Recognizing that fact, I am doubly grateful. I will not be keeping you long. I just want to say a few things about my book, why I wrote it, and what I learned in the process.

First of all, in the very beginning I had no idea a book was in the picture. All I wanted to do was honor my dear mother's dying wishes. You see, she had these experiences which I learned later are fairly normal for people who are at the end of life. She saw people around her whom I could not see. They spoke to her, apparently very clearly, but I, of course, could never hear them speak. She even saw geographic locations. Yet, so much of what she saw and heard remained a mystery to her—and certainly to me.

All she asked of me was to follow the clues, so to speak; and so I did. The clues took me initially to the state of Georgia. I got there only by literally unraveling clues shared through Mom's deathbed visions, and what is known as the symbolic language of the dying.

Before all of this began to reveal itself, I had little to no knowledge that any of my relatives came from the South. However, a persistent, mysterious, and faithful visitor to my mother's bedside was a fellow by the name of David. By following various leads and hunches, and without going into all of the details here, suffice it to say that this David turned out to be an ancestor of mine, a Georgian, and a veteran of the Confederate Army.

As I said, my mother's mysterious visitors were never visible to me at that time. However, during my journey after Mom's death two of those visitors became quite present to me—fleetingly and repetitively, but present nevertheless.

My journey, which I initially believed would take me a week, turned into several months of crisscrossing the Southern States. In the process I discovered six ancestors who fought for the Confederacy and two who fought for the Union. The discovery did not stop there. I learned that in many cases all eight came together at the same sites of conflict. The evidence even suggested that they had come to know each other.

In a very real sense these ancestors of mine, belonging to four distinct families separated by nearly 2000 miles in the 1860s, and joined together through my grandparents' marriage nearly 100 years later, had already become family during the War itself. That is the first thing I learned.

The second is that I went into my "odyssey," as my dear friend Gary here has described it, with a profound prejudice against the South. What I have come to learn is that the people today in the Southern states are just like you and I. I have my prejudices. So does the typical Southerner. So too does the typical Northerner; and, I suspect, so too do all of us in this room this afternoon.

Thirdly, I learned that not everyone in the South in the 1860s wholeheartedly approved of slavery. Most Southerners did not have slaves, and many who did felt uncomfortable with the so-called "Peculiar Institution." Some, like Robert E. Lee and his family, did all they could to prepare their slaves for what they considered the inevitability of the end of slavery.

Fourth, I learned that the Civil War at the start, like all wars, was at first widely believed on both sides to be a short war. The reality was, of course, a god-awfully long war. It was a war driven by government propaganda, like all wars, including the Iraqi War we are in the midst of right now.

Fifth, I learned just how resilient the South has proven itself to be. As Will Durant notes in his study of civilization: "Civilization does not die, it migrates, it changes its habitat and its dress, but it lives on."

I would at this time like to share this slide with you. The house shown here was the home of Sadie and Gene Sheppard, fairly well off plantation owners in Edison, Georgia. They were some of the ancestors I discovered. This house is no longer a Sheppard residence. This house no longer sits in Edison. This house was transported some 15 miles to outside of Morgan, Georgia. Within this house today, however, life, Southern style, goes on. Yes, to repeat Durant, "Civilization does not die, it migrates, it changes its habitat and its dress, but it lives on."

Similarly, I learned the wisdom of General Douglas Macarthur when he said, "Old soldiers never die, they just fade away." As you will read in my book, one old soldier, David L. Wooten by name, may have faded away, but he kept fading into my consciousness more times than a few.

Sixth, there is a fine line of distinction between being loyal to, in this case the Confederacy or the Union, right to the bloody end of the war; and being loyal to one's family even if it means being a deserter to one's nation in the time of war. I will say no more about that this afternoon, but you can read about that fine line in this book.

The fine line extends even further. It is a fine line between bravery and cowardice. Furthermore, it is a fine line between being friend and foe.

Seventh, despite the best efforts of governments through their propaganda machines to clarify in black and white terms, evil versus goodness, right versus wrong, godliness versus godlessness, the reality of war obscures and calls into question the rationalizations and justifications for it.

Eighth, the inhumanity of war is nearly indescribable. I for one have no stomach for even trying to do so. However, even in the midst of the inhumanity of war, humanity survives and can transcend the polarities created by the echelons of government.

Ninth, there is a realm to reality that we have yet to understand. This thing we call life is not the end. While I was engaged in my odyssey, I had the occasion more than once to meet some of my ancestors. My mother met some of them before she died. They came to her right here in Omaha, Nebraska. I met them on their own turf, you might say, in Morgan and Edison, Georgia, at Antietam, in Richmond, Virginia, at Point Lookout, Maryland, and at Kennesaw Mountain near Atlanta. Some would call it the paranormal, I suppose. I call it being open to phenomenon of the extraordinaire.

Tenth, I learned who Dave Benson really is. I have spent most of my life knowing I am Gay. Yet, I have also spent most of that time at once accepting and denying, mostly denying. It is difficult for me to fully explain, but it was my eight ancestors, whom I came to know during my journey and my research, who helped me come to terms with who I really am; and none of them to my knowledge were Gay! I hope you will glimpse at least a little of what I am talking about here today in my book. After all of these 50+ years, I have come to realize that the difference between being Gay and being Straight is also a fine line.

Finally, I want to say this: Gary and I have been friends, partners—yes, lovers for all of our adult lives. We had hoped to have our union recognized, authenticated, blessed and sacramentalized here at the First United Methodist Church. However, as you may know, the minister who was officiating at such marriages has long since been removed. So, tomorrow morning Gary and I head for Vermont. Sharon, here, also a longtime and close friend and her fiancé Peter will be going with us. We will be witnessing one another's weddings.

I spent months researching the Civil War, only to come face-to-face with my own internal civil war. I think I have won the war. However, there seems to be another civil war going on right now—a cultural war. This war involves an effort by one side to treat us, who have a different sexual orientation than the mainstream, as subhuman and to keep us enslaved in the role of the socially impure. I do not believe that my great, great uncles, Ben and Johnny Manry of the 51st Georgia Infantry and who died at South Mountain, or Horace Barnes of the 60th NY Infantry and who died at Kennesaw Mountain, gave their lives to perpetuate any form of slavery. In fact they have saved me from my own bondage.

To conclude, TJ and I went around and around a few months ago as we negotiated the date for today's book signing. As you probably know there are few book signings in this city on a Sunday. As a matter of fact, Combs' is never, except for today, open on Sunday. I believe that if you read my book, you will soon understand why September 14th is so important.

It is not because I wanted to violate the Sabbath. I only want in this special way to honor two of my great, great uncles who were killed on this day in 1862, as well as to honor my ancestors who were also engaged at the same spot, South Mountain, near Antietam Creek and Sharpsburg, Maryland. September 14, 1862 was also a Sunday and neither the Confederacy nor the Union refrained from desecrating the Sabbath that day. Today is the 20th time since 1862 that September 14th has occurred on a Sunday.

Thank you for coming and being part of my effort to make this day holy and sacred following a family tradition that I was completely unaware of until a few years ago. Indeed, I did not until then even know the family was mine.

Thank you.

Epilogue

The inspiration for this book came one day in October 2001. My wife, Linda, and I had just left a month long residency at the Hambidge Center for the Creative Arts in Rabun Gap, Georgia (northeast Georgia) and had traveled to Calhoun County (southwest Georgia) to do some genealogical research on her father's family (the Wootens). While at the County Courthouse in Morgan and digging through probate records, I said to Linda, "I smell a novel coming on."

So it is that this novel came to be a nascent thought. Research conducted at the Courthouse at that time, as well as information gleaned from the Calhoun County Public Library in Edison that October and visits to the cemeteries in Morgan and Edison inflated the thought. Research continued sporadically for nearly two more years. Then in April/May 2003 Linda and I were granted another residency at Hambidge where work began in earnest on what appears within these pages.

Prior to arriving at Hambidge in 2003 we accomplished considerable research at Antietam Battlefield, South Mountain, Point Lookout State Park, as well as at the Museum of the Confederacy in Richmond, Virginia. During the Hambidge Residency time was spent at Kennesaw Mountain Battlefield and the National Cemetery in Marietta, Georgia.

Most of the characters in this novel are real people. From the South: The Manry brothers, Ben, John, and James are Linda's great-great uncles. Sadie Ann (also known as "Annie Belle") Manry Sheppard is Linda's paternal great grandmother. All of the members of Sadie's family mentioned herein are in fact her siblings, parents, and grandparents. Sadie's husband Gene, his parents William Drayton Sheppard and Martha Sheppard Sheppard, plus

Sadie & Gene's children are also historical figures, as are David Wooten (Linda's paternal great grandfather), his wife Elizabeth and their children including Will Wooten and his wife Bessie Sheppard (Linda's paternal grandparents).

The fictionalized characters on the Wooten side of this story are: Anna (Annie) Wooten Barnes, Anna (Annie) Barnes Benson, Frank Wooten, Hodges (Hooten Tooten or H.T.) Wooten, and David Sheppard.

From the North: Horace and Johnny Barnes are my own maternal great-great uncles. All the members of their family mentioned here are historical personages in my family's lineage, with the exception of: Anna (Annie) Wooten Barnes and Anna (Annie) Barnes Benson.

Other fictional characters include Dave Benson, Frank Benson, Sharon, Ginny, Claire, Cathy, Penny, Jerome, Karen, A'Jamal, Gary Lee, Mrs. Colquitt, Mrs. Davidson, Noretta, Horace's friend Frank, and TJ Coombs. CJ's Brewery on Cary, Burnside's Café in Sharpsburg, and the Edison Historical Center are fictional entities. The protagonist, Dave, is a composite especially of two people who have enriched my life—two men who have walked the fine line of distinction of sexual orientation, Ron and Phil.

Seven of the eight highlighted here did in fact gather at the South Mountain/Antietam Battles, Johnny G. Barnes being the only exception. John Bird Manry and Benjamin Manry did die at South Mountain, and the chances are near 100% that they were among those dropped into Farmer Wise's well, and are now interred among the Unknowns in the Confederate Cemetery at Shepherdstown, West Virginia.

James Manry, Roach (James Roach) Wooten, David Wooten, WD (William Drayton) Sheppard did in fact stand with the Confederacy against the Union and Horace Barnes at Antietam.

Johnny Barnes did marry his brother Horace's wife, Caroline, upon returning home from the War. Johnny did not, as far as I know, come to make an acquaintance with David Wooten or James Manry, but they definitely could have met at City Point where Johnny was a Union Guard and David as well as James were granted their freedom.

Sadie Ann Manry Sheppard did in fact lose it all. Even her son-in-law, John Price, sued her for his deceased wife's (Annie Belle Sheppard Price) share of the ever-dwindling plantation. William Drayton Sheppard did, it seems, desert the Confederate Army soon after the Battle of Sharpsburg/Antietam.

The tragedy of losing a way of life and the consequent descent from wealth to poverty, compounded by a family history of nurturing painful secrets, may have contributed to on-going family tragedies for generations to come. Suicides and suicide attempts became common along with drug and alcohol abuse. But one of the authentic survivors was David Linton Wooten, son of Bessie and Will, grandson of Sadie and Augustus Eugene Sheppard, great grandson of William Drayton Sheppard and Martha Sheppard Sheppard, grandson of David L. and Elizabeth Colley Wooten, father of my wife, Linda Wooten-Green, and her six brothers (David, William, Larry, Tom, Jeff and Jim) and now deceased sister (Karen).

Citations document the historical accuracy of events. Most of the dialog and all of the diaries are fictionalized.

As I poured over the available records in courthouses, libraries, and family documents, I came to believe there is more to the story than one will ever really know. Therefore, as Robert Hicks notes at the end of his novel, *The Widow of the South*:

> *To understand what happened, I have tried to fill in the blanks and empty spaces, always studying the historical details to help create a novel, not a history. My hope was to use the tools of fiction to divine a greater truth...*

For those who may be disappointed that the story here did not go far enough, or that it went too far, or that my flights of imagination have crashed-landed, I apologize.

Sadie Ann Manry Sheppard with Siblings & Granddaughter at the
Sheppard Plantation House (c. 1940)

Sheppard Plantation House

Notes

Chapter Three:

"Grieving," Penny noted, "is a matter of relearning the world..." From Thomas Attig, *How We Grieve: Relearning the World* (Oxford, 1996).

"...grieving is the 'process of exhuming all that was....'" From Molly Fumia, *Safe Passage* (Conari, 1992).

Chapter Five:

"Perhaps Durant had it right when he said it is 'almost a law of history...'" From Will Durant, *The Life of Greece*, p. 222.

Chapter Seven:

"...and then there was something about 'chewing' or was it 'going to' gum? Inspired by, "The War-Time Journal of a Georgia Girl, 1864-65: Electronic Edition, Eliza Frances Andrews, b. 1840 (Academic Affairs Library, University of North Carolina at Chapel Hill, 1997) (Call Number 973.78 A56).

Chapter Eight:

"We cannot understand the Egyptian or man..." From Will Durant, Vol. I, p.197.

"He will have witnessed fields running red with the blood of at least 62,351 men..." Unless noted otherwise all casualty statistics are taken from *The Civil War Battlefield Guide*, Frances H. Kennedy, editor, (Houghton Mifflin, 1998, 2nd Edition).

"The sight inspired more satisfaction than discomfort..." From "The Battle of South Mountain, or Boonsboro: Fighting for Time at Turner's and Fox's Gap," by Daniel H. Hill, Lieutenant General, C.S.A., in *North to Antietam: Battles and Leaders of the Civil War* (Castle Books, 1956), p.p. 564-65.

"They had moved the whole thing, every rifle, canon, pistol..." From Lawton B. Evans, *A History of Georgia* (NY: American Book Co, 1898, 1908), 171.

"They not only escaped from their plantations, but they set the torch..."
From James C. Bonner and Lucien E. Roberts, eds, *Studies in Georgia History and Government* (Spartansburg, S.C.: The Reprint Co., 1974, 1940), 169.

"But, like in 1811 in New Orleans when the Andry slaves revolted..."
From Howard Zinn, *A People's History of the United States 1492–Present* (NY: HarperPerennial, 1995), 169.

"Mob riots raged in Northern cities protesting Northern enforcement..."
From John A. Krout, Arnold S. Rice, and C.M. Harris, *United States History to 1877* (NY: HarperPerennial, 1991), 152.

"A shirt that cost $2 in March at Lewis General Store was now listed at $2.20..." This and all subsequent gold prices in Union/Confederate exchanges are from *The Civil War Almanac*, John Bowman, ed. (NY: Bison Books, 1982).

"I bet they get married one of these days." Inspired by Agnes Lee's references to her educating of slave children in *Growing Up in the 1850s: The Journal of Agnes Lee*, Mary Custis Lee deButts, ed., (University of North Carolina Press, 1984).

"The fighting ended around 11 p.m. and all turned quiet." From "Fire on the Mountain: The Battle of South Mountain-Battlefield Guide," (Central Maryland Heritage League, American Battlefield Protection Program, National Park Service, 1998.)

"Certainly the engagement of September 14, 1862 could be so defined..." Estimated Casualties were 2325 Union, 2300 Confederate. *The Civil War Battlefield Guide* (Houghton Mifflin, 1998, 2nd edition, Frances H. Kennedy, ed), p. 117.

"Forever the north produces rulers and warriors..." From Will Durant, Vol I, p.397.

Chapter Nine:
"It is an interesting document entitled 'Forcing Fox's Gap and Turner's Gap," From Jacob D. Cox, "Forcing Fox's Gap and Turner's Gap," in *North*

to Antietam: Battles and Leaders of the Civil War (Castle Books, 1956), pp.583-590.

"The battle of South Mountain was one of extraordinary illusions and delusions..." From Daniel H. Hill, "The Battle of South Mountain or Boonsboro: Fighting for time at Turner's and Fox's Gap," in *North to Antietam: Battles and Leaders of the Civil War* (Castle Books, 1956), pp.559-60, 580.

Chapter Ten:
"A Great Rush to Join the 1st St. Lawrence, 60th NY Regiment..." These recruiting posters were inspired by those found at *The Civil War: Unedited Original Documents, Autorun CD* (Vintagechannel.com)

"There either is no God, or God has abandoned us all." Much of the background for the actual battle sequences is taken from "Federal Flank Attack at Dunker Church," by Robert C. Cheecks (*America's Civil War*, September 1997, pp.55-61); and "Sharpsburg," by John G. Walker, Major General, C.S.A., in *North to Antietam*, pp. 675-682.

"My God, my God, why have you deserted me?" From Matthew 27: 47 (The Jerusalem Bible, Doubleday, 1968).

"I am the Church of the bloodiest battlefield in all American history." From E. Russell Hicks who was a historian of Washington County, Md., and a member of the Church of the Brethren. A century after the battle he wrote (the words quoted here).

Chapter Eleven:
"This should be fun." This account of the afternoon's battle is based on the account of Jacob D. Cox, Major General, USV, in his "The Battle of Antietam," *North to Antietam*, pp.630-660. The Union uniforms worn by A.P. Hills's Division were uniforms captured at Harper's Ferry.

"These were the sounds of the 'unbroken moans of dying men.'" From "At Antietam, George McClellan and his 'bodyguard' dawdled throughout a long 'Fatal Thursday'," an editorial in *The American Civil War*, September 1997, p. 6.

"It is enough, O LORD." From 1 Kings 19: 4. (King James Version)

Chapter Twelve:
"Then, there was Deacon Turner's remark a few days before the wedding… " Based on "Calhoun County Georgia Biographies" (http://ftp.rootsweb.com/pub/usgenweb/ga/calhoun/bios/hturner/txt)

Chapter Thirteen:
The following account of life at Point Lookout Prison is based on: "Prison Life at Point Lookout," Rev. J. B. Traywick (Southern Historical Society Papers, R.A. Brock, ed., Vol XIX, Richmond, VA, January 1891, pp. 432-435).

"Point Lookout," Bob Allen (*America's Civil War*, March 2003), p. 41.

Clara Mildred Thompson, *Reconstruction in Georgia: Economic, Social, Political 1865-1873* (NY: Columbia University Press, 1915), 37.

Edwin Beitzell, *Point Lookout: Confederate Prisoner of War Camp* (Leonardtown, MD: St. Mary's Historical society, 1972).

"Malachi Bowden is his name—2nd Georgia." See Beitzel, p.61 for background on Pvt. Bowden.

"Got acquainted with C.W. Hutt of Westmoreland, Virginny today." See Beitzel, pp.65-87 for detailed information on Pvt. Hutt.

"Sidney Lanier is his name." See Beitzel, p. 24.

"The Eating House." See Beitzel, p. 86.

"… and 2) the PWC School." See Beitzel, p. 106 for commentary on the Prisoner of War School at Point Lookout POW Camp.

THE GOOD OLD REBEL See Beitzel, p.101.

"I think of Astyages, the ruler of Media…" See Will Durant Volume I, p. 352; Volume II, pp. 382, 366, 392. and 551.

Chapter Fourteen:

"We are all visionaries..." From Journal, 5 Feb 1853, tr. Mrs. Humphrey Ward, 1887 (Leonard Roy Frank, *Quotationary [Random House, 2001]*), 910.

"Their allowance, however, would not get them far..." See John S. Bowman, ed., *The Civil War Almanac* (NY: Bison Books, 1982), 727.

"Seems like he is always found by someone like me in the same spot..." This paranormal event is based ones similar to those described in, "Who's Afraid of Ghosts?" (www.dnr.state.md.us/naturalresource/fall2001/ ghosts.html).

"0600 hours: General Grant is informed by special courier that President Lincoln..." The following encounter with President Abraham Lincoln is based in part on the events described in "Grant's Headquarters: President Lincoln Comes to City Point," (www.cr.nps.gov/logcabin/html/cp2.html).

"Look at the birds in the sky. They do not sow or reap..." From Matthew 6:26a.

"Thank you, Son. I think I can use all the prayers I can get. I had another dream..." President Lincoln's account of his dream is based on the account in "Abraham Lincoln: A Deadly Premonition," (www.cr.nps.gov/logcabin/ html/a14.html).

Chapter Fifteen

"Everything that happens to us..." From *Carl G. Jung's Letters*, Volume One, p.78.

"This is a camp where from time-to-time POW's would be picked at random..." See especially: "Point Lookout Prison Camp for Confederates" (http://members.tripod.com/~PLPOW/PrisonHistory.htm); Beitzell, pp. 56-58, 60, 66-67, 74, and 99; See also: "MY Experience In the Confederate Army and in Northern Prisons," Written From Memory By John R. King (Stonewall Jackson Chapter No. 1333, United Daughters of Confederacy, Clarksburg, W. VA. 1937 and Reprinted 1994 by great-granddaughter of John R. King, Martha Stump Benson, compiled October 5, 1994; and "Point

Lookout," *America's Civil War*, March 2003, 40-44, 72.

"Private Hensley had been nurturing a blade of grass..." See Beitzell, p. 107.

"I know of at least 10 from my own Regiment, the 13th Georgia, who also died..." See Beitzell, pp. 123-175.

"Nearly 61% of the people in Calhoun County today are Black." All statistics for Calhoun County and the State of Georgia are from the US Census Bureau: State and County QuickFacts www.quickfacts.census.gov/qfd/states/13/130307.html).

"In fact Dave had found that in 1860 there were approximately 20,000 slaves...". An extrapolation from Map 1.2: "Distribution of African American Slaves in 1860. Charles S. Aiken, *The Cotton Plantation South Since the Civil War* (Baltimore: Johns Hopkins University Press, 1998), 11.

"It was that very same year, 1909, that cotton production in the South..." From Aiken, 56-67.

"He said he probably would have been captured and executed as a traitor..." See Maurice Melton, "Disloyal Confederates," (*Civil War Times Illustrated*, August 1977), 112-19 for background regarding treatment of deserters.

"This is the bird that often lingers..." See "Birds of America," (John James Audubon), *Ferruginous Mocking Bird (Brown Thrasher) [www.50states.com/bird/brthrash.htm]*.

Chapter Sixteen
"All situations are passing memory." From Pema Chodran, *Awakening Compassion* (Boulder, CO: Sounds True Audio, 1995).

"When Harrison finally got off the ground, he had himself a royal case of ..." Based on an account in Richard A. Baumgartner and Larry M. Strayer, *Kennesaw Mountain June 1864: Bitter Standoff at the Gibraltar of Georgia* (Blue Acorn Press, 1998), 35.

"I suggest that since profanity is such an inexcusable and yet heinous sin…" From the chaplain's own "memoir". See Richard Eddy, Chaplain, *History of the 60th Regiment, New York State Volunteers* (Published by the Author, 1864), 88, 341.

"Then in late April of '63 Horace found himself engaged in the ferocious battle…" From Chaplain Eddy's *History of the 60th Regiment*, 275.

"While we rally round the flag, boys…" From Chaplain Eddy's account at p. 341.

"By the time he arrived at Kennesaw Mountain, Horace had witnessed…" These and the battlefield statistics that follow are taken from *The Civil War Battlefield Guide*, pp. 120, 199, 212, 246, 248, 328-335.

"It was not uncommon for bodies to lie untended for a week or more." Much of the account here for this battle is based upon Richard A. Baumgartner and Larry M. Strayer, *Kennesaw Mountain June 1864: Bitter Standoff at the Gibraltar of Georgia* (Blue Acorn Press, 1998), 17.

Chapter Seventeen
"I got there only by literally unraveling clues shared through Mom's deathbed…" For background on deathbed visions see especially, Carla Wills-Brandon's, *One Last Hug Before I Go: The Meaning and Mystery of Deathbed Visions* (Health Communications, 2000). For background on the symbolic language of the dying See especially, Ron Wooten-Green's, *When the Dying Speak: How to Listen to and Learn From Those Facing Death* (Loyola Press, 2002); and Maggie Callanan & Patricia Kelley's, *Final Gifts: Understanding the Special Awareness, Needs, and Communications of the Dying* (Bantam, 1992).

"Civilization does not die, it migrates…" Will Durant, *The Life of Greece*, 66.

Epilogue
"To understand what happened, I have tried to fill in the blanks and empty…" See Robert Hicks, *The Widow of the South* (Warner Books, 2005, p. 411).

Bibliography

"Abraham Lincoln: A Deadly Premonition," (www.cr.nps.gov/logcabin/html/a14.html).

Aiken, Charles S. *The Cotton Plantation South Since the Civil War* (Baltimore: Johns Hopkins University Press).

"A. J. Johnson's Map of Georgia and Alabama, 1863"; Carl Vinson Institute of Government, The University of Georgia; www.cviog.uga.edu/Projects/gainfo/histcountymaps/calhoun1863map.htm

Allen, Bob, "Point Lookout," (America's Civil War, March 2003).

Andrews, Eliza Frances, "The War-Time Journal of a Georgia Girl, 1864-65: Electronic Edition, b. 1840 (Academic Affairs Library, University of North Carolina at Chapel Hill, 1997) (Call Number 973.78 A56).(Original published by D. Appleton and Company, 1908. Available electronically (c. 800k) from University of North Carolina at Chapel Hill, Wilson Annex).

"Antietam, The Morning, Midday & Afternoon Phases," (Antietam National Battlefield, Trailhead Graphics, Inc.), 1999.

"At Antietam, George McClellan and his 'bodyguard' dawdled throughout a long 'Fatal Thursday'," an editorial in *The American Civil War*, September 1997.

Attig, Thomas, How We Grieve: Relearning the World (Oxford, 1996).

Baumgartner, Richard A. and Larry M. Strayer, *Kennesaw Mountain June 1864: Bitter Standoff at the Gibraltar of Georgia* (Blue Acorn Press, 1998).

Beitzell, Edwin, Point Lookout: Confederate Prisoner of War Camp (Leonardtown, MD: St. Mary's Historical society, 1972).

Berry, Wendell, A Timbered Choir—The Sabbath Poems 1979-1997 (Counterpoint, 1998).

"Birds of America," (John James Audubon), *Ferruginous Mocking bird (Brown Thrasher) [www.50states.com/bird/brthrash.htm]*.

Bonner, James C. and Lucien E. Roberts, eds, <u>Studies in Georgia History and Government</u> (Spartansburg, S.C.: The Reprint Co., 1974, 1940),

Bowman, John ed. <u>The Civil War Almanac</u>, (NY: Bison Books, 1982).

"Calhoun County Georgia Biographies" (http://ftp.rootsweb.com/pub/usgenweb/ga/calhoun/bios/hturner/txt)

Callanan, Maggie and Patricia Kelley, <u>Final Gifts: Understanding the Special Awareness, Needs, and Communications of the Dying</u> (Bantam, 1992).

<u>C. G. Jung's Letters</u>, Volume One.

Cheecks, Robert C. "Federal Flank Attack at Dunker Church," (*America's Civil War,* September 1997).

Chodran, Pema, *Awakening Compassion* (Boulder, CO: Sounds True Audio, 1995).

Civil War: Unedited Original Documents (The) , (Autorun CD) (Vintagechannel.com).

Curzon, David, ed <u>The Gospels in Our mage—An Anthology of Twentieth Century Poetry Based on Biblical Texts</u> (Harcourt Brace, 1995).

DeButts, Mary Custis Lee ed., <u>Growing Up in the 1850s: The Journal of Agnes Lee</u>, (University of North Carolina Press, 1984).

"Delaware, District of Columbia, Maryland, Virginia," (AAA State Series, 2002).

<u>Diaries and Letters of Anne Morrow Lindbergh, 1936—1939</u>, (Harvest Book, 1976).
Durant, Will, <u>The Life of Greece</u>, (Simon & Schuster, 1939/1966).

Durant, Will, Our Oriental Heritage (Simon & Schuster, 1935/1963).

Eddy, Rev. Richard, *History of the 60th Regiment, New York State Volunteers* (Published by the Author, 1864).

Evans, Lawton B. A History of Georgia (NY: American Book Co, 1898, 1908).

"Fire on the Mountain: The Battle of South Mountain-Battlefield Guide," (Central Maryland Heritage League, American Battlefield Protection Program, National Park Service, 1998.)

Frank, Leonard Roy, *Quotionary {Random House, 2001}*.

Fumia, Molly, Safe Passage (Conari, 1992).

"Grant's Headquarters: President Lincoln comes to City Point," (www.cr.nps.gov/logcabin/html/cp2.html).

"Georgia/Alabama," (AAA 2001 Edition.

Kennedy, Frances H. editor, Civil War Battlefield Guide, (Houghton Mifflin, 1998, 2nd Edition).

"Kennesaw Mountain," (National Park Service/GPO), 2003.

Krout, John A., Arnold S. Rice, and C.M. Harris, United States History to 1877 (NY: HarperPerennial, 1991).

Kubler-Ross, Elizabeth, On Death and Dying. (Quality Paperback Book Club, 1992).

Melton, Maurice, "Disloyal Confederates," (Civil War Times Illustrated, August 1977).

"MY Experience In the Confederate Army and in Northern Prisons," Written From Memory By John R. King (Stonewall Jackson Chapter No. 1333, United Daughters of Confederacy, Clarksburg, W. VA., 1937 and Reprinted 1994 by great-granddaughter of John R. King, Martha Stump Benson, compiled October 5, 1994.

North to Antietam: Battles and Leaders of the Civil War (Castle Books, 1956).

"Point Lookout," America's Civil War, March 2003, 40-44, 72.

"Point Lookout Prison Camp for Confederates " (http://members.tripod.com/ ~PLPOW/PrisonHistory.htm)

Rilke, Rainer Maria, Letters to a Young Poet, Translation by M.D. Herter (W.W. Norton, 1962).

Sondheim, Stephen, "No One is Alone," from Into the Woods, 1987.

Thompson, Clara Mildred, *Reconstruction in Georgia: Economic, Social, Political 1865-1873* (Columbia University Press, 1915).

Traywick, Rev. J. B., (Southern Historical Society Papers, Volume XIX, Richmond, Va., January 1891, and available electronically at: www.censusdiggins.com/prison_ptlookout.

US Census Bureau: State and County QuickFacts (www.quickfacts.census.gov/qfd/states/13/130307.html).

Waters, Frank, Pumpkin Seed Point: Being With the Hopi (Swallow Press, 1969).

"Who's Afraid of Ghosts?" (www.dnr.state.md.us/naturalresource/fall2001/ ghosts.html).

Wills-Brandon, Carla , One Last Hug Before I Go: The Meaning and Mystery of Deathbed Visions (Health Communications, 2000).

Wilson, Edward O., The Future of Life (Alfred A. Knopf, 2002).
Wolfe, Thomas, You Can't Go Home Again (Perennial Library, 1989).

Wooten-Green, Ron, When the Dying Speak: How to Listen to and Learn From Those Facing Death (Loyola Press, 2002).
Zinn, Howard, A People's History of the United States 1492 – Present (NY: HarperPerennial, 1995).

www.ingramcontent.com/pod-product-compliance
Lightning Source LLC
Chambersburg PA
CBHW051148030726
47504CB00004B/1098